The Spartan Sacrifice

Also by Andrew Varga

The Last Saxon King
A Jump in Time Novel, Book One

The Celtic Deception
A Jump in Time Novel, Book Two

The Mongol Ascension
A Jump in Time Novel, Book Three

The Spartan Sacrifice

A Jump in Time Novel
Book Four

Andrew Varga

IMBRIFEX BOOKS

IMBRIFEX BOOKS
8275 S. Eastern Avenue, Suite 200
Las Vegas, NV 89123
Imbrifex.com

THE SPARTAN SACRIFICE: A JUMP IN TIME NOVEL, BOOK FOUR

Copyright ©2025 by Andrew Varga. All rights reserved under International and Pan-American Copyright Conventions. No part of this book may be used or reproduced in any manner whatsoever without written permission from the publisher, except in the case of brief quotations used in critical articles and reviews.

This is a work of fiction. All of the characters, organizations, and events portrayed in this novel are either products of the author's imagination or are used fictitiously. Any resemblance to actual persons, living or dead, businesses, companies, events, or locales is entirely coincidental.

IMBRIFEX® is a registered trademark of Flattop Productions, Inc.

Library of Congress Cataloging-in-Publication Data

Names: Varga, Andrew, 1969- author.
Title: The Spartan sacrifice / Andrew Varga.
Description: First edition. | Las Vegas, NV : Imbrifex Books, 2025. |
  Series: A jump in time novel ; book 4 | Audience term: Teenagers |
  Audience: Ages 12-19. | Audience: Grades 7-9. | Summary: "A
  seventeen-year-old time jumper Dan Renfrew and his partner Sam jump into
  Greece in the year 480 BCE just before the legendary Battle of
  Thermopylae"-- Provided by publisher.
Identifiers: LCCN 2025004522 (print) | LCCN 2025004523 (ebook) | ISBN
  9781955307109 (hardcover) | ISBN 9781955307123 (paperback) | ISBN
  9781955307116 (epub) | ISBN 9781955307130
Subjects: CYAC: Time travel--Fiction. | Greece--History--Persian Wars,
  500-449 B.C.--Fiction. | Thermopylae, Battle of, Greece, 480
  B.C.--Fiction. | LCGFT: Time-travel fiction. | Historical fiction. | Novels.
Classification: LCC PZ7.1.V39635 Sp 2025 (print) | LCC PZ7.1.V39635 (ebook)
LC record available at https://lccn.loc.gov/2025004522
LC ebook record available at https://lccn.loc.gov/2025004523

Cover design: Jason Heuer
Book design: John Hall Design Group
Author photo: Andrew Johnson
Typeset in ITC Berkeley Oldstyle

Printed in the United States of America
Distributed by Publishers Group West
First Edition: August 2025

For Vasileios (Bill) Kefalas, who was the fiercest Greek patriot I ever knew

And, as always, for Pam, Leah, Arawn, and Calvin

Ὦ ξεῖν’, ἀγγέλλειν Λακεδαιμονίοις ὅτι τῇδε
κείμεθα, τοῖς κείνων ῥήμασι πειθόμενοι.

Stranger, announce to the Lakedaimonians that here we are buried, having obeyed their commandments.

Epitaph to the Spartan warriors of Thermopylae

CHAPTER 1

Hoofbeats drummed across the dusky plain, pounding with a dull rhythm that set my heart racing with dread. The dark clouds that stretched across the sky flashed white with lightning, illuminating a lone rider only twenty paces away from me. He wore a long shirt of chain mail, belted at the waist, and gripped a shield in his left hand. A bloody gash snaked across his throat, while cold, glassy eyes stared at me from a gaunt face. His ragged mouth twisted with hate.

I stood rooted to the spot with fear. I knew the rider—he was the first man I had ever killed.

He pointed at me with an accusing finger, and from his lips came a gurgling moan. Thunder rumbled and, in another flash of lightning, more riders appeared behind him: Normans in chain mail from the Battle of Hastings, shaggy-haired Batavians from the Roman conquest of Anglesey. Skeletal hands gripped rusty swords and shattered spears, and each rider bore savage wounds that still oozed black blood.

I recognized every single horseman—I'd killed them all on my travels through time. And they were coming for revenge.

With a raspy cry, they spurred their horses and came charging toward me. I turned to run, but my legs felt like cement. At my feet, rotting hands reached out from the earth and clutched my legs. Around me, the ground began to erupt as corpses burst from their graves, their decaying flesh barely clinging to their broken limbs. With slow, deliberate movements, they shambled toward me.

My heart pounded in my chest. There were thousands of them, maybe millions—an endless tide of death that threatened to pull me under.

"You didn't save us," they droned, over and over, as they surrounded me.

I swung at them with my fists, trying to defend myself, but my hands barely moved, as if I was punching through honey. The dead swarmed over me, knocking me to the ground and swallowing me up in darkness.

"Dan," a female voice called out from somewhere.

The dead vanished, and Sam appeared at the top of a small hill, bathed in brilliant sunlight. She was dressed in the same green medieval gown she had worn when I took her to the homecoming dance, her fiery red hair spilling in a wild mass around her head. In her left hand, she held her bow while a quiver full of arrows peeked out from behind one shoulder.

At the sight of her, all my fear drifted away. "Sam!"

Suddenly, she was no longer on the hill, but standing right in front of me. "It's okay, Dan. I'm here." She smiled and reached toward me to run her fingers across my forehead. "It's all right," she soothed.

At her touch, my eyes blinked open. The gloom of the plains was gone, replaced by the brightness of a sunlit room where the aroma of roast chicken hung in the air. Instead of Sam, Jenna's face came into focus, staring down at me, her long, wavy black hair almost brushing my cheek.

What? . . . Where am I?

Across the room, one of Jenna's favorite cooking shows was playing on a TV that sat in front of a wall covered with pictures of Jenna and her family. I let out a long breath as comprehension cut through my disoriented fog. I was at Jenna's house, where I'd fallen asleep on the couch with my head on her lap.

Jenna stroked my forehead again. "You were having a nightmare." The corners of her deep brown eyes were creased with concern.

Groggily, I sat up and, with the heel of my palm, wiped away the last remnants of sleep from my eyes. "What time is it?"

"Just after six. Dinner's almost ready." She rested her hand on my knee. "Was it the usual nightmare?"

"Yeah." I stretched my neck from side to side to work out the kinks. "More horsemen chasing me." I didn't tell her about the army of dead people crawling out of the earth. That was a newer addition to my regular nightmares over the last few weeks.

Jenna's hand caressed my shoulder, her fingers just skimming the surface of my T-shirt. "You really should talk to someone. You've been through some pretty traumatic stuff."

"You mean like a psychiatrist?"

"Or a therapist."

I snorted. "I don't know much about doctors, but from what I've seen in movies, they can't help you unless you're completely honest with them. And as soon as I walk into an office and say 'Hi, I'm Dan Renfrew, and I get these awful nightmares because of all the horrible things I've experienced while jumping through time,' I know exactly what they'll think."

"Well . . . you could . . . talk to *me*?" She leaned in closer and raised her brow hopefully. "Just telling someone else about it might help."

This wasn't the first time she had offered. But I doubted talking would make my nightmares go away. They had started about a year earlier, when I first traveled back through time to Anglo-Saxon England and saw the horrors of medieval battlefields. They were just typical nightmares then, happening maybe once every few weeks. Usually I was being chased by cavalry or the men I'd killed. But in the three months since I had come back from my Mongolian adventure, they'd gotten a lot worse—ever since Victor Stahl had told me the details of his plan to wipe out a good chunk of humanity. Now, almost every night I woke up drenched in sweat and with my bedsheets kicked to the floor. I didn't need a psychiatrist to help me figure out my problems, and I definitely didn't want to tell Jenna what Victor was planning.

"I'll be fine," I said.

A pained look crossed Jenna's face. "You never let me in, Dan."

I grabbed her hand and held it to my chest. "I'm sorry, Jenna." I spoke quietly so her mom wouldn't hear me from the kitchen. "I know you want to help, but telling you what I've gone through won't make me forget." I squeezed my eyes shut for a second, trying to banish the memories from my mind. "We get the kid-friendly version of history in school. The real thing is horrible, especially when you're on the losing side." I shook my head. "You don't want to hear the gruesome details. And I don't want you to share my nightmares."

Jenna frowned and rested her head on my shoulder. "Fine. But I still think you need to talk to someone. What about Eric? You've been hanging out with him a lot lately."

"No, he can't help. He's not a time jumper."

"How about Sam, then? From the very, *very* few details you've told me, he's got to be a time jumper. Maybe you could talk to him."

Him.

In the three months we had been dating, I'd never corrected Jenna. At first, I'd kept the fact that Sam was female from Jenna because I didn't want to bring in any weird baggage that might threaten our brand-new relationship. Then, once Jenna and I were solid in our relationship, I held off from telling the truth about Sam because I was waiting for the right moment. I knew I'd dug myself into a huge pit that I'd have to crawl out of one day, but today was not that day.

"Sam and I talk only once a week. Never for long, and definitely not about stuff like this." I struggled to keep the sadness out of my voice. Even though we lived in different states, Sam and I used to talk every day. Video chats. Texts. Phone calls. We would talk endlessly about anything and everything. School, work, the weather, our hopes and dreams, and our darkest fears. She wasn't just my time-jumping partner; she had been my best friend. Then I messed everything up by telling her I loved her. Now our few short calls were strictly about time jumping, and all the warmth and intimacy was gone.

"Do you know that every time you mention Sam you get this little pouty look?" Jenna ran her finger in a small circle around my knee. "I don't know what's going on between you two, but I can tell you miss him. Why don't you invite him for a visit? Virginia isn't that far. I'd love to meet him."

Ooof . . . Now there's *a nightmare.*

"That's probably never gonna happen."

"Well . . . you still should talk to him. If he's seen the same things you have, he might be struggling too. It can't hurt to talk." She shrugged. "It might even make your nightmares ease up."

"I'll think about it."

Jenna rolled her eyes. "You and I both know you won't. Please, Dan. Seriously consider talking to someone. I'm worried about you."

"All right," I said in what I hoped was a convincing manner. "Now, can we watch TV or something?"

For a second, it looked as if she was going to press the issue, but then she picked up the remote instead. "Any preferences?"

"Anything but cooking shows," I mumbled, only too happy to be done with that conversation.

Jenna chuckled and started flipping through channels.

"Jenna! No more TV until your homework is finished," Mrs. Alvarez called from the kitchen. She was briefly visible through the doorway as she took some containers down from the pantry shelf.

"Already done," Jenna called out.

"Dan?" Mrs. Alvarez added.

"Me too, Mrs. A."

Mrs. Alvarez poked her head through the doorway. She had similar features to Jenna and the same long wavy black hair. "Are you staying for dinner?"

"It smells delicious, but I can't. I always have my club meeting on Mondays."

"Oh, yes, I forgot." She wagged her finger at me, and her face took on that serious mom look, which meant there was no room for arguments. "But tomorrow you're eating with us. No objections!"

I tried not to smile as she ducked back into the kitchen. Every day Mr. and Mrs. Alvarez attempted to sneak in a bit more parenting on me. It started the first time Jenna brought me home, when they found out that my own parents were dead and I was living on my own. Mrs. Alvarez started inviting me over for dinner every few nights, as if I was a stray cat that needed feeding. Then Mr. Alvarez started getting me alone so he could have career and life discussions with me. Their stealth parenting had even snuck into my homework. I didn't mind—it was kind of nice to be part of a family again. My mom had died when I was young, so I didn't remember her much, and Dad had done the best he could while he was alive, but he hadn't been that great on the little things, like making sure dinner actually tasted good.

Victor Stahl's smiling face appeared on the TV screen and my amusement vanished, replaced with the burning anger I always felt when I saw him. And unfortunately I saw him a lot. Every freakin' five minutes another one of his stupid political ads was on TV.

He was the source of my nightmares. *He* was the bastard who had killed my dad right in front of me. *He* was the nutjob who was plotting to plunge the world into death and anarchy so he and his allies could take over and rule. If I wanted to end my nightmares, I needed to stop Victor Stahl. I needed to figure out how his group of time jumpers was manipulating history to their advantage, and then destroy every last—

"Dan?" Jenna asked. "Are you threatening my TV?"

Somehow, I had picked up one of the throw pillows from the couch, and it now lay crushed and twisted in my hands.

Awkward.

I tossed the pillow back on the couch and gave it a few pats to plump it back into shape. "Sorry," I said sheepishly.

"What's your problem with him? Every time he's on, you get all cranky."

I'd told Jenna a lot about time jumping, but nothing about Victor and his plans. She had this exuberance about her that I couldn't bear to snuff out. "The guy's a complete tool," I spat, trying to make up some excuse for my animosity. "I mean . . . uh . . . look at him. He's like the uh . . . worst possible choice for president. A half-trained monkey would be better."

"Da-a-an," she said playfully. "Come on. I know you. And you don't care about politics. I also know when you're hiding something." She gave me a stern look. "So tell me what's really going on between you and Victor Stahl."

"I . . . just don't like him."

"Damn it, Dan! Let me into your life!" She got up from the couch and stood in front of me, her eyes locked on mine. "You've told me so many secrets, and I've kept them all. I've proved that you can trust me. Why do you keep hiding things from me?" She held her hands out to me. "I want to help you. Why won't you let me? You don't know how hard it is to care for someone so much and have them always pushing you away."

I winced. Unfortunately, I knew exactly how she felt. She had just summed up my entire relationship with Sam. Me always wanting more and her never willing to open herself up to me. In that instant, I felt so ashamed at the way I'd kept Jenna in the dark. I'd always justified it as being for her own safety. But if Victor was truly going to unleash hell on earth, how was I protecting her by keeping her ignorant?

"All right." I stood up and grasped her hands. "I'll tell you anything you want to know. But understand this: Whatever you hear, you can't unhear. Day and night, it will be the only thing you'll think about."

"Oh, come on. It can't be that bad." She was practically laughing at me. "What did big bad Congressman Stahl do to upset Dan?"

"He told me his plans if he gets elected. Billions of people are going to die."

Her eyes hardened. "I thought you were going to start telling me the truth."

"I am! I met him in Washington a few days after I came back from Mongolia. During that week when you wouldn't talk to me."

Jenna looked at me in disbelief. "And this guy who's on his way to becoming the next president just told a seventeen-year-old high-school student his top-secret plans?"

I tapped the tattoo of a four-pointed star within a circle that lay on the inside of my right forearm—the mark of a time jumper. "He wants me to join him."

Jenna inhaled sharply. "He's one of you?"

"He was. But he's gone crazy. He thinks the world is falling apart and the only way to fix it is to wipe out a good chunk of humanity and start over."

Jenna snorted. "What, like Thanos? I think you've been watching too many Marvel movies, Dan."

"Actually, yes," I said. "A whole lot like that."

Jenna cocked her head, ready to scoff again, but when she looked at my face, hers dropped. "Wait, what? You're serious?"

I nodded. "I'm sorry, Jenna. But this is the cold, hard truth. Victor Stahl is a madman, and I'm trying to stop him."

Jenna stared into my eyes, and I could see the desperation in hers. She wanted me to be lying, but, unfortunately, I wasn't.

"He and a bunch of other rogue time jumpers have spent the last twenty years making subtle changes to the past. These 'tweaks' have allowed them to build a secret alliance of some of the most powerful political, military, and business leaders on the planet. They're almost ready for the final step—taking over *everything*."

Jenna paled as my words sank in. "Why didn't you ever tell me anything about this?"

"Do you feel better now that you know?"

"No!" She wrapped her arms around herself and shivered. "I'm terrified. I feel so . . . powerless."

"Welcome to my nightmare. This is what makes me scream in my sleep."

Jenna bowed her head and began absent-mindedly picking the polish off her thumbnail. "So it's just . . . *you* against . . . all of this?"

"No. I have some help. But I can't tell you who."

Jenna picked harder at the polish, clearly pondering, then her eyes sparkled with realization. "Your medieval club!"

"What? . . . How? . . . uh . . . I mean, no."

She laughed. "You're such a bad liar. I knew there was something sketch about them. You never stay for dinner on Monday, no matter how much I beg. And you always give the same weak excuse, that you're hanging out with Eric and some dumb medieval club at Eric's campus. But come on. It's June. College is out for the summer. No *real* club would still be meeting."

"Fine." I raised my hands in mock surrender. "But there actually *is* a medieval club that meets every Monday, even in the summer. Most of the people there dress up and pretend they're in medieval times. The *real* meeting happens after they leave. That's when me, Eric, and a few of his college friends try to figure out how to save the world."

"But you told me Eric's not a time jumper."

"He's not. His dads gave him all the training, but he doesn't have a jump rod. So he's never gone back in time."

She shook her head. "Technicality."

"No, it's not. You can't call yourself a pilot if you've had all the classroom training but never flown a plane."

"Fine." She rolled her eyes. "What about the rest of them?"

"Same as Eric. Related to former time jumpers, but without the devices or any time-travel experience."

"Do you guys have a plan? Do you know how to stop Victor?"

"I don't think I should tell you anything more."

"Why not?"

"Because Victor kills people. Wanna know how my dad died? I watched Victor stab him through the chest with a sword. And he did it because my dad wouldn't surrender his time-jumping device." Jenna's eyes widened. "Victor also kills people for information, or if they know too much, or if he feels like they're a threat. And the more I tell you, the more I risk you becoming someone he views as a source of information. Do you really think you could hold back if they decided to torture you or your parents?" I didn't wait for her answer. "No. Your best chance of survival is to know only that on Mondays I go to a medieval club and chat with Eric."

Jenna's bottom lip quivered. She looked toward the kitchen, where her mom was getting plates out of the cupboard. "Do you think he'd actually come here?" A note of panic crept into her voice.

Seeing Jenna so scared made me feel awful. All these months I'd managed to hide the truth from her, and now I'd destroyed the happy little world she lived in. I wrapped my arms around her and hugged her tight. "No. Victor has more important things to do than worry about me or the people I hang out with."

Jenna trembled in my arms but said nothing.

"You okay?" I kissed her softly on the forehead. "I'm sorry for telling you all this."

"No . . . it's okay." She exhaled slowly, and her resolve seemed to grow. "I'd rather know the truth than live a lie." She looked at me expectantly. "What can I do to help?"

Jenna never ceased to amaze me. I had just dumped the most unimaginably horrific news on her, and, instead of freaking out or going numb with shock, her first response was to help. I gave her what I hoped was an encouraging smile. "Thanks. But we got this."

"So what now?"

I glanced at my watch: six twenty. "Gotta go. Medieval club starts soon."

I quickly said bye to Mrs. Alvarez, promising to be at dinner tomorrow, then Jenna walked me through the rest of her house and out the front door. On the porch, she placed her hands on my shoulders. "Whatever you end up doing tonight, be careful."

"Don't worry." I kissed her. "Nothing dangerous is going to happen."

I headed for my car in the driveway. *Nothing dangerous.* Not really a lie, but not the truth either. Like most things I told Jenna, it was in a gray area. If Victor ever found out about our medieval club meetings, it would probably mean death for all of us. But if we wanted to stop Victor, our little band of wannabe heroes had to take that risk.

CHAPTER 2

As soon as I swung open the door to the lecture hall where the medieval club met, I could sense something was wrong—an anxious vibe hung over the room like a dark gray storm cloud. The usual crowd of medieval geeks didn't seem to notice. They flitted around the room in their costumes, chatting about the wonders of yarn, or farming, or whatever stuff they usually talked about when the club met.

No, the anxious feeling seemed to affect only a smaller group: my little army of people whose lives had been torn apart by Victor. Adjoa, usually so animated in conversation, leaned against the wall and nodded glumly as someone spoke to her. Manuel sat slumped in one of the stiff plastic seats, scribbling furiously in a notebook, instead of walking around the room and shaking everyone's hand as he usually did.

"Damn," I muttered under my breath. After the drama I'd just gone through with Jenna, I'd been hoping for an easy evening.

Eric came rushing over the moment he saw me. He wore his customary Roman soldier outfit, so his leather sandals slapped against the floor. "Hey," he said, sounding breathless. "It's good to see you."

"Hey." I maintained a huge smile in case anyone from the regular club happened to be watching us. "What's wrong?" I kept my voice low so no one could overhear me.

Eric dragged a hand through his short brown hair. "It's Stewart. He's been acting weird since he got here. It's putting everyone on edge."

"That's it? Doesn't he always act kind of weird?"

"Not like this."

"Do you know what his problem is?"

"Us." Eric heaped a truckload of scorn into that one word. "He says we're not moving fast enough."

"What?" I exclaimed, drawing curious glances from people nearby. I leaned in closer to Eric and dropped my volume a few notches. "We've been meeting for only a few weeks. Victor's been planning for twenty years. What the hell does Stewart expect us to do?"

"No clue." Eric shrugged. "This came out of nowhere."

I spotted Stewart standing off to one side, talking with Tim, who wore a brown monk's robe with a white rope belt. Like me, Stewart never dressed up, preferring instead a pair of jeans and a T-shirt. His usually pale face was flushed with the passion of whatever he was talking about, and his arms flailed wildly as he spoke. It seemed to be a pretty one-sided conversation, as Tim merely nodded every few seconds, his lips drawn tight and his eyes darting around.

I couldn't hear what Stewart was saying, but the people near him were casting bewildered looks his way. *What an idiot.* The first rule of time-jumper club: Don't bring attention to time-jumper club. "We need to shut him up before he blows our cover and gets us all killed," I whispered to Eric. "Try to contain him for the next hour or so. We'll clear things up once the normals leave."

Eric nodded and strode across the room to where Tim and Stewart huddled together. Dressed in his Roman armor, Eric kind of clanked as he walked, so he announced his presence long before he got there. Tim and Stewart both threw him unwelcoming glares, but Eric merely waved, flashed a big smile, and kept heading toward them. With an irritated turn of his head, Stewart leaned toward Tim and whispered something. Tim nodded again, and the pair split to find seats, Stewart choosing to sit alone in the back corner of the lecture hall.

I sighed and found myself a spot near Stewart, where I could keep an eye on him. It was hard for me not to scowl. The fate of the world depended on me and my little group, and we were the most dysfunctional band of misfits I'd ever been part of. I sure as hell hadn't expected this drama when Eric asked me to lead his group a few months back. It sounded so cool at first—me, a simple high-school kid, leading a squad of college students Eric had gathered from around the world to prevent Victor from unleashing worldwide destruction. I hadn't realized that leadership would mean dealing with Stewart's constant attitude, or Sophie's fears, or Tim's near-crippling silence. Eric, Manuel, and Adjoa were solid, while Britney, Kate, and Pascal held their own, but we definitely weren't a team of superheroes like the Avengers. For all of our dreams and hopes of defeating Victor, we were more a team of super-zeroes.

At the front of the lecture hall, a girl was setting up for the evening's discussion. On a table, she had arranged some cloth samples, five or six spools of thread, and a small handheld loom.

Great . . . Just what I needed to add to my misery: another discussion about weaving. This was my eighth club meeting, and every one of them had included a presentation about medieval clothing or food—things I already knew way too much about, thanks to my travels through time.

As the girl started droning on about the wonders of weaving, I leaned back in my seat and tried to figure out the best way to deal with Stewart, my thoughts drifting to similar challenges I'd faced before. In Anglo-Saxon times, I'd used my martial arts skills on Wulfric, the annoying peasant who was pushing me around, and left him flat in the dirt. At school, I'd broken Nick's nose when he bullied me. And in Mongol times, I'd punched Jelme repeatedly in the face after he said something that struck a nerve.

Wow . . . I really need to work on my conflict-resolution skills.

Punching Stewart would probably make me feel better, but it wouldn't solve my problems. I'd have to use tact and diplomacy, and neither was one of my strong suits.

I glanced over at Stewart. He kept twisting and turning in his chair, looking as anxious as I felt. Our eyes met and his narrowed. He glared at me for a few seconds before turning away.

I clenched my fist and repeatedly tapped it against the top of my armrest. How could I get Stewart to understand that we couldn't rush into things against Victor? The guy had spies everywhere—one wrong move on our part and someone would die. The ten of us rushing down the street swinging swords over our heads weren't going to defeat him. We needed to be smart. We needed to be careful.

A smattering of applause derailed my train of thought. At the front of the room, the girl had finished her presentation and was beginning to pack up her display while everyone started wandering around the room and breaking into smaller groups to chat.

For the next hour, I flitted from conversation to conversation, pretending to listen, nodding every now and then, but always keeping my eye on Stewart. I needed to be prepared for anything. I'd seen him flip out at Britney before, when she accidentally dripped water from her water bottle onto his shoe. And during sparring sessions, only Eric and I were willing to go up against him because he never held back.

"It's eight thirty, everyone!" Eric announced. "We have to clear out."

In minutes, the last of the regular club members were gone, and Adjoa locked the door behind them. She taped a piece of cardboard over the window so no one could see in.

An ominous silence settled like a shroud over the ten of us, no one willing to speak. Stewart was leaning against the wall with his arms across his chest. His eyes hadn't left me since Adjoa closed the door.

I took a deep breath, clenching and opening my fists a few times.

First rule of leadership—confront your problems. "I hear you got some issues," I said to Stewart.

"Damn right," he replied. "We're moving way too slow."

"We're talking about taking out Victor Stahl—a guy who's survived twenty years of people trying to kill him. So, yeah, we're moving slowly. We have to plan and do things right."

Stewart snorted. "All we do is plan, and talk, and then plan some more. The election keeps getting closer. As soon as he wins, we're toast. Game over. We need to do something *now*."

"Come on, Stewart," Manuel said. "We're getting ideas together. We've all experienced firsthand what happens if Victor considers someone a threat."

A pained look darkened Stewart's eyes. "Like I don't know that?" His voice cracked with emotion. "Every single minute of every single day, I think about my family. So I know we need to be cautious. But we've been brainstorming"—he air-quoted the word—"for weeks, and name me one solid idea that we've thought of." He looked at everyone in turn, with a challenging scowl on his face, daring anyone to prove him wrong. "Yeah," he snorted, "that's what I thought." He raised his fist. "The time for talk is over. We need to *do* something."

Inwardly, I winced. Everything Stewart said, I'd thought myself a hundred times. Our group *was* stagnating. When Eric first asked me to lead them, I had all these great hopes and dreams that we could take Victor down. But hopes and dreams needed hard work and planning to come true, and we were woefully short in that respect.

Victor seemed invincible. How could we stop a guy with powerful allies, huge cash reserves, and the ability to alter the past in his favor? We all felt the hopelessness of the task, but none of us wanted to admit it. Instead, we held little training sessions where we sparred, or brainstormed, or thought up new anti-Victor posts for social media to hurt his chances of winning the election. But all this gave us was a false sense of doing something. Stewart was right: We needed to act, and I should point the way. But how could I lead when I had no clue which direction to go?

Eric raised his hands toward Stewart. "No one's arguing with you. We know we need a plan. We just have to make sure it's a good one. Do you know how many members of the time-jumping community with a hell of a lot more resources and experience than us have already died while trying to kill Victor? My dads have the names of each and every one of them, and it's a pretty long list. But Victor's survived *every* attempt against him because he's paranoid and super well-guarded."

"I don't care how paranoid or how guarded he is," Stewart said. "He has to make a mistake sometime. And I'll be waiting for him. One bullet is all it will take."

"I've been to Victor's office," I said. "He has armed guards and security cameras, and he hides behind bulletproof glass. If you try to attack him, you'll be throwing your life away."

Stewart looked at me like I was the stupidest person he'd ever seen. "Of course he's invincible inside his office. But he's running for president. He can't stay in his office forever. We just need him to come out in the open once."

"You won't get near him. Victor hardly makes any public appearances. And when he does, he has more guards with him than the actual president."

"And in a few more months, he'll be president and it will be too late. We have to do something now."

"So that's your plan?" Manuel crossed his arms over his chest and glared at Stewart. "To just wait for him at some campaign event and hope his security slips up? And if you get caught? Have you thought about that? Victor won't just kill *you*. He'll kill the rest of us too."

"He's going to kill us all anyway if we don't stop him," Stewart sneered. "Should I just sit here and wait for him to kill me?"

"You're crazy, man." Manuel waved his hands dismissively.

Stewart leveled a withering glare at Manuel. "Don't call me crazy."

Manuel raised his chin and returned the glare. "I call it like I see it. And if you think you can just find Victor and gun him down, then you *are* crazy." He jabbed a finger at Stewart. "If any of Victor's spies hear you talking like this, you'll get us all killed before we even have a real chance at stopping him. So shut up already!"

Stewart's hands balled into fists, and he puffed his chest out as a challenge.

This situation was getting ugly fast. These two idiots would be at each other's throats in seconds.

I stepped in between them. "Look, Stewart . . . Manuel. We're all on the same team here."

Stewart held his defiant pose a few seconds longer, then shook his head and grabbed his backpack off the floor. "I've been part of this group for a year." He pointed to Eric. "You promised me we'd get justice. Then you promised me that when Dan showed up we'd get leadership. What a joke."

"Justice is coming," Eric insisted. "I promise."

"When?" Stewart cried. "Do you know how long I've been waiting to make Victor pay? That bastard burned my house down and killed my entire family. My dad, mom, sister . . . all gone." His voice quivered with anguish. "I only survived because I was at a friend's house that night. It'll be five years ago tomorrow. Five damn years and Victor's only gotten stronger!" He flicked a hand dismissively. "You losers can stick around planning forever. Me, I'm taking my fate into my own hands. Anyone want to join me?"

"Stewart, please." Britney placed her hand on his arm. "I know you're upset, but you can't just rush off. All our lives depend on it."

The harshness in his eyes softened, and he patted Britney's hand. "Don't worry. I won't mess things up. I'll just do what all you cowards don't have the guts to do."

"Come on, Stewart," I said. "We need you with us."

His back stiffened, and he turned to face me. "What for? What do you actually need me for?"

He had me there. We didn't need him. He was hotheaded, not a team player, and any information he might have had about time jumping had been destroyed in the fire that killed his family.

He snorted at my silence. "Yeah. That's what I thought." He shouldered me aside and stormed for the exit. "You can thank me later, losers."

As he unlocked the door and began to open it, I slammed it closed again with the palm of my hand. He was going to get us all killed. "You can't just run after Victor."

"And who's going to stop me?" Stewart sniffed. "You?"

Good question. Short of kidnapping Stewart, there was nothing I could do. "No. I'm not going to stop you. But I hope you'll remember that all our lives depend on what you do. Please, don't do anything stupid." I stepped away from the door.

Stewart pushed past me. "I won't promise anything, but I will be careful." He swung the door open and stomped out.

Tim chewed his lip and scanned the faces of our group as if he was searching for an answer. He then bowed his head to avoid looking directly at the rest of us as he wordlessly followed Stewart out.

"Do you think . . . um, that we can trust them?" Sophie asked in her usual timid tone.

"We don't have any choice," Eric said.

"I'll go talk to Stewart," Britney suggested before chasing after the pair, the door slamming behind her.

I drew a hand across my face. If this was a test of my leadership ability, I'd failed miserably.

"The anniversary of his family's death has really hit him hard," Eric said. "But he likes Britney. She should be able to bring him back to his senses."

"And if she doesn't?"

Eric avoided my eyes, while Sophie and Manuel became suddenly interested in the floor. Only Adjoa had the courage to speak. "We need to give Stewart hope. To show him some way we can stop Victor without putting everyone's lives at risk."

For half a second, I thought about telling everyone about the two ideas I had in the works. Except both of them involved time jumping, meaning none of the group could help me, and both were just as one-in-a-million as Stewart's plan. So I kept quiet—we already had enough bad ideas for one evening.

"If we could just figure out how Victor and his gang are changing history," I said, "we'd have a place to start. We need to find notes for these jump rods. There are so many different symbols—there have to be more settings than the few we know." I turned to Eric. "Did you talk to your dads again?"

"Yeah. But they don't know of a setting that can take you wherever you want in history. The rods take you only to where the glitches are."

"Any luck getting your hands on their files?" Even to my own ears, my voice sounded desperate. I asked Eric about those files all the time. His dads, Brian and Dave, had been the archivists of the time-jumping community, back before Victor's schemes had ripped the community apart. They had kept track of all the different time jumpers, as well as where they went in history, who they met, what glitches they solved, and who they traveled with. I'd seen the files only once, and that brief view had blown me away with the detail. I was positive that somewhere in all that information were clues on how Victor was altering the past. But Dave and Brian were only willing to trade me the information in return for a jump rod, and I didn't have any extras. So I kept hounding Eric in the hopes he had somehow managed to sneak out a copy of the files.

Eric exhaled a long sigh of disappointment and shook his head. "They still keep their laptop locked up like it's made of gold and won't let me near it." He rolled his eyes. "They're doing this for my own protection," he said in a mock parental voice.

Damn it. It was always the same issue with the former members of the time-jumping community. Victor hadn't just taken their jump devices; he'd also taken their courage. None of them dared to do anything that might earn Victor's wrath. "Anyone else dig anything up?"

A bunch of blank faces stared back at me, just like every other meeting, when I asked the exact same question. I didn't blame Stewart for getting so upset—our current path was clearly heading nowhere. As long as Victor controlled the past, he could write the future, and our little group was just a speck of dust he could whisk off the page.

But he couldn't be completely invincible. There had to be some weakness, some loophole we were missing.

But what?

CHAPTER 3

The sun had set by the time medieval club ended, leaving the campus in darkness, with only a few street lamps providing the occasional cone of illumination over the path. I took a seat on a bench in front of one of the half-lit buildings and pulled out my phone to video chat with Sam, like I did every Monday night after the club meeting finished. And, same as every Monday, as soon as her face appeared on screen, my chest tightened and I felt the sting of embarrassment all over again. It had been three months since she'd stomped on my declaration of love. Even with Jenna in my life, I still hadn't gotten over Sam.

"Hey." I tried to keep my tone casual.

"Hey. How did the meeting go today?"

No pleasantries. No asking about my week. Not even a simple comment about the weather. The only thing we talked about anymore was time jumping. I knew she was trying to protect herself from feeling anything for me, but this didn't make the situation any less upsetting. "Stewart threatened to go rogue because we're not moving fast enough for him. He thinks a full-on assault, guns blazing, is the best option."

Sam's lips pursed and she shook her head. "What an idiot. Did you explain to him that people have tried that already—and got killed for their efforts?"

"We all told him. But he thinks he knows what he's doing. Britney is working on knocking some sense into him."

"Any new information about the jump rods from your little group?"

"Absolutely nothing," I said glumly. "Victor doesn't leave anything behind when he crushes people. We're still stuck with that same plan you and I talked about after Mongolia."

Sam tilted her head. "*Stuck with?* You're not having doubts, are you?" I could feel her annoyance as acutely as if she was right next to me.

For a second, I thought about denying it. After all, we had created this plan together, and I didn't want to sound like I was suddenly bailing on it. But Sam knew me too well; she'd know I was lying. "Yeah. I am. I mean . . . stealing a jump rod from one of Victor's guys in the past? Do you know how hard that's going to be? We were lucky on our Anglo-Saxon jump that two of them decided to stick around. But where were they on our Celtic jump, or in Mongolia?" I shook my head. "Not to mention that they'll be armed, too, and they will fight back. They're not just going to hand over their devices because we ask them nicely."

"I know how difficult our plan is. I understand the risks." Sam twirled a lock of her red hair around a finger and chewed on the end of it. "But you and I both know our biggest problem is information—we don't have any. So unless Dave and Brian have changed their minds and are suddenly willing to give us all their files for free, we need to get them a jump device."

Ever since I'd told her about the files, she'd been obsessed with getting them. We didn't have a conversation now that didn't focus on either getting the files or getting a jump rod to trade for them. She kept mentioning our lack of information about Victor's plot, and how she hoped Dave and Brian's files would fill that gap, but I knew what she really wanted—to find out who in the time-jumping community had killed her father and brother. Unfortunately, her obsession with uncovering the truth about them had clouded her usually rock-solid judgment. "But what is our actual plan? All we've got so far is 'Land in wherever. Search for Victor's guys. And take them out before they take us out.' That sounds like the most poorly thought-out, made-up-on-the-spot plan ever. And I'm the king of poorly thought-out, made-up-on-the-spot plans!"

"And you're just bringing this up now because . . . ?" Her voice sharpened.

"Because after hearing Stewart's stupid plan, I realized that ours isn't much better. We're relying completely on luck."

"Fine." She crossed her arms over her chest. "Give me a better plan, then."

Ugh . . . I knew she'd say that.

"Well . . . uh . . . Remember that city I saw outside the time stream?"

She gaped at me incredulously. "You think some half-baked scheme to visit a mythical city is better than our current plan?"

"*Mythical?* You still don't believe me?"

Sam rolled her eyes. "I'm sure you hallucinated something. But think about it. Why would there be a city in the time stream? And how could you even see it? When I'm traveling through time, all I see is a light so bright it hurts to keep my eyes open."

"I told you. That part of the time stream is all black."

"Completely bright or all black. Same thing. Either way, it should be impossible to see a city."

I'd been telling Sam about the city ever since I found it by accident during our Celtic jump. And no matter how hard I tried to convince her it was real, she always gave me the same response. She just couldn't believe I'd seen something out there. But I knew the city wasn't a figment of my imagination. I'd even gotten closer to it after my Mongolian jump, but only during a freefall and at speeds that would have left me a huge splatter on the ancient cobbled streets if I had proceeded any further. I was positive the city had something to with time jumping, but I still hadn't figured out how to land there without dying. And that was an even bigger problem than getting Sam to believe me.

"All right, we'll skip the city and try your plan," I said without enthusiasm.

She stared intently at me. "Are you sure?"

"No. But it's all we got right now."

Her eyes softened. "I admit our plan has some holes, but have some faith in us. We're not Stewart."

"I have tons of faith in us—it's Victor's guys that are the problem."

"We'll pass that hurdle when we get to it. You just make sure you're ready to jump out as soon as the next glitch happens."

"Don't worry; my gear is packed." I leaned back against the hard plastic slats of the park bench. "As long as I'm not at school or Jenna's when a glitch happens, I can be ready in maybe twenty minutes. Just text me to let me know. I hardly ever have my jump rod with me."

"Oh, yeah," Sam muttered. "I forgot you have the luxury of leaving it lying around at home."

"It's not lying around—it's safely hidden. What other options do I have? I can't take it with me to school. How would I get it through the metal detector? Don't tell me you actually bring yours to school."

"Of course I do. Ever since you blabbed to my mom that I jump through time, she's been snooping around my room a lot more than before. I can't risk her finding it. So I bring it to work, to school, to wherever."

My brow furrowed. "How do you hide it?"

"In my backpack. At least there's one benefit to living in the armpit of Virginia—the schools here don't have metal detectors, not yet at least."

"Oh . . . right. Hey . . . um . . . speaking of school, will you be okay missing class if we have to jump out?"

She snorted. "I'm not really worried about school anymore. The year is practically over anyway. Besides, if Victor has his way, a high-school diploma won't be that important in a few months."

I chuckled in a sad sort of way. "Yeah. It's getting harder to drag myself to class every day."

Sam held her phone farther back so that I could see her room in the background. For the first time, I noticed she was wearing the checkered work shirt from her job at a pizza place, with a white plastic name tag. "I probably should be going now. It's late and I still need to shower."

And there it was, the usual excuse to end the call. Ever since Mongolia, our longest call had been maybe ten minutes. "All right," I sighed. "Good night, Sam."

"Good night, Dan."

The screen went black, and I felt the now-familiar pang of disappointment. Every time we spoke, I expected there to be some spark of the old Sam, some sign that things were returning to normal between us. But she'd built her walls up high, and I doubted they were ever coming down again.

I shut the phone off and leaned back on the bench, my foot bouncing up and down off the pavement as the frustrations of the day boiled over. My crumbling relationship with Sam was the least of my problems. Stewart needed to be reined in. Victor needed to be stopped. And I felt powerless to do anything. I stared up at the crescent moon. My luck needed to change, and soon. I disagreed with Stewart on his methods, but he was right about one thing—time was running out.

CHAPTER 4

As soon as the lunch bell rang, I tore out of class, dumped my books in my locker, and raced for the cafeteria. The place was filling up quickly, but my usual table stood empty, like a little island of calm in a sea of chaos. I tossed my lunch bag onto it, flopped into an orange plastic chair, and waited for Jenna. Like clockwork, she appeared from the cafeteria line, carrying a tray with a plate of fries on it.

She gave me a huge smile as she sat down next to me, her leg brushing against mine. "Hey, Dan." She gave me a quick kiss. "How was last night?" Her eyes lit up. "Did you do anything exciting that you can tell me about?"

I opened my lunch bag and dug out my ham-and-cheese sandwich. "As promised, nothing dangerous." I kept my voice just loud enough for her to hear it over the buzz of conversations all around us. "I learned about the wonders of weaving—again."

Her shoulders sagged. "That's it?"

"Well, we did have a bit of drama. One guy in our group decided to—"

My phone buzzed, interrupting me. A text from Eric appeared on the screen. **Call me!!!**

Crap.

Eric wasn't into drama or punctuation, so something serious had to be going on. I punched in his number and held a hand over my ear to block out some of the background noise.

Eric picked up after the first ring. "Things are bad, man." He spoke rapidly, with a note of panic in his voice.

"Is it Stewart?"

"Britney just texted me. She went to check on him this morning, but he's gone. His roommate said he packed a bunch of stuff and took off around midnight. She tried texting him, but he's not responding. Tim's missing too."

I slammed my hand on the table. Clearly, Britney had failed to calm Stewart down. "We need to find them."

"How? They must be going after Victor, but we don't know which way they're headed. They could be heading to DC, or they could be trying to catch him wherever his next campaign stop is."

"Forget looking for Tim and Stewart. We just need to follow Victor—and his schedule is public. As long as we are close to Victor, we can intercept Tim and Stewart before they do anything dumb."

"Great plan, Dan," Eric replied sarcastically, "but I'm a college student, remember? I live on mac and cheese and ramen noodles. Where are we going to get the money to do all this?"

"How much do you think it would cost?"

"I don't know. It all depends on where we have to go and how long we're gone."

"You think ten thousand would do it?"

"Uh, yeah, I think that would cover it. But who has ten grand that they can just drop like that?"

"Um . . . me."

Eric sucked in his breath. "Are you serious?"

"Yup. Give me about an hour to ditch school and grab some things. I'll come by your house. We can be in DC before dark."

For a second, the phone went silent. "Um . . . I don't think you should come, Dan," Eric said, hesitation in his voice.

"Why not? I know where Victor works. I know what his bodyguard looks like. I know how much security he has in his building. How can you do it without me?"

"That's just it. Victor and his security team have seen you before. If I sit outside his office on a park bench, no one will notice or care. If he sees you . . . well, do you really want Victor to start asking questions?"

Damn. Eric was right. This was one battle I had to avoid. "All right, I'll float you the cash, but I don't think you should go alone."

"I'll text Manuel and Adjoa. One of them should be up for it. Give me a few minutes to figure things out, then I'll call you back."

The call ended and I stared up at the dirty white ceiling in frustration. I wasn't used to relying on others to do my work for me. I wanted to be part of the action, not sitting around, waiting for the results. But I was supposed to be the leader of Eric's little group, and leadership was all about delegating responsibility. So I'd have to get used to it.

Jenna grabbed my hand. "Is everything all right?"

"Nope. Everything's terrible."

"Can you tell me what's going on?"

I mentally went over everything she had already heard me say to Eric. Jenna was smart; she'd be able to figure out most of what was going on, even without my help. No use in keeping things secret now. "Some of the group are going after Victor Stahl," I explained in a low voice.

"To do what?" she asked. I waited for her to figure it out. "You mean . . . to kill him?" Her mouth hung open.

I winced. Even though she was speaking quietly, it sounded to me as if she had stood up on the table and shouted to the entire school. I glanced quickly around to see if anyone had heard her, but all I could see were uninterested people eating their lunches and absorbed in their own lives. "Yeah. And I have to stop them."

"Wait." Jenna's brow furrowed. "I thought you wanted him dead."

"I do. But the chances of Tim and Stewart succeeding are slim to none, while the chances of them getting caught are huge. And once those idiots gets caught, Victor will come after everyone in the club."

My phone rang before Jenna could respond, but the horrified look on her face said more than any words could.

"Manuel's in," Eric said. "Adjoa's joining Britney over at Stewart's place to see if his roommate knows where he's headed, and Kate and Pascal are going to search for Tim. As for Sophie . . . " Eric didn't need to finish the sentence. We both knew she was more a liability than a help.

"When do you think you can leave?"

"As soon as you send me the cash, we're out of here."

"Okay, on it. And Eric?"

"Yeah?"

I swung my head back and forth to make sure no one was listening. "If, through some one-in-a-million fluke, Stewart actually does get a chance to take Victor out, don't stop him, okay?"

"Gotcha."

I ended the call, spent a few minutes arranging the money transfer, and then tossed my phone back on the table. Jenna was just staring at me, an odd look in her eye. "What?" I asked.

"I'm kind of freaking out right now," she whispered. "You were just talking about . . . you know!"

"He needs to be stopped."

"I know . . . It's just so . . . real." Jenna began nervously drumming her fingers on the table top. "And did you seriously just give Eric ten thousand dollars? Where did you get that much cash?"

I shrugged.

She pushed her hair back over one ear. "Another secret?"

"Kinda. If I tell you, you have to promise never to tell anyone."

She leaned toward me, her face serious. "Is this another life-and-death thing?"

"No, it's more of an 'I don't want people bugging me for money' thing."

She put her hand over her heart as her brown eyes met mine. "I promise. I won't tell anyone."

"Okay . . . do you remember when we first met, and I told you that I'm living off my inheritance?"

Jenna nodded.

"Well . . . my dad had a two-million dollar life-insurance policy."

She jerked upright in her seat. "And it's just . . . yours? You're a millionaire?"

"Not so loud," I hissed, but there was so much noise in the cafeteria that Jenna's outburst seemed to have been lost in the din.

"Sorry." She leaned in closer to me. "So what do you do with it all?"

"Nothing, really. I pay bills and save the rest for emergencies, like this one."

"So you're sitting on millions of dollars, yet you choose to drive your dad's old car, wear ripped jeans and T-shirts, and eat homemade sandwiches for lunch?"

"What's wrong with sandwiches? I like sandwiches."

Jenna's eyes narrowed and she smirked. "So the guy I randomly asked out because he was kind of cute turns out to be both a time jumper *and* a millionaire? What next, you're some kind of royalty?"

"You can look at things optimistically like that, or you can look at things my way. I'm an orphan. I live alone. I have the weight of the world on my shoulders."

Jenna got up and stood behind me to wrap her arms around me. "But you're not alone in this. I'm here with you. And not just me—my parents think you're great, they'd do anything for you. And you have Eric and all your college friends supporting you too."

I closed my eyes and basked in the warmth of her embrace. She was right. I wasn't alone in my fight against Victor. Everything would be fine. Eric and Manuel would find Stewart and Tim before Victor did.

My phone buzzed again. Three simple words from Sam leapt off the screen.

TIME TO GO.

My momentary feeling of calm vanished and I jerked in my seat as I snatched the phone off the table. Half an hour, I texted back, my fingers flying over the keypad.

"Is everything okay?" Jenna asked.

"No. That was Sam. I have to go." I gently lifted Jenna's arms off me so I could get up from my seat.

"Now?"

"Yes, now. Please give your mom some excuse about why I can't make it to dinner tonight." I began wolfing down the last bites of my sandwich.

"What about school?"

Despite the urgency of the situation, I allowed myself a smile. Only a straight-A student like Jenna would worry about school at a time like this. "It's the end of the year," I said through a mouthful of bread. "A few missed classes aren't going to change my grades. Besides, this is a lot more important."

I gulped down the last of my orange juice, gave Jenna a quick kiss goodbye, then dumped my trash and headed for the cafeteria doors, mentally going over the list of things I had to do before jumping out.

A patter of footsteps warned of someone following me. A second later, Jenna appeared at my side. "I'm coming with you."

"What? Jenna Alvarez is ditching school?" I shook my head in mock disapproval. "Aren't you worried about potentially missing a pop quiz and messing up your spotless average?"

She laughed and punched me playfully in the shoulder. "I'm not *that* bad. Besides, you're jumping into history. I don't want to miss that."

We grabbed our backpacks from our lockers and hurried outside to the parking lot and my car. As I steered away from the school, Jenna craned her neck to watch the building disappear behind us. Only when the car was safely around the corner did she finally look forward and settle into her seat. "I can't believe you're jumping into history again." She patted my thigh. "Promise me you'll be careful."

I snorted. "I'm always careful."

"Really?" Although I had my eyes focused on the road, I still heard the disbelief in her tone and I could imagine the look on her face. "Then why did I have to two pull two arrows out of you on your last jump? And you've told me about all the stuff that happened on your first two jumps, and nothing there struck me as incredibly careful either. So how about being even more careful this time?"

"Trust me, it's not like I go out looking for someone to stab me. It just kind of happens." I glanced quickly at Jenna and shrugged. "I actually hate time jumping—it terrifies me. But I have to go. Victor needs to be stopped, and this is my best chance to do it."

"Do you think *I* could ever come with you?" She had this eager look, like she was waiting for a gold star from her teacher. I knew she wanted me to tell her how great a time jumper she'd be, but I was working hard on being truthful with her.

"Jenna, my dad trained me since birth in weapons and martial arts, and I still get my butt kicked. You're tough, but you wouldn't survive a minute."

Her eager look faded and her forehead creased. "Thanks for the vote of confidence."

"It's not just that. Even if you had a decade of training, time-jumping devices are in short supply. Someone told me there are only a few hundred in existence. The chances of me finding you an extra one are less than winning the lottery."

"Well . . . just think about it. I want to help you, Dan. You and Sam shouldn't be stuck doing this all by yourselves."

"Sure." A nice vague answer that kept me in that vast gray zone between outright lying and the truth.

I had barely pulled my car into its parking spot before I was racing toward the elevator with Jenna chasing after me. "Come on. Come on. Come on," I muttered to the elevator as I jabbed the button repeatedly.

Three minutes and one agonizingly slow elevator ride later, I flung open the door to my apartment and was met by the clutter of pizza boxes just inside the door. I could feel my cheeks flushing with embarrassment. "Don't mind the mess," I said sheepishly as I waved Jenna in. Because her parents were pretty strict, we always hung out at her house, so I had never bothered keeping my place clean.

She gingerly stepped around the pile of boxes. "You really like pizza, huh?"

"It's better than anything I could cook." I tried to remember how I had left the rest of my apartment. "Wait here a second." I hurried past her into the living room to make sure there wasn't any more garbage lying around. Thankfully, other than a pair of dirty socks on the couch and a few empty glasses on the table, the rest of the place looked clean enough. I grabbed the socks, rolled them into a ball, and tossed them into my bedroom. "Just make yourself at home. I have to get ready."

While Jenna sat down in the big armchair next to my couch, I selected a wooden staff from the large display of medieval weapons hanging on the wall. Most of them were from my dad's travels into history, but I'd managed to add a few to the display after my three time jumps.

"That's all you're taking?" Jenna asked. "No swords or armor?"

I shook my head. "Remember pulling the arrows? That was all because someone tried to steal my armor. I'm going light this time around. Hopefully people will leave me alone if I don't look like a threat."

Her lips drew tight with disapproval. "Are you sure that's the smart thing to do?"

If I wanted to be honest with Jenna, the answer would be no. Time jumps were completely unpredictable—I had no clue where in history

I'd land or how people would react to me. But an honest answer would only make Jenna worry about me. So I just gave her a reassuring smile. "Don't worry. I know what I'm doing." I then went to the laundry room and tugged at the shiny metal vent pipe behind the dryer, releasing it from the wall. A thick metal rod, a bit shorter than a ruler, clanged to the floor. It was hexagonal in shape, like a pencil, and divided lengthwise into six individual sections. Each of its faces had a strange glyph etched into it. When I picked up the rod, a slight chill ran through my hand: Somewhere in time, a glitch had occurred.

As I headed back over to my bedroom, I peeked in on Jenna. She was no longer in the living room, but I could hear her clattering around in the kitchen, opening and closing cupboards. "Cups are next to the fridge," I yelled as I started rummaging through the piles of clothes in my bedroom closet and then changed into my usual time-jumping outfit: a ratty-looking tunic and pants, leather boots, and a dark gray cloak. I strapped a leather bracer to my left arm, then tucked my jump device securely into it.

A quick glance at my phone showed that twenty-five minutes had passed since I last texted Sam. She would be expecting me any minute now.

I grabbed the leather backpack from the top shelf of the closet and checked the first-aid supplies and sewing kit I kept in a small felt pouch. Everything looked good. Now I just needed food.

I dashed over to the kitchen and found Jenna leaning against the counter, holding a cloth bag in both hands.

"What's that?" I asked.

"You need food, right?"

"Yes, but . . ." It was nice of her to do this for me, but I cringed at the thought of what she might have put in there. Little plastic-wrapped sandwiches that would spoil within a day? A bag of chips? Cans of soda? But inside the bag I found trail mix, protein bars with their wrappers removed, rice, and other dry foods all packed in little brown paper bags.

Jenna watched me with her eyebrows raised expectantly. "So?"

"This is awesome." I meant it sincerely. "How did you know what to pack?"

A smile crept across her face. "I listen. You told me how you can only bring things that don't draw attention to you in the past. So no plastic. No wrappers. No obviously modern foods."

"Impressive." I hefted the sack over my shoulder. "Now I just need—"

She picked up two filled leather water skins from the kitchen counter.

"Wow . . ." I leaned in and kissed Jenna. "You're awesome."

Was this what things had been like with my dad and mom? Had she known early on in their relationship that he was a time jumper? Had she been there packing his lunches as if he was heading off on a fishing trip with the boys, while knowing that he was off to some potentially dangerous trip into the past?

She wrapped her arms around me. "Come back in one piece."

"I will." I held her tight.

My phone buzzed. Reluctantly, I pulled away from our embrace and grabbed the phone off the counter.

Where R U? Call me!!!

I was just about to text Sam back and tell her to relax for a second, when I realized I had a major problem. Usually, when Sam and I jumped out, we did a countdown in unison with our phones on speaker. But with Jenna here, that was something I definitely wanted to avoid. Instead, I cranked the volume way low on my phone so that Jenna wouldn't hear Sam's voice, then called Sam's number, with the phone pressed tightly against my ear.

"Ready?" Sam asked the moment she picked up the phone.

"Yep. Um . . . by the way, Jenna's here."

"Yeah? So? What do I care?" I could picture Sam in the forest behind her home, dressed in her usual time-jumping garb, her bow slung over her shoulder.

Jenna pointed to herself. "Can I talk to him? I'd love to just say hi."

"No!" I yelped. "Um . . . I mean . . . no, we don't have time for that."

"*Him?*" Sam chuckled. "You told her I'm a guy? Maybe she *should* talk to me. I'm sure we could chat about all sorts of things."

"We need to go," I said tersely.

"You're no fun." Sam laughed. "But fine. Let's get going. And you can count us down, so that your precious girlfriend doesn't find out you've been lying to her."

"Thanks." I exhaled in relief. "Now?"

"Yes, go already."

Taking a deep breath, I spun the sections of the rod to the pattern for jumping out. "Three . . . Two . . ." I counted out.

Jenna stood watching me, a nervous smile on her face. "Be safe. I love you."

I love you. Neither of us had said those words before. I could feel myself staring at her unblinking, like a deer in headlights. *What do I say back? What do I do?*

"Hello?" Sam asked impatiently. "Are you still there?"

"One," I yelled. As quickly as possible, I shut my phone off and handed it to Jenna while blowing her a kiss, then shouted *"Azkabaleth virros ku, haztri valent bhidri du!"*

Jenna and my apartment disappeared in a blinding flash of light, replaced by the brightness of the time stream. All my senses disappeared. No smells. No sounds. No hard tiles beneath my feet. Just the harsh light pressing against my eyelids and the feeling of weightlessness, as if I was meandering down a lazy river on an inner tube.

This was usually the best part of a time jump, the half minute where I just floated along in the blinding glare of the time stream. It gave me time to collect my thoughts and mentally prepare myself for the grueling difficulties ahead. But this time, all I could think about was what Jenna had said. Her words shouldn't have surprised me. After all, we had been going out for three months and had been pretty much inseparable. But I hadn't been ready for it, and I'd responded terribly. I should have said something—anything. Instead, I just jumped back in time. The problem was, I had no idea if I loved Jenna. She was incredible in so many ways, and I definitely felt something for her, but Sam was still taking up so much space in my head that it was hard to define what I felt about Jenna.

I'd have to figure out my feelings for Jenna later. In roughly thirty seconds, the jump device would plunk me somewhere in history, and the hunt for Victor's men would begin.

CHAPTER 5

The brightness of the time stream vanished, and something solid materialized beneath my feet. I hurled myself down as I waited for the dizziness of time travel to recede, and for the purple spots in front of my eyes to fade away. Beneath my fingers, I felt dirt and grass, while the salty tang of seawater filled my nostrils. A gentle breeze stirred the air, carrying with it the cry of gulls and the lapping of waves against the shore.

I'd landed near the ocean. But where? It had to be someplace tropical; even though I'd been here only a few seconds, I could already feel the heat, especially with my heavy cloak wrapped around me.

I held my breath and strained my ears, listening intently for the sounds of people, animals, or anything that could pose a threat. Other than the normal beach noises, I didn't hear anything, which was a relief. The few seconds of time-travel sickness that I experienced on every jump always left me vulnerable.

Within a few heartbeats, my dizziness passed. Opening my eyes, I drew myself up into a crouch and spun in a slow circle to take in my surroundings. I'd landed on a narrow strip of land maybe two hundred paces wide and covered in dry, yellow grass. The grassland was bordered on the right by a salty marsh that drained into the sea, while on the left rose a rocky ridge that stretched to the sky. The lower part of the ridge had a gentle slope to it and was covered in a thick forest, but higher up, the ridge became steep like a wall.

The only sign of life was a lone boat in the distance bobbing gently on the waves. It had a wood hull with a single deck and one mast with an unfurled sail. Unfortunately, my knowledge of historical boats was pretty limited, and since this boat wasn't a Viking longship, or a Roman trireme with tons of oars poking out each side, or flying a pirate flag, I had no clue where or when I'd landed. People had to be close by, though, because a worn path had been beaten into the grass by the passage of many feet.

Keeping low, I dashed toward the forest at the base of the ridge and hid behind the first large tree I could find. With its rough bark pressing against my back and the low branches hiding me from sight, I felt safe for the moment. Now to find Sam.

I twisted the sections of the jump rod until the symbols lined up in the combination to detect other time jumpers, then swept the rod in a slow circle around me. It gave three sharp tugs, like a magnet pulling toward metal, all in the same direction. One of them had to be Sam, meaning the other two were Victor's guys. And, based on the strength of the pulls, everyone was close together.

Too close.

Sam was in trouble.

I leaped out of my hiding spot, all thoughts of stealth gone, and raced toward the stretch of forest where the jump rod pointed. My heart pounded in my ears as I trampled through the grass—my only focus the clump of trees ahead. I scanned it as I ran, desperately hoping to see a flash of Sam's clothing or her red hair through the trunks.

"Andreas, look out!" a male voice cried to the left from deep within the trees. "He has a bow!"

A second later, a cry of pain came from the right. "My arm!"

The Spartan Sacrifice

Sam had to be in the middle. But which way should I go? *Help Sam with the wounded guy, or go after the bigger threat?*

I lunged left and crashed through the trees, twigs snapping as I brushed them aside. About fifty paces ahead of me, a figure was barely visible through the branches. He was leaning with his back against a tree, and in his right hand he held a spear while in his left was the familiar shape of a jump device. His eyes widened when he saw me. "There's another one! Go home, Andreas!" He dropped his spear to the ground and began rapidly spinning the sections of his jump device.

He'd be gone in seconds. There was no way I could cover the distance between us in time. In desperation, I flung my staff at him, hoping to buy a few precious seconds. But it banged harmlessly off a tree trunk, and by the time it fell to the forest floor, he was gone.

I snatched up my staff and turned to help Sam, but stopped. There were no sounds of fighting, no panicked shouts, and no snapping branches. A quick check with my jump rod revealed that the other jumper had escaped as well.

A string of profanities erupted from my mouth as I whacked my staff against a tree trunk. *So close.* If only the stupid jump rod had landed me a bit nearer to Sam, our half-baked plan to steal a jump device from one of Victor's guys might have worked. But now Sam and I were stuck here fixing the glitch.

I whacked the tree trunk again.

"Umm . . . You know you're attacking a tree, right?" Sam said.

She was just visible through the maze of tree trunks, walking toward me. She wore her usual time-jumping garb of brown leather boots, gray pants, gray tunic, and a drab-green cloak with the hood pulled up. In her left hand, she held her bow, while her right hand gripped her jump device.

Sheepishly I lowered my staff and watched her approach. Based on past jumps, I knew she could walk through a field of dry twigs without making a sound. But after spending so much time with Jenna, I had a new appreciation for how stealthy Sam was. Where Jenna kind of bounced along, as if unable to contain her energy and enthusiasm, Sam stalked. Every footstep was placed with purpose, like a tiger sneaking up on its prey.

She stopped a few paces away from me and pushed back her hood, revealing her long red hair. "I was *this* freakin' close." She held up a hand with her thumb and index finger just a fraction apart. "If my arrow had been this much more to the left."

"You should have waited for me. I could have helped you."

"There was no time to wait; I landed right in the middle of them." She batted aside a leaf. "Fat lot of good that did me; they still got away." She shook her head in annoyance. "We probably would have been okay if you had helped me with the wounded guy instead of running off into the woods."

I bristled at her tone, as if *I* was the only reason for our failure here. "Don't dump this on me. I had to make a split-second decision, and I went for the bigger threat."

"Well, you made the wrong decision. You should have helped me."

I crossed my arms over my chest. "Maybe you shouldn't have missed with your arrow."

"Whatever." Sam rolled her eyes. "Well . . . what's done is done." Her tone softened. "And with Victor's guys gone, it looks like keeping history on its proper course is up to us—again." She sat down next to a tree and rested her bow across her lap, her gaze fixed on the marshy shore just visible through the tree trunks. "Any idea where we are?"

I sat down next to her and tried to get control of the emotions swirling inside me. This was the first time we had talked in person since that terrible afternoon, in the forest behind her house, when she had ripped my heart out. With her beside me again, I felt the familiar ache, wanting there to be more between us. But at the same time, I could barely look her in the eye—she had rejected me.

Get over it.

I wiped the sweat off my forehead with a sleeve. "Other than someplace hot, I have no clue. I guess it's too much to hope we're in Jamaica, and the time glitch can only be solved by relaxing on the beach?"

She chuckled, then pointed with her bow toward the marshy ground next to the ocean, where swamp reeds swayed in the breeze. "If this was Jamaica, I definitely would have expected some palm trees. What we have here"—she tapped the trunk of a tree with her gloved hand—"is a lot of oak."

I shielded my eyes with a hand and stared off into the haze-filled distance. Across the expanse of ocean, another long stretch of hill covered coast was visible. "Hot climate by the ocean, steep hills, oak trees." I snorted. "We could be anywhere."

Sam twisted her jump device to another setting and swept it in a slow circle. Her brow creased and she performed a second sweep, this one slower.

"Anything wrong?"

"I'm trying out the new Find Locals setting. It's . . . weird."

I spun my device to the same setting and performed a slow scan, not sure what to expect. Eric had told me about this setting only after my time jump to Mongolia. But, since none of the device functions worked in modern times, this was my first opportunity to try it out in the field. Sam was right; the device did feel weird. It had the usual pull I felt when searching for other time jumpers. But depending on where I pointed, it also felt heavier, as if gravity was tugging harder on it. "Strange."

"You feel it too?"

"Yeah. I figure the strength of the pull probably means that someone is close by, but what does the heaviness mean? More people? Less people?"

"Probably less people." Sam pointed her device straight out over the water toward the other coastline. "Because my jump device is practically falling out of my hands when I point it that way." She raised a hand to shield her eyes from the glare and stared across the water. "But all I see over there is forest and rocky hills."

"Makes sense." I spun my device to the setting that would direct us to the glitch that had brought us here. The rod pointed in an angle toward the same distant coast. "Whoa . . . That's weird. The time glitch is that way too."

"That can't be right." Sam fiddled with the settings on her jump device and swung it in a slow arc. She stopped with it pointing in the same direction as mine. "The glitch is way over there? Do you think it's in the forest? Or maybe it's on a boat anchored in some hidden cove?"

My stomach churned at the thought. I'd been on the ocean only twice in my life, and both times it had taken all of my willpower not to heave my lunch over the railing. "I really hope you're wrong about the boat."

"And if I'm not?" She raised an eyebrow. "Do you know how to sail?"

"Are you kidding? I grew up in the suburbs. I either drive, take the bus, or call an Uber. How about you?"

"Sure," Sam scoffed. "I sail every weekend. Right after my polo lessons."

"Check. No sailing skills for either of us. I guess that leaves us with our usual plan of heading toward the glitch and making things up as we go."

"Do we ever do anything else?" She sighed as she stood up and tucked her jump device inside the leather archery bracer that ran from wrist to elbow on her left forearm. "But if the glitch is straight across the water, which way do we go?" She pointed left, then right, then shrugged.

I pulled myself to my feet and stared intently at the distant shoreline where the glitch was located, trying to figure out which way we should go. "It actually looks like it kind of angles closer if we head left. Maybe if we head down that way, we can find a rowboat or something and then row across."

"Sure," she said with little conviction, then started walking.

I fell in step beside her. We deliberately picked a course that left us partially hidden by the trees, but still allowed us to see the ocean, as well as the path cutting through the field.

"So how are we going to do this?" I asked.

"Uh . . . the usual way. Find the glitch, fix it, leave." She gave me a confused look. "Did you already forget that we just scared off the only other time jumpers here?"

"That's not what I meant. I meant how are we going to handle things between us?"

Sam muttered under her breath and continued walking.

"Come on, Sam. I need to know the ground rules now that you dumped me. Do we—"

"Hold it." Sam stopped in her tracks and jabbed a finger at my chest. "I didn't dump you. We were *never* a couple."

"I didn't mean—"

"No! Let me finish! Don't get me wrong. I liked having you in my life. You made me feel less alone. But the two of us were *never* going to lead a normal life." She waved a hand toward the surrounding hills and ocean. "*This* is our normal. We don't get the luxury of holding hands and watching movies together. We get brutal jumps into the past, where it takes all our skill and focus to survive. We've been lucky so far, but one day, our luck will run out. I found out what it would feel like to lose you in Mongolia—and I'm *never* going to let myself feel that pain again." She pushed her hair back from her face. "So just forget about romance and focus on stopping Victor. That's all that matters." She fixed me with a challenging stare. "Can you do that?"

"Sure," I grumbled. "But that's the same thing you said months ago. As I was trying to say before you interrupted me, I just want to know the ground rules. Do we sleep side by side for warmth like we used to, or do we keep our space now? Are we still doing the strict 'no personal conversations' thing, or can we relax that a bit? Because we're going to be stuck with each other for a little while here, so I'd really like to know how to avoid pissing you off."

Sam rolled her eyes and let out an exaggerated sigh. "Yes, we'll still sleep side by side. And yes, you can talk about whatever—the weather, your sore feet, the dorks in your college club. I don't expect us never to talk to each other." She jabbed her finger at me again. "But no romance. Treat me like a coworker, or one of the guys."

One of the guys? Talk about impossible. No one, not even Jenna, made my heart quiver like Sam did. "I'll do my best." I began walking again.

She patted the trunk of an oak as she moved beside me. "After Mongolia, it's kinda nice to have a decent amount of forest to hide in again. Even if it is a bit on the steep side."

"You know that at some point we'll probably have to leave it, right? What are you going to do then?"

"Let's worry about that later. Right now, we need to figure out what we're dealing with here." She wiped her forehead with a sleeve.

"You look hot."

Sam inhaled sharply and her back stiffened.

I jerked back and raised my hands in apology. "That wasn't a come-on. I literally meant that you look hot. You know, the opposite of cold."

"Sorry," she said with an abashed smile. "I thought . . . you know."

"Wouldn't dream of it," I muttered.

She took off her thin leather archery gloves and stuffed them into her backpack. "You look the opposite of cold also. I wish these devices could tell us what sort of climate we're jumping into."

I glanced down at the jump device in my hand, with its multiple twisting sections. "Who knows? Maybe it can. I don't think we even know half of what these things are capable of doing."

"Too bad there's no owner's manual."

"My friends in the medieval club are piecing together what they can. Did you ever find out what happened to your dad's notes?"

"Nope. I'm still convinced my mom either hid them or threw them

The Spartan Sacrifice 55

out. She won't admit it, but you know what she's like." Sam grimaced. "I remember seeing Dad's notebook in my brother's apartment, but my *mother*"—she said the word with particular scorn—"emptied Steven's place out right after he died. So she probably found it and chucked it."

"As much as I hate to say this, it might not be your mom's fault. The people in my group are having a tough time finding information. Everything seems to have a way of disappearing: notebooks, USB sticks, laptops. It looks like Victor goes out of his way to make sure only people on his side know about time jumping." A bead of sweat trickled down the side of my face, and I wiped it away with my upper arm. "This is hotter than Mongolia."

Sam shrugged. "Yeah, it's hot, but it could be worse. At least there's shade, and a decent breeze coming off the ocean." She pointed to a shrub-covered hill visible through the trees between the coast and the steep ridge. It wasn't a huge hill, maybe about the height of a six-story building, but it was large enough to block our view of anything beyond it. "Why don't we climb up there to get a better view? Maybe we can figure out where we are."

A hill . . . a hot coastline . . . a narrow strip of land between a rocky ridge and the ocean? Something about this place seemed familiar. "I could swear I've seen this before."

"You mean you've *been* here?"

"No. It's more like . . ." My mind was a whirl of thoughts trying to snatch at a memory. "I don't know . . . It's like I've read about this place or seen it in a movie."

"And in this movie, was there a huge ambush hiding behind a hill?"

I scanned the area with my jump rod, searching again for locals. The device tugged forward sharply. "Maybe not an ambush, but I'm pretty sure someone's on the other side of that hill."

Sam nocked an arrow and held her bow at the ready. "Change of plans," she whispered. "We skip the hill and head higher up the ridge to scout from there."

I nodded and, with tentative steps, we crept up the ridge, pushing deeper into the trees and thick bushes that clung to the slope. After a few minutes, we managed to get high enough to see past the hill. Ahead of us, about five city blocks away, was a huge gathering of people. They filled the entire area between the cliffs and the ocean, blocking our way forward.

Sam ducked behind a nearby tree for cover, even though there was no way anyone down there on the plain could see us. "And, of course, there's a freakin' army," she muttered as she peered through the gaps in the trees. "Why can't we for once have a glitch that *doesn't* involve an army?"

I shielded my eyes with a hand and tried to make out details of the people ahead of us. "We don't know it's an army. Those white shapes are definitely tents, but it could be a . . . medieval Boy Scout Jamboree. I mean . . . look how they're separated into groups, all under different banners. Could be—oh. Those guys over there definitely have spears and shields."

"Told ya." She sighed and with little enthusiasm stepped out from behind her tree to stand beside me. "Can you see who they are?"

"No. We have to get closer."

"Of course we do," she grumbled. "But we're only getting close enough to figure things out." She waved a finger at me. "And we're not leaving the forest."

It took us about five minutes to pick our way along the tree-covered slope until we were close enough to the mass of people to see details more clearly. I counted ten groups, some fairly large, maybe a thousand or more men, and some less than a hundred. The groups were close to each other on the narrow plain but stuck to their own little packs. For the most part, everyone looked similar, with short black hair and olive-toned skin. No one wore armor, just loose tunic-like garments that ended just above the knee, and were worn either covering both shoulders or only one.

I rested my chin in my hand as I looked out over the assembled men. "I'd say we're somewhere in the ancient Mediterranean. These guys could be Greek, Roman, Carthaginian . . . maybe even Phoenician."

Sam scowled as her gazed drifted over the assembled men. "And would you look at that—not a single pale red-headed female in sight. Another time jump where I'm basically waving a sign above my head that says 'I'm not from here.'"

I wasn't really listening. My mind kept teasing me with flashes of memories that vanished before I could latch onto them. *Why do I think I know this place?*

A bit farther up the grassy plain, a low wall stretched from the ridge down to the coast. It was about a hundred and fifty paces long with a narrow opening in the middle of it through which the path continued. Hundreds of large, round shields, each with a different image painted on it, leaned against the wall. A group of men who looked different from the other groups was camped closest to the wall. While the rest of the soldiers had short hair and average builds, this group had long hair and looked more muscular, like they worked out regularly. And many of them skipped clothes altogether, strutting around naked with only a long blood-red cloak draped over their shoulders and a heavy spear in their hands.

Hot climate? Narrow pass? Muscular guys in red cloaks?

No freakin' way . . .

Goose bumps tingled along my arms despite the heat. "I know where we are!"

Sam tilted her head at me. "And?"

"See those guys at the wall—the ones standing around like they own the place, who everyone else is avoiding? How many of them would you say there are?"

"I don't know. Two hundred . . . maybe three hundred."

I crossed my arms over my chest to stop my hands from trembling with excitement. "And does the number three hundred mean anything to you?"

"No." She gave me a blank look. "Should it?"

"We're in Greece during the summer of 480 BCE!" I was so giddy that the words tumbled out of me. "Those guys"—I jabbed a finger in the direction of the wall—"are King Leonidas and his bodyguard of three hundred of the bravest and toughest Spartan warriors. The other guys are their Greek allies."

"So?" Sam shrugged. "Is the time glitch helping them find their lost clothes?"

"What?" I blinked in astonishment. "Have you not seen the movie *300*?"

"No," Sam scoffed. "I don't have time for movies; I have to work most nights. And if I do catch a movie, it sure as hell isn't going to be about a bunch of ancient Greek nudists having a picnic by the seaside."

"This isn't a picnic!" I sputtered. "This is the Battle of Thermopylae! One of the most famous battles in all of history! It is here that the brave King Leonidas leads his heroic group of Spartans in a last-ditch defense of Greece against the mighty forces of Persia."

"Brave King Leonidas? Heroic Spartans?" She laughed. "Are you some sort of fanboy or something?"

"Yeah? So? What if I am?" I stared at her defiantly, daring her to mock me. "Everyone needs heroes in their life, people they can look up to. Some people like basketball players or movie stars. Me? I'm all about the Spartans."

She raised a hand in mock apology. "Hey, if you want to geek out over a bunch of guys who dress like nude superheroes, that's your business." She jerked a thumb toward the Spartans. "What's so special about them anyway?"

"I don't know. They're just . . . badass. You have to understand; my dad never read me normal bedtime stories. There was a definite lack of happy ducks and curious kittens in the tales he told me. Instead, I got to hear epic blow-by-blow accounts of Leonidas and his three hundred warriors at Thermopylae, or the Spartan army at Plataea, or the Battle of Notium. Sure, Dad told me stories about other legendary warriors and battles, but none of them sounded even half as cool as the Spartans in their red cloaks."

Sam spun the sections of her jump device and pointed it in the direction of the army. A few seconds later, she moved it so that it angled almost straight out over the water. "I hate to disappoint you, but the glitch isn't with them; it's still way over there on the other shoreline."

"What the . . . ? That's not right. How could it . . . Oh . . ." My shoulders sagged. "The glitch is with the Persians."

"What Persians? I don't see any."

Memories came flooding back to me of sitting in my dad's study as he went over the details of Thermopylae. The troops numbers. The topography. The heroic events. "We're on the Malian Gulf, which is a huge bay. And that—" I pointed to hilly shoreline in the distance—"is just the other side of the bay. So the Persian army is somewhere over there."

Sam gave out a long, dramatic sigh. "Of course there's *another* freakin' army." She stared up at the sky and shook her head. "You can't have just one bunch of morons trying to kill each other; you always have to have at least two." She raised an eyebrow. "So, if the glitch is with the Persians and not your heroes, why did the stupid jump rods dump us on the Greek side of the bay?"

I blinked in surprise. "You're asking me? You're the more experienced time jumper."

"And you're the Spartan fanboy who knows all about this battle. So tell me—what are we supposed to do?"

Good freakin' question.

"I guess we should probably try to get closer to the glitch." I rubbed my jaw as I scanned the steep hills edging the near shoreline, searching for the easiest way to cross to the Persian side. But the Greeks had chosen this battle site for a reason—there was no way to get around the gulf except through the pass, or by using hidden mountain trails that the two of us would probably never find. "We could stay in the forest for a while and sneak along the hills, but over there"—I pointed to where the pass was narrowest—"the hills are steep, and the forest cover becomes impassable. We'll have to cut through a portion of the Greek camp."

"You want to 'cut through' an army?" Her eyes widened in horror. "This isn't a line in the school cafeteria. They're not just going to let us walk around."

I shrugged. "They might."

Sam placed her hands on her hips and gave me the are-you-freakin'-serious look that I knew too well. "Well, I'm not ready to 'cut through' an army because they 'might' let us pass."

Sam enjoyed being near armies about as much as cats enjoyed long soaks in a hot tub. And I couldn't blame her—I hadn't exactly had the best experiences with them either. But the glitch was with the Persians, and for some stupid reason, the jump rods had dumped us on the Greek side of the pass, so we had no other choice. "How about I go down there among the Greeks to scout things out a bit and see what sort of response I get?"

Sam snorted. "In our three jumps together, you've been"—she counted on her fingers—"stabbed . . . enslaved . . . shot with arrows. I have a pretty good idea how this one's going to turn out."

"Do you want to come with me, then?"

Sam exhaled slowly as she squeezed the bridge of her nose. "What *exactly* are you planning on doing?" She sounded tired, as if she was just waiting for me to present some stupid idea that she'd have to shoot down.

"Well . . . uh . . ." I waved my staff. "I'll just walk down there, like I'm some bored shepherd, and see how far I can get into their camp before someone challenges me."

She lifted an eyebrow and stared intently at me. "And do you think you can do that without getting stabbed or starting a fight?"

The old Dan would have given some sort of cocky answer about how he could handle things and not to worry. But that guy was kind of a moron who had nearly died on every time jump he'd been on. I wanted to prove to Sam that I was not the same guy—I was smarter and more cautious now. "Trust me. I know I don't look remotely Greek. I fully expect the first Greek I see to raise the alarm. But when that happens, I'm not going to stick around or cause problems, I'm just going to run like hell." I held my hands out to her. "I know the plan isn't the greatest, but we need to get over to the Persian side somehow."

Her brow furrowed as she chewed thoughtfully on a fingernail. "I guess you're right," she finally decided, then tossed her backpack to the ground. "Just *try* to stay out of trouble for once. I don't want to go near that"—she flicked a hand dismissively as if the Greek army was some wild animal that could just be shooed away—"unless I absolutely have to."

"Have some faith. I know I've done some dumb things on earlier jumps, but I've learned." I placed my backpack beside hers and turned to go.

"Um . . . aren't you even going to try and dress like a Greek?"

"Do you think it will make a difference?"

"Probably not." Sam shrugged. "But why stand out more than necessary?"

I hastily removed my cloak and boots, then yanked off my pants and socks, leaving me barefoot in just my tunic, which hung to midthigh. "How's this?"

"You need to cut your sleeves too. You look kind of dorky with long sleeves and no pants."

"Right!" Using my knife, I hacked off most of my sleeves, leaving me in the equivalent of a long T-shirt belted at the waist, with the bracer on my left arm. "Better?"

Sam cocked her head to the side as she looked me up and down. "Good enough, I guess. You're not going for the 'naked man in a cape' look like your heroes?"

"Hell no! I'm just trying to pass myself off as a shepherd, not a Spartan."

"Just a regular, tall, blond, blue-eyed, Greek guy, without a trace of a tan. Oh yeah. No problem." Her voice oozed sarcasm. "I'm sure you'll fit in *perfectly*." Shaking her head, she sat down next to our backpacks with her back against a tree trunk.

"Yeah, yeah. Maybe I look a *bit* different. But I'll think of some excuse. Hopefully all those guys will be too preoccupied with thoughts of the Persians to worry about me."

Sam shook her head disapprovingly but said nothing.

"Don't worry. I'll be right back."

With my staff in hand, I wove my way down the forested hillside, placing each bare foot carefully so I didn't scrape one on a rock or step on a thorn. Sweat covered my palms as I mentally prepared myself to enter the Greek camp. Hopefully no one would stop me and I could prove to Sam that we could safely pass over to the Persian side. The bigger question was: Would Sam actually come? The one thing I hadn't told her was the size of the Persian army. About two hundred thousand of them were currently marching along the opposite shore. If a few thousand Greeks were stressing her out, how would she react to an army thirty times larger?

CHAPTER 6

I broke through the tree cover at the foot of the ridge and stepped out onto the grassy plain. Ahead of me lay the entire Greek army. They hadn't noticed me yet, but they would. Then what? Sam was right about me looking totally not-Greek. And since the chances of me developing a decent tan and finding some dark hair dye in the next few minutes were nonexistent, I needed to quickly figure out an explanation for my strange appearance.

First: a name. Zeus? Definitely not. Theseus? Herakles? Double no.

Unfortunately, the only Greek names I knew were from mythology. Time to improvise.

Daneus? Not bad.

Danakles? That one had a good ring to it.

"Hi, I'm Danakles," I repeated to myself until the name rolled off my tongue with a tone worthy of a Homeric epic.

Next: a backstory. Nothing fancy, just something that would explain my presence. The simpler the story, the better. And since I was already committed to pretending to be a shepherd, I could just tell everyone I was from some far northern land. That would hopefully excuse my paler skin and lighter hair.

Now I just had to figure out *why* I was here. Since all the Greeks here had left their own faraway homes to stand against the Persians, I could probably pass off a sob story that my made-up homeland had been attacked as well, and I had fled here, traveling only at night.

Not bad. Not bad at all.

A warm feeling of satisfaction spread through me. For the first time ever on a time jump, I'd actually be somewhat prepared when I met the locals.

With my jump rod safely hidden inside the bracer on my left arm and my staff in hand as a walking stick, I strolled forward, heading for the Greek army. As I approached the first group of men, another problem appeared. Ancient Greeks were short. Not Oompa-Loompa short, but I had almost a full head advantage over all of them.

I'd never towered over an entire group like this. In school, I was just slightly above average height. And when I'd fought with other ancient peoples, like the Celts and the Anglo-Saxons, they were all shorter than me, but not by this much. Even with the Mongols, I hadn't noticed much of a difference because they did almost everything from horseback. But my height really stood out here. I hunched over my staff to appear shorter and pressed on.

A few heads turned my way as I strolled past the first group of men. My nerves stood on edge, waiting for someone to challenge me or move to stand in my way.

Nothing to see here.

With each step, my confidence grew. These men didn't seem to care that I was walking through the middle of their camp. I got a few curious glances, but nothing hostile.

As I sauntered along, I picked up various snippets of conversation, all of them automatically translated for me through the power of the jump device so that I understood everything as if I'd been speaking the various Ancient Greek dialects since birth. Some men spoke of their home and family, wondering if they'd ever see them again. Others spoke of the futility of trying to hold back the Persians long enough for reinforcements to arrive. Nobody was sounding optimistic about their chances.

After a few tense minutes, I passed through the main gathering of Greeks and approached the Spartan camp next to the short wall. This was going to be the toughest challenge. While the rest of the Greek "warriors" were actually merchants or farmers who had picked up weapons in a time of war, the Spartans were professional soldiers who dedicated their lives to training for battle. From the age of seven, every Spartan male underwent an education focused on hardship and discipline. They were given only one cloak to wear each year, and that had to act as their rain gear, blanket, and heavy clothing in cold weather. The boys were underfed so they would learn stealth by stealing food. They had to walk barefoot to toughen up their feet. And they were given lots and lots of training. Life in the *agoge*, their military training program, lasted until the age of thirty, when Spartan males were considered adults. This life of hardship created the toughest soldiers of the ancient world. They wouldn't be so relaxed about letting me pass through their camp.

The moment I stepped onto the empty stretch of dry grass separating the Spartans from the rest of the Greeks, a Spartan with shoulder-length black hair appeared in front of me, blocking my path with his spear. "Who are you?" he said gruffly. "Why do you approach our camp?" He was probably in his late forties or early fifties and taller than the Greeks I'd just passed, but he'd still be a bit shorter than I was if I hadn't been hunching over. He wore a pair of sandals and a red cloak over one shoulder, but that was it. Nothing else, not even a smile.

Time to see how far the dumb shepherd routine would take me. "I'm Danakles," I said cheerfully, the jump device automatically translating my thoughts so my words came out perfectly in his dialect of Ancient Greek. "I . . . um . . . want to see the wall."

He looked at me with disdain, as if I was some poor kid caught trying to sneak into the yacht club. "This area is for warriors only.

Shepherds belong over there." He pointed dismissively to where the rest of the Greek army camped.

"Let him see the wall, Areus," said another Spartan who was practicing his spear work. Thankfully, he wore a crimson tunic along with his red cloak. "He is at least brave enough to venture this way, unlike the rest of these *men* who are too scared to come near us."

Areus grunted and stepped aside. But as I walked past, he matched my stride and followed alongside me.

Just what I need: a naked shadow.

I began meandering through the Spartan camp, keeping a sharp eye out for any subtle hints, like a whispered order, or a discreet shifting of men, that would show the Spartans were planning to confront me. And deep down, the Spartan fanboy side of me was also hoping to see some of the incredible battle skills and legendary toughness that my dad had told me so many stories about. On both counts, I came up empty. Except for Areus, the Spartans didn't care one bit that I was in their camp. As for seeing something tough or warlike, the Spartans here were kind of disappointing. First off, all of them looked as old as Areus or even older. And, other than a few who were lazily practicing with their weapons, most of them just kind of hung out while servants rushed around, bringing them food, fetching water, sharpening weapons, or polishing bronze-covered shields until they gleamed in the bright sun.

Areus gestured to my staff. "And where are your sheep, O *mighty* Danakles?" The mockery in his tone was unmistakeable.

Around us, a few other Spartans laughed.

Great. I'd become their entertainment for the day. "I don't have any sheep," I muttered as we reached the wall—although calling it a wall was pretty generous. It was made of stone and only about waist high, like a wall someone would build around their garden. As a defensive fortification, it was adequate at best. It wouldn't stop a determined opponent, but it would at least slow them down. The gate had no doors and was wide enough to allow a cart through.

Beyond the wall, there was an empty field that gradually narrowed as the rocky shoreline came in to meet the ridge, until the field became just a thin stretch of land probably wide enough for only a few carts to drive through. This narrow strip of land, a few hundred paces long and draped in shadow by the looming hills next to it, was the famous pass of Thermopylae.

"So, O brave Danakles," Areus continued, "are you going to be the first of men along this wall, fighting off the Persians?"

I knew he was just trying to get me to say something dumb about the wall, so he and his buddies could have another laugh. In actual history, the Greeks fought far in front of the wall, where the pass was the narrowest and the superior numbers of the Persians would factor in the least. The old me would have probably tried to show off this bit of knowledge just to take Areus down a peg, but I was trying really hard not to get in trouble on this time jump. So I raised both hands toward the wall and dramatically shied away from it like I figured a shepherd would. "No, no! I don't want to fight."

Areus chortled. "The brave shepherd fears battle?"

"Yup. You got me. I'm just a cowardly shepherd who wants nothing more than to be left alone." Not one of my braver responses, but I wasn't here to impress Areus. The important thing was that I had made it all the way to the wall without any real challenge. Sam might be harder to get past everyone, but my idea of cutting through the Greek army to get to the Persian side didn't seem impossible. I turned away from the wall so I could head back to Sam and tell her what I'd found out.

"Wait!" yelled a Spartan who had been sitting on the wall staring off into the distance, with his red cloak draped around him. His long black hair was sprinkled with gray and reached just past his shoulders. He also had a strong jaw and fierce eyes, although the wrinkles on his face showed him to be older than the rest of the Spartans here. "Who are you?"

"He is a shepherd with no sheep," Areus snorted. "He is of no consequence."

"Do not be a fool, Areus," the Spartan said. "Look at the way his eyes move left and right, constantly searching for danger. And look at the way he stands on the balls of his feet, like a warrior alert for battle, not a shepherd."

Damn it . . .

Areus might have been duped by my simple shepherd act, but this new guy definitely wasn't. With a swirl of his cloak, he turned and hopped off the wall. Like all the Spartans, he stood confidently, like he owned the universe, even though he wore his blood-red cloak and nothing else.

"Stand up straight," he commanded.

I pulled myself to my full height. This new Spartan was taller than Areus, but still slightly shorter than me. "You are tall for a youth," he said. "Let me see your hands."

I laid my staff on the ground and held out my hands to him.

He grabbed my right wrist and ran a finger along the ridge of my palm. "You have used weapons before." He said it as a statement, not a question.

"Yes." No use denying it. The scars and callouses on my hands proved him right.

He picked up one of the spears leaning against the wall and shoved it into my hand. "Show us whether you can use a spear." Areus had addressed me with a constant mocking tone to his voice, but this Spartan actually sounded like he wanted to see my skill.

I peered at him intently. "Who are you?"

He placed a fist over his heart. "I am Leonidas, son of Anaxandridas, son of Leon. King of the Spartans."

CHAPTER 7

I sucked in my breath. Leonidas, king of the Spartans, leader of the three hundred, hero of Thermopylae, was actually standing right in front of me! Part of me was in awe. I'd heard so many stories about his bravery and his defiance against the Persians. The other part was quivering in fear. He clearly didn't believe my peasant disguise—so what did he want with me? I became aware of his scrutinizing gaze and the large number of other Spartans watching.

With shaking hands, I gripped the spear. It was about eight feet long, with a metal blade on one end and a thick, spiked counterweight on the other. Its size and weight clearly limited it to stabbing, not throwing. It felt incredibly balanced in my hands, much better than any other spear I'd ever used.

Leonidas stood by my side. "Show me what you would do if a Persian stood in front of you."

Last chance for me to act like someone who knew nothing about warfare. I could "accidentally" drop the spear, or flail around like someone swatting bugs, but I had a feeling Leonidas wouldn't believe either. Instead, I shifted into a fighting stance, with the spear held high over my shoulder. I raised my left arm as if it held a shield.

"He does not stand like a shepherd," someone remarked.

"No." Leonidas stroked his chin thoughtfully. "He does not."

My spear darted out and back as if I was stabbing an imaginary opponent.

"Bah!" Areus scoffed. "Even a simple shepherd can learn how to stand like a man. But does he have the strength of one?" He picked up a large round shield with a bull's head painted on it. "This shield was passed to me by my father, Telekles, who received it from his father, Archelaus, who received it from his father, Labotas, who in turn received it from *his* father. I and my ancestors have carried it with courage and honor into every battle, where we have triumphed over countless enemies." He passed it to me. "See if you can wield it like a man." He turned to face the other Spartans gathered around. "Now you will see the difference between a shepherd and a Spartan."

The shield was made of thick wood reinforced with bronze, with two large bronze loops on the back—one in the center and the second near the edge. I slid my left arm through the center one and gripped the other. The shield was probably twice as heavy as any shield I'd used before, but it was manageable. I went back into my fighting stance, shield in front of me, protecting me from chin to knee.

"You are right, Areus," said another Spartan. "I see the difference now. He is taller than you."

"Hold your tongue, Dienekes," Areus spat, his face turning red. He snatched the shield back from me and laid it aside. "I will prove to you all that he is nothing more than a mere shepherd." He wheeled around and jabbed his finger toward my face. "You! Fight me!" He crouched low like he was about to attack me with his bare hands.

The spear hung loosely in my grip. No part of me wanted to fight Areus. First, he was naked. And second, I didn't want Sam to be right about me always ending up in a fight. The smart thing would be for me to drop the spear and head back to Sam so we could worry about the glitch over on the Persian side of the bay. But all I could think about was how Sam couldn't understand why the jump device had dropped us right next to the Greeks instead of over by the Persians. It seemed like a mistake, but what if it wasn't?

"Um . . . I can't fight you. You don't have a weapon," I said, trying to buy some time while I figured things out.

Areus laughed and thumped his bare chest with a fist. "I am a Spartan. You are a shepherd. Do you think yourself equal to a Spartan, even with a spear?" A ripple of laughter flowed through the watching crowd.

Leave or fight?

Areus sauntered back in front of me, gloating. "The shepherd quakes with fear. I knew he was not a man."

Leonidas gave me a look filled with disappointment before he and the rest of the Spartans began to turn away.

I glanced down at my bracer where I had hidden the jump device. Why had this little hunk of mystery metal dumped Sam and me so far from the actual glitch? My head said it was probably a mistake, but my gut said it wasn't—the jump device had always landed us exactly where we needed to be to fix the glitch, and this time was no exception.

But which one was right?

There was only one way to find out.

"Go big or go home," I muttered to myself.

I let the spear fall out of my hand. It landed with a metallic clang against the hard earth. "You're right, I'm not your equal." I fixed Areus with my most arrogant stare. "I'm better."

Areus laughed. "Your father never taught you respect for your superiors. I will now give you the beating he neglected to deliver."

His threats would probably terrify the average Greek peasant, but I'd had my own version of the *agoge*—since I was old enough to walk, my dad had trained me in martial arts and medieval weapons. I'd fought with the Anglo-Saxons against Norman invaders. I'd fought with Celts against Romans, and with Mongols against Merkits. I knew about fighting, and some arrogant Spartan bastard wasn't going to intimidate me. I let all distractions slip into the background and focused on Areus.

He swaggered confidently toward me. Then, for the briefest of instants, his body tensed, and he exploded with a punch at my midsection. My years of martial arts training with my dad kicked in, and I dodged the punch, grabbed his wrist, and twisted it. He grimaced in pain, trying to fight back, but I twisted harder until he was forced to his knees. With my other hand, I then reinforced my hold on his wrist so he couldn't move.

"He knows *pankration*!" a Spartan gasped.

I stood there with a smirk on my face. *I'd done it. I beat Areus without actually throwing any punches. That would show Sam—*

Areus kicked at my knee, sending me to the ground. My hold on his wrist slipped, and he leaped back to his feet. I rolled along the ground and jumped up into a crouch.

Stupid. Stupid. Stupid. First rule of fighting: Make sure the fight is actually over before you start celebrating.

"You have some skill, shepherd," Areus conceded.

He rushed at me and sent a kick flying—a beautiful kick worthy of anything done in my karate dojo. I leaped to the side and caught his foot just before it hit my head and twisted his leg until he lost his balance and fell.

Areus jumped back to his feet. With a calm focus, he released a flurry of kicks and punches at my head, chest, and ribs. Step by step, he forced me back as it took all my skill to block these attacks.

He threw a huge lunging punch at my head that I just managed to dodge. His momentum carried him too far forward, and for a fraction of a second, his guard fell, allowing me to counter with a knee straight to his midsection. He doubled over from the impact, and, before he could recover, my elbow cracked against the side of his jaw, sending him sprawling flat onto the grass.

"If this is how the shepherds of his land fight, I would hate to meet their warriors," Dienekes chuckled.

Leonidas stepped in front of me. "Where did you learn *pankration*?"

I took a few deep breaths to calm my heart rate. I'd never heard that word before, but based on the precision punches and kicks Areus had aimed at me, it must have been some type of Spartan martial art. "From my father."

The Spartan king raised an eyebrow. "What else did he teach you?"

I shrugged, nervous at the sudden attention. "Umm . . . all sorts of things: fighting, how to survive in the wild, battle tactics . . . and . . . um . . . other stuff."

A murmur rippled through the crowd of Spartans.

"And who is your father?"

Oh, boy. There was a backstory I hadn't yet made up. Best to just go with the truth here. "James."

A puzzled look crossed Leonidas's face. "He does not have a Spartan name. But he has trained you in the Spartan manner."

Areus grunted and pulled himself up off the ground. He grasped his jaw and moved it back and forth to shake off the effects of my elbow. "He fights like a Spartan. Could his words be true?" Before he'd looked at me with arrogance, but now he seemed puzzled.

Leonidas eyed me. "Take off your chiton."

"Chiton?"

"Your covering."

I gulped. When the Spartan king told you to do something, it wasn't a suggestion; it was an order. And with three hundred Spartan warriors watching, it was a command that better be obeyed quickly.

I yanked my tunic over my head, leaving me with just my bracer along my forearm and my boxers. Luckily, I was wearing boring gray cotton, not something flashy that would stand out. Hopefully the Spartans weren't going to ask me to take those off too.

"He has strong arms and chest," someone remarked.

"A broad back too," another man added.

"Look how pale his skin is. Does he never see the sun?"

The irony of my situation sank in. I had hoped to casually walk into the Greek camp and not attract attention, but now I was the center of a ring of Spartans, all of them studying me like I was some weird creature that had landed in their midst.

"He bears a mark upon his arm," one of them observed.

Leonidas grabbed my right wrist and twisted it so the tattoo on the inside of my forearm became visible to everyone. He glanced at it for a second, and his brows narrowed. "What does this signify?"

"Um . . . I don't know. My father had it done when I was young." A weak answer, and I knew it. But the truth would only cause more problems.

Another Spartan peered at my tattoo. "Could it be a Persian mark? Is he a spy?"

"But he wears it openly," Areus said. "No spy would announce his presence so freely. And why would the foul Persians send a spy who is so clearly not one of us? They have already conquered many Greek lands; they could have picked any number of Greek men to spy for them."

Leonidas stroked his chin, clearly pondering. "Fetch Megistias the Seer," he called to a servant. "Maybe he has seen this mark before."

As the servant rushed off toward the main Greek camp, Leonidas poked me in the bicep. "He has the physique of a Spartan."

"And battle scars too." Dienekes walked slowly around me, his fingers tracing over my skin. "I see one on his shoulder and one across his brow."

The Spartans continued poking and prodding me, commenting on my posture, my height, my skin color, my muscle mass, and my scars. I'd had less intrusive checkups at the doctor.

Areus stood in front of me, a bewildered expression on his face. "How old are you, shep—Danakles?"

"Almost eighteen." This set off another murmur.

"And where are you from?"

Although probably no one would believe it, I stuck to the original backstory I had created. "I'm from a small village north of here."

"It must be *very* far north of here." Dienekes's tone hinted at his disbelief. "Why are you here?"

I scrambled for an explanation. The Spartans weren't hostile yet—I was just a curiosity they didn't understand. But what happened when I ran out of answers to their questions? "I'm here to . . . uh . . . help?"

Areus gaped at me incredulously. "With no weapons? No armor?"

Ugh . . . I didn't have an answer for that one. "I . . . uh . . ."

"Let me see the mark," commanded a deep voice, saving me from answering.

All heads turned toward a gray-bearded man who stood just outside the little group surrounding me. He wore an ankle-length tunic of deep green and held a long staff in his right hand. But while my staff was a weapon, he leaned on his for support.

With a reverence I'm sure they afforded no one else, the Spartans moved aside, and the old man shuffled slowly through their ranks until he stopped right in front of me. He peered through cloudy eyes, his wrinkled face scrunched up as he scrutinized me like a scientist with a new discovery. When he caught sight of my tattoo, his eyes widened. "I know that mark," he said, his voice noticeably hushed.

My ears perked up. "Where have you seen it? Does someone else here have this mark?" I whipped my head around, paying close attention to everyone else's forearms. Was one of Victor's men somehow hiding here among the Spartans, and Sam and I had missed him?

The seer's bony fingers reached out and traced the outlines of my tattoo. "I saw a symbol like this when I was a young man. Except the star within a circle had eight points, not four." He stroked his beard and his eyes glazed as he tried to recapture the memory. "It was on a piece of stone that had been part of a triumphal column from a distant land."

My heart pounded. I *knew* the mark was ancient. Could it be Greek? Did he know what it signified? Did he know how the time devices worked? "Can you tell me anything about it?"

He clasped my hand and bowed his head toward me. "The piece I saw was very small. No doubt, when intact, the original column would have reached high into the sky. I would very much liked to have seen it. But, even from that small fragment, I learned that it came from a very ancient and powerful people."

Leonidas's brow furrowed, and he eyed me intently. "Are any others from your village here?"

"No," I responded, still in a daze. If this weird eight-pointed star that Megistias had seen was related to the symbol on my arm, then my tattoo clearly belonged to a people who predated even the ancient Greeks. My thoughts flew back to the city I'd seen in the time stream. It had looked kind of Greek, but not quite. Had the stone that Megistias had seen come from this same city?

Leonidas threw a fatherly arm over my shoulder. "And what news do you bring from the north? How do their lands fare under the yoke of Persian tyranny?"

"Um . . . terrible."

He nodded as if mulling over my words. "Is that why you are here, to help us defeat the foul Persian plague that overwhelms our lands?"

That sounded better than any excuse I'd made up so far. "Yeah . . . sure."

"Excellent!" He beamed a huge smile and clapped me on the shoulder. "You will fight with us, then!"

The blood drained from my face. That was the worst idea I'd *ever* heard. I didn't want to be remotely near these guys when the battle started. But how could I disobey a king?

Before I could think of a response, one of the Spartans inhaled sharply, and his back stiffened as if he had been personally insulted. "What? He is not a Spartiate."

Leonidas raised a hand and held it out for silence. "He does not need to be a Spartiate to fight with us, Charilaus. Both *helots* and *perioikoi* bear arms when Sparta calls."

"But he is neither. He has never lived in Sparta. He does not know our ways."

Silently, I kept willing Charilaus to win this argument, but Leonidas merely shrugged. "Then I will make him my *trophimos*, and we can teach him."

Charilaus's face turned red with anger. "This incredible honor is supposed to be given only to the children of noble non-Spartans, so that they may train for war with our sons in the *agoge*." He jabbed a finger at me. "He is not the son of a noble. And this is a field of battle, not the *agoge*."

"What better training could we give him than right here, right now?" Leonidas asked.

"But he is a babe who has not even grown his first beard," Charilaus argued. "We do not let children of fewer than twenty summers fight."

Leonidas sniffed as if insulted. "I would never let a boy like him hold a spot in our phalanx. But the gods led Danakles here for a reason, and I believe that reason is to help us."

"Gods?" Charilaus scoffed. "More like the Persians. I do not trust him."

Leonidas clapped a hand on Charilaus's shoulder. "I hear your words, old friend, but my decision has been made. Danakles has shown his bravery by coming here. He has shown his skill by besting Areus. He is clearly as strong and as tall as any of us. And Megistias the Seer says he comes from an ancient and honorable people. We could use him here with us, even if only to throw spears from behind our formation." He waved his hand dismissively toward the non-Spartan Greeks. "Our allies bring only shepherds and farmers, so I have no illusions upon whose backs the brunt of the fighting will fall. If Danakles here truly wishes to be of use in our fight against the Persians, then I will adopt him as my *trophimos* and, in the short time before the battle starts, we can teach him what he needs to know." He turned to me. "What say you, Danakles? Do you accept?"

I wanted to shout out *Hell no!* at the top of my lungs. But with Leonidas, my hero, staring at me expectantly, all I could do was mutter a weak yes.

As Leonidas gave me a proud nod, I choked back the bile rising in my throat. This scouting mission had gone horribly. All I had to do was see if there was a way for Sam and me to get safely past all the Greeks and make it over to the Persian side. It should have been a simple job, but somehow I had messed up horribly and become an honorary Spartan instead. I felt myself trembling with dread, and my heart hammered in my chest, a steady beat that seemed to carry in the wind.

Wait a minute . . . That's not my heart.

The Spartans heard the noise too. They looked past me, out over the water. Across the bay, thousands of Persian cavalry rode slowly along the coast, just visible through a haze of dust and humidity. The hooves of their horses pounded along the shore, creating a steady rumble like thunder.

Whoa . . .

The Persians were coming, thousands upon thousands of them, and I'd just volunteered to join the Spartan army.

CHAPTER 8

I'd seen forty thousand Mongol horsemen thundering across the steppes of Mongolia. I'd seen eighty thousand Celtic warriors massing on the shores of the Menai Strait as they prepared to battle twenty thousand invading Romans. But none of these armies came close to the size of the Persian force. I could feel my mouth hanging open as I shielded my eyes from the sun and watched the ribbon of troops approaching. From this distance, they looked like one long black snake slithering along the curve of the bay. I couldn't even see the end of the army; it just went on forever.

"There are more Persians than I thought." Dienekes scratched his chin thoughtfully. "I should have brought more spears."

Areus's gaze traveled slowly along the length of the dark smudge. "A few thousand more men would have been better."

"Those men will come," Charilaus said. "We just need to hold out long enough for the Carneian festival to end. Then the full might of Sparta will send these invaders back into the sea."

"This will be no easy task." Leonidas scanned the thousands of approaching Persians. "Many of us will find a glorious death before we see victory."

Areus waved a hand dismissively. "We knew when we volunteered to come with you that the Fates would not be kind and that few of us would see our homes again. I have already said goodbye to my wife, and my son looks forward to bearing my shield after I die."

"So he is eager for war, like his father." Leonidas placed a hand on Areus's shoulder. "Do your best to disappoint him."

"I will," Areus grinned.

Leonidas took one more look at the Persian army on the distant shore and then clapped his hands together. "Enough standing here like sheep! Let us prepare for war!" With that he strode purposefully toward a section of the wall where a large shield, painted with a sunburst design, stood next to a stack of neatly piled armor.

Prepare for battle now? At the pace the Persian army was currently moving, its lead elements would take a good chunk of the day to get around the bay. Why would Leonidas want to put his armor on now? He'd only end up standing around in it for hours under the hot sun.

But Leonidas didn't collect his armor. Instead, he rummaged through a cloth bag and retrieved a small clay jug and a wooden comb.

Some Spartans retrieved their own combs and jars, while others rushed to the open space in front of the wall and started stretching, wrestling, or doing sprints.

What the . . . ? A trip to the beauty salon and pre-battle Zumba class were definitely not in the movie *300*.

"Danakles," Areus said as he poured oil from a small jar onto his head then massaged it into his long black hair. "You wear your hair long in our manner. So why do you not prepare it now for battle?"

"What does my hair have to do with fighting? I just strap on my armor and pray to whatever gods might be listening that I don't die."

"A good prayer." Leonidas chuckled. "They have listened so far."

"It seems that although you were trained like a Spartan," Areus said, "some of your teaching may have been neglected." He drew a comb through his hair, spreading the oil so his hair took on a shiny look. "We wear our hair long to show that we are free men—not slaves with their heads shorn." He raised a clenched fist, and his voice grew louder in intensity. "And before battle, we oil and comb our hair so our foes will know they face proud and strong free men, and we drive fear into their hearts!"

I felt a goofy smile spread across my face. Only the Spartans could turn something as bland as combing their hair into an epic expression of toughness. I had almost told Areus that I only had longish hair because I was too lazy to get myself a haircut. That little bit of honesty would never pass my lips now.

"What about those guys?" I asked, pointing to a bunch of Spartans who were racing and wrestling each other. "How does that prepare them for battle?"

"They do not prepare for battle," Areus corrected me. "They prepare for death. Many of us will not survive these next few days. Our sport is the last chance many of us will have to engage in friendly competition and say goodbye to lifelong companions." He glanced at me sideways. "You said you would join us in our fight. Do you have anyone you wish to say goodbye to?"

And again, the Spartans had managed to turn something monotonous like wind sprints into a deep and meaningful expression of brotherhood. "I do have someone I need to talk to." With the Spartans engrossed in their pre-battle rituals, now would be a good time to check in on Sam and tell her everything that had happened.

I put my tunic back on, then nodded to Areus. "I'll be back."

"Do not be too long," Areus said. "Your skill at *pankration* is superior to mine, and I wish to learn more."

"Yeah, sure . . . later." I ran off before he could respond.

I jogged through the Greek camp in the direction of where I'd left Sam—way past the farthest group of Greeks. Once I was clear of the camp, I ducked into the trees and pulled out the jump device to search for her.

Huh? She was nowhere close to where I'd left her. She had moved to a forested section of hillside directly overlooking the Spartan camp. I slowly followed the tugging of the rod through a maze of trees and up the slope.

It took me about ten minutes to find her. She sat with her back resting against a tree in a small clearing, a book in one hand, while her other hand lay on the jump device next to her leg. She had gone through a wardrobe change since I'd last seen her. Like me, she had ditched her boots, pants, and cloak. She now wore just her tunic like a mini-dress that reached the midpoint of her thighs. She had also hacked off her sleeves completely, baring her pale shoulders and arms.

"Hey," she said without looking up.

"Um . . . How'd you know it was me?"

Sam laid the book down beside her, cracked open, pages down so she wouldn't lose her spot. "I have the jump rod set to Find Locals, so I knew none of them were coming up the hill. Plus, you have a distinctive stomp."

"You're looking pretty chill. All you're missing is a fruity umbrella drink. Should I come back later?"

Sam laughed. "This is definitely not my normal look. But I saw you were doing okay down there, so I figured I could relax a bit. After all, we *are* in Greece, and even in the shade, it's still like a sauna."

I looked around. All I could see were trees. "How were you watching me?"

She patted the spot next to her. "Come sit and I'll show you."

I sat down next to Sam and she pointed to a gap in the trees that was only visible from close to the ground. Through it she had a clear view of the wall and the Spartan camp. "Ugh . . . I guess you saw my fight then, huh?"

Sam rolled her eyes. "Yeah. I saw it. I told you you'd end up in one."

"Well . . . yeah . . . um . . . Hey! I saw you brought a book. Why?"

It was obvious that I was trying to change the subject, but Sam didn't seem to notice. Instead, she slapped her hand over the cover of the book to hide it. "I always bring a book on jumps. They're a great way to pass time when things get boring. And when I'm done, the pages make great fire starters."

"I never saw you reading during other jumps."

"You mean when I was surrounded by thousands of Mongols or saving you from a life of Roman slavery?" she said sarcastically. "I didn't quite feel like reading then."

I tried to peek at the book's cover picture between her splayed fingers. I couldn't see all of it, but I caught glimpses of what looked like a male werewolf and a female vampire. "You're reading *Darkness Beckons*?" I laughed.

A blush crept up her lightly freckled cheeks. "What's wrong with that?"

"Nothing, I guess. I just never had you pegged as liking the whole vampire-werewolf romance thing."

She snapped the book shut and placed it cover-down on the far side of her. "At least I read. All you ever talk about is movies. What's the last book you read?"

I raised my hands defensively. "I never said there's anything wrong with cheesy romance novels. I'm sure they make great toilet paper."

"Don't you have some naked men to go fight with?"

I snorted. "Why do you think I'm up here?"

"I guess to make fun of my book choices."

"Actually, I was hoping we could talk about the glitch and what we're going to do about it."

"Oh, yeah." Sam sighed. "The glitch." She picked up the jump device and pointed it toward the Greeks and then the distant Persians on the other side of the bay. The device angled down slightly when aimed toward the Greeks, but it plunged straight to the ground when focused on the Persians. "By the way, I figured out how the Find Locals setting works. I had it backward before: The heavier it feels, the *more* people there are. So I'm guessing—by the fact I can hardly hold it up—that there are a ton of Persians coming." She glanced at me sideways. "How *big* is this battle?"

"Well . . . there were about seven thousand Greeks."

"And *how* many Persians?"

"Two hundred thousand?" I replied quietly.

Her head jerked back and her eyes widened. "Two hundred freakin' thousand! Don't tell me. Let me guess." She put up a hand to silence me. "The Greeks lose?"

"Yeah."

"So why are we here? Why is this battle so important to history? Because I can see it being over in about ten minutes."

I remembered the fire that would appear in my dad's eyes when he spoke of the Battle of Thermopylae. How his voice pitched with enthusiasm as he described the heroic Spartan defense. "This battle isn't important because of the Greeks losing. It's the Spartans who are important here. Instead of running away like most of the Greeks, the Spartans fight to the last man so the rest of the Greeks can escape. Their act of sacrifice becomes a morale boost for the Greek states. It shows them that a small group of determined warriors, in the right terrain, can hold off or defeat a larger force." I closed my hand into a fist. "A month from now, the outnumbered Greek navy is going to use the lessons of Thermopylae to win the Battle of Salamis, and the Greeks will follow up that victory with another one on land, at the Battle of Plataea, with the full might of the Spartan army, effectively ending the Persian threat. But it all starts here. The Spartans have to die heroically to inspire the rest of the Greeks."

Sam's brow furrowed. "Um . . . if the Spartans have a full army available, why'd they only send three hundred guys to such an important battle? That sounds kind of dumb."

"It has to do with their religion. The Spartan people are celebrating the festival of Carneia right now, in honor of the god Apollo. And during the festival, they were forbidden from waging war. Leonidas knew how

The Spartan Sacrifice 85

important it was to stop the Persians, so he decided to venture out here, with his bodyguard of three hundred men, and see what they could do just by themselves—without an official declaration of war."

Her eyes had a hunted look to them as she stared intently across the bay. "Are there seriously two hundred thousand Persians?" There was an uncharacteristic quiver in her voice.

"Unfortunately. The Persian empire was the largest in existence at the time. It stretched from Egypt to India, so King Xerxes brought in people from all his conquered lands to help him defeat Greece. They even have people from former Greek lands in their army."

Sam wrapped her arms around herself as she continued staring straight ahead, unblinking.

"Are you okay, Sam?"

"No." Her entire body trembled and her voice dropped to barely a whisper. "I was lucky in Mongolia that nothing happened to me. But two hundred thousand? I . . . I just can't."

"It's okay." I moved to put a comforting hand on her shoulder but stopped myself. "I have a plan so that neither of us have to risk going to the Persian side."

She turned toward me, a hopeful expression on her face. "What is it?"

"Well . . . you know that little martial arts display that I put on down there? The Spartans were kind of impressed by it, and they sort of volunteered me to join them. So if I hang out with them, I can keep a constant eye on the Persians from this side of the pass." I raised my hand to cut off Sam's response. "I know it's not the ideal situation, but I got a hunch it's the right thing to do. After all, you even said you couldn't understand why we were dumped on the Greek side instead of the Persian side." I raised my index finger. "Plus, in actual history, the Persians camped out for four days before they attacked, waiting for the rest of their army to show up, so that will give us four days to get more information about the glitch before we make a decision about what we need to do."

I braced myself for all sorts of scathing responses. How it was foolish of me to risk our chance of fixing history just because of a hunch. How I always got into fights, and I should have just walked away. But Sam didn't say anything. She merely stared out across the bay, chewing on a lock of red hair that she had twisted around a finger. I wasn't sure if this silence was actually better.

"So?" I ventured.

"It's not a terrible idea." She sounded like she was trying to convince herself more than me. "So on day five, the Persians attack, right?" She snorted. "How long does that battle last? Five minutes? Ten?"

"Actually, the Greeks kicked major butt for two days straight. On the third and final day of the battle, a Greek traitor led a portion of the Persian army along a secret mountain pass, so they could appear to the rear of the Greeks. If the Spartans hadn't gotten attacked from the back, they might have held out long enough for reinforcements . . ." My voice trailed off as a bolt of inspiration struck me. "What if that's the glitch? What if the Persians don't send that bit of their army around the back?"

"So? You said the Greeks win eventually. What difference would it make if they ended up winning here instead of at the next battle?"

My excitement faded. "You're right. It doesn't make sense."

Sam tapped two fingers against her lips. "What if the Spartans don't do this heroic stand?"

"You think they'd just run away?" I could barely keep the disdain out of my voice. "They would *never* run. A Spartan who surrendered or ran away from battle was considered a disgrace to society. His own family would cast him out, and he would be shunned by everyone."

"It doesn't have to be that. What if, through some fluke, the Persians fight so well that the Spartans get overwhelmed in the first day of battle?"

I tried to envision how history would unfold. "Well . . . without the Spartan heroics, some of the Greek cities might believe that defeat is inevitable and surrender, so who knows how that might affect the Battle of Salamis. And, without the victory at Salamis, the battle at Plataea would definitely be out." The thought of Sam's prediction coming true made my stomach churn. "But how likely is that? All the glitches we've fixed so far were caused by one person. How could one guy make the entire Persian army fight so much better that they beat the Spartans in one day?"

Sam shrugged. "You're the fanboy who knows everything about this battle. I'm just trying to brainstorm." Sam spun her jump device to the setting that detected glitches and swept it in a slow arc from right to left over the water. She ended up pointing just past the Spartans, and deep down the narrow pass of Thermopylae. Her brow furrowed. "That's weird. Whatever the glitch is, it just got a lot closer."

"That can't be right. The Persian army should have taken hours to arrive." I grabbed my own jump device from out of my bracer and did my own check. Sam was right, the glitch was rapidly approaching the Greek lines.

"I gotta go!" I turned away from her and began crashing through the trees and down the hillside, my heart racing.

Was the glitch going to happen right now?

What even was the glitch?

How could I stop it?

So many questions, and history depended on two measly teenagers to set everything right.

CHAPTER 9

As I left the cover of the forested hillside and ran out onto the dry plains, I saw many of the Spartans staring in the direction of the narrow pass, watching someone or something. Leonidas didn't seem to notice, though. He was still at his spot on the wall, combing his long black hair while singing to himself.

I ran over to his side, ready to warn him of whatever was in the pass, just as Charilaus approached. "Riders," he said casually as he motioned with his chin to where the outer guard now blocked a small group of Persian horsemen from coming any closer.

Leonidas jumped to the top of the wall, his red cloak flapping behind him in the breeze coming off the bay. With a hand shielding his eyes, he peered off into the distance. "They look like messengers." Hopping down from the wall, Leonidas signaled to two of his men. "Telekles. Maron. Rouse the other leaders. It looks like the Persians wish to speak with us."

As the pair sprinted off toward the scattered camps of the various Greek city-states, I casually stretched out my left arm. The jump device hidden in my bracer definitely pointed to the group of horsemen.

The messenger is the glitch?

I'd have to get closer to be sure. And my best bet for doing that was to tag along with the Greeks when they went to meet the Persian delegation. Fortunately, it didn't take long for the rest of the Greek leaders to arrive. All of them were older men, wearing colorful tunics embroidered with gold and silver thread, and many of them wore large gold chains to denote their higher status.

"The Persians have sent messengers." Leonidas pointed to the small group of horsemen gathered in the middle of the pass. "Does anyone here speak their wretched tongue?"

No one stepped forward.

"No matter." Leonidas picked up his spear and shield. "What we must say now does not need words."

What if this was the glitch? What if, because of some misunderstanding, the messenger convinced the Persians into attacking now instead of waiting four days? I pushed my way forward. "I speak their language." Or at least I hoped that the jump rod strapped to my arm would allow me to.

Leonidas raised an eyebrow. "You bring many surprises." He rested his spear on his shoulder. "So be it. We will hear the words of the Persians." He motioned to me, then to Areus, Dienekes, Maron, and Charilaus. "Follow me."

He turned on his heel and marched through the empty gate, his red cloak trailing behind him. The four other Spartans fell into step a few paces back, two on each side. Oddly, none of them had stopped to put on armor or even a proper tunic. If I was heading off to meet a Persian emissary, I would try to make myself look as impressive as possible. But the five Spartans remained naked except for cloaks, spears, and shields. They strolled along the worn path through the yellowed grass as if confronting a huge army was an everyday occurrence for them. The rest of us could only follow meekly in their wake.

It took us only a few minutes to cross the distance between the wall and the narrowest part of the pass, where the Spartan outer guard blocked the messengers. Here, the sun was completely hidden by the high ridge to our left so we walked in the shade, which provided a welcome relief from the heat. There were nine Persians, all of them mounted, but one stuck out from the rest. He had olive skin and a thick black beard that glistened with oil. Ornate gold brooches held his tunic in place at the shoulders, and gold rings flashed on his fingers. And while the others rode chestnut mares, he rode a huge white stallion with precious gems studding its bridle, and silver and gold inlay decorating the saddle.

On each side of him rode a pair of boys, dressed in white, whose sole function was to hold the four poles of a large square white sunshade above him. Behind them all, four soldiers in matching sets of leather armor sat statue like on their horses. They carried spears and had bows slung over their shoulders, but they held their spears pointing downward.

As our group approached, the jump device strapped to my forearm started pulling like crazy, pointing directly at the Persian delegation.

I moved to one side to check if I'd misunderstood the reading, but even when I angled myself so the messenger had the wide-open expanse of the bay behind him, the device still pointed directly toward him.

A surge of adrenaline thundered through my veins, switching my senses to high alert. The messenger was definitely the glitch—the history-altering event was probably about to happen!

The Spartans, with the rest of the Greek leaders following just behind them, came to a halt directly in front of the Persian delegation. The two groups stared at each other for a few seconds, giving me enough time to slip further to the side so I was halfway between the Greeks and the Persians. From there I'd be close enough to translate for Leonidas, but more importantly, I would be just a few steps away from the messenger in case he tried anything unexpected.

The messenger gave us all a broad smile, clasped his hands together, and bowed from the saddle. "Xerxes, most esteemed of kings, sends his greetings."

I was about to translate, but Leonidas cut me off. "You speak our tongue?"

"Yes. I am Megasthenes of Abydos." The friendly smile did not leave the messenger's face, and his voice oozed pleasantness. "I bring you greetings from the most merciful Xerxes, King of Kings, ruler of Persia, ruler of Babylon, ruler of Egypt, and bringer of prosperity and peace."

Leonidas's face remained cold and hard. "And what does your *most merciful* Xerxes want from us?"

Megasthenes reached his hand out as if offering a gift. "Wise and noble Xerxes requires only your loyalty. He orders all here to give up their arms, then to depart unharmed to their native lands, and to become his loyal allies. To all those who accept his most generous offer, he will give more and better lands than they now possess."

Behind Leonidas, a murmur rippled through the crowd of Greeks.

"A fair offer," one of them declared.

"You are touched by the gods if you believe these lies!" spat another.

"Quiet!" Leonidas commanded, without turning around. He leveled his harsh gaze upon the messenger. "Does your king have anything else he wishes to offer?"

The messenger's brow furrowed in confusion. "No. Only peace, friendship, and better lands than what you already possess. What else could he possibly offer?"

Leonidas nodded. "We will discuss your offer and bring you our response shortly."

With a swirl of their cloaks, Leonidas and the other four Spartans turned in precise formation and began striding back toward our lines. The Greeks who had previously been directly behind them had to scramble out of their way before following. I trailed after their group, pausing every so often to glance over my shoulder and watch the messenger, hoping to catch an insight into how he could muck up history. But the man merely sat on his horse, back straight, and hands clasped in front of him, the picture of hospitality.

Once we'd retreated far enough that the messenger could no longer hear us, Leonidas stopped. He stamped the butt of his spear against the ground and stared at each of the Greek leaders in turn. "I will gut any man who thinks of accepting the Persian offer," he warned.

"But we cannot fight this army; it is too large," insisted an older man as he nervously stroked the gold chain that hung around his neck. "We must flee back to the Peloponnese. The Persians will have a harder time attacking us there."

"We. Cannot. Retreat," insisted another man, his fist pumping emphatically with each word. "I bring with me a thousand men from Locris. Our rulers surrendered to the Persians, offering them earth and water, and we promised to seize this pass for Xerxes. But when we heard that the Spartans were coming, we broke our promise and instead seized this pass for the defense of Greece." He cast a horrified glance over his shoulder toward the Persian camp. "Xerxes will punish our city harshly for our betrayal if we do not stop him here."

"And I bring four hundred men from Thebes." A warrior in a bronze breastplate thumped his chest with his fist. "Our city exiled us because we refused to submit to Persian rule when the rest of our city bent their knees to these foul Persians. We stand with you here as free men, ready to fight and die if need be. We most certainly do not wish to flee."

"What of Phocis?" chimed in a new voice. "It is only a half day's walk from here. What of its people—will you abandon them to the Persians? Let us make our stand here, while we send for more fighting men."

"But if we retreat back to the Peloponnese," declared another Greek, "we will be able to get even more men to join our cause."

"More will come," Leonidas said. "We will send messengers to the nearby cities, demanding they send help. We need only to hold here until they arrive."

"But how can we stop them?" another man asked, his voice rising in panic. "The Persians bring so many warriors that their arrows will blot out the sun."

Dienekes glanced at the sky and shrugged. "Then at least we will fight in the shade."

"How can you jest at a time like this?" the panicked Greek demanded.

"It is better to jest in the face of death like a man than to cry and scream and allow my last actions be those of a coward."

Dienekes's response set off a chorus of shouts and counter shouts as some men argued for a retreat and others to stand firm. Hands flailed wildly in the air—pointing skyward to the gods, or pointing to the Persians, or pointing to the homes and lands that all had left behind.

Luckily, the current argument was one I could avoid. I hung back to keep an eye on the messenger. Still seated on his horse, he was staring straight ahead, a slight smile on his face as he watched the Greeks argue. Nothing seemed the slightest bit off about him at all.

"Silence!" Leonidas roared, bringing my attention back to the Greeks.

The group of leaders had physically split in two: the stay-and-fight faction on one side, and the chicken-out-and-run-away faction on the other side.

Leonidas strode slowly down the sliver of dried grass that separated the two. He was half a head taller than even the tallest of the other Greeks, and he made sure to stare down each and every man who had suggested retreating. None of them could meet his eyes for any length of time before looking away in shame.

"O men of Greece!" he said. "Now is not the time to show fear. Yes, the Persian force is mighty, and we are few. And yes, if we stand against them, many will never see their homes and loved ones again. But we will hold, for this spot is well chosen." He gestured with his spear to the thin stretch of land between the rocky cliffs and the churning sea through which the Persians must approach. "The land here is narrow, so their horses will be of no use, nor their chariots. Here it will be only men fighting other men. And any man among us is worth at least a hundred

Persians." He turned in a slow circle, defying anyone to contradict him. "So do not fear the might of Persia. For they bring an army of men who have marched long distances. They are tired. They are hungry. They serve a cruel king who has enslaved their lands." His voice grew louder and stronger, like the rumble of an avalanche. "It is the men of Persia who should be fearful. For each of us here is a free man. We fight for our homes. We fight for our families. We fight for all other free men—and women—throughout Greece."

Goose bumps tingled up my arms, and I could feel myself hanging on every word.

"Hold your courage fast to your chests, O men of Greece," Leonidas continued. "Three hundred warriors of Sparta will make their stand here at Thermopylae, along with the men of Phocis, Locris, Thespiae, and Thebes." He thrust his spear skyward. "And you can either stand with us as men, or you can run back to the Peloponnese to your wives. Just remember, when you safely reach your home cities and you pass other men in the streets, to tell them that you were at Thermopylae with the Spartans. Tell them that instead of fighting honorably and gloriously in defense of Greece, you ran home." He stabbed at the earth with his spear. The sound of the sharp blade slicing into the earth had an ominous finality to it. "Make your choice now, O men of Greece. Will you fight with us here, or will you run away?"

A mixture of tepid half cheers and bloodthirsty roars arose from the men. Everyone would stay and fight—some with reluctance. And I couldn't blame those who wanted to run away—the odds here stank.

Leonidas flung his red cloak over his shoulder and spun around on his heel. "Let us tell the messenger of Persia what we have decided."

"Wait!" said the leader of the Phocians. "I must warn you." He leaned in close to Leonidas and his voice dropped. "There is a path through the mountains that comes out near the village of Alpenoi. If the Persians were to discover it, they could attack us from behind."

"You bring us ill tidings." Leonidas's brow creased. "Can this path be held?"

"I brought with me a thousand men," the Phocian said. "With them I could hold that path if the invader discovered it. And if the Persians bring too many men against us, we could at least defend it long enough to send warning to the rest of you."

Leonidas turned his head as he slowly scanned the rocky hills. "So be it. We must take this risk. We will make our stand here."

He started back toward the Persian delegation. Dienekes, Areus, Maron, and Charilaus fell in beside him, and the rest of us rushed after them. There they were, just five guys completely naked except for their red cloaks, shields, and spears. Somehow, with their backs straight and their heads held high, they looked more terrifying than if they had worn armor—almost like gods instead of men.

At that moment, I finally understood the Spartan view of clothing. Sandals? They were for wimps who couldn't handle a few rocks in their path. Tunics? They were for losers who got cold or complained about the rain. The Spartans' nakedness told the world they were too tough to be bothered by the elements. Where merchants and craftsmen and farmers put on clothes for protection or comfort, a Spartan stood as he was born, saying, *I am a warrior and I am tougher than all of you.*

For the first time ever, wearing clothes made me feel less confident. My ratty tunic told the Spartans that I was some little wimp who couldn't handle too much sun or a little rain. Part of me wanted to just rip it off and show the Spartans I could be just as tough as they were. But the saner part of me thought about how foolish I'd look strutting around in my underwear, so I just kept walking.

Leonidas stopped in front of the messenger and again rammed the end of his spear into the ground. "We have weighed the offer from your king, Xerxes," he said to the messenger, who still wore a welcoming smile. "If we should be allies of the king, we should be more useful if we kept our arms. And if we should have to wage war against him, we should fight all the better for our freedom if we kept them." He waved his hand toward the mountains and the coast that lay behind him. "As for the lands he promises to give us, the Greeks have learned from their fathers to gain lands not by cowardice but by valor."

The messenger's smile vanished as his eyes widened in shock. "This is madness! The all-powerful Xerxes leads an unbeatable army. He offers you generous terms, yet you still wish to defy him? You will die if you fight him. Please, give up your weapons, and you shall live."

"An honorable death as a free man is better than a long life as someone else's slave."

For a moment, the messenger could only gape at Leonidas, then he shook his head. "I will regretfully inform the most noble king of your decision." With that, he turned his horse and began riding back to the Persian lines, his little entourage of umbrella holders and guards following close behind.

That was it?

I thought for sure the history-altering event would happen during this meeting. But if not now, then when?

"Do you think they will attack today?" Areus mused.

"The day is half gone." Leonidas glanced up at the blazing sun sitting in a near cloudless sky. "Only a portion of their army has yet arrived. They will most likely come against us tomorrow."

Charilaus watched the retreating backs of the Persian delegation. "And if they do not choose to wait?"

"They will wait," Dienekes said. "They have traveled a long distance. Even Xerxes would not be so foolish as to make his troops fight after such a long journey."

Leonidas shifted his focus out to sea, where the lone boat bobbed gently on the waves. Its sail was still down, and any oars had been pulled in. With several broad sweeps of his arm, Leonidas waved out to the ship, and a responding wave could be seen. "Our fleet at Artemisium still holds the sea, so Xerxes cannot bring his troops past us by water.

There will be no attack today," he announced with finality. "We will leave some men here to hold the gap. As for the rest of us, we shall gather our strength and make ready for battle tomorrow." With a whirl of his cloak, he headed back to the Greek camp, the rest of the Spartans following.

The muscles in my back and shoulders grew tense as I trailed along behind the Greeks. Leonidas might have felt confident that it was too late in the day for the Persians to attack, but I didn't. Now that I knew the messenger was the source of the glitch, I kept thinking of ways he might screw up history. So far I'd come up empty.

I stopped and looked one last time at the messenger, still visible as he and his little entourage wound its way through the pass.

What am I missing?

CHAPTER 10

When we finally made it back to the Spartan camp, I wasn't sure whether to be relieved or worried. While the Greek leaders dispersed to their own camps, I sat on the stone wall facing the Persian lines. The advance units of the Persian army had come to a halt on the other side of the pass and were now clearing trees for firewood, setting up a perimeter of guards, unsaddling horses, and making all the other preparations necessary for an army to settle down. The messenger had disappeared somewhere into the mess. Everything looked normal. But was it?

"Pantites!" Leonidas yelled, drawing my attention back to the Spartans. "I have a special mission for you."

A Spartan rushed over and stood straight at attention in front of Leonidas. Although muscular, he was leaner than most of the Spartans, and he looked a few years younger as well, maybe in his early forties. He pounded a fist on his chest. "What do you need of me?"

"You must hurry to Thessaly and demand they send us men."

Pantites's face pinched as if he had just been given a whiff of my gym socks. "Please do not send me, O great king. I joined you so that I could kill Persians, not to become a messenger." He pointed to one of the many servants rushing around. "Why not send one of the helots instead?"

Leonidas's face softened, and he clapped Pantites on the shoulder. "I know you want to stay with us, brave friend. But you are the swiftest runner among us, and I cannot trust a matter of this importance to a helot. Would the Thessalians listen if a helot begs them for men? No, they will scoff at his bearing, his clothes, and his spirit. And if the Thessalians dare to ignore our call, would a helot be able to shame them into action? I am sorry, my friend, but a helot will not do. I need a Spartan to stand there, spear in hand, and demand from them more men."

"I will go." Pantites sagged, his voice drained of enthusiasm. "But know that if you gave me the choice, I would stay."

Leonidas smiled. "I have no doubt you would fight like twenty men. But if I send you now, you could bring me back a thousand more men. That is why you must go."

Pantites nodded glumly. "So be it." Without another word, he hefted his spear over his shoulder and retrieved his shield from a pile of armor lying next to the wall. He raised a fist and scanned the faces of the Spartans. "Fight well, my brothers! But be sure to save some Persians for when I return." He then began jogging, with long steady strides, out of our camp.

"Danakles!" Leonidas shouted as soon as Pantites had disappeared from view.

"Yes!" I snapped to attention, my heart pounding. What could Leonidas want from me?

He pointed to the sword, jumble of armor, and extra spears that Pantites had left behind. "If you are to support us in our struggle, you must be armed. That armor and those weapons are yours until Pantites returns."

I wasn't sure what to say. From my dad's stories about the Spartans, I knew they considered their shields sacred family heirlooms, and it was pretty much the ultimate dishonor to use someone else's shield in battle.

Did the same rules apply to armor? Would I be insulting generations of Pantites's ancestors if I borrowed it? "Are you sure? They belong to Pantites."

"And he is not here," Leonidas replied gruffly. "When the Persians attack, should we let his armor lie against the wall, protecting dirt, or should it be worn by one who may see battle?" Leonidas grabbed a sleeveless set of body armor made of what looked like hardened cloth. "Put this on. We will need to adjust it to fit you."

Disobeying a king would probably get me into even more trouble than using someone else's gear. So I grabbed the lightweight armor and began pulling it over my head, trying my best to ignore the fact that its interior was covered with sweat stains. I managed to wriggle into the armor, but the hard plates of what looked like laminated linen squeezed against my sides, forcing me to suck in my breath. "A little tight," I wheezed.

Areus adjusted the leather straps at the back and I could breathe again. "How is that?" he asked.

"Much better."

Off to the side, Charilaus watched me with his lips curled in a disapproving sneer. Surprisingly, he said nothing.

"Good." Leonidas tugged at the shoulder plates and nodded. "Put the rest on."

The remainder consisted of two bronze greaves for shin protection; a heavy leather bracer for my right arm; a pair of thick-soled leather sandals that a servant brought over; and a bronze helmet that fully covered my face and head, with two oval eye slits to see out of, and a vertical slit from the base of my nose to beneath my chin to breathe through. Most of the armor fit well enough, although the greaves needed to be widened a bit to fit my calves and the helmet was a tight squeeze. I wished I had a mirror to check myself out; with my armor on and a spear in my hand, I felt pretty damn awesome, like I could take on anything.

Leonidas nodded appreciatively. "You look like a proper Spartan now."

Charilaus sniffed. "I still think this is madness. He does not know our commands. He does not know our way of fighting. He will be as useful as one of those donkeys." He jabbed his spear toward the other Greeks.

Areus clapped me on the shoulder. "We can teach him." He sounded confident, almost proud, like a father talking about his son. Ever since I'd beaten him up, he'd been like this, and it kind of weirded me out. I was more comfortable dealing with people like Charilaus, who didn't like me and had made his reasons clear: I was a newcomer, I wasn't a Spartan, and I hadn't proved myself. Hell, if I was in his sandals, I wouldn't trust me either.

I ducked my shoulder out from under Areus's hand and quickly stripped off my armor, leaving it lying next to the wall in a tidy pile with all the other Spartan gear. As I looked around, trying to figure out what to do next, Areus appeared again.

What now?

"Danakles. Will you show me your *pankration* now?"

Oh, right. He had asked earlier for me to teach him some martial arts. I guess I could do that. And, since I wanted to stick close to the Spartans in case the Persians didn't end up waiting four days before attacking, like history expected them to do, then hanging out with Areus would be a great way to do it.

"Sure. Where?"

He pointed to the grassy area past the wall where a few nude Spartans were exercising. Without waiting for my response, he removed his red cloak, leaving him completely naked, then rested his spear over his shoulder and headed toward the gap in the wall.

Crap . . . I forgot that in ancient Greece, all exercises, even the Olympics, were done in the nude. My mind raced in search of any excuse to avoid him but came up empty. Unfortunately, I needed to stick around here and keep a close eye on the Persians until I could be sure there would be no battle today.

"All right," I said with zero enthusiasm. "Let's get this over with."

I took a deep breath, as if I was about to plunge into cold water, and yanked off both my tunic and underwear, leaving me completely naked except for the bracer strapped to my forearm where I kept the jump device hidden.

A brief chuckle escaped my lips. *Not what I expected for my first-ever trip to a nude beach.*

I cast a glance toward the tree-covered hillside to the south. Somewhere up there, Sam was probably watching me through the branches and making herself sick laughing. Good thing we couldn't bring cell phones on our time jumps, because she'd probably record the whole thing if she had the chance.

Yup, this had to be one of my life's most embarrassing moments—I'd get an earful tonight from Sam, that was for sure.

With a sigh, I followed Areus out into the grassy space in front of the wall.

The things I had to do to save history.

CHAPTER 11

If I'd had to rate my afternoon with Areus, I'd have given it a solid two out of ten. Which was pretty generous considering that I was stuck slowly baking to death in the intense Greek sunshine while trying to teach some naked old dude how to do karate. I focused on the basic punches, kicks, and blocks, making sure to avoid all the holds and throws; the farther I could keep his sweaty body away from me, the better.

In return, every time Areus learned a new move, he insisted on returning the favor and teaching me something. If you'd told me a week ago I'd be learning Spartan battle tactics from a real-life Spartan, I'd have been totally geeking out. Too bad the reality stank. Areus skipped all the cool fighting stuff and stuck to the tactics and commands the Spartans would be using here at Thermopylae. This meant I got to learn about forming a proper phalanx, attacking in a line, retreating in a line, and rotating lines. Every single thing I learned was about fighting in a stupid line—and I already knew a bunch of that from when I'd fought in the Anglo-Saxon shield wall during my first time jump.

Areus seemed pretty excited to be teaching me all this stuff, as if he was passing down sacred knowledge from father to son. I just kind of smiled and nodded as he went through it. After all, I didn't plan to be around for the actual fighting. My only goal was to figure out the glitch and get the hell out of Greece before the fighting started. Until then, hanging out with Areus was the best way for me to keep an eye on the Persians.

Fortunately, every time I checked on them, they remained on their side of the pass, not making any hostile moves, just like history expected them to.

It took forever for the descending sun to hit the top of the ridge. But as the shadows crept over the grass, I let out a sigh of relief. The day was almost over—no way the Persians would attack now. "Wow, it's getting kind of late," I said to Areus in a sort of *Can we be done here?* tone.

He glanced up at the darkening sky. "Where has the time flown?" He stared at the shadows for a few seconds, as if deciding what to do, and then clapped me on the shoulder. "I have learned so much today. But you are right, it is late. We should end our training now and go eat, so we can keep our strength for battle tomorrow."

Finally! While I was out here making sure history didn't mess up, my stomach had nearly collapsed from hunger—an emptiness made only worse by the smell of roasting meats wafting through the air. Hundreds of fires had sprung up all over the Greek camps, although naturally the Spartans had fewer and smaller fires than everyone else's. Knowing them, they probably figured that needing fully cooked food or even a light at night was a sign of weakness.

Areus grabbed his spear, slung it over his shoulder, and strode purposefully back to the Spartan camp with me on his heels. Once we passed the gate, we put on our tunics and sandals, then he guided me toward a small circle of about fifteen men where Leonidas and Charilaus were both sitting. Thankfully, everyone else had their tunics on as well.

Areus motioned for me to take a spot. "Now we shall feast. No doubt you are as famished as I am."

Charilaus's head whipped up. "You wish him to eat with *us*?"

"Why not?" Areus asked. "He trains like a Spartan. He has the armor of a Spartan. Why should he not eat like a Spartan?"

"Because he is *not* a Spartan," Charilaus replied firmly.

"But he has willingly joined us," Areus said.

So much drama. I turned to Areus. "You know what, I'll pass on the meal. I'm not very hungry."

"You would not sit and eat with the king?" Charilaus reeled back as if I'd just punched him in the face. "Against my advice, Leonidas has made you his *trophimos*, and now you insult him?"

I shook my head and tried to control the frustration welling up inside me. I clearly couldn't win with this guy. Now he had everyone else glaring at me like I was some ungrateful little snot who thought he was better than everyone else. "No! I'd love to have dinner with Leonidas! It's just that . . . um . . . he's a king, and I didn't consider myself worthy of sitting with him."

Leonidas nodded thoughtfully, as if I'd just scored a perfect answer to the hardest question on a test. "Come! Sit!" He pointed to a spot of grass beside him. "I made you my *trophimos*, so of course you are worthy to join our circle."

Charilaus scowled and took a sip of wine, his hate-filled eyes peering at me over the rim of his cup.

Don't worry, buddy. The feeling's mutual.

As soon as I sat down, a servant rushed over and handed me a mug of wine, a thick slice of rye bread, and a piece of cheese. That was it. Nothing else. Disappointed couldn't come close to describing what I felt about my dinner. The wine was weak and the cheese was . . . cheesy. I ate carefully, mimicking what was obviously the Spartan way of eating: slow, quiet, with only a few sips of wine between mouthfuls. Laughter and shouting carried in the breeze from the other Greek camps, but no one spoke here among the Spartans.

The silence felt so strange. I knew that, if history flowed properly, the Persians would wait four days before attacking. But the Spartans didn't know that. So there should have been some discussion, some recognition that this might be their last night alive. I'd eaten with Anglo-Saxons, Celts, Mongols, and all of them knew how to feast before battle. They drank, they laughed, they celebrated their life. This quiet Spartan approach to dinner just seemed wrong. It was like we were eating dinner at a funeral.

I didn't dare speak and break the silence, so I just sat there, slowly munching my food and listening to the rest of the Greeks feasting.

The meal couldn't end soon enough for me. As soon as Leonidas dismissed us, I leaped to my feet and grabbed my backpack and wooden staff from next to the wall.

"You are leaving us?" Areus asked.

Him again. My constant shadow. "Yes. I'm . . . uh . . . going for a walk. I might even sleep in the forest, where it's . . . uh . . . quieter." I waved a hand toward the Greek camps, where loud shouts and laughter could still be heard.

Areus looked surprised. "You will not stay here with us? What of the Persians? You said you wished to help us against them."

"Don't worry about me. I'll be here bright and early, ready to hand out spears or whatever else you need me to do."

Before Areus could say anything else, I raced toward the hillside. A few times, I glanced over my shoulder to make sure he wasn't following, but in the fading light, I couldn't see him.

Once I had reached the safety of the trees, I pulled out the jump device from under my bracer and set it to find Sam. By now the sun had almost completely disappeared, so finding my way up the slope was tricky. Branches smacked me in the face, and I kept tripping over roots and rocks.

As the jump rod pulled harder against my arm, signaling I was closer to Sam, she called out to me through the trees. "I hope you're not naked."

"Very funny," I muttered as I emerged from the cover of the woods. "You know I put my clothes back on."

Sam was still in the clearing, sitting next to her usual tree, although with the sun down, she had given up trying to read. In front of her, the remains of a roasted rabbit hung on a spit over the glowing embers of a fire.

"I see you made a friend down there." Sam smirked. "Is this going to be a repeat of the Celtic jump? Do I hear wedding bells again?"

"Four seconds," I sighed.

"What?"

"It only took you four seconds to make a comment about me sparring with Areus." I sat down next to her under the tree. "I'm doing this for us, you know. The Spartans are the front line against the Persians, so me staying with them is our best hope of solving this time glitch. And if that means letting everything hang out, I'll do it."

"Sorry," Sam muttered. "So what did you learn?"

"The messenger is the glitch."

"The messenger?" Sam's nose crinkled with confusion. "You sure?"

"Positive. My jump rod pointed right at him."

"But that doesn't make sense. Messengers are usually the glitch when they have to travel long distances and end up dropping the message or dying on the way. But look at how far this guy has to go—less than the distance from my house to my school. How hard is that?"

"I know. That's what's bugging me about this. He has one simple job, but somehow he screws it up and changes history. I'm going to have to keep hanging around the Spartans until I find out how he manages to mess things up. How about you? What are your plans?"

Sam picked up an oak leaf from the ground and slowly tore pieces from it. "I can't really do much, can I? The only women down there are cooking or fetching water, and they're only in the other Greek camps; I don't see a single one with the Spartans. Not to mention that with my hair color and skin tone, I'll stand out even more than you do." She tossed the remains of the leaf aside. "So unless something glaringly obvious happens that needs my attention, I'm going to stay here in the forest, watching over you, and making sure that you don't get into anything you can't handle."

"For four days? Sounds boring."

"What you call boring, I call awesome. That's four days of no one trying to kill me. Four days of no homework, no school, no job, no mom bitching at me and getting on my case for every little thing I do." I could hear the exhaustion in her voice. "I wish it could be *more* than—" Sam's head shot up and her back stiffened. "There's someone out there," she hissed.

"You sure?"

"Positive," she whispered. "My jump device is set on Find Locals." She swept her arm around in a circle and then her lips drew tight. "They're all around us!"

Crap!

Were the Persians doing a sneak night attack through the mountains? Is this how the messenger messed up history?

Slowly and quietly, I grabbed my staff and scanned the forest. It was eerily quiet. Too quiet. No sounds of birds or small animals. I whipped my head around, trying to peer into the thick trees but couldn't see anything in the twilight.

"How far away are they?"

Sam silenced me with an irritated wave of her hand. "Hide!" she mouthed, before wrapping her gray cloak around herself and disappearing silently into the brush.

I kicked dirt over the embers of the fire, extinguishing the few glimmers of light left in the clearing.

My heart was beating so loud I couldn't hear anything else. How did the Persians get up here? How many were there? And where exactly were they? I needed to hide until I could warn the Spartans. Crouching low, I crept toward a large clump of bushes, in the hope it would give me enough cover.

"Do not attempt to run, traitor!" a voice called out from the darkness. "We will kill anyone who flees."

I stood there frozen with fear. I couldn't see who was out there, but they could clearly see me. How could I get out of this?

Wait . . .

Only one person would put that much hatred for me into his tone—Charilaus. Meaning those weren't Persians out there; they were Spartans. A knot formed in my stomach. Why had he followed me?

"I'm not a traitor!" I yelled, panic making my voice crack.

"Yet as soon as our meal ends, you rush into the forest to meet with a Persian?" Charilaus called back, his voice getting closer. "We heard you speaking with the Persian spy in their foul tongue. Bring forth the Persian now, and perhaps Leonidas will show mercy."

He heard us? But we weren't speaking Persian. We were—

Oh . . . he heard us speaking English.

"Sam," I whispered into the forest behind me. "You have to come out. They know you're here."

"Uh-uh. No way," she whispered back. "I can outrun these guys."

"Don't do it!" I warned. "They'll kill you if you try to run."

"Silence!" Charilaus yelled. "Drop your weapons and step forward."

I tried once again to peer into the forest, but my vision just couldn't penetrate the gloom. I knew the Spartans could see me; they were trained to fight in almost total darkness, so this semi-darkness was nothing to them.

I couldn't run.

I couldn't fight.

With slow, exaggerated movements, I tossed my staff to the ground, then motioned for Sam to come out of hiding.

For a second, I didn't know whether she was going to run. But then a gray shadow rose off the forest floor, and Sam hesitantly stepped out into the clearing. With her cloak wrapped around her and her hood raised, she was almost invisible in the twilight.

"As I expected." Charilaus strode into the clearing in his usual arrogant manner. "Leonidas will kill you himself when he sees this spy." He yanked Sam's hood back and her fiery red hair spilled around her pale face.

"That is a Persian spy?" said an amused voice from the trees. "I might have to go join the Persians myself if that is what their spies look like." From another spot in the forest came an amused chuckle.

Charilaus stomped in a circle around the clearing. "Danakles is a spy, I tell you!" he shouted at the forest.

With a whisper of movement, Areus, Maron, and Dienekes all emerged from the thick cover of trees.

Areus is here! I'd never thought I'd be so glad to see him. Hopefully, he'd be able to calm Charilaus down.

Dienekes looked Sam up and down and then shook his head and laughed. "You are a fool, Charilaus. If Danakles is a spy, the only information he seeks is what is under this girl's dress."

"But they were speaking Persian!" Charilaus raged.

"No, we weren't," I said flatly, finding my voice. "We were speaking the language of our own land."

Areus added some twigs to the campfire and then blew on it to bring it back to life. A warm glow gradually enveloped our little circle, revealing everyone's face more clearly. Charilaus wore his usual scowl, while Dienekes had an amused grin. Sam's eyes kept darting back and forth while she chewed her lip nervously. It was pretty obvious she was ready to bolt.

Areus held up both his hands in a soothing manner and took a step toward her. "I am Areus of Sparta. Do you speak our tongue?"

"Y-yes," Sam said.

"How old are you, girl?"

"Seventeen."

"Seventeen." Areus gave her a warm smile. "And beautiful, too. With skin and hair like no Persian or Greek I have ever seen." He turned to Charilaus. "She is no Persian and Danakles is no spy. We wrong them both by being here. Let us quit this place."

Charilaus's lips twisted as he jabbed a finger into my chest. "You may have these three fooled, but know that I will be watching you, Danakles. I still do not trust you." He turned on his heel and stomped out of the clearing.

Areus watched Charilaus disappear into the dark forest, then turned to me. "Enjoy your evening, Danakles. Do not fret about Charilaus. He trusts few. But for those who he calls friend, he is the best of men." With silent footsteps, Areus left the clearing, followed by Maron. Dienekes gave me a wink and a nod as he passed me by.

Sam exhaled long and loud, as her shoulders sagged in relief. "So those are your friends, huh?"

"More like acquaintances."

"Who's the guy with the attitude?"

"Charilaus. He's founder and president of the I Hate Danakles Club."

"Danakles?" Sam smiled. "Cute."

I shrugged. "Yeah, well, best I could do on short notice."

"It works." Her gaze traveled down the hill toward the Spartan camp, where a few small fires flickered in the darkness. Her smile faded. "Just watch out for Charilaus."

"Don't worry. I will. I know he's got it out for me."

"So . . . are we going to pull watches?"

"Yeah. After what just happened, we probably should. You can sleep first. My heart's racing so hard right now I probably won't be able to sleep for hours."

Sam looked at me as if I'd just said the stupidest thing ever. "And you think I can?"

"No. Guess not." I poked at the fire with a stick and small sparks flew skyward. "I guess we're both taking first watch, then."

"Sounds good." Sam sat down facing the fire, with her back resting against a tree. Her bow remained cradled in her lap.

The fire cast flickering shadows across her face. On all our other time jumps, this part of the day, where Sam and I just sat by the fire, had always been my favorite. No stress. No drama. Just the chance to relax for a moment and try to forget that tomorrow someone might try to kill us.

It was at times like this that Sam and I had shared so many deep conversations, talking about our hopes, our dreams, our lives. I knew Sam better than anyone else—even Jenna. I ached to talk like that with Sam again. But, ever since we'd arrived in Greece, all we'd talked about was the glitch, the Spartans, or the weather—all the nice, safe topics that allowed Sam to keep her emotional distance from me.

Did she miss our talks? Did she miss how things used to be between us? In the weak light of the fire, it was impossible to read her face.

Eventually I gave up trying to find ways to break the cavernous silence between us and instead leaned back against a tree trunk and stared through the leafy branches toward the beach. Stars had begun to appear in the night sky, and moonlight glinted off the waves. A gentle breeze blew in from the ocean, bringing with it the smell of salt air and the gentle rhythm of the surf.

Except for Sam, my first day in Greece hadn't gone too badly. I'd met the legendary Leonidas and hung out with the Spartans, so from a getting-to-know-my-childhood-heroes point of view, this day had gone awesome—maybe a bit too awesome in the case of Areus. But in the case of solving the time glitch, things weren't that great. The messenger thing really bothered me. How could one man, and not even someone that important in the great scheme of things, mess up history? I had this overwhelming feeling that I was missing something.

But what?

CHAPTER 12

For the next three days, my life followed the same pattern: wake up, say goodbye to Sam, train with Areus all day long, have a quiet dinner with the Spartans, go back up into the hills to sleep.

I should have been overjoyed that these days were easy and that history looked to be flowing on its proper course, but instead my nerves were stretched nearly to the breaking point. I spent my days watching the Persian lines, fearful of an attack that never came. Every shout, every scouting party, every practice drill from the Persians produced a terrified panic that they were attacking and that I'd failed to fix the glitch.

The lack of fighting was putting the Greeks on edge too. Nothing's worse than knowing your death lies only a short distance away, and then having to wait for it to come. Although the Spartans retained their cool under this pressure, the other Greeks weren't nearly as calm. As the days wore on, men's nerves began to fray. Minor disagreements blew up into fistfights, so Leonidas and the other leaders spent most of their days keeping the men busy.

I woke up early on the morning of my fifth day in Greece and rubbed the sleep from my eyes. I'd slept terribly. My dreams had been filled with nightmares of the Persians attacking at night and taking everyone by surprise.

The sun hadn't risen yet, so I still had time to think things out before the battle started. According to history, today was the day when roughly two hundred thousand Persians would come pouring through that little pass with just a handful of Greeks trying to stop them. Part of me was kind of glad—the fact that the Persians had delayed this long meant history was still flowing normally. The other part of me was terrified. The battle would start any minute now, and I still had no clue how the messenger was going to mess things up. I needed to find and fix the glitch before the arrows and spears started flying.

I sat up and rifled through my backpack for the dwindling bag of mystery mix that Jenna had packed for me. Thinking was always easier on a full stomach.

"You're up early," Sam murmured.

"Sorry. I didn't mean to wake you. I couldn't sleep."

She sat up and shook her hair out of its ponytail before brushing the knots out with her fingers. "Today's the day, huh?"

"It has to be. I mean, we're on day five, the day that history says the Persians finally attack. So the messenger is running out of time to mess things up." My shoulders slumped. "I just hope I fix the glitch before the fighting starts."

Sam slid over to sit cross-legged in front of me. She grabbed both my hands and held them tightly in hers, sending a tingle of warmth through me. "I know you're worried. But even if you don't figure out the glitch before the battle starts, what are the chances you're actually going to have to fight?"

"No freakin' clue. Why?"

"For four days you've been gushing about how awesome the Spartans are. And you've told me that, in the real history, the Spartans hold back the entire Persian army for two days, and they only get defeated because they're attacked from the rear on the third day. Well,

I've seen the size of the Persian army. And if the Spartans can hold that huge group back for two days, then they really are badass." She tilted her head at me and smiled. "Do you actually think a band of warriors that tough will ask some random seventeen-year-old kid to fight on the front lines?"

For an instant I bristled at her suggestion that I wasn't good enough to be a Spartan. Then the weight of her words sank through, and the tension that was in my shoulders released. "You know what? You're right. They won't. The Greeks will fight, and I'll be free to hang out in the rear, trying to solve whatever glitch might happen." I sprang to my feet and gathered up my backpack and blanket. "Thanks, Sam! I needed that."

Sam stood up also. "Okay, but still be careful out there. If you get into the slightest bit of trouble, jump to safety. I know I haven't done anything so far here in Greece, but I'm still around to fix things if you have to leave."

"Thanks, Sam. But don't worry; I'll be careful."

She raised her eyebrow. "Do you know how many times we've had this conversation? And yet you end up in trouble every time." She crossed her arms and fixed me with a stern look. "I'm serious, Dan. Don't be a hero."

"Trust me." I pulled out my jump device and spun it to the setting that would allow me to jump out before a glitch was fixed. "Panic button primed and ready. If I see a single spear flying my way, I'm out of here."

She rested her fingers on my arm, her still-pale skin standing out in sharp contrast to the wicked tan I had developed over the past few days. "Just be safe."

Her green eyes held me in place. At moments like this on previous jumps, we'd shared some of the most awesome kisses of my life. Deep and passionate, fueled by our fears, with neither of us sure if I'd make it back. I so longed to kiss her again like that, to have things how they used to be between us.

But even after four nights of hanging out together, I hadn't managed to break through the wall she'd built around herself. Our few non-glitch conversations had all been superficial, like two coworkers talking at the coffee machine. They'd been nowhere close to the deep and personal talks we used to have.

If all went well, this would be our last moment together in Greece. I wouldn't see Sam again until our next time jump, and who knew when that would be. So we'd be back to our weekly video chats, with all the warmth of a job interview. I couldn't let our last moment be this awkward. I spied her book lying on her blanket. "Just make sure you don't leave *Darkness Beckons* behind," I teased. "In the wrong hands, a book that cheesy could destroy history."

Sam smiled and playfully punched me on the shoulder. "If only you knew how to read, you might actually enjoy that book."

I slung my backpack over my shoulder. "See ya, Sam. I'll text you once I get home." I began stepping carefully down the tree-covered slope toward the Greek camp, while swinging my staff in a spirited fashion. If Sam was watching me, she wouldn't know how bummed out I really felt. Part of me had hoped this jump would give me a chance to rebuild our friendship—to make things how they'd been before. But I had hardly spent any time with her. And now our time here was over, and I didn't feel like anything had changed.

That seemed to be how things always turned out between me and Sam. From the first time I'd seen her, I'd had a major crush on her. And the more I'd gotten to know her, the more I'd fallen for her. But, no matter how hard I tried, she wouldn't let herself feel the same about me. There were times it almost seemed like she did, but the memories of her dead dad and brother always got in the way. She refused to allow herself to care for anyone again.

I sighed as I picked my way through a thick stand of pines. Why did I keep chasing Sam? In addition to being pathetic, it was totally unfair to Jenna. She was the best girlfriend a guy could ask for, but she went right out of my head as soon as Sam showed up.

A smile crossed my lips as I thought of Jenna's relentless optimism and boundless enthusiasm. Jenna didn't have all the emotional walls Sam had. She accepted me as I was and gave me nothing but love. She deserved better than second place in my heart.

I broke out of the cover of the woods just as the sun rose over the cliffs to the east, bathing the Greek camp in sunlight. Men were stirring, gathering their gear or eating breakfast. From the Persian side of the pass came a tumult of activity that hadn't been noticeable there the past four days. It sounded like . . . well . . . an army of two hundred thousand men getting ready for war. No trumpet calls or marching feet yet, so we still had some time, but the battle would be happening today.

I reached the Spartan camp just as they sat down to their morning meal.

"Good morning, Danakles," Areus said, with a huge smile on his face. He turned to Charilaus. "See, I told you he would come, that the sound of Persian preparations would not scare him off."

Charilaus snorted. "Showing up to break his fast does not show that he will fight—it only shows he is hungry."

"It makes me question the soundness of his mind," Maron said. "Only a man touched by the gods would leave such a beautiful maiden alone in the woods to join our ugly bunch."

"Speak for yourself," Dienekes quipped. "I am quite handsome."

This set off a round of laughter among the Spartans. I joined in as I sat down in their breakfast circle. Areus passed me a haunch of roast lamb, and I snapped my head back in surprise. No completely tasteless slab of dry bread for breakfast today? All around me, men were digging into hunks of lamb—not a chunk of bread to be seen.

Leonidas stood up from our little circle. "My friends and brothers," he called as he hoisted his wine cup in front of him. "It looks as if battle will finally be upon us today! Let us fight well and make Xerxes rue the day he decided to set his sights on our fair lands."

Around me the Spartans raised their cups and cheered. I suddenly felt too choked up to eat. Here they were, three hundred guys who surely knew they were heading to their death, all to save Greece, and not a single man looked hesitant or upset. In the face of certain death, they shared a sense of brotherhood like I'd never seen before. Everything Dad had told me about the Spartans had been spot on: They were heroes in every sense of the word.

After our meal, we suited up for battle. In full armor, and once they put their helmets on, each Spartan looked almost exactly the same as the man standing next to him. The main distinguishing feature was their shields, each with a different image painted on it. Areus carried the one with the bull, Dienekes had the one with three fish, and Charilaus's bore a coiled snake. Two things separated Leonidas from the rest. His shield had a sunburst on it, and his helmet was decorated with a tall crest of red hair that ran from just above his forehead to the back of his neck.

"So where do you guys need me to be?" I asked Areus.

"You will be at the rear," Areus said sadly, like this was the worst news. "Bring us fresh spears when ours shatter. Bring water when we thirst. I know that, like my son, you are eager for battle, but you cannot stand with us."

Woo-hoo! Best news I've heard all day.

"I understand," I said, trying my best to sound disappointed.

"Spartans!" Leonidas raised his spear. "We march to battle!"

As a group, the men raised their shields and began marching through the gate, spears in hand and helmets tucked under their shield arms. I followed after the last group of twelve, a kind of half Spartan, with the armor but not the shield. After me came the rest of the Greeks: Malians, Thebans, Phocians, Locrians, and a bunch of men from other cities all across Greece, fighting here together to hold off the Persian horde.

The Spartan Sacrifice

Although I planned to stick around only long enough to fix the time glitch, the stomp of marching feet and the clatter of armor still had the blood pounding in my ears. It always did. There's a certain undeniable excitement about heading into battle.

As we neared the pass, the Persian army became visible, waiting at the other end of it in all their might. An endless sea of men and weapons trailing into the distance. In their middle, towering over them, stood a huge golden throne on which Xerxes, king of the Persians, sat watching.

Everything looked set. The Greeks were playing their part by marching valiantly out to battle. The Persians were doing their bit by meeting them at the pass. Everything was lining up just like it should. *So what could possibly go wrong?*

As if on cue, the messenger emerged from the pass riding toward us, with four boys on horseback holding a large white cloth sunshade above him as four guards in ornate armor trailed.

"Shield wall!" Leonidas yelled.

The Spartans responded instantly to his command, standing shoulder to shoulder across the messenger's path in a solid wall of bronze six rows deep and fifty men across. On their right lay the ocean and on their left the steep ridge.

"I think he is coming to surrender," Dienekes declared loudly, and a ripple of laughter ran through the Spartans.

If the messenger was going to mess up history, this would be the right time for it. I had maybe a minute to get into place and stop him. Stretching up on my toes, I peeked over the heads of the Spartan wall in front of me, trying to figure out how to get myself past them. But I'd have better luck getting through a real wall—the Spartans were packed solidly together with no room for me to weasel past them.

Time for Plan B.

If I couldn't go through the Spartan wall, I'd have to go around it.

I ran down the length of the Spartan line until I reached the far end of it at the base of the ridge. Without stopping, I scrambled up the steep rock face, clutching at the stunted trees to keep myself from sliding back down the slope. A few seconds of careful stepping took me around the left flank of the Spartan wall. I now had a clear view of the entire pass and was still only about fifty steps away from the messenger and his group.

The man halted about twenty paces in front of the Spartan lines. Then he bowed in the saddle. "O great Leonidas," he called, "I bring you word from, Xerxes, King of Kings. My most merciful lord does not wish to see your blood shed. He offers you one more chance to give up your weapons and flee this place."

Leonidas strode confidently forward, his helmet tucked under his arm and the bronze rim of his shield gleaming in the sunlight. "He desires our weapons so badly?" Leonidas pointed his spear at the messenger. "Then tell him to come and take them!"

As one, the entire mass of Spartans thumped their spears once against their shields. "Hurrah!" they yelled, their voices shouting out in defiance.

The smile faded from the messenger's face. "Very well. I will tell the great and glorious Xerxes of your decision." He walked his horse in a tight circle. His little group of sunshade holders and guards shifted along with him, keeping the same exact distance from him.

Leonidas turned and faced the Spartans, with his long black hair waving in the breeze coming in from the ocean. "Now is the time we must stand fast. For the fate of Greece depends on us. We are the . . ."

I let his speech drone off into the background as I thumped my fist repeatedly against my thigh. The battle was about to start; this had to be the moment when the messenger messed up history. My entire body trembled in anticipation as I tracked him with my eyes. *What was he going to do?*

But he wasn't doing anything. He was just turning his horse around so he could ride back to Xerxes.

Then a flicker of motion caught my eye. Beside the messenger, one of his sunshade bearers turned in his saddle. With one hand still holding the wooden sunshade support, he reached inside his tunic and pulled out a sling. He began twirling the sling to one side, building up speed.

Oh . . . crap . . . I could feel the blood drain from my face. The messenger wasn't the time glitch—it was the kid next to him!

"No!" I yelled.

I leaped from my hiding spot and raced across the dry grass. Spartan spears were designed for stabbing; they were heavy suckers that didn't throw well. I needed to get closer!

My lungs heaved with panic as I sped across the plain. I had only one shot. Missing was not an option.

Almost there.

I raised the spear over my head and prepared to do a running throw . . . just as the boy released the sling stone.

Like a bullet, the cherry-sized stone sped toward the Spartan lines. In real history, the kid either never took the shot or missed. But as I stood there watching helplessly, the stone hit Leonidas in the back of the head with a sickening thud, right at the base of his skull.

Leonidas arched backward for a moment, his eyes wide and his mouth open in surprise. Wordlessly, he sank to his knees, then collapsed face-first into the dirt.

The constant chill that had emanated from the jump rod disappeared, and an electric-like charge I'd never felt before began to build up along the length of the device. My arm dropped to my side, and the spear tumbled out of my grasp as the horrible meaning of this electricity became clear.

History had just been altered. Leonidas, king of the Spartans, hero of the Battle of Thermopylae, was dead.

CHAPTER 13

The electric spark from the jump device grew in intensity, sending spasms up my arm as a banshee-like keening echoed inside my head. I clapped my hands to my ears to try to block out the noise as images of a horrible new future flashed through my mind, almost as if the jump device was tearing pages out of a history book and showing me the revisions to be inserted in their place.

With Leonidas dead, and the decisive leadership the Greeks needed gone with him, many of the non-Spartans would flee. The few remaining Greeks would still fight valiantly, but the story of the battle would change. Instead of Thermopylae becoming a symbol of defiance and solidarity, it would be remembered as the battle where the Greeks ran away from the overwhelming might of the Persians.

Without the heroic stand at Thermopylae acting as a rallying call to the Greeks, the Persians would easily rampage through Greece, conquering its cities and states one after another.

The Persian fleet wouldn't be destroyed at the Battle of Salamis.

The Persian army wouldn't be defeated once and for all at the Battle of Plataea.

The Persians would go on to a long history of dominating Greece. Democracy wouldn't flourish. Persia would instead become a superpower and clash with Rome. The entire history of the Middle East and the Mediterranean would change, the path of European and Western civilization forever altered.

The images faded from my mind, and the enormity of the glitch left me feeling drained and helpless. The threads of history were unraveling by the second, and I had to stop them. But how? Leonidas was dead. There was no coming back from that.

Think, Dan! Think!

My mind scrambled for options as the jump rod screamed even louder inside my head. Areus let out a terrible howl and beat at his chest with his fist. Dienekes sank to his knees and held his head in his hands. Charilaus rushed to Leonidas's side and cradled the king's lifeless body in his arms.

My feet pulled me forward as a glimmer of an idea formed. The Greeks needed Leonidas. However, he had just been lying face down in the dirt, a rock embedded in the back of his head. But the average Greek couldn't tell the Spartans apart: They only knew the difference between shields and helmets. And with a wall of Spartans blocking everyone's view, none of the other Greeks could have possibly seen Leonidas fall.

My eyes zeroed in on the king's shield. As more Spartans crowded around Leonidas's body, I picked it up.

Charilaus's head whipped around toward me, his features contorting with rage. "How dare you touch his shield?" He lowered Leonidas's body to the ground and leaped to his feet to confront me, his face just inches from mine.

I backed up a few steps; Charilaus looked ready to kill me. "S-s-someone needs to take his shield," I stammered. "They need to lead the army in his place." I thrust the shield toward Charilaus, hoping he'd take it from me. "The Greeks can't know Leonidas has died. If they do, Greece will fall."

"You insult me!" Charilaus's eyes narrowed and his nostrils flared. "While I live, I will never let my shield fall." He raised it so the coiled snake emblazoned on it was glaring at me. "Return with your shield, or on it—that is the Spartan creed. I will never dishonor my ancestors by putting my shield aside for that of another." With a hiss of metal, he drew his short sword from his scabbard and pointed it at my chest. "And you will put his shield down now! You dishonor it by even touching it. He was a great king and man. And you . . ." Charilaus sniffed. "You are not even Spartan."

"Okay! Okay!" Pure terror made my reply come out as a squeak. "I'm putting it down." I reverently lowered the shield to the ground, my eyes not leaving Charilaus. With every second, the keening in my head grew even louder, as if history itself was screaming as it was torn apart.

Over the din, a new sound emerged: the steady stomp of thousands of Persian feet as they marched through the pass. Time was running out!

I held up my hands in what was hopefully a calming motion. "But someone needs to carry his shield. The Greeks need to see Leonidas. As soon as they find out he's dead, half your army is going to run away." A crowd had built up around us now. I recognized a few of the shields and I pointed to each of the bearers individually. "Areus? Dienekes? Maron? Will any of you take up Leonidas's shield and save Greece?"

Areus removed his helmet and tucked it under one arm. His eyes lingered for a moment on Leonidas's shield, lying on the ground, and then he pulled his own shield tighter into his body. "Your words bear the weight of truth, Danakles. Many of our allies will flee once they hear of our king's death. But no man here will take up Leonidas's shield. We would dishonor our own ancestors by carrying the shield of another." He pointed at the shield on the ground and raised his eyebrow at me. "But you can take it up. You can don the guise of Leonidas."

I recoiled from the shield like it was a rattlesnake. Picking it up would mean a heroic death at the front of the Spartan army. "No. I can't."

I was about to launch into every excuse imaginable about why I shouldn't pick up the shield, when Charilaus jumped in again. "No! That *boy* will not insult the memory of Leonidas by holding his shield. We will inform our allies that Leonidas is dead. No doubt they will wish to honor him by fighting bravely in his name."

Areus snorted. "Half our army wished to flee even when Leonidas was alive. Danakles is correct: They will run back to their homes if they know of our king's death. We must therefore hide it from them. I say we let Danakles carry the shield, for he and Leonidas are of similar height."

Charilaus stared at me, his cold, hard eyes reflecting only hate. I couldn't tell whether he was weighing Areus's words or just considering the best place to stab me.

Suddenly, Charilaus blinked in surprise and his gaze drifted over my shoulder toward a point behind me. He squinted for a moment, as if trying to make out the details, while his head tilted to the side in confusion.

From anyone else, I would have assumed this to be some sort of sucker ploy intended to make me turn around so that he could stab me in the back. But this was Charilaus; he wasn't the subtle type. Something weird was going on behind me—even stranger than Leonidas dying before the battle had even started.

I glanced over my shoulder and felt just as confused as Charilaus. In the yellowing grass near the water, midway between the Spartan lines and the approaching Persians, a dark figure crouched low. As I squinted, another materialized off to the right. First there was nothing but grass, then—*Bam!*—a person appeared from out of nowhere. The person staggered around for a few seconds as if dizzy, and then fell flat to the ground, nearly disappearing from view amid the tall grass.

Time jumpers! Victor's guys were actually stepping up for once, coming to save history like they were supposed to.

With a sense of giddiness almost overwhelming me, I turned slowly in a complete circle, noticing more and more time jumpers appearing by the second.

The Spartan Sacrifice

"The gods appear . . ." Charilaus murmured. His sword fell from his hand and his mouth hung wide open.

The one in the grass stood up and started edging toward us, as the other jumpers kept low while recovering from their time-travel sickness. He took slow steps, approaching cautiously with his jump device sweeping the area before him. He wore jeans, a T-shirt, and running shoes, and his only weapon was a sword at his hip that he kept sheathed. His eyes darted toward the rows of Spartans in their battle lines, and then back to our little group immediately around Leonidas. Even from this distance, the tattoo of a four-pointed star within a circle was clearly visible on his forearm.

Charilaus pointed a shaky finger toward the man. "The gods bear the same mark as Danakles." He turned toward me, and all the hate and anger disappeared from his face, replaced by awe. He picked up Leonidas's shield and, dropping to one knee in front of me, he bowed his head and thrust the shield into my hands. "You must lead us, O great Danakles. Forgive me for doubting you."

I held the shield far away from my body like it would bite me. History was unraveling by the second; the constant howling in my head kept me fully aware of that. But I didn't want the shield. I didn't want to pretend to be Leonidas. I didn't want to lead the Greeks, and I definitely didn't want to fight in this battle.

In the pass, the lead Persians had reached the midpoint. One of the most famous clashes in history would begin any moment now. I had only seconds to figure out a new plan.

Areus picked up Leonidas's distinctive helmet, with its bright red crest. "Take the shield and helmet, Danakles. Lead us now, like Leonidas would."

Charilaus rose to his feet and thumped his fist across his chest. "I will follow you!"

"I will follow you!" echoed Dienekes.

"I will follow you!" shouted Telekles and Maron, and then a thunderous chorus of Spartan voices.

They all looked toward me, waiting for me to accept the shield.

The wailing in my head had reached almost ear-splitting proportions, like history was howling its last death throes. The painful noise reverberated through my skull, making me clench my teeth just to stop them from chattering.

The other time jumpers must have heard the noise, too, but they didn't seem in a hurry to fix things. They were still inching forward, their heads swiveling between the two armies as if expecting either one to attack. And even if they got close, there wouldn't be enough time to get them fitted out in Spartan armor before the fighting started.

There was only one person here who could take over for Leonidas and save history.

Damn it!

I tossed my helmet to the ground and slammed Leonidas's on my head. *Please let this work*, I begged the universe as I looped my arm through the shield's leather straps.

As soon as my hand wrapped itself around the shield's grip, the keening in my head vanished, and the regular sound of waves and seabirds again filled my ears. Inside the bracer along my forearm, the jump rod suddenly felt . . . normal.

It wasn't hot. It wasn't cold. It just felt like a regular piece of metal, as if I was back home in my apartment. I'd never felt it like this before while on a jump. It was either cold—signifying a problem—or warm, signifying that I could go home. This weird neutral feeling probably meant something bad, but I didn't have time to worry about that right now. "Move Leonidas's body out of sight behind our lines," I ordered. "But tell no one who he is. We will give him a proper funeral later."

Six Spartans stepped forward and hoisted the king's corpse up on their shoulders.

Across the field, the various jumpers slowly began disappearing again, blinking out from the field as quickly as they had appeared.

But the first time jumper to appear didn't leave with the others. Instead, he edged closer to the Spartan lines, stopping about twenty paces from me. He was probably my dad's age, with short, thinning black hair. A confused look passed over his face as he pointed the jump device in a slow circle and found it pointing at me.

He bowed low toward me and then straightened. "Forgive my ignorance, great warrior," he called over to me. "But are you Leonidas, king of the Spartans?"

"Nope, I'm Dan." I pointed to the body of Leonidas as it was carried away through the Spartan lines on the shoulders of the six Spartans. "*That* was Leonidas. I just took his place."

The man spun his jump device to another setting and it pointed right at me. His eyes widened. "You're one of us!" He turned toward one of the few remaining jumpers, whistling loudly with two fingers in his mouth, then waved frantically to call him over.

"What's going on?" I asked. "Why are you guys leaving? Why is my jump device not saying the glitch is fixed?"

"You seriously don't know what's happening?" he asked.

A shiver ran down the back of my neck. "No. I was here trying to fix a regular glitch, but then Leonidas got killed. I'm kind of taking his place for the moment, because I could tell history was going to unravel if I didn't."

A blast of trumpets came from the Persian lines, and their lead elements came to a halt about two hundred paces away. As soon as they charged, they'd close the distance in seconds.

"Archers moving into position!" Areus warned.

The time jumper glanced behind him at the Persians and then shook his head at me, his expression unreadable. "I'll keep this short, because things are going to get pretty pointy in a minute. Right now, the most important thing is to keep history flowing properly. You have to do everything exactly as Leonidas would have done here."

I felt like a knife had just been rammed into my gut. "But Leonidas dies in this battle!"

The man shrugged, then he and his partner began walking through the Spartan lines toward safety. The Spartans moved aside for them, heads bowed in deference to these men they thought were gods.

"Don't worry, kid. We'll stick around to make sure you get it right," the jumper called out over his shoulder. "All of history is counting on you."

CHAPTER 14

As the two time jumpers headed to the rear of the Spartan lines, I could only stand there, my mouth hanging open and a hollow ache growing in the pit of my stomach.

If I stayed and pretended to be Leonidas, I died. And if I left, history would spin out.

I was so screwed.

"Hurry, Danakles!" Areus yelled. "The battle is about to start!"

What am I doing? Twenty bazillion troops were about to come screaming through that pass, and I was standing there with my back to them? "Where do I go?" I yelled to Areus. "What do I do?" Everything was piling on so quickly. My mind was a complete blank, and my nerves felt like they were going to shatter.

Areus pointed over to the right side of the Spartan line, next to the small cliff edge that dropped off into the ocean. "The far-right side is the place of honor and command. That is where Leonidas would have stood, and where you must now stand." He started to go back to his spot in the middle of the line, along with Charilaus and Dienekes.

"Don't leave!" I yelled. "I need you guys beside me."

All three stood a little taller. "Are you sure?" Areus asked.

"Yes! You need to make sure I don't screw up. Please!"

They rushed with me to the far side of the Spartan phalanx. The men already there moved aside to let us flow seamlessly into their formation. Charilaus took up his place on my left, Areus stood directly behind me, and Dienekes moved into position behind Charilaus.

A horn sounded again, and in one fluid motion, the Persian archers reached for their arrows.

"Rain coming!" Dienekes yelled.

I squeezed my fist tighter around the leather-wrapped grip of my shield. In seconds, this hunk of bronze-covered wood was going to be the only thing protecting me from an agonizing death.

With a loud creak of wood straining under pressure, the Persian archers pulled back on their bows and angled them skyward.

"Give the command," Areus urged.

The Persians loosed their arrows, and a storm of pointy shafts hissed through the air toward us.

"What?" *Oh yeah, I'm in charge.* "Shields up!" I yelled as four days of training with Areus flooded back to me. I gripped my shield in front of me and knelt on the ground. The command was relayed on down the line and, like a set of dominoes, the first row of Spartans knelt and anchored their shields against the ground. The second row gripped their shields at waist height so that they overlapped ours, and the last rows held their shields overhead, always extending over the row in front. The bright Greek sunshine disappeared, and I was locked in a world of shadow.

For a second, there was the eeriest of silences, then the plain reverberated with the clatter of thousands of arrows striking shields. I curled my head into my chest and tried to make myself as small as possible behind my own shield. Vibrations traveled up my arm from the shield as arrows bounced off it or embedded themselves into the wood.

In the semidarkness, Charilaus casually turned his head toward me, as if crouching behind a shield was a daily occurrence in his life. "O great Danakles, would you be willing to tell this humble mortal which god you are?"

I took a deep breath before responding, not wanting my voice to crack or shake with fear. "I'm not a god. I'm just a normal man."

"Just a man," Charilaus scoffed. "Yet your friends appear as if sent from Mount Olympus, and then disappear again just as quickly."

Okay, that was kind of hard to explain.

"Are you Herakles?" Areus asked from behind me, raising his voice to be heard over the constant crash of arrows.

"Herakles?" Dienekes laughed. "He has not the bull-like arms or legs of Herakles. But maybe a god of not so mighty stature, like Apollo?"

"I'm not a god!"

They ignored my protests.

"Gods can change their shape," the man on the far side of Charilaus suggested. "He could indeed be Herakles."

"What should we call you?" Areus asked.

"Danakles is fine," I muttered. "Or Leonidas whenever the other Greeks are around."

"He could be Ares," Charilaus continued. "It would be only fitting that the god of war comes join us in our fight."

Sigh . . . I wasn't going to win this argument, especially since the reality of my situation was even weirder than anything they could think of.

As the arrows continued raining down on us, the Spartans carried on with their discussion about whether I was a god, a demi-god, or just blessed by the gods like the heroes in the Iliad. I ignored them and focused on the more important issue: the fact that right now I was stuck in the role of Leonidas. Everything he had done, I would also have to do. My dad had told me so much about Leonidas and the Battle of Thermopylae, but unfortunately all I could remember right now was from the movie *300*. And all Leonidas did in that was make a few short speeches, show off his abs—and kill lots of Persians. Nothing in that movie had prepared me for leading the united forces of Greece into battle. I was trying to pull off an impersonation of a man who I'd known for only four days, and the only thing I really knew about him was that he kicked ass and then died.

I didn't know how long I'd been kneeling there on the dusty ground, shaking in fear as each arrow hammered against my shield and sent shudders up my arm. We could have been there for five minutes . . . ten . . . There was just a constant drumming of bronze points against our wooden shields until another trumpet sounded from the Persian lines and the incessant pounding ending.

"The rain has stopped," Dienekes remarked lightly.

A sigh of relief escaped my lips. No more arrows. Now we'd be fighting hand to hand. I could do that. "Just remember," I muttered to myself. "Act like Leonidas."

"Spears out!" I yelled. On this command, the shield wall broke apart with a rhythmic clacking. To my relief, all our men returned to their standing positions. Not a single arrow had snuck past our huge shields.

In front of us the ground was littered with arrows, as if an arrow factory had exploded. Twelve of them had even embedded themselves in my shield, but one sweep of my sword slashed through them all.

On the Persian side of the battlefield, the archers retreated and infantry took their place. Only two hundred paces separated our armies. I picked up a clod of dirt and crushed it into my fist to try and sop up some of the sweat on my palms. Two hundred measly paces.

Another horn sounded from the Persian ranks, and the infantry came marching toward us, bearing small wicker shields and short stabbing spears.

A hush fell across the Spartan lines. Each man stood statue-still, spears and shields held in perfect sync. A strong wind blew off the ocean, and gulls circled above us.

The Spartan Sacrifice

I gripped my spear tighter while sweat trickled down my brow from underneath my helmet. This was it, the actual battle. Over both my shoulders jutted the long spears of the men behind me, presenting a deadly wall of points to the Persians. We had better armor, larger shields, longer spears, and infinitely better training. We had the advantage here as long as we didn't get overwhelmed by the enemy's sheer number.

One hundred paces.

"Here is courage," Charilaus shouted, as if challenging the entire universe. "Mankind's finest possession."

"Here is the noblest prize that a young man can endeavor to win," Areus added from behind me, joining his voice to Charilaus's as the pair recited the same words.

A roar of Spartan voices joined in. "It is a good thing his city and all the people share with him when a man plants his feet and stands in the foremost spears relentlessly, all thought of foul flight completely forgotten, and has well trained his heart to be steadfast and to endure, and with words encourages the man who is stationed beside him."

Goose bumps rose along my arms. I had no clue what they were reciting, but they all knew the words, like it was some kind of sacred battle cry. And the power of those three hundred voices raised in unified defiance was like nothing I'd ever felt before.

"Here is a man who proves himself to be valiant in war," the entire Spartan line thundered as they hammered their spears against their shields. "With a sudden rush, he turns to flight the rugged battalions of the enemy and sustains the beating waves of assault."

Only fifty paces separated us now from the Persians, close enough for us to see their faces clearly. Each face held the same look—fear. And, with each step closer, their fear seemed to grow, while my own confidence increased.

"And he who so falls among the champions and loses his sweet life," the Spartans continued, "so blessing with honor his city, his father, and all his people, with wounds in his chest, where the spear that he was facing has transfixed that massive guard of his shield, and gone through his breastplate as well. Why, such a man is lamented alike by the young and the elders, and all his city goes into mourning and grieves for his loss."

Only seconds now until the Persians would be upon us. The power and energy of that Spartan poetry was contagious, infecting me with both bravery and defiance.

Every Spartan was shouting now, with a swelling of energy and sound that blocked out everything else. "His tomb is pointed to with pride, and so are his children, and his children's children, and afterward all the race that is his. His shining glory is never forgotten. His name is remembered." The entire Spartan line then let out a bloodthirsty howl. "And he becomes an immortal!"

My every nerve was on fire. The Persians were only steps away, within reach of our long spears.

"Attack!" I roared as I thrust my spear forward. Its heavy blade sliced through the wicker shield directly in front of me and sank into a Persian warrior's poorly armored stomach. I wrenched it out and the Persian crumpled to the ground, his eyes wide with disbelief.

The energy and courage that had surged through me evaporated as the wounded Persian stared at me with accusing eyes. His hands that had gripped a spear looked hard, but not warrior hard, more like a farmer's. And his face? Just a face filled with pain and confusion, wondering why he had marched for such a long distance only to die on a distant coast.

This wasn't me. I wasn't a killer. How could I pretend to be Leonidas?

"Watch out!" Charilaus yelled.

The man I'd stabbed had somehow found the strength to lift himself to his knees and thrust his spear at my groin. Charilaus's spear slashed sideways and caught the Persian across the throat, sending a spray of blood into the air. The man collapsed to the ground, dead for sure this time.

The Spartan Sacrifice

"You said you were a fighter—then fight!" Charilaus barked at me. "And you now bear the shield and helmet of Leonidas—so lead like he would!"

I cringed at my own stupidity. He was right. I didn't have time for doubt or pity, or any of a thousand other thoughts that might interfere with what I had to do. If I wanted history to flow correctly, I couldn't be Dan the dumb teenager, the guy who couldn't figure out which girl to give his heart to . . . even when he should be worrying more about Victor. I had to act like Leonidas, king of the Spartans. And history needed me to get my act together—now!

Another Persian had already stepped into the space left by the dead soldier. I jabbed at his face, but he raised his shield and blocked my strike. With a twist of my arm, I swung my spear around and sliced him across his shins. The press of bodies from behind shoved him forward, and he fell sprawling at my feet. Without hesitation, I rammed the bronze edge of my shield down on his unarmored skull. With a sickening crack, he collapsed lifeless to the ground.

I felt a momentary twinge of guilt but sucked it back. I'd have to deal with the nightmares later.

The battle became a blur of attack, attack, and more attack. The only constant was the pressure of Areus's shield against my back, supporting me, holding me in place in the line so that I would not back up or falter.

Like a viper, my spear kept darting out in search of a target. Wicker shields split. Armor parted. Blood flowed. Bodies fell.

This wasn't battle. This was butchery.

The Spartans had years of fighting experience. They were battling for their homes, their families, and their pride. They fought with ferocity and skill against a Persian army that seemed to be comprised only of farmers and conscripts. Corpses were piling up in front of us, a blood-soaked wall of flesh that did nothing to slow the tsunami of Persians.

My spear lashed out for what seemed like the thousandth time, when another enemy showed itself—fatigue. Sweat poured down my face and my left shoulder ached from holding my heavy shield up for so long. I realized I had maybe only a few more minutes left in me before I needed a rest.

Would Leonidas also have become exhausted at this point of the battle, or was I just being a wimp?

On my left, Charilaus was still holding his shield close to his body so that it protected him from knee to chin. But his spear seemed to be moving with less intensity and speed. That made up my mind for me. If we were going to continue fighting for a full two days, I would need to get the next row of fresh troops in.

"Areus," I yelled over my shoulder. "Prepare to move forward."

"Second rank ready!" he yelled, and the same command was repeated down his row.

I took a deep breath and tried to steady my nerves. We were about to execute probably the hardest move in the whole Spartan playbook, and I'd only had a chance to practice it a few times with Areus—but never with a whole line, and never under combat conditions.

"Second rank forward!" I barked.

I jabbed at the face of the Persian in front of me. He reeled back a few steps to get out of the way of my spear, allowing me a blip of free time.

In that same instant, I pushed my shield as far out in front of me as possible while twisting to the side to leave a slight gap between me and Charilaus. A second later, Areus squeezed through the gap and stood in front of me. His heavy shield collided with the small wicker shield of a short Persian spearman, sending the man sprawling into the dirt. As he scrambled to get back to his feet, Areus's spear sank deep into his chest.

All down the line the fresh second row leaped ferociously into battle, allowing me and the rest of the exhausted first row a chance to back out of the fight. The rearmost ranks of Spartans gave us room to pass through them, and my line snuck to the back before taking our places as the last row of the phalanx.

Servants rushed toward us with jugs of water and long strips of cloth for binding wounds. I waved aside a mug of water and rushed down the length of my line. A few men tended minor wounds, but a quick count showed fifty tired and bloody Spartans in this newly formed last row.

My spirits soared. *I did it.* I'd survived my first taste of battle with the Spartans, and no one in my row had died. Maybe I could pretend to be Leonidas after all?

With a confident spring in my step, I returned to my spot at the far right.

Charilaus passed me a clay cup. "Here, drink. You fought well."

"Thank you." I tilted back my helmet, wiped the sweat from my brow with the back of a blood-spattered hand, and took a sip of the cool water. A few steps ahead of us, the battle raged on. Men screamed, spears shattered against shields, and blood flowed. I motioned with my cup toward the first row. "Do they need me to lead them?"

Charilaus had tilted his helmet back so his face was exposed, allowing him to drink from his own cup. "No. Areus holds the far right now. He will know what to do. Our task is merely to recover our strength so as to be ready to fight again."

After an incredibly short water break, my line of fifty men took up position as the sixth row in the Spartan shield wall. Here, in the back, our spears weren't long enough to reach the Persians, and we didn't have bows or slings. Our job was to firmly plant our shields into the backs of the men in front of us and provide additional strength to the phalanx.

Standing there doing nothing seemed even worse than fighting. At least in battle I had adrenaline pumping through me, masking all sorts of irritations. But in the back row all I could think about was the sun beating down on me, the soreness in my arms, and the rivers of sweat trickling down my ribs and back.

"Second line forward!" came the cry from the front ranks.

With Spartan precision, Areus's line extricated itself from the battle and moved to the rear. Not all the men returned on their own strength, though. One man was carried on his shield through our lines. And when the shield was lowered to the ground, no one attempted to bind his wounds. Instead, a trio of servants wrapped the corpse in a red cloak with the face covered.

Areus grabbed a quick drink of water then took his place behind me in the phalanx. Noticing my stare fixed on the servants as they covered the dead Spartan, he explained. "Polydoros has fallen." He then shifted his gaze toward the east and their path home. "But he died in a noble cause. All of Greece will know of his sacrifice."

His words made me wince. Yeah, if I succeeded here, all of Greece would know of Polydoros and Areus and Charilaus and Dienekes, and everyone else in the Spartan line. But what about me? If I got stuck here and died, would anybody know or care that I gave up my life so that over two thousand years of history wouldn't get destroyed?

Sam would remember. And those two jerks who worked with Victor would know. But so what? Would anyone raise a monument to me? Would anyone get to know my story? The Spartans became legends because of their brave sacrifice here. But I wouldn't share their fame—I would be quickly forgotten.

Would Jenna even know what happened to me? Sam might manage to contact her, but so what? I'd be dead.

And what about Eric and the gang? The group already seemed to be on the verge of fracturing. Would they still try to take Victor down or just go their separate ways if I didn't make it back?

Areus must have sensed my discomfort. "Do not look sad, Danakles. All men die—but few get to choose their death." He waved his hand toward the rows of Spartans in front of us battling the Persians. "Each and every man here chose to march with Leonidas to defend this pass. We know we risk our lives, but our lives are a small price to pay for the safety of all Greece. Not a single man here would have chosen otherwise."

The Spartan Sacrifice 143

That's what it all came down to: choice. And I had made mine. I had picked up Leonidas's shield because saving history was more important than saving my own measly life. I snorted and shook my head—I guess I was more Spartan than I'd thought.

"To the rear!" Charilaus yelled.

In the Spartan army, you learned to obey immediately, no matter how weird the command might seem. I slammed my helmet down over my face, whirled around, and with my heart racing, I braced for the next attack.

Just in front of me, Areus and Dienekes spun around also, their shields already locked and their spears out, forming a small wall in front of me.

A group of ten men headed toward us from the Greek camp. I recognized them as the leaders of the other Greek armies.

"We wish to speak with Leonidas," bellowed a man I remembered as the leader of the Thebans.

My heart began racing even faster. The rest of the Greeks hadn't seen what happened to the real Leonidas. They didn't know that an imposter led the Spartans. But now they wanted to meet with me. If I screwed up here, the Greeks might still decide to leave . . . and history could come crashing down.

Should I tell them the truth about Leonidas, and hope they would accept me like the Spartans did? Or should I try to fake it?

"We are in the middle of battle," Areus replied. "Why do you wish to bother him?"

"It is about the battle," said the leader of the Locrians. "We wish to slay Persians as well."

Areus turned around and locked eyes with me. Then, he nodded almost imperceptibly toward me.

I took a deep breath. How would Leonidas have stood? What words would he have used? Could I fake his voice? Everything rested on me pulling this off.

I made sure to hold my shield in front of me so it covered as much of my body as possible. My skin might have developed a decent tan over the last few days, but I still looked nothing like Leonidas. "You will get your turn," I said in what I hoped was a deep enough voice.

The leader of the Thespians peered intently at me, no doubt trying to see my face through the small openings in my helmet. "You are Leonidas?" he asked, his voice thick with doubt. "I remember him not so tall, but broader of shoulder."

Areus slammed his spear into the ground. "He is our leader. What you choose to remember is not relevant to the battle at hand."

"But when I last saw him, he—"

Charilaus pushed past Areus and Dienekes and leveled his spear in front of him. "I am Charilaus, son of Labotas, son of Alkamenes. I fought at Sepeia when the forest ran red with Argive blood. Countless have fallen beneath my attack." He moved his spear in a slow arc so it pointed at each of the Greek leaders in turn. "Do you think I would follow some man other than my rightful king into battle?"

The Greeks paled and took a step back.

It was a good thing my helmet covered most of my face so no one could see the smile curling my lips. Less than an hour ago, Charilaus had been ready to kill me for just touching Leonidas's shield. But now he stood ready to fight the other Greeks for not believing I was Leonidas. Life was so much easier when people thought I was a god.

The leader of the Malians raised his hands. "We mean no offense. We only wish to take our turn in battle. We came to fight for Greece, not to simply watch Sparta earn all the glory."

Although there were tons of books and movies about the Spartans' heroics at Thermopylae, I knew from my dad that the other Greek contingents had played a huge role. "You will have your chance," I said.

"When?"

Good question. In the Spartan ranks, it took all our skill just to switch a line. How would we switch out an entire army when the

Persians were constantly attacking? "Have your men ready. And when the time comes, I will let you know."

I could tell by the sour looks on their faces that they weren't pleased with my answer. I actually thought it was a pretty good one. It hinted at giving them what they wanted without promising a single thing. And it even had an undertone of Spartan arrogance to it—a perfect answer.

"We will be ready." The Arcadian leader thumped his chest with a fist.

With that, the Greek leaders turned and began walking back to their separate groups.

Dienekes watched their retreating backs until they were safely out of hearing range. "Think of the fun we could have if we gave Leonidas's shield and helmet to a different man every time our new allies came to speak with our king." He turned toward us and dropped into a battle-ready crouch with his spear extended. "I am Charilaus," he said, mimicking Charilaus's harsh tone. "I fought at Sepeia. And even if I should put a goat in armor and call him a king, you will not contradict me."

Charilaus's back stiffened, and through his helmet's eye slits, he gave Dienekes a menacing glare. He held that pose for a second, and I thought he was going to punch him, but then he doubled over laughing, a sight I'd never thought I'd see; the guy never even smiled.

"Ah . . . Dienekes," Charilaus gasped through his laughter. "When the time comes for the vultures to eat the flesh from our bones, I will miss you."

Areus laughed along with the pair of them and then tapped my shield twice with his fist. "You did well, Danakles. Now come, let us discuss how to share the glory with our allies, so they will have tales of victory to share around their home fires as well."

We resumed our positions in the Spartan phalanx. My line had moved up to the third rank by now, so I'd be back into the thick of fighting again soon. I pressed my shield into the back of the man in front of me. "So how do we swap armies?" I yelled over my shoulder.

"Give it time," Areus said. "You will know when the moment arrives."

I gripped my spear tighter and stared at the pack of massed Persians ahead. They filled the pass for as far as I could see.

I hoped Areus was right.

CHAPTER 15

The ground at our feet had become slick with blood, and the bodies had piled up in front of us before we finally had a break in fighting. The Persian troops refused to advance, even with their overseers shouting for them to move forward. Every battle I'd been in had a point like this, where one side faces so much death that they can't press on. I knew that this was only a momentary lull, but it was the moment that I needed.

"Spartans!" I raised my spear up high. "Retreat!"

The command was relayed down the line, and the center of our formation flowed backward, like a bursting dam, before splitting apart, allowing a huge hole in our line. At this sight, the Persians howled and rushed forward to renew their attack. But, before they could take advantage of the situation, the leader of the Arcadians shouted out a string of commands, and a group of Arcadian troops hurried into the gap.

The Spartan wings peeled away as more and more Arcadians rushed to take their place, and within seconds, the Spartan phalanx had completely separated from battle, to be replaced by the Arcadians, who spanned the pass with almost twenty rows of men.

I pumped my fist in the air. "Yes!" We had executed the swap of armies flawlessly, and for the first time today, the Spartans were completely out of the battle.

Areus pounded me on the back. "Well done!"

With a bounce in my step, I strode back, with the rest of the Spartans, to our camp just inside the crumbling stone wall. Men crowded around the gate, cheering us as we stepped through. I didn't acknowledge their cheers, and instead tried my best to keep a large circle of Spartans around me. After all, the less the other Greeks saw me, the less chance that they would figure out that Leonidas was dead and an imposter had taken his place. Luckily, the Greeks were used to Spartans being aloof, so me ignoring them wasn't considered an insult. They filtered back to their own camps, leaving me and the rest of the Spartans alone in ours. Servants rushed around, binding the wounds of injured men or bringing water and collecting gear, which brought a new problem. Did Leonidas's servants know he had been slain? How would they react to seeing me in his armor?

Wait a second. While every other Spartan had a crew of servants around him, not a single servant had come near me. I looked around the camp, searching for Leonidas's servants, and saw three men huddled together, whispering to each other and casting fearful looks my way. No, not fearful, terrified. Whoever had brought Leonidas's body back must have told the servants about my "god" status.

I looked around to make sure no non-Spartans were in sight, then pulled off my helmet and shook the sweat from my hair. "It's okay," I called to the three men, while waving an encouraging hand.

With tentative steps, they crept forward, building up the courage to offer me a large clay pitcher of water and to take my helmet and shield. I took the pitcher and went to sit on the shady part of the wall, facing the battle. It felt so good to put my heavy shield down and be out of my sweaty helmet. For a little while, I could stop acting like Leonidas and be Dan again.

All around me, men were smiling and clapping each other on the back, celebrating their success so far. Even I felt happy. Yeah, maybe on the third day, everyone here was going to die, but at this moment, we had a victory in our hands, and no one could take it away from us.

Charilaus's smile vanished, and he lowered his head. "The other gods approach," he said in a hushed voice.

Victor's two time-jumping stooges were making their way through the Spartan camp with a swagger to their step, like they owned the place. And wherever they passed, men bowed their heads and scrambled to get out of their way. Even Areus, Dienekes, and Charilaus began edging away.

"Where are you going?" I asked them.

"We must not stay near when you talk with the other gods," Areus said. "We will cause offense."

"But we're not—" I stopped myself before I said the word *gods*. The Spartans had seen Victor's men magically appear and then disappear again; I would never convince them we were just normal guys. But I wanted the Spartans around me for protection. After all, the two guys headed my way were Victor's men. Whatever they wanted to talk to me about was probably going to be bad. They might even be coming for my jump device. And there was no way I could fight them both off without the Spartans backing me up.

Unless . . .

"All right, go," I said to the Spartans. "But if I *ever* point with my shield hand at them, I need you to kill them instantly."

"You fear these gods?" Charilaus asked.

"Let's just say we are not on the best of terms." I hopped off the wall and tugged once at the sword belted at my side to make sure it would come clear of its scabbard easily.

"But how could we slay them?" Areus asked. "They are gods."

"Trust me," I said quietly. "You'll be able to. Now go! And tell the others."

Dienekes, Areus, and Charilaus hustled away, just as the two time jumpers approached. The older of the two, the one with short black hair and a thin mustache, stopped a few steps away from me and crossed his arms over his chest. "You okay? You wounded or anything?"

"Why do you care?" I looked them both up and down, trying to figure out what they wanted. Surprisingly, the younger one looked like he was only a few years older than me. He wore a black dress shirt with silver accents, dress pants, and black leather shoes. But what really shocked me was that his longish black hair was slicked back with gel.

He caught me staring at his hair and scowled. "What, you never seen gel before?"

"Not on a time jump."

"Not that it's any of your business, but I was about to go out on a date when the black event hit. I didn't have time to change."

Black event. That must be what these guys called it when history started unraveling. Had they heard the same howling inside their heads and seen the same visions of history being torn apart?

The older jumper gestured at the younger one to be quiet. "So?" he asked me again. "Are you okay?"

"Yeah, I'm okay." My words came out heavy with irritation. "But don't pretend you care."

He raised his hands. "Please. Let's not fight. What's important here is making sure history doesn't fall apart."

"Yeah," said the younger jumper. "We have to make sure you last two more days."

If I hadn't already suffered way too many talks with Victor, the time jumper's disregard for my life would have annoyed me. Instead, it just proved that anyone allied with Victor was a smug idiot who didn't give a damn about anyone else.

But they did care about history.

I thought things over for a moment. Some sucker needed to stick around to save history, and currently that sucker was me. But

I specifically remembered that I'd set my jump device to the setting that allowed me to leave before the glitch was fixed. If I left now, these guys would be forced to take my place. All they would need would be Leonidas's helmet and shield, both of which were sitting there next to the wall.

I took one last glance at Areus. For the last four days, he had been like a second father to me, teaching me what it meant to be a Spartan and supporting me when Charilaus had doubted me. It had been Areus's shield in my back that had braced me in the phalanx, and it had been his spear that had hovered over my shoulder, protecting me when any Persian got too close. Of all the Spartans, I'd miss him the most. But I would miss my life more.

I raised both my middle fingers toward the two jumpers. "So long, suckers!" Before they could react, I yelled the command to jump home. "*Arbah rostvos orokol biradelem!*"

Nothing happened.

I was stuck on the same dusty Greek plain, staring at the two time jumpers, both my middle fingers raised.

The younger one laughed and turned to his partner. "He's too dumb to know what's going on."

"*Arbah rostvos orokol biradelem!*" I yelled again.

Still nothing.

I slowly curled my middle fingers back into my fists.

Awkward.

"I'll give you a hint, kid." The older jumper looked at me almost sympathetically. "Where was that command supposed to take you?"

"Home," I said sheepishly. "To the place where I jumped out from."

The younger jumper laughed at my obvious confusion. This guy was already getting on my last nerve and I'd just met him. A part of me felt like smashing the butt of my spear into his gut to see how funny he found that. But I held back. These guys had answers, and without them I was stuck here.

"What's going on?" I pleaded. "Why won't my jump device work?"

"You know how the time stream mostly fixes itself," the older jumper said, "and we're only called in to fix the *big* issues, like kings dying at the wrong time or battles being fought at the wrong spots?"

Sam had told me pretty much the same thing on my first time jump. She'd told me that you never had to worry about accidentally killing Einstein's great-great-great-grandfather because the time stream would still make sure he was born. "Yeah? So?"

The older jumper nodded. "Let's look at this from the time stream's perspective. It needed a Leonidas, and it had you running around with Leonidas's shield and helmet, and with all the Spartans already listening to you as if you were their king. What do you think the time stream ended up doing?"

"Oh . . . crap . . ." My jaw hung open and I stared at him in horror. "Are you telling me the time stream decided to make *me* Leonidas?"

"Yup. This is your home now, kid."

"No . . . no . . . you're wrong. That can't be true." Despite my denial, deep down I knew he was right, and the dead jump device hidden inside my bracer proved it. I wasn't just pretending to be Leonidas—from history's perspective, I *was* Leonidas. I looked at him with pleading eyes. "How am I going to get out of this?"

"That's what we're trying to tell you." The younger jumper smirked. "You're not. You're stuck here. Now where's your partner? We need to talk."

CHAPTER 16

I'm stuck here. And in two days, the time stream would expect me to die in a heroic defense of Greece.

"You listening, dumbass?" the younger man snapped. "Get your partner down here."

He wanted the impossible. "Why do you need my partner?"

"Because we don't want to risk getting a sword in the back," the older man replied. "Now either you get him down here, or we'll find him ourselves and drag him down here."

The younger man extended his right arm and slowly pulled it across his chest with his left hand as if he was stretching. Just as slowly, he swung his right arm in the other direction. To a casual observer, it might look like he was trying to get a kink out of his shoulder. But I knew better; he was searching for Sam with his jump device. "He's hiding in the woods," the jumper said. "Close to the Phocian wall."

The older jumper snorted. "Your partner hides away in the forest while you put your life on the line? That's pretty cowardly. How's he supposed to have your back?" He waved aside his words. "Doesn't matter. Call him over."

His arrogant manner, so typical of one of Victor's men, set my teeth on edge. Like I was some dog that was supposed to fetch on his command. But he forgot I wasn't just some stupid teenager. History had thrown me into the role of Leonidas, and right now Charilaus, Areus, and the rest of the Spartans were all watching us. They weren't obvious about it, as not a single Spartan dared to look directly our way. But every one of them had turned so we remained in their peripheral vision. All I had to do was jab my left hand toward these two morons and they'd be human spear targets.

I opened and closed my left fist a few times as I stared at the two jumpers. *But should I?*

No.

I needed these guys. They clearly knew more about time jumping than I did. If I wanted any chance of leaving Greece, I'd have to do what they said—and that meant getting Sam down here.

"Give me a few minutes," I muttered as I headed toward the forest, the two jumpers close behind.

A few steps away from the treeline, I stopped. Somewhere up on that slope, amid all those shadows, bushes, and tree trunks, Sam was hiding. I waved my arms over my head like a stranded person signaling for a plane. Nothing stirred within the woods.

Come on, Sam. I need you.

She had to be able to see me. I was the only Spartan in the entire army waving his arms like an idiot in the middle of that dusty field.

I stood there waving for about two minutes before an arrow point slowly peeked out from behind the trunk of a large oak, followed a second later by a bow, and then Sam. She was still dressed in only her sleeveless tunic, but she had put her boots on. Swiveling her bow back and forth, she targeted the two jumpers. "What are they doing here?"

The younger man laughed. "Your partner is a girl? No wonder your side is such a mess."

"Oh . . . damn," the older jumper exclaimed, his words sounding almost fearful.

"What?" the younger one asked.

"It's *her*."

"Oh . . ." The younger jumper's cocky smirk vanished, and he suddenly looked unsure of himself.

"What the hell's going on?" Sam turned her head slightly toward me but still kept her bow trained on the other two.

"I'm screwed. The time stream thinks I'm Leonidas, so my jump rod doesn't work. I'm stuck here."

She motioned with her bow toward the two jumpers. "And why are they here?"

"Samantha, right?" The older man beamed a smile, and his voice had this sickening cheerful tone, like he and Sam were long-lost friends, finally reunited. "I'm Jerry." He jerked his thumb toward his partner. "And this is Chris. We're here to help."

Sam's eyes narrowed. "How do you know my name?"

"You probably don't remember me—you were very young." Jerry placed a hand over his heart. "But I knew your father. I was even at your house a few times. I remember you, with your little red pigtails and your unicorn nightgown, jumping up and down on the couch when Robert tried to put you to bed."

Sam inhaled sharply and, for the briefest of instants, her eyes were filled with sadness. But, just as quickly, her expression hardened again. "What do you want?"

Jerry hesitated for a moment. "We're here to make sure that the time stream doesn't collapse again. Dan did a fine job saving it the first time, and we just want to make sure he follows through to the end."

"Excuse me?" I sputtered. "Tell her the truth. You're here to make sure I die at the right moment."

Chris snorted. "If you want to put it that way . . . you got yourself stuck in this situation, so yeah, we're here to make sure you don't mess things up."

Sam sighted along her arrow and aimed it at Chris. "Both of you, back up."

"Whoa! Whoa!" Jerry raised both of his arms. "We don't mean you any harm."

"Just move." Sam motioned with her bow.

The two of them moved back a few steps, and Sam leaned close to me, so she could whisper in my ear. "Do you trust them?"

"Nope. They're with Victor."

Sam turned her focus back to the two jumpers. "Follow us and I'll shoot you," she warned, then retraced her steps backward into the forest. I had no choice but to follow her, and together we retreated until we were completely covered by the shade of the stunted oak trees. She sat down facing the ocean, the bow resting across her thighs. From here, she had a clear view of the Spartans, the two time jumpers, and the battle raging between the Arcadians and the Persians.

She crossed her arms over her chest. "How is it that just when I think things are bad, you always find a way to make it worse?"

I sat down next to her and laid my spear on the ground beside me. "Come on! Do you think I *planned* this? Before Leonidas took that rock to the head, I was all set to go home. Tell me, did anything flash in your head when Leonidas died?"

"Yeah . . . I saw history going all to hell." The harshness in her voice vanished, and there was a slight tremor in her tone, as if she'd been scared by what she'd seen.

"Exactly! I saw the same. History needed a Leonidas, and me picking up his shield was the only way to fix things." I stared at Sam defiantly. "What would you have done differently?"

Sam held up her hands. "Sorry. You're right. I'm just overwhelmed." She rested her hand on my arm, and the hard lines in her face softened. "You did the right thing."

I snorted. "Yay me. I saved history. But now if I leave, history crumbles. Or, I should say, if I *could* leave—my jump rod doesn't work anymore. I'm stuck here."

Sam spun the settings on her jump device and did a quick search. The rod ended up pointing directly at me. "That's weird. *You're* the glitch."

"Me?" I looked at her jump device pointing at me like an accusing finger. "I guess it makes sense. No part of me wants to stay here. The jump device probably knows that and thinks I might run away before history is completely fixed."

Sam twirled a strand of her long red hair around a finger and nibbled on the end of it as she mulled things over. "Can't you just fight for two days and then jump out with me, like you did in Celtic times? That should be enough to make history happy, right?"

Horrific memories of that trip flashed through my mind. My own jump rod had been stolen, so the only way for me to get home was to hold on to Sam while she jumped out. The trip had been like nothing I'd ever experienced. No light, only complete darkness, like being in the deepest cave. The horrible wind that tried to rip me away from Sam. Me desperately clinging to her, trying not to fall. And the city hiding there in the darkness. Despite the stifling heat, I shuddered. "It's a huge risk. Even when I was legitimately trying to head home to my own time, the wind in the void still almost killed me. How would it react to someone it considers as being from *this* time period?"

Sam gazed off toward the ocean and sighed. "All right, we'll leave that as a last resort." She plucked on her bowstring a few times like it was a guitar, its toneless twang an odd contrast to the shouts and clash of weapons from the battle below. "You swapped into the role of Leonidas by taking his shield; can you swap out of it with someone?"

"Nope. The Spartans would never accept the shield. It's an honor thing. They will never let their own shield willingly drop." I motioned toward the Arcadians as they stood valiantly against the Persians. "And

I can't ask the rest of the Greeks. As soon as they hear Leonidas is dead, they'll start stampeding for home."

Sam pushed her hair back with both her hands. "Geez . . . what a mess." She shook her head, a grim expression on her face. "I promised myself I wasn't going to get dragged into your drama," she muttered, more to herself than to me. "But you always manage to suck me back in."

"Do you think I wanted this?"

"Nope. But you found it. Just like you have in *every* time jump so far." She exhaled loudly, then motioned toward Victor's two men. "Why are you even talking to them?"

From the safety of the forest, I watched the pair. Servants had raised an awning above them so they were in the shade, and both sat propped up on pillows with trays of food and pitchers sitting between them. They ate and drank while they observed the battle raging in the distance. They looked more like two guys watching a football game on TV than time jumpers. "Because they know a hell of a lot more about time jumping than we do. They're my only hope of leaving this place."

Sam snorted. "Do you really think they'll help you? These guys are evil. Everyone they come close to dies. My dad. My brother. Your dad."

For a second, the heartbreaking image of Victor's sword piercing my dad's chest flashed through my mind. "Trust me. I know they don't care about me. But they do care about history flowing correctly, and they also seem to care about you. They were complete buttheads to me before you showed up. Then they . . . changed. Almost like they didn't want to offend you. Maybe I can use that to my advantage."

"That doesn't make sense, though. So he remembers me from when I was a kid. Who cares? Why would that matter?"

"I don't know. These guys have answers, though. And the only way we'll find those out is by both of us talking to them."

Sam's lips twisted as if she had just bitten into a lemon. "The only way, huh?" Her eyes drifted to the Spartans in their camp. "If I come down there, will I be safe?"

I looked her straight in the eyes. "I promise you. The Spartans will not lay a finger on you."

"How can you be so sure?"

I pointed to the Spartans. Most of them rested against the wall, while servants rushed among them carrying food and drink. A few others were lying in the shade or sharpening their weapons. Not a single one was within twenty steps of Chris and Jerry. "See how much space they're giving Victor's guys?"

Sam nodded.

"The Spartans think time jumpers are gods."

"What?"

"Did you see all the time jumpers appear when Leonidas died?"

"Of course."

"Well, so did the Spartans. And now they think we're gods." I swirled my finger in the dusty earth. "That's why they let me take over for Leonidas. And that's why they won't touch you."

"And the rest of the Greeks?"

"They do whatever the Spartans tell them to do. Trust me, you'll be safe."

Sam sighed and reluctantly got to her feet. "All right," she said without enthusiasm. "Let's get this over with."

Just as glumly, I pulled myself up off the ground and picked up my spear. Together we left the cover of the trees and moved through the Spartan camp. I led the way, my eyes sweeping from Spartan to Spartan, hoping that everyone would react favorably to the sight of Sam. I'd just given her my word they wouldn't touch her, but what if I was wrong?

Maron was the first to see her. His eyes went wide, in a completely un-Spartan expression of surprise, then he blinked repeatedly as if he couldn't believe what he was seeing. "Artemis . . ." His voice was an awestruck whisper. He bowed his head and dropped to one knee, keeping his eyes focused on the ground.

"Artemis!" The cry carried through the ranks, and like magic, the Spartans parted before us, heads bowed.

One Spartan, who I didn't recognize, fell to his knees in front of Sam with his hands clasped in front of him. "Thank you, O great Artemis." His voice cracked with emotion. "I sacrificed to you when my son went missing in the forest. You returned him to us two days later, safe and whole."

Sam's nose crinkled with uncertainty. "Umm . . . you're welcome." She turned to me and leaned in close. "Is this"—she waved her hand toward all the bowed heads—"normal?" Her voice had an uncharacteristic giddiness to it.

"No." I glanced around, trying to figure out what I was missing. The Spartans thought I was a god, too, but none of them treated me like this. "They must really like Artemis."

"What's she the goddess of?"

"Hunting. She always carried a bow and was found primarily in the woods."

"Cool." Sam smiled and an even more uncharacteristic spring entered her step.

We stopped just inside the shade of the little pavilion that had been set up for the two time jumpers. They lounged on their cushions, a plate of cheese and meat between them. They both eyed us, neither giving a hint as to what they were thinking.

"We're back," I said. "What now?"

Jerry looked sideways at Chris and then turned to Sam. "We think you should go home, Samantha. It's not safe for you here."

"Why do you care so much about my safety?" Sam asked. "My father and brother are dead because of bastards like you." Her eyes narrowed. "Wait . . . How do I know it wasn't you who killed them?"

"Whoa! Whoa!" Jerry raised his hands. "I would *never* have done anything to Robert. He was a good friend."

"Good friend?" I snorted. "Friendship means nothing to you guys."

Jerry looked imploringly at Sam. "You have to believe me. I want to help you, Samantha."

Sam's back stiffened. "Why do you care so much about my safety? I don't know you."

Chris raised his goblet of wine and winked at her. "Orders from Victor."

Victor! Every time I heard that name, I wanted to smash something. He was the source of everything bad in my life. And yet somehow he was connected to Sam. He seemed to want to protect her, but I couldn't figure out why. I'd gone through tons of different possibilities in my mind, but none of them seemed remotely plausible.

"I don't care about your orders. I run my own life." Sam jabbed a finger at the ground. "And I'm staying here."

Chris gave her a cheesy smile. "I admire your spirit, but it's dangerous out here. Especially for a pretty young thing like you." His eyes traveled up and down her body. "You shouldn't have to risk your life, beautiful, to save some idiot who shouldn't be time jumping in the first place."

Sam's nostrils flared as her fingers tightened on her bowstring. "My name is not Beautiful! Or Babe! Or whatever condescending crap you can think of! My name," she growled, "is Samantha."

"Sorry!" Chris held his hands out in front of himself as if he was sorry, but the grin on his face said otherwise. "But my point stands. Your loser of a partner is stuck here, and you shouldn't risk your life to save him."

Sam drew an arrow out from her quiver and began slapping it with a slow, ominous rhythm against her leg. "I'm going to speak slowly so that even your little pea brain can understand." She raised the razor sharp tip of the arrow so that it hovered just in front of Chris's face. "I'm staying. Understand?"

Chris's grin disappeared and he swallowed hard. "Y-yes."

"Good." Sam nodded. "Now are you two clowns going to do anything to help Dan?"

"As we've already told him," Jerry said, sounding almost apologetic, "we can't. As far as the time stream is concerned, he *is* Leonidas. Helping him will change the course of history."

"We don't need to talk any more, then." She motioned to me. "Come on, Dan. These guys are less than useless. Let's figure out our next move *without* them."

CHAPTER 17

Sam and I strode across the brittle yellow grass, heading for the forest. "I actually thought you were going to kill him," I said the moment we were out of hearing range of Chris and Jerry. "When you pulled that arrow out, I thought for sure that was the end of Chris."

Her eyes narrowed, and her jaw stiffened. "I almost did. The guy's such a creep—reminds me of my stepdad." She visibly shuddered. "I feel like I need a shower."

"I'm kinda glad you held back. I know he's about as useful as a box of moldy gym socks, but I still have hope that Jerry might help out somehow."

"And if he doesn't? Do you have any idea how to get out of this mess?"

"Nope." I glumly shook my head. "But I do think you should come down from the hill and stay with me and the Spartans."

Sam tossed her hands up. "Of course. Why not?" Her tone oozed sarcasm. "We're on another time jump with *another* huge army, so the best idea is for me to be in the middle of it."

I pointed back to Chris and Jerry. "The Spartans aren't the danger. Those two are. With their jump devices, they can find you no matter where you're hiding. Do you think they'll leave you alone in the woods the next time I'm stuck in battle? Not to mention that I need you, Sam. I can't figure a way out of this mess on my own. How are we going to brainstorm if you're way up in the forest?"

For a second, Sam said nothing as she clearly tried to think of some other option, then she exhaled slowly and her shoulders sagged. "No," she grumbled. "You're right. It's better if I'm here with you, stuck in the middle of an army—again." She waved her hands in mock celebration. "Yay."

"Relax. You're a goddess, remember? The Spartans won't come near you. Just look at them." The Spartans were so obviously giving us a wide space.

She glanced over both her shoulders. Every Spartan in the path of her gaze bowed his head or turned away, not daring to make eye contact. "All right, but I still don't feel comfortable standing right here in the middle of them. Why don't we go there so we can talk privately?" She pointed to the far left of the Spartan camp, where the short stone wall disappeared into the steep wooded hillside.

"Yeah, sure."

The Spartans who had gathered at that section of the wall practically scrambled out of the way as we approached, then remained at a respectful distance while casting furtive glances toward us. Sam and I sat down on the rough stone, facing the battlefield where the Arcadians were still battling the Persians in the pass, and the contingent of Malians had formed up, ready for their turn to fight.

I found myself just staring at the battlefield, barely registering what was going on. All I could think about was being trapped in Greece and that I had only two days to figure out a way home.

Sam placed a hand on my shoulder. "I know you're scared, but we've been in bad situations before. We'll think of something." She was trying to sound positive, but her words rang hollow.

"Don't lie to me, Sam. We both know nothing short of a miracle will get me out of this mess." All my fear and anger welled up inside me, forcing the words to just keep tumbling out. "I've screwed myself so royally. What am I going to do? I can't run. I can't even hide behind the rest of the Spartans or the Greeks—they expect me to lead them. And history expects me to die here in two days."

"You could still jump out with me."

"Could I? The time stream made me Leonidas. I don't think it will let me leave." The breath caught in my throat as tears welled up in the corners of my eyes. No matter how much I needed Sam's strength and the comfort of her hand on my shoulder, I didn't want her to see me like this. After everything that had gone on today, I was stressed and tired and scared and ten seconds away from completely breaking down. "Why don't you go get your gear from your camp?" It took all my effort to stop my voice from trembling. "Then we can figure out where you'll sleep tonight."

"Yeah . . . okay." She hopped off the wall and disappeared silently into the trees.

A tear trickled down my cheek, and I stared blankly at the Malian troops waiting for their turn in battle. Hundreds of men, standing in the bright Greek sunshine, with shields in hand and spears resting on their shoulders. If any of them felt fear, they didn't show it. They stood tall and proud. Like heroes.

I bowed my head and covered my eyes with a hand as a sob racked my chest. Why hadn't I figured out the kid was the glitch? If I'd just clued in a bit quicker, I could have stopped him. Hell, I never should have come to Greece in the first place. Sam was right—on every single jump, I wound up in trouble. But I still let her convince me that jumping again was a good idea, even though I knew her idea of capturing one of Victor's men wouldn't work. "Stupid doomed-to-fail plan," I muttered.

"What did you say?" Sam asked from behind me.

I nearly fell off the wall in surprise. I whipped around to see Sam standing just inside the treeline, almost hidden by the branches. "W-w-what are you doing back? Why aren't you getting your stuff?"

"I changed my mind. You're my partner; I couldn't leave you when you're so clearly hurting." She stepped out from the trees and cocked her head to the side. "Why, during all this, would you be complaining about some plan?"

"Nothing. Don't worry about it." I felt the sting of shame creep up my cheeks. "Everything's fine." I returned to staring at the fighting in the pass, hoping that Sam would take the hint and leave.

The soft padding of her footsteps behind warned me she hadn't. "No. I want to know. Are you seriously blaming this mess on our plan?"

I wiped my eyes with the back of my hand then turned to face her, hoping I didn't look as terrible as I felt. "Wouldn't you if you were in my situation? The only reason we jumped was to ambush one of Victor's guys and steal their jump device. How many times did I tell you it wouldn't work?"

"Oh, so this is my fault?" Her nostrils flared. "You had plenty of time over the last few months to tell me you hated it. But did you ever actually say to me, 'Sam, I don't want to do this plan'?" She jabbed a finger at me. "No! And did you ever suggest some other plan that wasn't your dumb mythical city? A big fat no on that one too."

"How could I? You barely talk to me! We used to talk every day, but you've completely ghosted me. You only let me dare contact you once a week, and even then all you want is a status report—you can't wait to hang up on me."

"Don't give me that," she snapped. "You had plenty of opportunity to say something. But fine, let's say I do accept the blame for dragging us out here. It was *you* who decided to be Leonidas."

"What was I supposed to do? Let history unravel?" I shook my head incredulously. "I would have been more than happy to let *anyone* else take my place, but there was no one else." I jabbed an accusing finger at Sam. "You scared off all of Victor's guys with your one-woman assault. You could have waited for me, but noooo, you had to rush in and try to take them down yourself. When I do stuff like that, you call me impulsive and reckless." I snorted. "But when you do it, it's 'seizing the advantage.'"

"Fine." Sam raised her hands. "Maybe I screwed up there. But you screw up every freakin' glitch. Do you even bother thinking, or do you just blindly rush into every disaster you can find?"

My back stiffened. "I'm actually putting my life on the line trying to get things done—sorry that doesn't always work out perfectly. We can't both just sit back, relax, and read a book in the woods during a time jump." I flicked a dismissive hand at her arm. "Look at yourself. We've been here four days, in the blazing summer sun, and you're still paler than a ghost."

Sam jerked her arm back. "I burn easy. I have to be careful."

"That's the thing—you have the luxury of being careful because I'm the one risking my neck. And then, if I mess up, you sit there on your high horse looking all smug while telling me what a terrible job I'm doing. And your 'let Dan do everything' attitude doesn't just happen on jumps. Back home, I've made contact with other jumpers. I've confronted Victor in his office. I've become part of a team that's trying to take Victor down. What are you doing?"

"Screw you, Dan. I'm doing my best."

"How? I'm the one putting my life on the line to save history."

"And I'm the one constantly putting my life on the line to save your stupid ass."

"Well, in two days I'll be dead, and you won't have to worry about my stupid ass anymore." I pulled the jump device out from my bracer and slammed it down next to me on top of the stone wall. "Here. Since you wanted an extra jump rod so badly, you can have it. I'm sure I can figure out the few ancient Greek words I need without it."

Sam crossed her arms over her chest and fixed me with a withering glare. "Why are you being like this?"

"Because I'm hot. I'm tired. I'm scared. And I have two days left to live. What should I be doing?"

Sam gave me a pitiful look and shook her head. "I'm done here. I'll come back when you've finished acting like an idiot." She turned toward the forest.

"Of course you're leaving. That's all you do. As soon as anything becomes remotely difficult—relationships, time jumping, it doesn't matter—you're out."

Sam spun around and her eyes narrowed. "Is that what this is all about? Because I said no to having a relationship with you?" She jabbed a finger at me. "Yeah, I might run when things get tough, but you're no saint. You're the neediest person I know." She lowered her voice to mimic mine. "I'm Dan. I'm an orphan. I'm so lonely. I love you." She rolled her eyes and then pretended to vomit. "You're not the only one who's had it rough. My dad's dead. My brother's dead. I'm stuck living with my bitch of a mom and my disgusting sleazeball of a stepdad. But do I whine about it constantly?"

"That's because you have no friends to whine to!"

"Oh, please. You get one girlfriend and suddenly you think you're Mr. Popular?" She snorted. "You are so clueless. Does she know you're rich?"

"What does that have to do with anything?"

Sam raised her index finger in front of my face. "She knows you jump through time and"—she raised a second finger—"she knows you have a few million bucks in the bank. Let me give you a clue, genius. She probably would have ditched your whiny butt ages ago if it weren't for those things."

I bristled at her comment. "I'm sorry—are *you* giving *me* relationship advice? Have you even been on a date?"

Sam's cheeks flushed, but she said nothing.

"Yeah, that's what I thought," I continued. "You put up this massive wall around you so no one can get in. The only warmth or affection I've even seen you give is when you hugged one of your dumb little stuffed unicorns."

The Spartan Sacrifice

"Leave my unicorns out of this," Sam warned, her voice low. "My dad got me those. He was the only one who ever cared about me."

"It always comes back to your freakin' dad." I rolled my eyes. "You really think he cared about you? Now it's my turn to give *you* a clue—he didn't. From what you've told me, he just tossed you a bow and told you to go play outside while he spent every second he could with your brother—instead of you."

The instant the words left my mouth, I knew I'd gone too far. Sam recoiled as if I'd hit her. "Screw you, Dan." Tears welled up in her eyes. "Screw you."

"I'm sorry, I'm sorry, I'm sorry." The apologies tumbled out of my mouth. "I didn't mean that. Sam, please—" I reached for her shoulder, but she tore herself away.

"Don't touch me!" she screamed, then raced for the forest.

I chased after her. "Sam! Stop! Please! I'm sorry!"

At the edge of the tree line, she whipped around and pulled the jump device from inside her bracer. Tears streamed down her cheeks as she stared grimly at me, unbelievable pain and sadness in her eyes.

"What are you doing?" I asked. "Please. I'm sorry."

As if in a daze, she spun the sections of the jump device to a new setting.

"Please, Sam, I didn't mean what I said."

"It's too late." She sniffed back her tears. "You said it."

"Just give me a chance—"

"*Arbah rostvos orokol biradelem!*" In a flash of light, Sam disappeared.

"Nooooooooooooooo!" I sank to my knees, staring at the spot where Sam had just stood.

She was gone. The one person in the world who I trusted with my life had just left me when I needed her most.

I was trapped and alone.

And it was all my fault.

CHAPTER 18

A scuffling in the dirt behind me warned of someone approaching. It was a forced sound, as if this someone had intentionally kicked the earth to announce their presence. I grabbed my jump device from the top of the wall and jammed it under my bracer, then whirled around to see Areus only a few steps away. His head was bowed, to avoid direct eye contact, but he stood lightly on his feet, ready to run, and his entire body looked tense, as if he was approaching a dangerous animal. Or, in my case, an angry god?

"Danakles?" he ventured. "Is all well?"

I snorted. No. All was not well. Things had never been worse. "Just leave me alone," I muttered. "You wouldn't under—"

I stopped myself. Like me, Areus chose to be here because the alternative was even worse. But while I had left nothing behind, he had left his wife and kids back home so he could hold off an entire Persian army with three hundred of his friends. So yeah, he'd get it.

The only thing he wouldn't understand was why I insisted on whining about my decision. Both of us had chosen a path that led to death, but Areus and the other Spartans handled the situation like heroes, while I complained about it every chance I got.

I sighed and shook my head. Sam was right: I did have a tendency to see only my own problems and not the problems of others. Too bad this insight into my own personality had come too late to stop her from leaving.

"Wait, Areus." I smiled to put him at ease. "I'm sorry. Don't go. I could use a friend."

Some of the tension left Areus's stance and he moved a few hesitant steps closer. "I apologize. But I could not fail to overhear some of your argument with Artemis. I do not wish to offend, but may I talk with you about it?"

"Sure." I sat down in the shade of the trees so I still had a view of the ocean. The water glistened like diamonds in the sun and birds wheeled through the sky. For a second, I closed my eyes and inhaled the salty air, trying to forget my situation. But the clash of weapons and the howls of men from the battlefield wouldn't let me forget, even for a second. "What do you want to talk about?"

Areus took a seat next to me. "Artemis is angry with you?"

That was an understatement if I ever heard one. "Yeah, she is. I upset her."

"Does that bode ill for us?" His brow knit and an uncharacteristic note of worry entered his voice. "We have always worshipped her above all other Olympians. We would hate to lose her favor now, when we need it the most."

Now I understood his hesitation. He'd just seen me piss off someone he considered a goddess. And, in Greek myths, that never turned out well for anybody.

"You don't have to worry. Artemis is only angry at me. Nothing will change for the Spartans or the other Greeks. All will go as it should."

The strain on Areus's face disappeared.

"As for me," I continued. "Well . . . let's just say I won't be seeing Artemis again." My voice caught in my throat on that last sentence. The finality of it was like a dagger in my chest. It had to be said, though.

The Spartan Sacrifice

Sam was gone, and, like the Spartans, I would die here. The quicker I accepted that, the quicker I could move on and save history.

"You will see her again," Areus said confidently. "For you are gods, and you live long lives. Even a goddess must grow weary of her anger at some point."

"No. She's gone for good."

Areus squinted at me from one eye and nodded knowingly. "Trust an old married man. She will forgive you. In twenty years, I have tasted my wife's fury many times." He sighed in remembrance. "But rarely could I find fault with her anger. I was not the best husband, yet my wife always forgave me. That is the way of women: Over time, they forgive—but they never forget." He glanced east toward the path home, and a wistful smile crossed his lips. "I hope my wife marries well after I fall. She deserves a better man than me."

Areus's calm acceptance of his fate made me feel embarrassed for myself. He was a true hero—fighting for what he believed in, no matter the cost to himself. I wanted to assure him that everything would be all right, that he'd see his wife and kids again. But I couldn't lie to him. Instead I clapped my hand on his shoulder. "Come on. Let's go save Greece."

The battle against the Persians raged all day long as the sun slowly traversed the sky. The once-dry earth became soaked with the blood of the fallen until it turned into a thick brown mud. The brittle yellow grass lay flattened from the passage of thousands of feet, and only corpses and arrows now sprouted from the field in front of the Greek lines.

With each Persian wave, their attacks grew more hesitant as they trod over the dead and the dying from their previous assaults. The Persians surely realized this would not be an easy victory. They were fighting desperate men who could not afford to lose this battle. The

Persians' advantage lay in their numbers; they could keep sending in fresh troops. Their supply seemed endless, while the Greeks continuously rotated their warriors to get the most out of them.

Four more times, I ended up in the front line, with Charilaus to my left and Areus's shield planted firmly in my back. And four more times, Persians fell before my spear.

As the sun lowered in the west and the mountains began to cast long shadows over the battlefield, a horn sounded from the enemy lines and the Persians finally retreated. The Spartans weren't engaged in combat at this point—the Thespians had that honor—but we watched from the safety of the wall, along with the rest of the Greek warriors.

Loud cheers erupted all around me as the Thespians began their triumphant march back from the battlefield, leaving behind them a field strewn with Persian corpses. Their own dead, which they carried on shields supported by four men, were few, although many other men bled from their wounds.

A spirit of celebration spread throughout the Greek army. They had fought back against a seemingly invincible Persian army and won a momentary victory. Even though everyone was tired, they still broke out jugs of wine and toasted each other, sharing tales of their heroism.

Every inch of me wanted to toss my armor aside, grab some food, and then pass out from exhaustion. I couldn't, though. The movie *300* might have been glaringly inaccurate on most things but, according to my dad, they had gotten one historical detail right: The toughest battle of the day was still coming. So I leaned against the wall and let the victory celebration continue. The Persians were still retreating out of the pass; I had a few minutes before I had to spoil everyone's fun.

Areus came up beside me. He had taken off his helmet, and his black hair lay matted with sweat against his scalp. "You do not celebrate. Why?"

I stared grimly out over the narrow pass. "The fight isn't over yet."

"But the enemy retreats and the day nears its close. Surely they will not attack again today."

"Trust me. They will."

I watched the last stragglers of the Persian group disappear from view, then I leaped up on the wall and banged my heavy shield with my spear for attention. Expectant faces looked up at me, probably expecting a heroic speech or words of praise. They were about to be really disappointed.

"Spartans!" I yelled as I looked out over the mass of troops. "Get ready for battle!"

These men had been standing for a whole day in the hot sun. Wave after wave of the enemy had broken against their spears without them ever giving ground. They had seen friends and allies die and had been pushed to near exhaustion. Any other group of men would probably have told me to stick it where the sun didn't shine. These were Spartans, though, the toughest soldiers in the ancient world. Despite all they'd gone through, not a single one questioned my order or even grumbled. Each man sprang to attention and began gearing up for battle again. Within minutes, we stood shoulder to shoulder, once more blocking the pass.

From deep within the Persian army, a horn sounded, and the rhythmic thump of thousands of feet resonated off the hillsides. An army was on the march, but it sounded different from the previous Persian groups. Those had made a lot of noise, but it had always been random, everyone putting his foot down when he felt like it. This now was the synchronized step of ten thousand men marching into the pass as one. These were the Persian king's best troops. His elite. The legendary Persian Immortals.

I took a deep breath and gripped my spear tighter. If the Spartans were the best troops in the ancient world, the Immortals were at least in the top five. How hard a fight would they give us? How many Spartans would fall?

"Fight well, Danakles," Charilaus said.

I nodded. "Fight well, Charilaus."

The Immortals marched steadily toward us, their sandaled feet stomping over the corpses of those who had fallen. No looks of fear on their faces. No hesitation in their step. Their spears held perfectly upright as they marched.

"Shields up!" I yelled when the Persians were only fifty paces away.

With a metallic clanging, the Spartans locked their shields together and raised their spears above their heads. A feeling of invincibility overcame me. The shield now covered my body from chin to knee. Metal greaves guarded my legs, and a bronze helmet sat heavy on my head. As long as my shield didn't drop, I had a full wall of metal facing the Persians. Behind me, the comforting weight of Areus's shield pressed up against my back, and the point of his spear stuck out past my shoulder, reassuring me that he was watching out for me.

I can do this.

The Immortals stopped mere steps away from our line. For a moment, the two armies stood facing each other, the only sounds the crashing of waves against the short cliff to my right and the moans of the dying who still had not been cleared from the field. My arm trembled with anticipation as I held my spear at shoulder level, ready to strike.

A shout rang out from the Persian lines, and the Immortals surged forward. My spear darted out, but my opponent had more skill than the men I'd faced previously. He deflected my thrust with his shield and stepped in to stab with his own shorter spear, glancing it harmlessly off my shield. From behind me, Areus jabbed his long spear at my opponent's head. As the Persian raised his shield to block that thrust, I stabbed forward to impale him in the stomach. The Immortal crumpled to the ground, clutching my spear shaft as he fell. I yanked it hard, trying to pull it out of his grasp, but he held on tightly.

Another Immortal rushed at me, stabbing for my head. I ducked and wrenched harder at my own spear, trying to free it, but the dying Persian would not let go.

"Take my spear!" Areus yelled.

I let go of my spear and reached up over my head, with my hand open like a runner in a relay race. A thick wooden shaft smacked into my palm, and I stabbed forward, spearing the second Persian in the shoulder. His shield dropped for a moment, and my second thrust took him in the chest.

The Immortals kept coming, a never-ending tide of troops that threatened to push us back. If this had been a fair fight, we'd have been overrun in seconds just because of their sheer numbers. But it wasn't a fair fight—the Immortals might have been the best troops in the Persian army, but they still carried those short spears and small wicker shields.

My spear kept lashing out, and my shield vibrated in my hands each time it blocked another spear thrust. The Immortals pressed so hard that I barely had a chance to breathe. In just a few minutes, sweat dribbled down my face and back, and my arms felt cramped from holding the shield and spear. I desperately needed to swap out of the front row. I kept looking for that opening: an instant where I could get the Spartans to switch lines. But it wasn't happening.

My breath grew increasingly ragged in my chest as my lungs gulped for air. I knew I couldn't hold out much longer. I needed to think of something quickly—the entire front row was slowing.

What would Leonidas have done?

I didn't have an answer, though. I had maybe two more minutes of hard fighting left before my shield arm collapsed from fatigue.

As my spear weakly jabbed out again, a horn sounded over the battlefield, echoing off the rocky hills. For a second, I stood there, petrified that this this would signal a hail of arrows or a full-on press by the Immortals, but, to my relief, the Immortals began pulling back from the fight, dragging their dead along with them. The battle was over for the day.

I didn't cheer. I didn't pump my fist in victory. I just let my arms drop so the edge of my shield and the heavy tip of my spear rested against the ground. "Spartans!" I called, my voice rasping out through a parched throat. "Return to camp!"

I limped back to the Greek lines along with the rest of the Spartans. The Greeks cheered us as we returned, but I ignored them all and sat slumped against the wall, waiting for them to leave. Only then did I let Leonidas's servants loosen my armor and take it, my shield, and my sword.

"You forgot this." I pushed my spear toward one of them.

He shied away from it like it was cursed. "Please, my lord. I cannot take it."

"Why not? Just put it with the rest of my stuff."

The man's head whipped back and forth and his lips trembled. "I beg you. Do not make me take your spear." He raised his hands and took another step back.

What the hell?

Charilaus rushed over and grabbed the spear from my hand, burying it point first into the ground between my feet. "You gods may not have many enemies, but we Spartans do. If you wish to act like Leonidas, then you must never let your spear get out of reach." He turned to the servant. "Go!"

As the servant scurried away, I wrenched my spear from the ground. "Better?"

Charilaus nodded and left, and since he had already scared off my servants, I was actually alone for a moment. I let my gaze drift over the Spartan camp as I changed into a red cloak and a crimson chiton that Leonidas would have worn. Not a single Spartan was out of arm's reach of a spear. I had kinda noticed this during my four days of hanging out with them, but figured it was just part of their readiness in case the Persians attacked. But the sun was going down, battle was done for the day, so what were the Spartans worried about?

The fear I had seen in the servant's eyes triggered a memory of sitting in the kitchen while my dad explained the Spartan social hierarchy.

The Spartan Sacrifice

I hadn't paid much attention at the time, because all I wanted to hear about was the cool fighting. But I remembered him saying that the Spartans had three social levels. At the top were the Spartan citizens. These were the guys who trained since birth to be warriors and fought in all the battles. Underneath them were the perioikoi—merchants and craftspeople who weren't full citizens of Sparta but performed a valuable service to Spartan society. They also fought in Sparta's wars alongside the regular Spartans, although none of them had come to Thermopylae. And at the bottom of the social hierarchy were the helots—people bound to the land and forced to grow crops and serve their Spartan masters. Every Spartan had a few helots as servants, and during desperate times, the helots would even be called to fight, but they wouldn't be given armor—they were expendable.

With horrible clarity, I realized who the Spartans were afraid of—their *servants*. This was the dark reality of Spartan life that movies and books tended to gloss over. The Spartans were the biggest slave owners in all of Greece, and, from what I remembered my dad saying, they weren't the kindest masters either. Every Spartan always kept his weapon close at hand in case the helots decided to revolt.

I felt sick to my stomach. I'd been so preoccupied with the glitch and being stuck in Greece that I hadn't realized I'd been surrounded by slaves. The helots had been giving me food and drink and helping me change in and out of armor and basically doing everything for me, and I just . . . let them.

I stared at the dirt, the sting of shame creeping up my cheeks. I hated that the people helping me were enslaved. On my second time jump, I'd spent a week as a slave of the Romans, and it had been the worst experience of my life. I couldn't imagine what it was like for these poor helots. Trapped in an entire life of slavery. I had to do something. But what?

For a few seconds, I sat there, searching for an answer. Then it hit me. There was absolutely nothing I could do. I couldn't just clap my hands and shout "You're all free! Go home!" No matter how terrible I felt, history needed to remain on track, meaning the helots had to remain here and die with the Spartans.

With a heavy heart, I grudgingly accepted some food from one of the helots and sat down to eat with the rest of the Spartans. While the other Greeks raised huge bonfires blazing into the night and celebrated the day's victory, the Spartans remained quiet. For them there were no bonfires, no feasts. Only a few small fires burned, with goat meat roasting above them.

Like me, most of the Spartans reclined back against the wall, exhausted from the final battle of the day. We drank watered-down wine and ate bowls of thick black soup or slices of roasted meat that the helots provided.

Maron hoisted his cup of wine. "We lost some brothers today. They fought well, but the Fates deemed that their time had come. Let us not forget them."

"Let us not forget them," everyone echoed as they raised their cups in silent salute.

After dinner, I ignored the complaints of my tired and aching muscles and staggered to my feet—I still had one more thing I needed to do. With the light waning, I picked my way up the hill and found Sam's camp. Her gear lay neatly stored in the clearing, with her book resting beside her backpack. Despite what she had said before about burning the book, all its pages were still intact. I studied the cover with its picture of a male werewolf and a female vampire locked in a passionate embrace, and a pang of sadness burrowed into my chest. We were supposed to be a team, but I'd let all my fear and anger get the better of me and said things that never should have been said.

Now she was gone.

With flint and steel from Sam's backpack, I started a small fire. One by one, I tore sections out of the book and fed them to the flames, watching the pages first curl in the heat, then burst into flame, and finally crumble into ash.

So many of my hopes and dreams were now burned to ash, like these pages. Victor had destroyed what he could, and I'd done the rest myself.

I tossed the remaining pages of the book onto the fire and watched the last reminder of the life I'd known go up in flames. There were so many things that would continue without me. Maybe Stewart would actually succeed in killing Victor and stopping his plan. Maybe Eric and the rest of the group would figure out another way to defeat him. Or maybe Sam would figure it out all on her own.

None of this was my concern now. History had cast me in the role of Leonidas, and I could not fail.

"Goodbye, Sam. Goodbye, Jenna." As the last page of Sam's book turned to ashes, I kicked dirt on the remains of the fire, extinguishing it.

I picked up Sam's backpack and headed back to the Spartan camp. Darkness clung to the hillside, but the moon and stars provided enough light to see by. In front of me, dots of fire showed where the Greek army was settled in for the night. This was my home now, and they were my family. And if the next two days were to be my last, I would make sure history would never forget the courage of Leonidas and the Spartans.

CHAPTER 19

Thousands of seagulls, crows, and vultures flocked above the battlefield the next morning, squawking relentlessly as they fought over the few remaining corpses, each bird trying to peck out a soft eyeball or tear off an ear. During the night, men from the Persian side had dumped the majority of their dead off the short cliff into the water, so now only a handful of forgotten bodies remained on the battlefield, along with the few waterlogged corpses that were snagged on the rocks and hadn't been pulled out to sea.

I stood there in line, ready for battle with the rest of the Spartans, watching this carnage with a dispassionate eye. A year ago, I would have thrown up multiple times at the sight of crabs scuttling over the remains of a headless man or birds fighting over a severed finger. That Dan was gone. I'd become harder over the last year. Colder. I wasn't sure I actually liked what I'd become, but it was the only way to survive.

Not that I had much time left—if all went according to plan, my short life would come to an abrupt and painful end sometime tomorrow. But I had to get through today first, and that didn't look like it would be easy. At the far side of the pass, the first wave of Persians was already marching toward us, their numbers obscured in a huge cloud of dust raised by their pounding feet.

Charilaus's gaze swept across the advancing ranks. "Who will they send this day to die?"

"Maybe they will try a new tactic and send women," Dienekes suggested from behind him. "Because their men have shown they have no skill in war."

I squinted into the distance, trying to see what new horror the Persians had in store for us today. Dad had told me all sorts of stories about Sparta and the battle of Thermopylae, but I had only latched on to the cool stuff. I knew day one had the Immortals getting their asses kicked, and day three had seen the death of all the Spartans, but what had happened on day two?

Think, Dan! Think!

"I am getting too old for this," Areus muttered. "I should be spending my nights at home in bed next to my wife, not here sleeping on some forgotten piece of dirt."

"You make it sound bad," Dienekes chuckled. "At least you are sleeping *on* the ground. You could be sleeping *in* it."

"That might still come," Charilaus said. "By the time help arrives, not many of us will survive to carry our shields home."

Help? We weren't getting any. The lone Greek ship still bobbed gently at anchor out in the bay, but no fleet was about to rush in to save us. I knew from my dad that the Greeks had sent their entire navy to Artemisium to battle the Persian fleet there. The lone Greek ship anchored offshore was only there to watch our battle and report back to the main fleet. As for the messengers that Leonidas had sent out, they weren't going to come back with thousands of men in support. We were it. A few brave Greeks holding back the endless hordes of Persians.

With a rush of wings, thousands of birds took flight, drawing my attention back to the pass. The Persians were descending upon us, an avalanche of men streaming at full speed toward our line.

The Spartan Sacrifice

What the . . . ?

This didn't feel right. Yesterday's troops had been cautious; they'd advanced tightly as a group, trying to keep some form of phalanx together. This group charging at us now clearly had no thought for their own safety; they were just a mass of wild-eyed, howling men stampeding forward.

Oh, crap.

Xerxes wasn't trying to beat us with skill; he was trying to overwhelm us with an avalanche of bodies.

"Shields up!" I yelled, and was instantly rewarded with the sound of hundreds of Spartan shields snapping into an overlapping wall of protection.

My chest rose and fell rapidly as I gripped my own shield tighter and braced for the impact. The howling grew even louder as the horde got closer and closer. Suddenly, my spear shivered in my grasp as a man impaled himself on it. Before I had a chance to free my weapon, another Persian slammed into my shield; only Areus's shield supporting me from behind kept me from falling backward. Stubby fingers curled around the edges of my shield, trying to rip it away from me. I tried to hold on, but the Persian just dug in and pulled harder. My shield dipped forward, and another Persian jabbed a spear at me. I sucked in my breath, trying to dodge, but the spear struck me in the right side. I howled as it tore through my armor and scraped along my ribs.

A sudden chill settled upon me as shock took over.

Can't die here! Can't die here! Can't die here!

I let go of my spear and in one fluid motion drew my sword and slashed downward. Four stubby fingers fell to the dirt, and I yanked my shield back into place before the spear could strike again. Areus's spear darted out, catching the Persian in the stomach. Despite the mortal wound, the Persian grabbed Areus's spear with both hands, not letting go. Another Persian took a running leap and launched himself over Charilaus's shield and into the middle of our phalanx.

My eyes darted around the battlefield as my breathing accelerated to almost hyperventilation levels. We weren't fighting men; we were fighting an unstoppable zombie horde.

Leonidas had somehow survived this onslaught, but how? Our spears were useless against so many attackers at once.

"First line! Swords out!" I yelled in desperation. We had to hold.

I yanked my shield up and slammed an enemy under the chin. An instant later, my sword sliced open his throat, sending a spray of blood through the air. Another Persian leaped wildly at me, but I slashed him across the chest and he fell to the ground.

The panic that had been rising within me began to fade. With my sword in hand, I actually felt like I had a chance.

The enemy hurled themselves at us like rabid wolves, trying desperately to break through our lines. Over the clash of weapons and the screams of men, the snapping of whips was constant as Persian commanders kept spurring their men onward, a relentless wave that threatened to wash over us. We couldn't retreat. We couldn't even switch over to fresh troops. We could only fight on or die where we stood.

Time lost all meaning as I fought, measured only by the beats of my heart, the rise and fall of my blade, and the path of my shadow as the sun crossed the sky. In this one small patch of windswept seaside, I fought longer and harder than ever before. Sweat poured out of me, and my throat felt like I'd swallowed a bowl of dust. I'd reached the point where the cut across my ribs spasmed with every breath, and my arms ached. The few sword swings I still managed were weak and slow, easily parried by whoever I was facing.

Beside me, Charilaus looked just as horrible and, along the row, numerous Spartan bodies lay where they had fallen. We had reaped a bloody harvest in return, but if the Persians continued like this, we would break.

I ducked under a spear aimed at my face and felt its blade ring off the side of my helmet. Areus jabbed weakly with his spear, and it struck the Persian lightly in the shoulder. I was safe for another second, maybe two at the most.

But then what? Another spear would be aimed at me. And, with my reactions getting slower by the second, it was only a matter of time before I fell. Something had to change. We needed some genius tactic to save the day.

Retreat? No. That would just open the floodgates and allow more of the Persian wave to hit us. We could barely hold ground at six deep. If we spread ourselves too thin, the Persians would obliterate us.

Surrender? Not an option.

That left only one alternative. "Areus," I yelled behind me. "Call all the Greeks together, even the helots. Tell them to bring all their spears."

"We can barely hold," Charilaus yelled from beside me, his voice ragged and breathless. "Those farmers and merchants will never survive."

"They won't be fighting," I panted as I knocked aside another spear shaft with my shield. "I just need their spears."

Areus relayed the command to those behind him.

"Spartans hold the line!" I yelled as I dropped into a purely defensive stance. I swung my sword now only to block, trying to conserve as much of my waning strength as possible.

"Spartans hold the line!" Charilaus repeated. The command echoed down the ranks, and the Spartans altered their fighting pattern to conserve their remaining energy.

A thousand heaving breaths later, Areus yelled to me over the clamor of the battlefield. "The Greeks are in place."

"Get them to throw all their spears. Every single one."

"That will leave them weaponless."

"Just do it!" I snapped. "We don't have time to argue." The pressure of Areus's shield in my back eased for a moment as he relayed my order to all behind him.

A few agonizing seconds later, volley after volley of spears and javelins began flying over our heads and crashing among the Persians. The heavy Greek spears easily pierced the enemy's flimsy shields and armor. Their men died by the hundreds, some struck by two or three spears at once. For the first time all day, we had a short break in the battle, as the front lines of the Persian army lay shattered and bleeding on the plain.

"Spartans!" I howled, as a new energy surged through me. "Attack!"

A roar emanated from the Spartans as the command echoed down the line. We surged forward and plowed into the still reeling front ranks of Persians. Areus's shield pressed even harder into my back as I leaned into my own shield. With every ounce of strength left in me, I pushed forward. My feet dug into the bloody ground, slowly shoving the Persian in front of me backward. Areus's spear darted over my head and the same Persian fell at my feet. I stomped over him, jabbing my sword into his chest in case he was only wounded and was planning to rise up and stab me from behind.

Step by painful step, the Spartan wall moved forward. Men groaned under the strain, but our wall did not waver. Spears from the second and third rows kept lashing out, striking enemy soldiers and adding to the ranks of the dead.

Like a bulldozer, we drove at the Persians, our solid wall of shields pushing them back against their own ranks. Without freedom of movement, they became easy targets for our swords and spears, dying by the hundreds. Men turned to flee our onslaught, which made it only easier to hack them down. The overseers at the rear kept lashing their whips, forcing more men forward against the fleeing masses and packing them even tighter together.

Chaos descended on the Persians as their front line crumbled. Men dropped their shields and ran, only to find their way blocked by their own troops. On the right wing, some Persians threw themselves off the short cliff and into the ocean, trying to swim back to their lines. The waves dashed them against the rocks, or the weight of their armor pulled them under the surface. Others fell to the ground and were trampled in the disorderly press, or died by Spartan steel.

The Spartan Sacrifice

Step by bloody step, we pushed forward, slashing and stabbing until the entire Persian force was in flight. Only when we reached the midway point of the pass did we stop. The Persians had fled to the far end, leaving behind trampled bodies and discarded shields.

I lowered my shield and exhaled slowly. The battle had ended for us for the day. Already a fresh batch of Greek troops had appeared at our former positions, ready to hold the line for the next wave of Persian attacks, while others rushed around gathering the thousands of spears that lay strewn across the battlefield.

My last bit of adrenaline faded, bringing a world of hurt with it. The slash across my ribs burned with every breath. The blisters on my hands had popped, leaving behind open red sores. My arms felt like they were going to fall off, and my legs shook as if they were going to collapse underneath me at any second.

Charilaus took off his helmet to run a tired hand through his sweat-drenched hair. A large gash ran across his right arm just above his bracer. "Thank . . . the gods . . . ," he panted, each word struggling to come out. "The battle . . . is over." He gave Dienekes a tap on the greaves with his spear. "No comment?"

"Too . . . tired," Dienekes panted.

A weak smile appeared on Charilaus's face, and he bent over with his hands on his knees. "Now . . . I have seen . . . everything."

With only Spartans around me, I removed my helmet and threw my head back, relishing the cool air coming off the ocean. Above us the birds had begun circling again now that the din of battle had ceased.

Areus surveyed the wreckage of the Persian army. "We have avoided death for another day."

His words made me wince. Tomorrow would be the big day—the day all of us would die. And none of us deserved that fate. We'd fought with almost superhuman courage and strength, performing unbelievable acts of heroism, and all it would bring us would be death tomorrow.

I plunked my sweat-soaked helmet back on my head. "Come on. Let's go get some rest."

With few words, we gathered our dead and placed them on their shields for a final, triumphant journey from the battlefield. We'd lost over fifty men, and the rest of us had been beaten down to the point of exhaustion. I barely acknowledged the cheers of the other Greeks as we returned to camp. My attention was solely on placing one foot in front of the other and trying not to fall over.

Once we reached camp, I flopped to the ground and sat with my back propped against the short wall. Two helots rushed over and removed my armor and shield, while another brought me a cup of watered-down wine and a slab of roasted goat. Another two helots inspected the gash along my ribs. I was lucky—my armor had taken the brunt of the damage. The gash still looked like hell, though: about the length of a pencil and as wide as my finger. Dried blood caked my side all the way down to my waist. I sucked in my breath and gritted my teeth as one helot sewed up the slash, using twenty small, meticulous stitches that stung with each tug of the thread.

When he had finished, I dug down into my last reserves of strength and pulled myself to my feet. My legs nearly buckled underneath me, but I held onto the wall until I felt steady. Even though Death and I were going to meet tomorrow, there were still a few things I wanted to figure out before I died.

And Chris and Jerry had the answers I needed.

CHAPTER 20

It wasn't hard to find Jerry and Chris. The two arrogant bastards were still lounging in their shaded pavilion, eating and drinking their weight in food and wine as servants fawned over them. At their feet lay a small pile of coins and gold rings. I always figured that Victor's men had stolen from the past, but I'd never actually seen evidence of it before. Seeing their blatant greed firsthand just made me hate these two guys even more.

I glanced over my shoulder to make sure the Spartans still had my back. Despite their exhaustion after battle, none of them were sitting. They were milling around, eating, talking, and casting glances my way, waiting to see if my left hand dropped and pointed at either Chris or Jerry to signal their death.

The two morons didn't even notice me approaching until I stopped in front of their little party pavilion and nudged their treasure heap with the butt of my spear.

Chris blinked at me through bleary eyes. "Hey! It's hero boy!" He raised his mug to me in a mocking salute, his speech slurred from too much wine. "Good job surviving another day. It's looking like you might fix this glitch after all."

"Screw you." I leveled my spear at him and tried to keep its point steady, despite the ache in my arms. "I want answers!"

"Relax! No need to threaten!" Jerry raised his hands. "Put the spear down. Then we can have a chat."

I lowered my spear and ground it into the dirt so I could lean on it to keep myself from collapsing from fatigue. "Tell me the truth. Can you see any way out of this for me?"

Jerry sighed and shook his head. "I've seen this type of situation only once before, and back then it took us about three weeks to get our guy out." He tilted his head and shrugged. "Sorry, kid. If we had more time, maybe. But not in one day, and definitely not in the middle of one of the most important battles of history."

A big fat no on that one. Not that it surprised me. Sam and I had come up empty there too. I squeezed the bridge of my nose as I tried to fight through the fatigue and formulate my next question. "Can you at least tell me why Victor keeps protecting Sam?"

"Why?" Chris asked. "You jealous?"

"No. Just curious. He doesn't seem like the caring type."

Chris waved a hand dismissively. "No clue. I just know she's off limits."

I turned to Jerry. "What about you?"

Jerry rubbed his jaw and eyed me for a moment, clearly deciding how much he could reveal. At first I thought he was going to ignore my question, but then he gave a slight nod, as if agreeing with himself. "Sam's father, Robert, was a very good friend of Victor's. So when Robert died, Victor took it upon himself to watch over his family."

"You're kidding, right?" I scoffed. "According to Victor, he and my dad were great *friends*. Yet Victor still murdered him. So I don't buy your story. Victor wouldn't protect Sam just out of friendship. Hell, he probably killed Robert and Sam's brother Steven also."

Jerry shook his head. "Believe what you want, kid. But I'm telling you Victor didn't kill Robert. I'd swear to it on my life. And none of us would ever have dreamed of harming Steven. He was a good kid. Whoever took him out was sloppy—some amateur hit-and-run job, way beneath our ability."

I didn't know if it was the utter exhaustion clouding my better judgment, but I actually believed Jerry. "Who was it, then?"

"No clue about Steven." Jerry stared into his wine cup as he slowly swirled its contents. "I have some hunches about who killed Robert, but nothing definite. No one in the community ever stepped forward to admit it." He looked up at me from his pile of cushions. "Anything else you want to know?"

I had tons of questions, but so far not a single decent answer. Time to switch things up. "I saw everyone jump in when history looked like it was going to unravel, so clearly you guys do care about the world. You also know how much death Victor's plan will cause. Why do you side with him?"

"It's a no-brainer." Chris raised his cup and pointed it at Jerry. "He's getting Italy and I'm getting Sweden."

I shook my head. The guy was such an idiot. "So? What's the point? Most of the people there will be dead."

Chris's arrogant smirk faded and his eyes hardened. "I don't care." His voice came out angry and bitter. "I'm twenty-seven years old with a crappy job and a mountain of student debt. Unless I win the lottery, I'll work my ass off until I die, paying off my loans, plus a mortgage, all while hoping to make it to middle management." He thumped his chest with a fist and his tone sharpened. "But I'm a time traveler! I deserve respect. I deserve power. I don't care if there are ten million or two million people left alive—they'll all be bowing to me."

"So that's it?" I stared at them with pure disgust. "You two sold out the entire human race just so you can become dictators of your own little kingdoms?"

Jerry jerked his thumb at Chris. "He might be in it only for the power, but for me there's more to it than that." He tilted his head and eyed me for a second. "Why don't you sit while I explain? You look like you're going to collapse, and you need to be fresh for tomorrow."

The stubborn part of me wanted to tell him that I was fine—to show him that I didn't need his pity. The exhausted side of me won, though. I sat down at the edge of their pavilion with my spear resting across my lap and my shoulders slumped forward.

"Look at them." Jerry gestured to the Spartans. "They were the greatest warriors of the ancient age. They dedicated their entire lives to training for battle so they could defend their lands. The whole world remembers their heroism with monuments and movies and books."

I caught Charilaus's eye, and he nodded ever so slightly toward me, indicating he was ready for my signal.

"Now look at us," Jerry continued, not realizing how close to death he was. "The time-traveling community is just like the Spartans. We train from birth and put our lives on the line again and again to save our world. But do we get monuments? Do we get recognition?" He shook his head. "People don't even know we exist. We throw our entire lives into training and self-sacrifice and receive nothing in return."

"A lot of people do crappy jobs without recognition," I snapped. "You don't see them trying to wipe out half the human race."

"It isn't just about recognition. This is about fighting an endless fight to save history and then realizing that the world isn't worth saving. Look at the news on any day. You have murders, wars, pollution, greed, and corruption. We've become a world that sits on our phones and computers all day long, somehow connected to everyone in the world but at the same time disconnected from what is immediately around us. The human race is headed toward its own destruction. It is our duty as time travelers to set the world on the right path before it's too late."

"You're full of it," I said. "At least Chris is honest. He's just a power-hungry jerk. But you want me to believe that killing off half the world and enslaving the rest is making the world a better place?"

"The world is already enslaved. Do you think the kid in a sweatshop who sewed your T-shirts *wants* to be stuck in a factory earning pennies a day? Do you think the people who use food banks *want* to rely on handouts to survive? We live in a time of economic slavery. People work long hours at terrible jobs just to afford the basic necessities. You just don't see it because you were fortunate enough to be born into a family at the higher end of the pay scale. But as automation and artificial intelligence take more and more jobs, the number of poor around the world will only increase. Cities will crumble because they will not have the tax base to maintain infrastructure and social programs. Lawlessness will reign as governments lose control. This is already happening in some countries today, and it will only get worse. The world needs us to take over. Only the members of the time-traveling community have the vision to lead. We have proven ourselves to have only the world's best interests at heart."

"Best interests?" I sputtered. "You want to kill billions!"

Jerry stared grimly into his wine goblet. "Unfortunately, there is no other way. All revolutions demand bloodshed. The only way for ours to succeed is to destroy all the institutions that bind people. Only when the world is in complete chaos and despair will they be open to the new world order we plan to bring. With the leaders of the time-traveling community at the top, and the rest of the world following along into a new future of prosperity for all. Where people will finally be free of division and strife, and the world will live in harmony under our watchful eye."

I'd heard the same speech from Victor, but it still made my stomach churn. It sounded all noble, but I couldn't see someone like Chris ruling benevolently, guiding people to prosperity. I could see him abusing his power and taking everything he could, and then demanding more. And how long would people suffer under his rule until they started to rebel, and Chris became like the Spartans, always armed, and always dreading that the people he oppressed would strike back? I shook my head in disgust. "You guys are delusional!"

Jerry laughed—the last thing I expected from him. "I believe the term is 'visionary.' We have the courage to do what needs to be done to stop humanity from wiping itself out and taking the rest of the planet with it. Our methods might seem cruel to some, but they are necessary." He drained his cup and wiped his mouth with the back of one hand, then raised his chin to stare defiantly at me, as if challenging me to find fault with his argument.

But I didn't care about arguing with him. All I cared about was that he'd started talking, which meant I might be able to get the answer to the one question I wanted to know more than anything else. "And how do you actually change the past to get your plan to work?"

Jerry's eyes narrowed. "I don't know what you're talking about."

"Don't lie to me. Victor already told me you've been making tweaks to the past during your jumps. So I'm curious—how do you pull it off without messing things up in history?" I pulled the jump device out of my bracer. "And if you're worried about me telling anyone—don't. This thing is still just a normal hunk of metal, so I'm guessing I'm still the time glitch." I shrugged. "Anything you tell me dies with me tomorrow."

Chris jutted his chin out at me. "What's it worth to ya?"

I tapped the nonexistent pockets of my tunic. "I seem to have left my wallet in my other chiton."

"How about your jump device, then? Like you said, you won't be needing it."

There was no hope I'd ever give my device to him. I jerked my thumb over my shoulder and pointed to the battle still raging in the pass. "Did you forget about that? I still need my device to translate for me." I turned to Jerry, since he was clearly the brains of the operation. "What harm will it do to tell me?"

Jerry tapped a finger against his lips, clearly trying to figure out whether he should tell me. "Fine," he finally said. "Here's the big secret—the time stream doesn't care who does something; it just needs the event to be done."

"Huh?"

Jerry pointed to the Spartans. "Look at them. They need to lose here. That's what history demands. But the time stream doesn't care who leads them; it cares only that *someone* leads them." He waved his hand toward me. "That's how you got stuck here."

"Okay . . . but that doesn't really tell me anything about the plan."

"Did you ever hear the name Elisha Gray?"

"No. Who is she?"

"*He* is an American inventor who filed a patent for the telephone on the exact same day, and with similar technology, as Alexander Graham Bell. Except Bell's patent, despite accusations that he copied Gray, was approved. Now imagine if Gray's patent had been approved. The telephone would still exist. The world wouldn't change. But Elisha Gray would be rich, and Bell would be some inventor no one had ever heard of."

"Yeah, yeah, I get it. History just needs the event, not the person. But I don't understand how that helps you."

"Now imagine if one of us time jumpers happened to be there in 1876 fixing some glitch when all this happened, and we made a deal with Bell to support him in his efforts, maybe even broke into the patent office and fiddled around with a few things? That would give us a *very* loyal ally. And if we also happened to tell a few influential people of that time period that they should invest in Mr. Bell's great idea, and not Gray's, then we've made even *more* friends in the past."

"I'm still missing something. Who cares if some guys in the past get rich?"

Jerry grinned. "The guys who get rich care." He spread his arms wide. "But it's not just the rich. In our efforts to resolve glitches in history, we in the time-traveling community are fortunate that we interact with so many great decision-makers of the past—kings, queens, warlords, religious leaders. And when our advice helps someone stay in power or make a fortune, they begin to look on us very favorably. Some might even say they are in our debt."

I pinched the bridge of my nose and tried to make sense of everything Jerry said. He was clearly hinting at something, but I was just too tired or too dumb to connect the dots. "So some people in the past owe you a favor. How does that help you in the present?"

Jerry chuckled. "It's simple. We tell these people in the past to help their friends get rich and to spread the word of their good fortune—all quietly, of course. But all this wealth and power comes with a condition"—he held up a finger—"everyone must follow *any* instructions we send."

I ran that sentence again through my head, just to make sure I hadn't misheard him. But there was no mistaking what he said. "You *send* instructions to the past?"

"Not directly, of course. Because we're handcuffed by the limitations of the time-travel devices, we can only go into the past whenever a glitch occurs. But over the past twenty years, while venturing into the past, we've earned the goodwill of hundreds of influential people throughout history, who in turn have made thousands of their friends rich. These people have become a secret society, working together across history and the world, and pulling more and more people into our web. They have chapter houses in every major city. We have allies in churches, in government, in palaces, in the military, and in the major trading companies of the past, and the major corporations of modern day. If a glitch sends me anywhere in history after the year 1600, I will be able to find one of our houses." His eyes took on an intense focus. "And then, if I choose to, I can show them my tattoo and give them a command. It can be something simple, like 'On the morning of February 28, 1976, make sure that Joe Blow's parents never meet at the only coffee shop in their little town of Hickville, Ohio.' This command will be written down and passed from chapter to chapter through the ages. Eventually, someone in the local Ohio chapter in 1976 will open up their book and see that hundreds of years in the past someone gave the command, and they'll follow through with it. We've passed down tons of commands over the last twenty years. Most have made our followers wealthy and bought their unflinching loyalty, while the select few have made sure that those people who were causing problems got erased from history."

I could feel the blood drain from my face. "You're the Illuminati?"

Chris laughed. "The Illuminati are a myth. If they did exist, they'd *wish* they could be as powerful as we are." He snapped his fingers. "We could wipe them out just like that."

"And what happens if you mess up? What happens if through all your scheming and plotting, you create a glitch?"

Jerry shrugged. "Except for your device and a few others, we control all the time-travel devices. If we accidentally create a glitch, we just fix it."

The enormity of their plans left me speechless. They'd created a plot that spanned continents and centuries. Even if I somehow survived Thermopylae, how could I have a hope of stopping this?

Jerry grinned at Chris. "I think the kid has finally realized what he's up against." He turned back to me. "Did you really think you had a chance of stopping us? One scribble in a book becomes a death sentence to anyone we choose. We control *everything*."

I swallowed hard. "And the people in the present who follow you, do they know about your plan?"

"A few. Most just know that following our commands brings wealth and power." Jerry snorted. "And sadly, that's enough for them. Like I said, our world is heading for its own destruction. Greed rules all." He raised an eyebrow. "That answer your question?"

I staggered back to my feet, my mind reeling. "Yeah."

But what now? Did I just ignore everything they told me and go back to fighting the Persians?

No. I had to do something. Slowly I clenched my left fist. All I had to do was point, and a flurry of Spartan spears would strike them down.

"Yo!" Chris said in his usual arrogant tone. "Whatcha looking at?"

"Leave him alone, Chris," Jerry said. "He's exhausted, and there's more fighting ahead for him."

I lowered my hand. Not yet. I needed to think over everything Jerry had told me, and maybe I'd have a few more questions before all this was over.

With slow steps, I made my way back to the Spartan camp. Now that I'd left Jerry and Chris, most of the Spartans had finally sat down to recover from our exhausting battle while helots rushed around bringing them food and drink.

I sat on the wall facing the battle still raging in the pass. The current Persian attack lacked the ferocity of this morning, when we had almost been overwhelmed, so the Greeks who were currently holding the pass looked like they would be all right without Spartan help. My gaze drifted out to the water, and I watched the rhythmic crashing of waves against the shore while the shouts and noise of battle carried through the humid air.

My conversation with Jerry kept replaying in my head. I had learned so much, but so what? Even if Jerry had given me step-by-step instructions on how to defeat Victor, I was still stuck in Greece.

For the rest of the day, the battle continued against the Persians. The Greeks fought. The Persians died. Eventually, battle ended for the day. As history expected, we had defeated the Persian attack for the second day. While the other Greeks celebrated another victory, I ate a silent dinner with the rest of the Spartans. Then, as the sky darkened and the first stars began to appear, I lay down to sleep. But even though every muscle in me felt cramped with fatigue, I just couldn't close my eyes and get the rest I so badly needed. My thoughts kept returning to tomorrow's battle. I'd seen the movies. I'd heard the stories. Tomorrow was it—game over. All of us here would die.

Leonidas had been super smart when he'd chosen his three hundred men. He had only picked men with wives and sons. Men who had known victory in other battles. Their names would be remembered by those they left behind. But what had I done in life? I hadn't even finished high school. And the one battle I had to win, the one against Victor, I had lost. Except for Jenna and Sam, my name would be forgotten. And would either of them survive Victor's plan?

Like a prisoner on death row, I thought of all the things I'd done wrong in life that had brought me to this point. I should have been more decisive. I should have fought harder against Victor. I should have hung out with my dad more and learned about time jumping. I shouldn't have lied so much to Jenna. I shouldn't have hurt Sam.

So many failures in such a short life.

The crunch of footsteps derailed my depressing train of thoughts. In the glow of the starry night, I could see Areus and Charilaus approaching. Areus's face had an ashy look to it. His brow was creased, his lips drawn tight.

"What is it?" Slowly I managed to drag myself to my feet. Every muscle in my body ached, and the stitches in my side felt like they were about to rip open. I stroked my hand over the wound to try to ease the pain.

"Two deserters have crossed from the Persian lines," Areus declared, not sounding panicked, but definitely not as cool and calm as usual. "They are good, honest men from Lemnos who were conscripted into the Persian army when their state was defeated. They bring tidings of grave danger. Xerxes has discovered the path that leads through the mountains, and even now a large force of men is traveling along it. By morning, they will emerge behind us." He ground the heavy end of his spear into the dirt. "What are your orders? How shall we confront this new threat?"

I'd been expecting this news, and I hated myself for what I was now about to say. "Don't worry. Leonidas knew something like this might happen. He sent the Phocians to guard the pass. They'll hold."

Even in the darkness, I could see the hesitation on their faces. They clearly didn't believe the Phocians were capable of holding the pass.

And the truth was, the Phocians wouldn't. History had recorded that they had been outnumbered twenty to one, and they crumbled like a stale cracker once the Persians attacked.

A knot of guilt weighed heavily on my chest. No matter how much I liked the Spartans, I couldn't bring myself to tell them the truth. It would be so easy for all of us to pack up in the night and leave. But no, for history to flow properly, we all had to stay here and die tomorrow.

"And if the Phocians cannot hold the pass?" Areus asked. "What then?"

"Trust in Leonidas," I said. "The Phocians have a thousand men, and they know these mountains. They'll be able to hold." The knot in my chest grew even larger. I hated lying like this. "Now go get some rest," I ordered. "Tomorrow will be another hard day for us."

After the pair of them left, I lay down on my little patch of ground and stared up at the night sky. The jump device was still a hunk of dead metal stuck in my bracer. I knew I had to die tomorrow to save history, but deep down I still held out the smallest hope that I'd figure a way out of this and the jump device would spark back to life.

"Come on, universe," I whispered. "Bring me a miracle."

CHAPTER 21

"Danakles! Wake up!" A hand shook my shoulder. "You are needed." Areus knelt beside me in full armor, with his shield and spear already in hand.

With the back of my hand, I wiped the sleep from my eyes. The morning sun peeked over the mountains, revealing a crowd of Greeks trying to push their way into the Spartan section of the camp, while a wall of Spartans held them back. "Are we under attack?"

"Not yet. But a messenger has come from the Phocians, and he insists on speaking with you. I fear the worst, as do the rest of the Greeks." Areus passed me Leonidas's distinctive helmet with its red crest. "Put this on. And hurry!"

I plunked the bronze helmet on my head and hefted my shield bearing the sun sign of the Spartan king. We both hurried through the Spartan camp, stopping in front of the Greek contingent. In their midst stood a short, wiry man, dressed only in a light tunic, weaponless. He was bent over, with his hands on his knees and his sides heaving in and out like a bellows. As soon as he saw me, he pulled himself upright and snapped to attention. "O great king Leonidas," he said, his breathing labored. "I have come from the Phocian camp. The Persians have sent a massive army through the mountains. We cannot . . . hold them back . . . we will be overrun. You must flee."

His announcement set off a flurry of muttering and grumbling.

"How long until they arrive?" asked the leader of the Tegeans.

"I do not know," the messenger gasped. "I ran with great haste through these mountains taking paths that no army would dare follow. But I have no doubt that they will be upon us before the sun has risen the width of two hands."

Cries of despair rose from the Greek leaders. "We must escape while we have the chance," shouted the leader of the Maniteans, glancing uneasily over his shoulder.

"Run?" scoffed one of the Thespians. "We have wounded men who must be carried. How fast do you think we can flee with them?" He stomped his foot. "We must stand and fight."

What would Leonidas do here? The obvious choice would be to run now while we had the chance. But, to keep history flowing properly, I needed to somehow convince the Greeks to throw their lives away and fight while surrounded. How had Leonidas persuaded them to stay? And, more importantly, why?

"If we must fight the enemy, we should retreat to Alpenoi," added one of the Locrians. "We can hold that town better than we can hold this pass."

Charilaus glared at the man. "Tell me. How long could we hold the town?" He waved a hand. "Here, it is still narrow, so only a few Persians can attack us at a time, no matter which side they approach from. The farther we retreat, the more the land widens. Then the Persian cavalry will easily catch up to us and kill us as we flee. Standing firm here is our only option."

"You are a fool," the Locrian spat. "Standing here will mean your death."

Charilaus's knuckles turned white as his grip tightened around his spear. "Unlike you"—his voice held a deathly calm—"I am not afraid to die for my family and country."

If Charilaus hadn't been a Spartan, the Locrian probably would have punched him. Instead, he vented his anger by shoving a nearby Thespian hard in the shoulder. "You are all madmen and fools."

The Thespian shoved him back even harder. "And you are a coward, unfit to stand here among men!"

More and more voices rose as the shoving match spread to the others. Insults flew until the men looked just as ready to fight among themselves as against the Persians. At least I knew what Leonidas would do in this situation. "Silence!" I banged repeatedly on my shield with my spear.

Angry and frightened faces snapped in my direction. "We don't have time to argue," I shouted. "Those who want to run will need to go now. But make sure you take the wounded with you."

"And what of you?" shouted the Locrian.

No matter how much I wanted to get the hell out of here, there was only one option available to keep history on the correct path. "I make my stand here." I slammed my spear into the soil and slowly glared at each of the Greek leaders in turn.

Charilaus nodded appreciatively and then took his place beside me. "I am Spartan. I do not run, no matter what the Fates may throw at me." He pounded his chest with a fist.

Dienekes glanced up at the sky and then nodded. "The sun is shining brightly. It will be an excellent day to die."

Areus looked at his two friends and a slight smile creased his lips. "Let us die well, my brothers."

I stood there with an intense feeling of pride swelling my chest. Even after all the heroics I had seen the Spartans perform on the battlefield, this final act of brotherhood and bravery left me speechless.

"You will all die!" the Locrian shouted, almost as if the mere thought of staying here terrified him.

"Yeah, we'll die," I said. "But the rest of you will be saved. Three hundred of us is a small price to pay for the lives of thousands."

Demophilus, the leader of the Thespians, stepped forward and brought his fist up to his chest. "You will not stand alone, for the men of Thespiae will join you. It is better to die here as free men than go back home and live as Persian slaves."

"The men of Thebes will join you as well!" yelled Leontiades, their leader.

Heads turned, looking for other volunteers to hold the pass. None of the remaining Greeks stepped forward. They looked at the ground, avoiding eye contact.

"You are all cowards," Megistias the Seer declared as he limped through the crowd, leaning heavily on his walking staff. "Even I will stay—for I am too old to flee. It is better to face a good, honorable death than a life of shameful cowardice." He turned his head slowly, taking in all the Greeks, who shrank before him. "Go then, *men* of Greece. Flee back to your homes. But makes sure that you tell your wives, your families, and all who you meet of the bravery of the men who bought your lives at the cost of their own."

The remaining Greeks quickly slipped back to their camps, a few uttering half-hearted shouts of encouragement.

"Look at the cowardly dogs run," Dienekes muttered. "I hope they trample each other in their haste to flee this place."

"Let them run," Charilaus said. "They would be of little use in battle."

I looked out over the men who had been brave enough to stay. Four hundred Thebans, seven hundred Thespians . . . and two hundred fifty wounded and battle-weary Spartans. Rounding out our numbers, we had one old man and nine hundred poorly armed helots who might just as likely stab us in the back as fight. This small group of misfits would now be standing against 200,000 Persians coming at us from two sides. If we could hold out longer than a few hours, it would be a miracle.

"Go! Gather your weapons and armor," I ordered. "Have one last drink with your brothers. But hurry! The Persians will be here soon."

As the remaining troops dispersed back to their camps, I returned to my spot by the wall to strap on my armor. Areus approached, carrying a bowl of warm grains with chunks of meat. "Eat. A man should not do battle on an empty stomach." He passed me the bowl.

"Thanks, Areus." I sat on the wall, removed my helmet, and idly stirred the goop with my wooden spoon. My last meal. Despite the hunger gnawing at my stomach, no part of me felt like eating.

Areus must have sensed my discomfort. He sat down next to me on the wall. "You led us well these last days. The real Leonidas would have been proud of how you carried his shield."

I knew he meant it as a compliment, but it didn't make me feel any better. "Thanks," I muttered.

"This battle weighs heavily on you, Danakles. Tell me, why do you stay?"

"Because I'm stuck here."

"But how? You are not Spartan. Leonidas was not your king. You should be free to go back to wherever you call home, without fearing humiliation and shame." He cast his eyes to the ground and his lips drew thin. "Your children will not hate you for returning to them." His voice sounded quiet, distant. "The people will not scorn you if you dare to flee this place and enjoy more of your life." He closed his eyes briefly, then shook his head. "So why do you stay? I saw Artemis disappear before my eyes. Why do you not do the same?"

He raised an excellent point. Now, with the Spartans and their few allies ready to make their final stand, history was firmly back on its proper course. I could probably sneak away from this last fight and the time stream wouldn't notice. But what sort of life would I lead? The jump device was still a hunk of dead metal strapped to my arm. I'd be trapped in Greece with no home, no family, and soon, with all the Spartans here about to die, no friends.

What would I do? Wander ancient Greece, hoping some village would take me in? Maybe, after a few decades of back-breaking work, I'd be able to create my own time glitch, and have jumpers pop in to rescue me. But would I even want to go back to a world controlled by Victor?

I tapped my spoon on the edge of the clay bowl. "I guess I'm stuck here, like you."

Areus nodded, and his eyes had a tenderness to them that I had never seen before. "I hope my sons grow up to be honorable men like you, Danakles. You would have made an excellent Spartan." He turned and left me alone with my breakfast.

I managed only a few bites before the slap of approaching feet made me look up from my meal. My muscles tensed—Jerry and Chris were heading my way.

Chris strutted through the camp with a cocky look on his face, probably relishing the way the surrounding Spartans gave him a wide space. Over his shoulder, he carried a cloth bag that rustled with a metallic chime at every step.

"Well, kid," Jerry said, "it looks like everything's almost back to normal." He stuck out his hand. "Good job."

I ignored the hand and remained seated on the wall. "So is the glitch fixed?"

"Not yet. The time stream is always a bit touchy when it's swapping a new person into someone's role. But as long as you lead the Spartans to their deaths, like Leonidas would have done, then everything should be fine."

Behind the pair, the Spartans had stopped what they were doing and stood watching at a respectful distance. All of them had their spears in hand and their eyes fixed on me, just waiting for my command.

"Yo! Where's your jump rod?" Chris demanded.

"In my bracer. Why?"

Chris slung the bag off his shoulder and held it open in front of me, like a kid at Halloween, revealing a heap of gold coins and jewelry. "You don't need it any more. Toss it in."

I put my hand on my sword hilt. "Come and take it."

The Spartan Sacrifice

Chris's back stiffened, and he reached for the sword at his side.

"Leave it." Jerry rested a hand on Chris's arm.

"But he's letting a perfectly good jump rod go to waste," Chris spluttered, his cheeks turning red. "We could easily take him."

"Forget about it." Jerry raised his index finger as a warning to Chris. "He might still need its translation ability for his last fight. We don't want to mess up history over one little device."

"Fine," Chris muttered.

I smirked at Chris. "You could always follow me into battle and wait until I die."

His eyes darted quickly to the Persian side of the pass, then he snorted. "Yeah, no thanks."

Jerry and Chris brought out their jump devices and twisted the sections into the pattern that would send them home.

"Wait," I said. "You're not staying until the end?"

"No," Jerry said. "The fact that you're still standing here tells me that you're going to follow this through." He put his hand over his heart. "I know you don't like us, but I deeply respect what you've done here."

Chris winked at me and gave me a thumbs-up. "Besides, I'm sure you can manage dying on your own."

I set my breakfast bowl aside and stood up on the wall. My entire body trembled as I raised my left hand, almost as if to wave goodbye.

Could I do this?

If I dropped my hand now, I'd be flat out executing the two. I wouldn't be saving history. I wouldn't be protecting myself. I'd just be a murderer. I'd be sinking to Victor's level. What would Dad say to that?

Nothing. Because he was dead—murdered by Victor.

He had been the good guy all his life, and all it got him was an early death. How many more good people would die because of murderous fiends like Chris and Jerry? There was only one way to protect the world from them.

"Wait!" I called to them. "I forgot to give you something."

Chris's eyes lit with greed as he opened his bag. "You change your mind?"

"No. It's a gift . . . from the Spartans." My left hand sliced down and pointed at the pair.

Jerry's eyes went wide. *"Arbah rostvos orokol biradelem!"* he yelled, his words nearly tumbling over each other in his rush to get them out.

A rain of spears flew through the air and slammed into Chris. He crumpled to the ground, his bag of loot and jump device falling to the dry grass beside him as his sightless eyes stared up at the clear blue sky.

But Jerry was gone.

Good. Let him tell Victor what happened here.

Charilaus wrenched his spear from Chris's body, his brow creased with concern. "What manner of god was he that our spears could wound him so?"

I jumped off the wall and nudged Chris's body with my foot. I anticipated a rush of satisfaction to fill me at the death of one of Victor's idiots.

Nothing. No sadness. No remorse. No joy.

I just felt . . . tired.

"He wasn't a god," I replied in a monotone. "He was just a man. An arrogant, lazy, and stupid man."

I picked up Chris's jump device, praying to whatever gods who were listening that maybe, just maybe, it would be cool to the touch.

Nope. It was just as dead as the one strapped to my forearm.

"Are you sure he was just a man?" Charilaus asked hesitantly. "The gods are not kind to those who affront them."

"Yes, he was a man. Trust me. The whole world is better off now that . . ."

The low boom of Persian drums came rumbling through the pass like thunder before a storm. I stuffed Chris's jump device in my bracer alongside my own. "The Persians are coming," I said to Charilaus. "Let's go now and die with honor."

CHAPTER 22

Within minutes, what was left of the Greek army had reassembled at the Spartan camp. With the help of the helots, I had decked myself out in my armor in record time. I hopped up on the wall again to face a sea of tired, worn faces. Even the Spartans seemed to lack their usual bravado. If any group was ever in need of a pep talk, it was this one.

I knew from history that it was on this morning that Leonidas said his famous line "Eat well, for tonight we dine in Hades." The line always gave me chills when Gerard Butler said it in the movie *300*, but now the words felt fake, hollow. Were these really the last words Leonidas had said to his friends, to men who had willingly followed him to their deaths? I wanted to give these men, my brothers, a *real* speech, something that reflected the seriousness of this moment. But what could I tell them? Inspirational words fled from my thoughts and only the cold harsh reality of our situation remained. We were all about to die.

Then it dawned on me. I wasn't just trying to motivate these men; I was trying to find inspiration for myself too. What do you tell a bunch of people who knew they wouldn't see the end of the day? I owed them a meaningful death.

"Men of Greece!" I shouted. "Today our death is at hand. We have made the choice to stand and hold this pass with our lives, so we could protect our homes and our families beyond. But now we have one more choice to make. We can choose *exactly* how we are remembered."

I jabbed my spear in the direction of the lone Greek ship rocking gently on the waves over in the bay. "That ship sits there, ready to take news of the outcome of this battle to the rest of Greece. What will the crew of that ship be telling the world? Do they tell the story of how a small group of Spartans, Thebans, Thespians, and helots huddled behind their shields and were slowly surrounded and killed by the Persians?"

A few half-hearted *no*s came from the crowd.

I raised my shield high so the sun symbol of the Spartan kings was visible to everyone. "Or does the crew of that ship tell the story of the world's most heroic battle? Do they tell the tale of how two thousand of Greece's bravest men stood up to the might of the Persians and took the battle to them, bringing so much death that our example will inspire men throughout all of history?"

A few shouts of *yes* came from the crowd while other men nodded.

"Then fight with me, heroes of Greece!" I yelled. "No longer are you men from scattered city-states. No longer are you either free men or slaves. You are the last heroes Greece has. And yes, we will likely die today." I thrust my spear skyward. "But we will make sure that no one *ever* forgets us!"

A loud cheer rose as the men battered their shields and stomped their feet.

"Here is courage!" Charilaus shouted above the din. "Mankind's finest possession."

"Here is the noblest prize that a young man can endeavor to win," the other Spartans continued, reciting the same lines they had called out on the first day of battle.

Row upon rows of helots stood silent behind the Greek ranks. They must have heard this poem countless times. They probably knew it by heart. Yet they kept silent, most likely because they weren't allowed to recite it. I couldn't give them their freedom, but on this day I could at least make them not feel like slaves.

I pointed at them with my spear and encouraged them to join in. Only a few recited the next line, but as I kept encouraging them, their voices grew stronger and louder as more and more helots joined in.

Areus nodded to me as the whole plain echoed with the thunder of voices. Goose bumps rose along my arms as they belted out the last line. "His shining glory is never forgotten. His name is remembered. And he becomes an immortal!"

As the echoes faded, I could feel a change in the army. They had purpose now. They wouldn't be dying as forgotten men—they'd be dying as heroes.

I hopped off the wall and jogged toward the pass. The stomp of feet and the wooden rattle of shields and spears filled the air as the Greeks proceeded, in a pack, along with me. At the far end of the pass, the Persian army was just beginning to muster itself into lines. Not all of them were in place yet. There were gaps in the ranks, and their phalanx was not fully formed.

My heart pounded as my legs churned across that narrow strip of rocky land forming the pass. Adrenaline coursed through my veins, dulling the pain from the gash along my ribs and erasing the fatigue that had weighed me down. Every nerve felt alive, and every sense amplified.

Like lions in pursuit of sheep, we roared out of the far end of the pass and straight into the mass of Persians. Bloodlust raged through my system, and I had only one goal in mind—to take down as many Persians as possible before my short life ended. My spear splintered in my grasp as it rammed through a man's breastbone and emerged from his back. Without pausing, I picked up his fallen spear and went after my next target.

As a mass, we stampeded forward, our previously close-knit formation now forgotten. My shield no longer overlapped Charilaus's; a helot had pushed his way between us so he could share the glory. And I no longer felt the reassuring presence of Areus's shield in my back. He'd moved up beside me, and a Theban now had my rear.

The battlefield became a never-ending sequence of sharply focused events: my spear plunging into a man's chest, my shield battering a man's face, shifting to avoid a sharp point jabbing at me, and then me striking again. Attack. Defend. Counterattack. I fought by instinct, no conscious thoughts slowing my actions. And in my wake, I left a stack of bodies and ground that grew slick with blood.

A loud bellow drew my attention. Charilaus was punching a Persian repeatedly in the face until bone cracked and the man collapsed, while the Persian's spear remained stuck in Charilaus's belly.

Charilaus wrenched the spear out of his gut and flung it into the Persian ranks, striking another man in the throat. "Dienekes!" he shouted over the clash of weapons. "My time is short now."

"As is all of ours," Dienekes replied from the other side of him. "We will meet soon enough in the fields of Elysium."

"You have been a good friend, Dienekes," Charilaus yelled. "And I wish you a glorious death." With that, he pulled out his sword and launched himself into the Persian ranks, hacking and slashing as he went. The Persians recoiled from his ferocious attacks and he pressed deeper and deeper into their ranks until he became completely surrounded. For a second, his shiny bronze helmet was visible above the masses of shorter men, and then it dropped from sight. With maniacal howls, the Persians rammed their spears into him, as if desecrating this one Spartan corpse could somehow make up for all their failures over the past two days.

"No!" Fury burned like an inferno within my chest. Charilaus deserved a better fate. I hurled myself at a tall Persian with a thin beard. Our eyes met for the briefest of seconds, then his widened in fear.

Without warning, my knee buckled as I tripped on a Persian corpse. The ground rushed up to meet me, and I landed face-first, with arms flung out to the side on the bloody dirt. Time seemed to slow, and only the tall Persian and his spear existed for me. He stomped on my large shield, pinning both it and my arm to the ground. I grasped for my sword, trying to free it from its scabbard, but I couldn't pry it out from under my body.

With horrible clarity, I realized this was it: my death.

The Persian inhaled sharply as he raised his spear over his head for the kill.

My body tensed as I waited for its sharp point to plunge into my back and end my life.

I'm sorry, Dad.

Suddenly, the pressure on my shield relaxed and the Persian tumbled backward, a gray-fletched arrow buried in his chest.

Arrows? What the . . .? How?

"Artemis!" someone yelled. "Artemis has returned!" A cry went up from the Spartans, and they attacked the enemy with even greater fury.

For the first time in days, a faint spark of hope ignited in my chest. Was it true? Had Sam really come back? With my heart racing, I scrabbled to my feet and took a glance behind me. Through the thin wall of Greek troops, I glimpsed a shock of red hair.

An arrow flew past the heads of the Greek soldiers and arced straight toward me. It whizzed underneath my armpit and thudded into the chest of another Persian who was rushing at me. "Move!" Sam yelled, her voice just audible over the clash of weapons.

Her words shocked me back into action, and I turned my full attention to the Persians. With my spear, I held the nearest ones at bay, then retreated through the thin Greek lines.

As I broke through the press of men, I found her. She was wearing the exact same outfit she had worn when she left me two days ago, except now she looked as if she had just jogged a huge distance in the sun. Her arms and shoulders were red with sunburn while beads of sweat trickled down the side of her face. A tempest of emotions roiled within me: happiness to see her again, fear for her safety, elation that I hadn't died. So many words wanted to come pouring out. But one thing had to be said more than anything else. "Sam, I'm so sorry for everything I said." I moved in closer so my shield would protect her from any stray spear.

"Yeah, yeah." She flicked her hand dismissively. "We don't have time for this."

"I know. But I still wanted you to know." I drew in a deep breath, my fingers trembling nervously on my spear shaft. "Please tell me you've figured a way to get me out of this mess."

Sam tilted her head at me and raised an eyebrow. "Do you really think I'd jump back in time and stick myself in the middle of a battle if I didn't have a plan?"

"But how? My jump device is still useless. History still needs Leonidas to die today."

"That's the thing. You're not Leonidas. You're Dan." She rapped my shield with her knuckles. "Leonidas is whoever carries that shield and wears that helmet. You need to switch them with somebody else."

"But no one will take them. That's how I got stuck in this mess in the first place."

A smile played across her lips. "That's your problem—you were looking for someone alive to take them. All you need to do is find a dead Spartan, swap your helmet and shield with him, and that should do it."

It seemed simple enough; we had plenty of dead Spartans. Many of them to the rear of our lines.

Crouching low, I snuck to the first dead Spartan I could find and then quickly swapped my shield and helmet with his. My hands trembled as I waited for the jump rods to spring to life.

Nothing.

"It's not working!" I said to Sam.

She chewed on her lip. "Maybe the Spartans have to see you die?"

"What? You mean I have to fake my death?"

The Spartan Sacrifice 217

She shrugged. "I don't know."

I sighed and picked up Leonidas's helmet and shield. I knew what I had to do. "How many arrows do you have?"

She pointed at the quiver jutting over her shoulder. "Thirty."

I drew my sword and inhaled a few deeps breaths to psych myself up. So many things could go wrong with this plan. I took one last look at Sam. "If this doesn't work, I'm still glad you came back for me . . . Thanks."

She rested a hand on my shield arm. "I couldn't leave you here." Her eyes, filled with concern, locked with mine.

A familiar ache formed in my chest. This could be the last time I ever saw her. I wanted to tell her how amazing she was. How I couldn't have gone through all the drama of this last hellish year—with my dad's death and Victor's plot and multiple time jumps—without her. But I held back. The battle was still raging, and we needed to focus on getting my sorry butt out of Greece.

"Cover me!" I said as I slammed the helmet back on my head.

I plunged into the Greek lines and pushed my way to the front. We'd been holding a fairly static line for the last few minutes. Time to get this army moving again.

"For Artemis!" I yelled as I threw myself forward. The rest of the Greeks surged after me, and step by bloody step, we pushed the Persians back. My sword was like a living extension of me. It hacked through limbs and tore through flesh, leading me ever closer to my goal. Blow after blow rang off my shield, but I just kept moving forward, my progress made easier by the almost constant stream of arrows whizzing past my head and thunking into Persians.

I reached the spot where Charilaus's body lay amid a heap of Persian corpses. He was almost unrecognizable from the savagery inflicted on him by the enemy.

As the battle continued raging around me, I slashed out at a Persian and then let my shield drop as if by accident. I crouched and picked up Charilaus's shield instead and used it to protect myself as I quickly removed his helmet. An instant later our helmets were switched, too, and I sprang back to my feet.

The hub of battle had already moved past me, leaving me staring at the backs of my own army.

Okay, swap's done. Now how do I get the Spartans to believe it?

"What are you doing, Danakles?" someone shouted.

I whipped my head around and saw Areus standing slightly back of the battle, tying off a bandage around a bloody gash in his arm. He leveled his spear at me in accusation. "Why do you dishonor Leonidas by discarding his shield?"

Oh, crap.

"It's not what it looks like, Areus." I raised my hands and took a step backward. "I'm not trying to dishonor Leonidas . . . or Charilaus either." The words tumbled out of my mouth. "I just can't . . . die here. There are bigger battles I need to fight."

"And you hope to do this by stealing Charilaus's shield? Were you going to flee from the battlefield and bring shame upon his name?" Areus stomped over the field of Persian corpses to stand in front of me. I couldn't see the rest of his face because of his helmet, but his eyes burned with anger.

"No!" My voice raised an octave in panic. "I just wanted the Spartans to think that I . . . I mean that Leonidas was dead. That he had died in battle."

"But you said earlier you could not leave. Has that changed?"

"Maybe . . . I don't know. All I know for sure is that someone else needs to bear Leonidas's shield and helmet."

Areus tilted his helmet back, revealing his face. The lines around his mouth looked deeper and his eyes had dark circles under them. "Are you truly not a god, Danakles?" His tone was less harsh.

"I already told you that I'm not."

"And you have truly only seen seventeen summers?"

The Spartan Sacrifice

I bowed my head. "Yes."

A faint smile crossed his lips, and he rubbed the graying stubble on his jaw. "I remember my seventeenth summer. Wrestling with my friends. Stealing chickens from the helots. Sneaking into the forest with beautiful girls." He looked me up and down and then nodded as if he had come to a decision. "No man should see his life end at seventeen." He removed his shield from his arm and placed it next to Charilaus's body.

"Wait . . . what are you doing?"

Areus picked up Leonidas's sunburst shield. He hefted it a few times and then nodded. "The real Leonidas would never have let you fight in his place." He pointed with his spear to the Spartan line only a few steps ahead of us. "We are all old men, and we have sons who will carry on our names." He placed his hand on my shoulder. "You are young. You should not be here." He glanced toward Sam, who steadily fired arrow after arrow at any Persian who managed to break through the Greek lines and come near us. "Go now. Flee this battle. Live a long life. Know the love of a woman. Father many sons. Bring honor to your name." He released my shoulder and pounded it twice with the bottom of his fist. "And tell everyone of this battle. Tell them what we did. Tell them of our bravery. Do not let our deeds ever be forgotten!"

I couldn't believe what Areus was doing. He had just thrown aside centuries of Spartan tradition and given away his shield so he could save my life. A lump formed in my throat—this was the most selfless thing anyone had ever done for me. "I will, Areus, I promise."

Areus bent down and gently removed Leonidas's crested helmet from Charilaus's bloodied head. He then carefully placed his own helmet in its place and, with his fingers, smoothed Charilaus's eyelids closed. "I will see you soon, my friend." He stood up and pulled Leonidas's helmet firmly down over his head.

The two jump rods strapped to my forearm suddenly developed a nice chill, signifying that they no longer considered me part of this time period.

"Farewell, Danakles." Areus raised his spear high and bowed his head once to me, then turned to face the raging battle. "Sparta!" he cried as he rushed off to join the other Spartans.

As I watched him plunge into the fray, Sam came up beside me. "Did it work?" she yelled as she loosed another arrow.

"Yes! I'm a time jumper again!"

"Why's the rod still cold?"

I remembered what Jerry had told me about the time stream swapping people out. "History's still adjusting to getting *another* Leonidas. But the glitch should be fixed soon." I looked to where Leonidas's red-crested helmet was at the front of a group of Spartans.

Farewell, Areus.

"Then let's go!" Sam grabbed me by the hand and dragged me back to the middle of the pass, where only rocky ground and trampled grass lay. There, she removed her jump device from her bracer and spun it to the setting to send her home. "I guess I won't be seeing you for a while."

I tilted my helmet back on my head and then spun my own jump device to the proper setting. "Nope. Probably not."

She nodded. "Be safe."

Before I could say anything, she shouted the words to send herself home, and only her footprints in the bloody dirt remained to show she had been there.

I sighed and took one last look at the bravest heroes I'd ever known. "Goodbye, Areus. Goodbye, Dienekes. Goodbye, Charilaus."

"Arbah rostvos orokol biradelem!" I howled.

The blinding glow of the time stream wrapped itself around me.

I was heading home.

CHAPTER 23

The glare of the time stream vanished, and the distinct smoothness of a tile floor materialized beneath my sandals. For a second, I managed to hold myself upright, and then a swirl of dizziness knocked me off balance. I threw my arms out to steady myself, and my hand smacked against a wall.

Bright spots danced across my vision, and I shook my head to clear them away. Something was deeply wrong here. The air smelled of cinnamon, while my apartment normally smelled like pizza boxes. Had the jump device brought me to the wrong place?

A shadow moved toward me just outside the range of my blurred vision.

"Who's here?" I wrenched the sword free from its scabbard and thrust it out in front of me. My heart pounded in my chest as I struggled to get my vision in focus.

"Dan!" Jenna exclaimed. "It's me!"

"Jenna?" I lowered my sword. "Where am I?"

"In your apartment." Her footsteps pattered across the floor as she hurried to my side. "Oh my gosh! You're bleeding. You need an ambulance!"

I slumped against a wall and then slid down it until my butt hit the floor.

Home. I made it.

The sword tumbled from my hand and onto the tiles. "I'm okay," I sighed. "Not much of this blood is mine."

"Are you sure you're okay?"

The spots cleared away from my vision as the inside of my apartment came into focus. Everything looked familiar yet different at the same time. The pizza boxes normally stacked by the door were gone. The dishes that usually filled the kitchen sink had disappeared, and a single large candle flickered on my coffee table—no doubt the source of that cinnamon smell.

I removed my helmet and patted myself down with both hands, checking to see if I had been seriously wounded and didn't yet realize it. Small cuts and scrapes covered my arms and legs—nothing major—just some more scars to add to my collection. I did, of course, have the slash across my ribs, but that seemed like old news now.

I pulled off my left greave and let it fall to the floor. "Yeah, I'm about as okay as I can be. What day is it?"

"Wednesday. You've been gone for a day."

"One day," I chuckled maniacally. "One measly day." I wiped the sweat off my brow and stared blankly at the opposite wall. "You'd never believe what I've gone through."

Jenna knelt in front of me, wearing jeans and a black T-shirt that I could have sworn was mine. "Do you want to talk about it?" she asked.

"No . . . not now. Some other time. I need sleep." My gaze drifted to the dancing flame of the candle. "What are you doing here? Shouldn't you be in class?"

"School's over. I came here right after. I was hoping to surprise you when you came back." She looked over her shoulder. "I did some cleaning while I waited."

"Thanks," I muttered as I removed my other greave. "Do you know where my phone is?"

"It's on the counter. But if you're worried about Eric, he's all right. He and Manuel are in Washington, looking for Stewart."

"You talked to him?"

"Well . . . he texted right after you left." A blush crept into her cheeks as she shrugged. "And I kind of know your password. Since I thought his message might be important, I answered him. We've been texting. Everything seems okay so far." She bit her lip and looked at me timidly. "Are you upset that I used your phone?"

"No." I leaned my head back against the wall and basked in the coolness of the tile floor. "All's good."

"Are you sure you're okay?" Jenna edged closer and rested her hand on my arm. She studied my eyes, as if searching for a hint of anything wrong. For a second, she held this pose, then pulled the hand slowly away and held it far away from her like it had become an alien creature. Blood covered it from wrist to fingertips.

"Yeah . . . I'm good. Just really, really tired . . . and thirsty."

She sprang to her feet. "Let me get you some water."

As Jenna dashed into the kitchen, I struggled to untie the long, winding straps of my sandals. From the kitchen came sounds of running water and vigorous scrubbing. She returned moments later and passed me a glass of water with ice.

"Thanks." I drained the glass and left it on the floor beside me. All I wanted now was a hot shower—something to wash away all the blood and ease the soreness in my muscles and the constant pain from the gash across my ribs.

Jenna passed me my phone. "You want to text Eric?"

"No. He'll be fine. I need to check something." I flipped on my phone and saw that Sam had messaged me. She'd only written **Back**, but I was still relieved she'd made it home safely and had actually texted me. One day, I'd give her a huge apology. But not today. Not with Jenna staring intently at me. Instead I texted I'm home, then placed my phone on the floor beside me.

Jenna flicked her middle fingernail anxiously with her thumb. "About your phone." Her voice had an odd edge to it.

"Don't worry . . . that crack was already there."

"No . . . Not that. When I was texting Eric to tell him that you were away in history, I thought I'd check out your pictures to see if you have any good ones of us that I don't already have."

I slapped my hand against my right bracer to untie its leather straps. But they were slick with blood and my fingers kept slipping across the knots. "Did you find any?"

"I did." She folded her arms across her chest and her expression grew serious. "But I also found pictures of you and this redhead."

If I wasn't exhausted, I'd probably be panicking that she'd discovered the pictures of Sam from our trip to Wales last winter. I struggled to remember if there was anything in there that might piss Jenna off. As far as I could remember, there were a few shots of me and Sam at various scenic locations. Maybe one or two of us snuggling in a chair by the fire. Nothing terrible.

"She's pretty," Jenna continued, as she froze me with an icy glare. "Is she your ex?"

I slowly hauled myself to my feet, taking care not to pull the stitches along my ribs. Every muscle ached as I moved, and a bloody handprint marked the wall where I touched it. I'd known this day would come. Time to man up and tell Jenna the truth. "That's Sam."

Jenna took a step back and clenched her fists at her side. For a moment, they trembled as if she was struggling to contain her anger. "You said Sam was a guy!"

I raised my hands to try and calm her down and grunted at the effort. "Nope. Never did."

"Yes, you did!" She pounded her fist against her thigh and her face flushed red.

"Nope. I admit that I've lied to you tons of times before, and for that I'm really sorry, but I never lied to you about Sam." With a flick of my wrist, the bracer fell to the ground, and I started working on the other one.

Jenna's face knotted in concentration. I knew she was trying to think of any time I had referred to Sam as a *he*. But she couldn't, because I never had. I'd always remained intentionally vague.

Jenna shook her head slowly and for a moment closed her eyes. Her nostrils flared as she took a few deep breaths to calm herself. When she opened her eyes again, they looked glassy with tears. "Hiding the truth is just as bad as lying about it." She wiped the back of a hand across her eyes. "Were you a couple? You look pretty happy in these pictures."

"No," I said quietly, trying to keep the disappointment out of my voice. "We never were."

"Then why bother hiding all this from me? So you have a female partner. Who cares? I'm not some stupid kid who gets jealous just because you look at someone else."

With a flick of my wrist, the other bracer fell to the floor. "Because I didn't want this discussion. I hoped to keep my two lives separate."

"But they aren't separate! All those pictures were taken here . . . not in history."

"But you saw the pictures. We were wearing parkas and sweaters. They were taken a few months before you and I met. That's the last time we hung out together. Anything we might have had is over."

Jenna sniffed back a tear. "And what did you have?"

"Absolutely nothing." My gut twisted at the truth. No matter how strongly I felt for Sam, she would never return the feelings.

"Do you love her?"

I wanted to tell Jenna no. I wanted to tell her that she was the only woman for me. But I couldn't lie to her anymore. "It's complicated."

Jenna winced and her body sagged.

"Please, Jenna. You have to understand. She's saved my life so many times. Even on this jump, when I thought all hope was gone, she came in to save my butt." I held out my hands to Jenna, hoping she'd understand. "How could I not love her?"

A tear trickled down Jenna's cheek. "If you love her, then why are you here with me?" Her voice cracked as she spoke.

I loosened the straps of my chest armor. "Because Sam and I are time-jumping partners and nothing else. We save history together. That's it." I reached out to touch Jenna's face but stopped. Dried blood still caked my hand, and I didn't want to taint her beautiful face with the carnage that covered me. "You're the one I spend my days and nights with, not her."

Some of the pain left Jenna's face and she raised an eyebrow. "So there's nothing going on?"

With both hands, I pulled my chest armor off and let it clunk onto the floor. A second later, my gross, sweaty tunic and underwear followed it.

Jenna's eyes widened at my nakedness but, after a week with the Spartans, I didn't feel the slightest bit embarrassed. "Nothing. We kissed a few times, and that's all."

Jenna took a deep breath as if gathering her courage. "And do you love *me*?" Her eyes were wide with hope and expectation.

I looked down to the floor like a fortune teller searching for answers in the entrails of my discarded armor. *Did I love Jenna?*

I looked back up. Her brown eyes, usually so sparkling and alive, were red-rimmed with tears. How much pain had I caused her because of all my deceit?

"I'm going to tell you the truth. No more lies, no hiding, no evasion. I'm literally standing naked in front of you. I don't know if I love you, but I do know that the best part of my day is being with you. You're pretty and smart and fun to be around, and you constantly push me to be a better person. But I can't get Sam out of my head."

Jenna's face became a stony mask, her thoughts unreadable. "So where does this leave us?"

"I don't know. All I know is that I just came back from the worst time jump I've ever experienced. I've seen good friends die, and I honestly killed so many men that I lost count. I'm tired, sore, covered in blood, and I still have to figure out what's happening with Eric. So I can't talk about this right now."

"That's it?" she asked incredulously. "You tell me you love someone else, and then you kick me to the curb like yesterday's trash?"

"No . . . No . . . Not at all." I shook my head. "Jenna, I'd love it if you stayed, but I don't expect you to. I know what a terrible boyfriend I've been. I fully expect you to storm out, dump *me* like yesterday's trash, and find someone who will appreciate all your awesomeness—like I do, but without all the grief." I gazed at her for what would most likely be the last time as her boyfriend. "I'm going to shower and wash all this blood off me and then go figure out what Eric's doing. As much as I hate it, the world depends on me. I don't get the luxury of having time to worry about you *or* Sam."

Without waiting for Jenna's response, I spun on my heel and marched into the bathroom, closing the door behind me. The mirror reflected a blood-spattered man severely in need of sleep. At least the stitches across my ribs hadn't gotten infected. I turned the shower lever to hot and stepped in. The water cascaded down my hair and onto my back, bringing a deep, relieving heat.

Had I been too much of a jerk to Jenna? I told her the truth and didn't hold back for once, but it might just be more than she could bear. She was most likely gathering up her things and storming out the door. I didn't know if I could fix our relationship after this. Losing her would leave a huge hole in my life, but right now I was too tired to feel anything.

I let the hot water wash away the blood, the pain, and the horrible memories of Thermopylae. It couldn't take away the pain of my real life, though. I knew the two most awesome women in the world, and I'd managed to blow things with both of them. Part of me kept thinking about all the ways to beg their forgiveness, but the other part of me kept thinking of the greater picture. Stopping Victor required *all* my attention.

My bathroom was a cloud of steam when I finally shut off the water. Wrapping a towel around my waist, I opened the door to head for the kitchen. All I wanted right now was a few slices of cold pizza and then a nice long sleep.

"Wow, you take long showers."

I whipped my head toward the voice. Jenna was watching me from the couch in the living room.

"Y-y-you didn't go?" I stammered.

She exhaled slowly before standing up. "I thought about it . . . a lot . . . but I never made it out the door." With purposeful strides, she crossed the room and stopped, facing me. "So now I'm standing here in front of you. Nothing to hide. No lies. Only the truth." She drew her hands through her hair to push it back from her face. "I said I love you, and I meant it. But I have to face reality. I'll never jump back into the past with you. I'll never save your life. Sam is always going to win there." She reached up and put her hands over my shoulders so her body was pressed against mine. "I don't like losing. Chess matches. Debates. Bowling. Doesn't matter. I have to win." She tilted her head toward me, and for a second her eyes took on a wolf-like ferocity. "If I can't beat Sam at her game, I'll just have to change the game."

CHAPTER 24

Jenna stood next to my bed, hovering over me as I pulled the blankets up to my chin. *Bed. I missed you.* She reached down and brushed a strand of wet hair from my face. "Have a good sleep, Dan."

"Will you be here when I wake up?" My words came out barely audible, even to me. I was so exhausted from Thermopylae that even talking had become a chore.

"Probably not," she said with an amused sparkle in her eye. "You look like you're going to sleep for days. I'm surprised you're still awake now."

My eyelids sagged closed, and I struggled to pry them open. "I'm not."

She leaned over and kissed me on my forehead. "Thanks for saving history. Maybe when you're awake, you can tell me what happened."

I stared up at the blank expanse of the ceiling, trying to clear the memories of death from my mind. "It was the worst fighting I've ever been in. They just kept coming . . ."

She kissed me one more time and flicked off the lamp on the bedside table. "You're home now. You don't need to be a hero. You just need to sleep."

Hero.

That word hung in my thoughts. I'd heard it before. *But where?*

No . . . Not hero . . . Hero boy.

That's what Chris had mockingly called me back in Greece before the Spartans made sure he'd never annoy anyone again. Too bad Jerry made it out before I could kill him too.

I jerked straight up in bed, wide awake. "Crap!"

Jerry! He'd tell Victor that I killed Chris and stole his jump rod! Victor would be coming for me!

"What?" Jenna startled back.

"No time to explain!" With my heart pounding, I leaped out of bed and raced to the door. *Bolt in place? Check.* Not that a simple deadbolt would keep Victor out, but it would delay him a few seconds. And every second mattered. Now what?

I needed to ditch Chris's jump rod.

Screw that. I needed to hide before Victor found me.

I snatched up the two jump rods and my sword from the pile of discarded armor on the floor, then tore off back into the bedroom, where I almost collided with Jenna. "What's happening?" she asked. Her eyes had a trapped animal sort of look to them. Mine probably looked the same.

"We gotta get out of here!"

Where the hell are my clothes? Damn it! Jenna had cleaned my bedroom too. Usually I just tossed my laundry on my chair or on top of the dresser, but I at least always knew where it was.

I flipped through the drawers and threw on the first T-shirt and pants I could find, then jammed my wallet into my back pocket.

Jenna's hands trembled as she held up her phone. "Should I call the police?"

"And tell them what? That a bunch of time jumpers may or may not be coming to my apartment to kill me?" I found a backpack, tossed both jump rods in it, then grabbed Jenna's hand. "No. We've got to get out of this on our own."

In the front hallway, we hurriedly put our shoes on, and then I squinted through the door's peephole. No one right outside. With sword in hand, I stepped into the hallway and looked around.

All clear.

Jenna made a move as if to run to the elevators, but I held up my hand to stop her. "Wait. Let me think." Victor's guys could be in the stairwell, or they could be waiting in the lobby. Either way, we would never make it outside unless I could distract them somehow.

The fire alarm next to the stairwell caught my attention.

Bingo!

"Stay here." Sword in hand, I raced along the hall and pulled the alarm. A loud whooping noise tore through the hallway.

I ran back to my apartment and slid my sword along the tiled floor of the entrance. I'd have felt a hell of a lot better keeping it, but it would be hard to blend in with my neighbors while waving a weapon around. "Come on!" I said to Jenna, who stood frozen with fear.

I grabbed her hand and pulled her out into the hallway, while other residents came pouring out of their units. Since it was late afternoon, most of my neighbors weren't home yet, but there were still enough of them around to provide a small crowd. Like a herd of obedient sheep, we shuffled down the stairs, our numbers growing larger as we passed other floors. Jenna didn't say anything, but I could tell by the way she gripped my hand that she was scared. I tried to give her a reassuring smile, but I was petrified—we were moving so freaking slowly down these steps. The narrow stairwell seemed to close in on me, and everyone became a potential threat.

As soon as we made it out into the sunlight, Jenna and I broke away from the herd and raced along the street. In the distance, sirens wailed over the whoosh of cars passing by. I stopped at the edge of the road, trying to figure out the best getaway. My car would be the fastest but also the most obvious choice.

Across the street, a bus had stopped at the red light. I pulled Jenna with me just as our light turned yellow.

With the gash in my side aching from the exertion, I paid the fare, then Jenna and I found seats near the back. As soon as the bus rolled forward, I exhaled loudly. No one had followed us onto the bus—we were safe from Victor for now.

"Where are we going?" Jenna kept her tone hushed.

"*You're* going home." I looked out the window, checking to see if anyone had attempted to follow us on foot. "You need to stay as far away from me as possible until I get things sorted out."

"What about you?"

"I'll figure something out." I leaned my head against the window and tried to gather my thoughts. Now that my adrenaline rush was beginning to fade, my exhaustion was returning and I could barely think. All I knew for sure was that I needed to ditch the two jump rods; Victor would be coming for them. As our bus reached the next stop, a dim outline of a plan began to form. I ordered an Uber to pick me up and take me downtown.

"I'm going to get off here," I said to Jenna. She opened her mouth to object, but I cut her off. "You just keep heading home. I'll call you when I can."

She bit her lip fearfully. "Be safe."

"I will." I kissed her, then hopped off the bus and jumped into my ride as soon as it appeared.

I leaned back into the seat and took a few deep breaths. I was safe for the moment, but it wouldn't last. First order of business: ditch this extra jump rod before Victor found me and forced me to give it back to him.

I need your help, I texted Eric.

What's up?

What's either of your dads' cell numbers?

Why?

I found something they might be interested in.

My phone rang. "Did you get what I think you got?" Eric asked breathlessly.

"Yeah."

"Forget my dads! Give it to me!"

I glanced out the rear window to check if any suspicious-looking cars were following me. "But you're in DC, and I need to get rid of it *now*."

"Can't you just hang on to it for a bit? I can be there in a few hours."

I leaned forward and placed a hand over one ear to block out the road noise. "Did you find Stewart yet?" I said quietly.

"Nope. But Manuel's here. He can keep up the search while I fly back."

"I can't give you this. I need the info from your dads' laptop."

"Screw the laptop! Nothing they have has helped them—it won't help you. Give it to me, and *I* can be your partner." There was a desperation in Eric's voice that I had never noticed before. "We can fight Victor as a team!"

Eric being my time-jumping partner had never been part of any plan—why was he bringing it up now? "I don't need a partner. I need information." Fatigue made my voice sound harsher than I intended. "Now are you, or are you not, going to give me the phone number of at least one of your dads?"

"Fine!" The line went dead, but Eric did send me Brian's number, and I called it.

"Hello," came Brian's voice.

"Hi. This is the man from the van at the back of the shoe store," I began cryptically, just in case Victor had tapped Brian's phone. "I'm interested in a used laptop."

"What?" Brian's voice was thick with confusion. "Who is this? I'm not—" His voice dropped to a whisper as he caught on. "Can you meet our terms?"

"Yes."

"When can we meet?" he asked, excited.

"Now! I gotta get rid of it quick!"

Brian sighed. "It's that bad?"

"Yup. I'm headed to the spot where we first met. Can you meet me?"

"No. But tape it to the underside of the dumpster, and we'll come pick it up."

"That's it? What if someone finds it there before you do?"

"Don't let anyone see you and everything should be fine. The biggest risk is us being spotted together. Just do this, and we'll be safe."

Safe? Yeah, right. He'd be safe. But I'd still have Victor's goons kicking down my door. "All right. And when do I get my stuff?"

"Dave will arrange a time and place to meet with you."

"You can't just email me the files, or upload them somewhere?"

"You're getting the whole application installed on a laptop and linked to the motherboard. It's the only way we can be sure you never create a copy for anyone else. You either do it this way or no way."

I squeezed the bridge of my nose to fight off my mounting headache. "All right," I muttered.

I asked my driver to make a quick detour to a hardware store so I could pick up some duct tape, then walked the last few blocks to the same dingy alley where I'd met Dave and Brian. It reeked even worse than before of urine and garbage. Trying to ignore the stench, I snapped off a generous length of tape and secured a jump device underneath the lone dumpster. It seemed insane to be leaving one of the most precious items in the world taped to the bottom of a dumpster, but that's what Brian wanted.

I hurried back to the main street and found a UPS Store, where I sent the other jump device to Sam using their most secure service. Not the best plan in the world, but at least if anything happened to me, the device would be in good hands.

I caught the first bus I saw and tried to figure out what to do next. The jump rods might be safe, but Victor would still be coming for me. It wasn't a matter of whether but when. I needed a plan, but, unfortunately, my brain had stopped cooperating. Stringing two simple thoughts together was almost impossible—I needed sleep so badly.

C'mon, Dan! Stay awake!

If I stripped my situation down to its barest elements, there were only two options: stay and wait for Victor to get me, or empty my bank accounts, get a flight to wherever, and disappear.

Both options sucked. If I bolted, I'd spend the rest of my life on the run, leaping at every sound and startled by every movement. Not to mention that I'd never be able to see Sam, Jenna, or Eric again. But if I stayed . . .

A shudder ran through me. If I stayed, Victor would find me and kill me, and it probably wouldn't take long.

A life on the run was better than no life. Sure, I'd miss Jenna and Eric, but not enough to risk my life. And, once Sam sent my jump device back, I'd still see her on time jumps.

Crap . . .

My passport was at home. I wouldn't get very far from Victor without it. I'd have to go back and get it.

About half an hour later, I hopped off the bus and shuffled, almost zombie-like, along the sidewalk back to my condo. The gash across my ribs burned intensely and my legs and arms felt like they were filled with lead. Only the thought of survival kept me moving.

As I turned down the driveway to my building, I did a quick scan of the street, searching for anything out of the ordinary. A couple with a stroller. A lady walking her dog. Two guys on skateboards doing tricks on the wide strip of concrete in front of the entrance.

No vans with tinted windows or strange guys lurking in the bushes. I walked quickly along the sidewalk.

"Hey, Dan!" one of the skateboard guys yelled. "How's it going?" He waved.

He didn't look even the slightest bit familiar. Did he go to my school? "Tired," I mumbled as I kept walking.

The wheels of his skateboard rumbled across the asphalt as he skated along the road beside me. "Hey, whatcha doing later? Me and Mike are heading up to my place to play some video games. You want in?"

He acted like he knew me, but I couldn't figure out how I might know him. Then again, I could barely remember my own name. "Nah, I'm gonna crash. Maybe some other time."

"Okay, cool." He kicked the tail of his skateboard to hop up onto the sidewalk, and then just as quickly hopped back onto the road again. "Hey! You dropped something."

"I did?" I stopped walking and turned around.

A sharp pain, like a hornet sting, hit the back of my leg. I slapped my hand down on my hamstring and felt a small dart. As it dawned on me that I'd been drugged, a numbness descended over my body, wiping out all my pain. My vision blurred and my muscles became so weak that I could barely hold myself up. The world began to spin as my phone tumbled out of my hands and clattered to the pavement.

The skateboarder slung his arm under my arm and propped me up before I could fall. "Whoa! Dan, man! You don't look too good," he said loudly. "Don't worry. Me and Mike will get you home."

Mike rushed over and wedged himself under my other arm to keep me upright. The pair half walked and half dragged me around to the back of the building. Through the thick fog that clung to my brain, one thought stood out—I was being kidnapped, but I couldn't even attempt to struggle; it took all my energy just to stay conscious.

Seconds later, a delivery van drove up, the door slid open, and I was shoved inside. I lay there on the cold metal floor of the van, too weak to resist as someone zip-tied my hands and feet.

Then the world went black.

CHAPTER 25

My right side was throbbing. It didn't really hurt, just a dull pulsing in my ribs. The rest of me felt . . . fuzzy . . . numb.

I opened my eyes but saw only blackness. Pure black, like all the light in the universe had been extinguished. It reminded me of the darkness outside the time stream, except without the wind.

Where am I?

It was hot and muggy . . . but only around my head. The rest of me felt a bit cold. The throbbing in my side grew in intensity to the point where it started to sting. I remembered the source of that pain now—a Persian spear had struck me there.

As the numbness in my body began to fade away, I noticed an ache in my shoulders as well. They felt stiff and cramped. I tried to shift position to loosen them up, but my arms and legs wouldn't move. There was something pressing down on my wrists and ankles, holding me in place.

What the . . . ? Why can't I move?

"Master Renfrew," a deep voice began, "how nice of you to grace us with your presence."

Fear swept like fire through me, burning away the remaining fog around my mind. I knew exactly where I was—tied to a chair with a hood over my head.

The hood was yanked off, revealing a small room. Concrete walls. Single fluorescent fixture casting a dim light. Concrete floor with a rusted drain in the middle. No furniture except for the chair I was strapped into and a gray steel folding chair set up directly in front of me.

Like the angel of death, Victor loomed just off to one side, dressed as always in a suit that cost more than most families would earn in a week. In the corner, his bodyguard, Drake, stood silently like a statue, arms folded across his chest. I expected Drake, since Victor never went anywhere without him, but I didn't expect to see Jerry. He stood right beside Drake, wearing a simple dress shirt and jeans. He glared at me with hate in his eyes.

"Now, Daniel," Victor continued. "I believe you have something of mine, and I want it back."

"It's gone." My voice emerged as a squeak.

Victor leaned into me so his face was just inches from my own. I could almost taste the stench of his cologne. "That is not a suitable answer," he hissed.

Even though a river of sweat ran down my back and my hands were trembling, I tried to put on a brave face. "It's the only answer you're going to get," I replied defiantly.

Victor turned his head to Jerry. "It seems young Daniel has grown in courage since I last met him. How unfortunate, as fear is an excellent motivator." Victor fixed me with a hardened look. "Now, Daniel. You do realize that your stubbornness only delays the inevitable. I *will* get this information out of you."

I swallowed hard. I knew that I'd eventually break, but I couldn't just throw Eric's dads under the bus. I needed time to figure out another option. "I don't care. I'm not telling you."

"Give me five minutes and I'll get it out of him," Jerry said. His voice had a harshness to it that hadn't been there in Greece.

"Not yet." Victor straightened and nodded to Jerry. "I am sure we have other ways to motivate young Daniel without resorting to common violence." He walked slowly around my chair, his thick-soled shoes echoing loudly in the small room. "What is that girl's name again?" he mused. "Jenna?"

"Leave her out of this!" I snarled.

"Ah! The courageous Master Renfrew has a weakness after all."

"You're the one with the weakness," I spat. "First Sam, now Jenna?" I glared at him. "Is that why there's no Mrs. Stahl? Got a thing for teenage girls?"

Victor's fist crashed into my jaw, whipping my head to one side. Stars floated in front of my eyes, and I tensed in preparation for his next blow.

But Victor didn't hit me again. He just slowly opened and closed his fist a few times. Maybe he hurt a knuckle when he punched me. *Good*.

"You have truly become annoying, Daniel," he sniffed. "However, you are correct. Threatening young women is not something to which I should lower myself." He pulled up the other chair and sat directly facing me so that our knees were almost touching. "But there is something else I think you value equally. I refer, of course, to your precious little group."

I sucked in my breath and Victor chuckled. "Yes, I know about your college friends and their ridiculous plans. Did you truly think you could hide them from me?" Victor wagged a finger, as if admonishing me like I was a small child. "How naive. You should know by now that I am aware of *everything* you do."

Victor stood and began walking around my chair again. He stopped right behind me and put his hands on my shoulders. I tried not to tremble and give him the satisfaction of knowing how scared I was.

"Let us think about them for a moment," Victor mused. "So young. So full of life and potential. What a shame it would be for an accident to happen to any of them. Yet the world is full of so many dangers. One moment of carelessness and you can run in front of a bus or drive your car into a river."

"Bastard!" I pulled against my restraints but my hands were tied too tightly. I tried to think of some sort of argument, some sort of appeal to him that could save my friends. But Victor was a murderous psychopath who planned on killing billions of people—why would he care about hurting a couple of my friends?

Victor was right: The group was a weakness. As their leader, I needed to protect them. I couldn't sacrifice them for the sake of a jump device . . . but I couldn't sell out Dave and Brian either.

I was screwed. *Unless* . . .

"All right, you win," I muttered. "I'll tell you exactly what I did with the jump rod. But you have to promise me you won't harm any of them."

Victor walked slowly around my chair to face me. "Agreed."

"No. I need your word that, in return for me telling you what I did with the rod, you won't have them harmed in any way. You can't get Drake to do it, or Jerry to do it, or hire other people . . . or have Drake hire anyone, or . . ."

"Yes, yes, yes, I understand," Victor said impatiently. "You have my word that, from this point onward, none of your precious little group members will be harmed. Now tell me what happened to the device."

"We have a deal, then?"

"Yes! How many more times must I say it?"

If there was one positive thing I could say about Victor, it was that he always stuck to his word. *Sucker!*

"At about five fifteen this afternoon, I taped the device to the bottom of a rusty green dumpster in the northwest corner of an alley behind a vacant store at 295 Williams Street. I think the store might have once sold shoes, but I'm not sure."

The Spartan Sacrifice

"Who cares about the store!" Victor snapped. "Who retrieved the device?"

I gave him a smug grin. "I promised to tell you *exactly* what I did with the jump device, and I did. I taped it to the bottom of a dumpster. I've fulfilled my end of the bargain. If you don't like my answer, maybe you should have phrased your question better."

Victor's nostrils flared as he clasped his hands together in front of him. I knew he was weighing his response, and I braced myself for another punch. It would be worth it, though. In previous conversations, he had always lectured me about being precise in my speech. This was the first time I'd ever had the chance to give him the same lecture.

Slowly Victor exhaled before unclasping his hands. Then he smiled—a menacing smile, full of teeth. "You have changed, Daniel. You used to be amusing, like a toddler taking his first steps. But with three of my men dead by your hands, I no longer find you amusing. You have become an irritation." With one finger, he lazily pointed to the circular drain that lay between our feet. "But you are correct. I should be impeccable in my speech." The menacing smile faded, and his face turned cold and hard. "Tell me what I want to know, or you will not leave here alive."

Bile rose to the back of my throat. "Wait! You can't kill me!" I blurted. "You need me to protect Sam on her time jumps. I know you don't care one bit about me, but you do care about her."

For the briefest instant, a flicker of doubt flashed across his face. Just as quickly, it disappeared, replaced by that calm mask he wore so diligently. "Yes, I do have a slight fondness for Ms. Cahill, because of my past friendship with her father, but I would never allow you to live solely on her account."

I knew Victor a hell of a lot better than I wanted to. I knew how he spoke and how he emphasized his words. And everything he had just said about Sam had come out way too emphatically for him. Almost like he was trying overly hard to convince me he wasn't protecting Sam.

No . . . he wasn't trying to convince me. He was trying to convince . . . Jerry?

"I have kept you alive so far," Victor continued, "because you have proved to be a remarkably successful chrononaut. Would anyone else have been able to take on the role of Leonidas and save us from the first black event in over two decades?" Victor clapped me on the shoulder in what I could only call a fatherly way. It made me want to puke. "We all applaud your efforts at saving history. The unfortunate war in the chrononaut community has taken a dreadful toll on our ranks, killing many of our most skilled members. We need more young, talented individuals like you."

"We'd have even more members if he didn't keep killing them," Jerry interjected. "I say we get rid of him now before he takes another one of us out."

Victor paced back and forth across the small room, stroking his chin thoughtfully. "What should I do with you, Daniel? My better judgment tells me I should kill you. But keeping you alive serves my interests as well."

"You still need me!" I pleaded. "I—"

"Just kill him," Jerry said. "A nice long, slow, painful death."

But Victor made no move toward me, just narrowed his eyes, deep in thought. It was almost like he legitimately didn't know what to do with me. It seemed like a part of him wanted to keep me alive to protect Sam, while another part of him wanted me dead. I'd never seen him so indecisive before.

Then it hit me—Victor didn't want to appear weak in front of Jerry. He didn't want to admit he had kept me alive in order to protect Sam. If I wanted to ever leave this room alive, I'd have to work on Jerry.

I gave Jerry the most sincere expression I could muster. "I'm so sorry I killed Chris. I know it was wrong. I shouldn't have done it. If I had the chance to take it back, I would."

Jerry's face twisted with rage, and he lunged across the room. His fist collided with my chin, snapping my head back and making my ears ring. Before Jerry could throw another punch, Drake hooked his arm and pulled him off me.

"You executed my son!" Spittle flew from Jerry's lips as he struggled to free himself from Drake's grasp.

Son? No . . .

My heart pounded. The next words coming out of my mouth would probably decide my fate. But what could I say?

A bead of sweat trickled down my temple.

I looked to Victor, then to Jerry, then back to Victor again. Who should I turn to? Which one of them could save me? I had only one chance to leave here alive. "What do you want from me?" I asked Victor.

"Want?" Victor's mouth curled upward into what I could only assume was a smile. "I want the same thing I wanted from your father, but which he was too stubborn to give." He held his hand palm up in front of him and then curled it into a fist. "I want your loyalty."

"What?" Jerry jerked back in surprise. "You're letting him live? He's killed three of our men. He killed Chris!"

Victor wheeled around angrily. "And history itself would have been rewritten if not for his actions in Greece, as you admitted yourself. We must *never* forget our first and foremost goal: to repair the anomalies that appear in the time stream and keep history flowing correctly. Otherwise, the rest of our plans are for nothing."

Jerry muttered under his breath but said nothing else.

Victor stared me straight in the eye. "So, Daniel, will you give me your loyalty?"

My skin crawled at the thought of throwing in with the man who had killed my dad, but did I have a choice? "What does loyalty to you mean?"

Victor clasped his hands behind his back and began pacing in front of me. "For you, loyalty will mean two simple rules. One: You will never again bring harm to any of my people. And two . . ." He stopped pacing and faced me. "From now on, you will be at the beck and call of your time-travel device. Anytime it signifies an anomaly in history, you will be the one who fixes it."

It took a second for his words to register, but when they did, dread settled in my gut. "I have to fix *every* glitch? That's a death sentence."

Victor waved his hand dismissively. "Maybe. But you have shown incredible skill and luck so far; perhaps your luck will continue to hold out. Either way, I will be rid of a pesky thorn in my side. But answer me now. My time is precious."

All I could think of was that little drain between my feet and how, if I didn't say yes, the last sight I'd ever see would be my blood flowing slowly into it. I knew my dad had fought Victor to the end. But Dad was braver than I was. I was just a tired, scared kid fighting desperately for his life.

Sorry, Dad.

"Deal," I said quietly, shuddering with shame.

"Do not disappoint me." Victor's voice was ominously flat. "I rarely forget, and I *never* forgive. I am keeping you alive because you are currently useful to me. Do not lose your usefulness." He leaned in closer to me. "And keep Ms. Cahill safe," he whispered so that only I could hear it.

"That's it?" Jerry stamped his foot. "You're letting him go? What about Chris's device?"

"I am done here. You, however, are free to use whatever means you deem necessary to extract that information from him, and at the same time convey the extreme sense of loss you are feeling after the recent execution of your son." Victor nodded to Drake. "Just make sure Master Renfrew survives. He works for us now."

As Victor strode toward the doorway, Jerry's eyes lit up with a sadistic glee I'd seen only in horror movies. With slow, measured steps, he moved in front of my chair. "Don't bother screaming," he said as he cracked the knuckles of one fist and then the other. "There are no Spartans around to save you this time."

CHAPTER 26

Pain...
   So... much... pain...

Every breath sent a torrent of agony across my bruised ribs. Blood spewed from my broken nose, and I'd already spat out two teeth. My right eye had swelled shut, and I couldn't move three fingers on my left hand.

I gritted my teeth to stop myself from sobbing as Drake and Jerry carried my limp body up the dimly lit stairs; I wouldn't give Jerry the satisfaction of knowing how much he had hurt me. Drake gripped me under the armpits while Jerry held me by the knees. Each thumping footstep they took was its own separate agony as my sides pulled and twisted as if my body was about to snap in half.

At the top of the stairs, Drake kicked open the door, and a rush of cold air blew down the stairwell. They carried me a few more steps, then dropped me like a sack of trash in the middle of the alley outside.

Jerry loomed over me, his features distorted with rage. "Where is it, you bastard?" He fired another kick into my ribs and a haze of pain darkened my vision.

I clenched my one good fist and tried not to scream. My ribs felt like they were caving in.

Jerry drew his leg back again and I wrapped my arms tightly around my sides for protection.

"Enough!" Drake barked.

"But he still hasn't told us what he did with it!" Jerry yelled back.

"Face it," Drake said flatly. "The kid's not going to break. And Victor wants him alive."

Jerry tilted his head toward Drake. "We should have killed this kid ages ago, but Victor still lets him live. Victor's gotten weak, and you know it."

Drake's face remained unchanged. "I have my orders, and I say that's enough."

Jerry crouched and grabbed a fistful of my hair and jerked my face toward him. "It's not over between us. I'm going to make you suffer. Whatever pain you feel now is nothing." He released my head abruptly, letting it thud off the pavement. My skull echoed with the impact and stars swam in front of my eyes.

Footfalls pounded through the alley as Drake and Jerry walked away. Seconds later, the heavy door slammed shut.

Tears started to flow. First a trickle, and then a flood, as all the pain and fear and anger I had held back over the last few hours erupted. Everything hurt so much—and it wasn't over yet. I still needed to get out of here.

"Help . . ." I moaned. "Help . . ." I could barely hear my own pitiful cries—no way anyone else would.

Above me the sky was black, the moon a pale sliver partially obscured by clouds. If I didn't want to die in this alley tonight, I'd have to get out of here.

Taking the utmost care not to jostle my ribs, I dragged myself to my hands and knees and then, using the wall for support, pulled myself to a standing position.

I took a few shaky steps and then paused to rest.

I clenched my teeth and hobbled along the narrow alley. My right hand dragged across the worn face of the brick wall on one side, while my other arm wrapped around my torso to brace my ribs.

I lurched out of the alley and into the street, where a pathetic whimper escaped my lips. I had thought getting as far as the street would get me rescued, but I was standing in the middle of a block of abandoned-looking industrial buildings, under the yellow glow of a street light. Graffiti covered the age-stained brick. Most of the window frames were empty. Grass and weeds grew from between cracks in the sidewalk, and the empty parking lots were filled with potholes. Not a single person was out, and the only cars on the road were rusting hulks that had been abandoned ages ago.

I fought the overwhelming panic that bubbled up inside me—I had survived Thermopylae; I could survive this.

About five blocks away, a lone traffic light turned red. A flicker of hope sparked in my chest. A light meant traffic. And traffic meant people.

As I shuffled along the cracked sidewalk, I imagined Areus's shield against my back, holding me up, propelling me onward. And I imagined Charilaus beside me, urging me on, giving me strength.

One block...

Two blocks...

Three blocks...

The hum of a car engine pierced the stillness of the evening. I whipped my head up, searching for the car. Headlights were coming toward me. I staggered into the middle of the street, praying the car would stop in time. Seconds later, tires screeched and headlight beams shone brightly at me. Raising my good hand to shield my eyes, I squinted into the blinding light. A car door slammed and a dark silhouette approached against the glow of headlights.

What if Jerry had come back to finish me off?

I rocked on my feet, using all my strength to keep myself standing. If Jerry was back, I was done.

The figure stepped out of the glare. A kindly looking older woman, with a schoolteacher sort of look to her, crept hesitantly toward me, and my body sagged with relief. "You're going to be okay," she soothed. "I've called an ambulance."

"Thanks," I groaned. That one word seemed to take the last of my strength. I sank to my knees and fell sideways onto the pavement. My eyelids grew heavier.

"Just keep talking," the lady encouraged as she knelt over me. "What's your name?"

"Dan . . . Where am I?"

She said something, but her voice sounded like it was coming from the end of a tunnel and the world began to spin.

"Huh? Can you repeat . . ."

The world went black.

CHAPTER 27

The nurse's rubber-soled shoes squeaked across the floor as she approached my hospital bed. "You have visitors," she said cheerily, as if I was supposed to feel excited that more cops were going to come barging into my room and ask me questions I couldn't answer.

I pulled the covers up under my chin. "Can't you tell them I'm sleeping?"

"Sorry," the nurse said with an amused smile. "Too late."

I rolled my eyes and stared up at the ceiling. How many more times were the cops going to interview me? I'd already told them all I could. Well, at least all they'd believe. I was lost in the city, two guys tried to mug me, I fought back, and they kicked my ass. Sure, my story had a few holes in it, especially when I had to explain how I'd ended up in DC without any luggage or a place to stay, but I'd come up with some plausible excuses. And the police had already given me the "Is your phone worth your life?" lecture. What else could they want?

The nurse left and, a few seconds later, Eric and Manuel strode into the room, both wearing jeans and wrinkled T-shirts. Neither looked like they had slept in days. Seeing them made me feel almost as good as the painkiller dripping into my arm through the IV. "Man, it's great to see you guys."

"*Madre mia . . .*" Manuel crossed himself. "What the hell happened to you?"

Eric looked over his shoulder toward the doorway. "And don't give us that mugging story we heard the cops talking about in the hall. I've sparred with you. No mugger did this."

"How'd you find me?"

"Jenna," Eric said. "The police found your wallet in the alley. Your cash and credit cards are gone, but your ID was still there. The cops tried to find your next of kin, but all they found was Jenna in your apartment. They told her, and she told us." He spread his hands wide. "And ta-da . . . we're here." He motioned with his chin. "So what really happened?"

"It was Victor." I kept my voice low. "I hid something of his, and he wanted it back." Because Manuel was around, I didn't say anything else. The fewer people who knew that Eric's dads had the extra jump device, the better.

Eric stiffened. "Did you tell him where to find it?"

"Nope. That's why he beat the crap out of me."

Eric's body sagged with relief. *Thanks,* he mouthed from behind Manuel.

"Did you find Stewart and Tim yet?" I asked.

Manuel rubbed his jaw as if trying to choose the right words. "Well . . . the police found them."

"Did they arrest them?"

Manuel and Eric exchanged glances but neither said a word.

"What's going on? Tell me!"

Manuel dropped his gaze to the floor and gave a sad shake of his head. "They're dead."

"No!" I sank back into my pillows, feeling completely overwhelmed. "How?"

Eric turned his head to the door, eyeing the two policemen standing outside. "The cops say they both had accidents. Tim was hit by a bus and Stewart drowned when he drove his car into the river. But I'm not buying it—especially after what happened to you."

Victor had practically given me a confession: *One moment of carelessness and you can run in front of a bus or drive your car into a river.* My entire body felt cold. "When?"

Eric turned his head back to me, his eyes narrowing. "Probably yesterday morning, if you can trust the cops. It took a while for us to find out."

A low moan escaped my lips as I remembered how cocky I'd felt when I had bargained with Victor for the safety of my group. I thought I had been so freakin' smart. But Victor, like always, had been the smarter one. He had already killed Stewart and Tim before he had agreed to our deal.

"But how did Victor even find out about them? *We* barely knew their plans."

Manuel walked over to the window and looked out over the street. "I don't know, man. But it's got me wondering how we're ever going to stop Victor. He seems to know what we're doing even before we do."

How did Victor do it? How did he find out that two guys with no specific plans were after him, and then take them both out, all while making it look accidental?

I pressed a button on my bed's control panel and the head of my bed rose mechanically a few inches. "So what happens now?"

"We *were* going home," Manuel said. "But we can wait until they discharge you."

"Nah, you can head home. I'll catch up with you in a few days."

Eric jerked his thumb toward the cops out in the hall. "No way we're leaving you alone with DC's finest. Any one of them could be on Victor's payroll."

"Thanks, guys." My voice caught in my throat, and it took all my effort not to look away in shame. I wanted to tell them the truth: We were all safe. I had traded my freedom for our lives. But no matter how hard I tried, the words would not come out. With Tim and Stewart dead, I'd sound like some gullible idiot who'd been conned by Victor.

The sun shone brightly in a nearly cloudless sky. It was a beautiful day, one Jenna and I should have been spending outside by a pool or at a beach. But there we were, standing in a cemetery with hundreds of other mourners as the priest said nice things about Stewart. He spoke of a charming young man, eager to help others, who was beloved by all. Maybe Stewart had those qualities, but I'd never seen them. I could only remember him as angry and impulsive—the two traits that had gotten him killed.

His grieving relatives huddled together around the grave site, some of them casting curious glances toward me. With my face all bruised and battered from Jerry, and three fingers of my left hand in a splint, they probably thought I'd been with Stewart in the car. I hoped they didn't try to talk to me about him. What could I say about a guy I barely tolerated?

After the service ended, Jenna and I muttered condolences to the family and then we went to join the rest of the medieval club members in the shade of a large oak. Jenna and I walked slowly; even on pain meds, my ribs still ached. She gripped my arm tightly as if expecting me to fall over at any minute.

This was the first time I'd seen the group together since the night Stewart had stormed out. I almost didn't recognize them without their medieval club garb. Manuel had gone all out for the funeral, dressing in a black suit and tie, while Eric was more casual in black jeans and a dress shirt. Adjoa and Britney both wore dark dresses, although

Britney's looked more like something to wear to a club than a funeral. Everyone looked a lot more tired than I'd ever seen them.

"Hey, guys." I gave them a half-hearted wave. "Jenna, this is Manuel, Eric, Britney, Kate, Pascal, and Adjoa." I pointed to each in turn. "And, guys, this is Jenna." I looked around. "Where's Sophie?"

Adjoa looked me up and down, her lips curling as if she was staring at a smear of dog crap on the bottom of her shoe. "She's gone."

I brushed off her harsh reaction. We were at a funeral after all, and emotions were tense. "Gone?"

"Yeah. Gone. She got freaked out, so she decided to go stay with her aunt and uncle in Kansas." Adjoa put her hands on her hips and turned her head away from me, as if she couldn't stand looking in my direction. "Not that you care."

What was her problem? Was she blaming me for what happened to Stewart and Tim? I turned to Britney, who took a quick step back, like she was afraid to be near me.

"Dan." Jenna tugged on my arm and her voice had a wary edge to it. "I think we should go."

"What's going on here?" I asked Adjoa.

"Don't ever talk to me again," Adjoa snapped.

No sugar coating. No niceness. Just a blunt statement that smacked me like a hammer to the chest. "What? Why?"

Manuel crossed his arms and gave me a look full of disappointment. "I used to idolize you, man. You were this badass—you killed two of Victor's men and had all these wild stories about saving history." His eyes narrowed and he shook his head, almost like he was mad at himself. "Not once did I ever doubt you. Never once did I wonder, how can this guy kill off Victor's guys and still be alive . . . still have his jump rod?"

My heart was banging in my chest. Had the entire group turned against me? "Look, I don't know what's going on here, but I've always been straight with you guys."

"Really?" Britney asked incredulously. "That's not what I heard."

"I don't care what you've heard." I pointed to Stewart's coffin sitting in the distance among the headstones. "That is not my fault."

"Oh, yeah? What about Victor? I heard you're now his little pet time jumper."

My eyes went wide. "How do you know about that?"

"Guy named Jerry." Britney stood straighter, as if emboldened by my response. "He said he was the one who beat you up. And that you're in Victor's pocket."

This was going downhill fast. I couldn't lose this group; besides Sam and Jenna, they were the only friends I had—the only people who understood what was at stake if Victor took over.

I raised my hands to try and calm the situation down. "I had no choice. He would have killed me—and probably all of you—if I hadn't agreed." I looked each one in the eye, imploring them to believe me. "Any one of you would have done the exact same thing. But that doesn't mean I betrayed Tim and Stewart. I was in ancient Greece on a time jump. Victor found out about them some other way."

Kate's eyes lit up like I had just admitted to murder. "So you don't deny that you're working for Victor?"

"I'm not working for him! I'm just stuck jumping through time for him."

"And what else did you agree to do?" Pascal got right in my face. "Spy on us? Warn him of any other attempts on his life?"

I could feel a little piece of me dying. Whatever Jerry had told them had obviously spread like a poison. Nothing I could say would win back their trust. To them I was one of Victor's people now.

I turned to Eric. "Are you with them, too?"

He cast his eyes to the ground. "Sorry, Dan," he mumbled.

His words stabbed me like a knife in the back. "Screw you! Screw all of you! I know none of you will believe me, but I did not sell out Tim and Stewart."

I could feel six icy stares tearing holes through me as Jenna and I started down the long path through the cemetery.

"Is what they said true?" Jenna asked me the moment we were out of hearing range. "Did you really join Victor?"

"Well, no, but . . . yeah, I guess I did." I bowed my head and stared at the dull pavement. "But I did it to save everyone's lives, including yours."

Jenna covered her mouth with her hand. "That's horrible! I'm so sorry."

I nodded. What could I say?

"What are you going to do?"

Good question. If I crossed Victor in even the slightest way, he'd make me and everyone I ever cared about suffer. Plus, I had my own personal nemesis in Jerry, who had sworn to make my life miserable and gotten off to a great start. And even if I did have a clue about what to do, my body needed several weeks to heal before it would be in any shape to do anything. "I don't know." My words sounded empty . . . just like my hopes.

We walked in silence a few more steps, then Jenna's phone rang. "Hello?" She nodded a few times. "I'll try." She held the phone out to me. "It's Eric. He wants to meet."

"Tell him to piss off."

"He wants to apologize."

"Too late."

Jenna stopped walking and rested her hand on my shoulder. "You really should talk to him. I know you're hurt, but hear him out. You two are friends. You shouldn't throw that away so easily."

I already knew Jenna well enough to know that no matter how hard I tried to argue against it, she'd bombard my stubborn refusal with logical arguments until I looked stupid, and then I'd end up meeting with Eric anyway. Might as well surrender before the battle started. "All right," I sighed. "I'll give him five minutes."

Jenna relayed this message back to Eric, and the two of us headed across the street to a coffee shop. It was a tiny place with antique-looking wooden tables, dim lighting, and the aroma of coffee hanging thick in the air. The place was crowded, but Jenna and I found a table, then placed our order and waited.

Eric appeared a few minutes later. He paused in the doorway to allow his eyes to adjust, then headed over to our table.

"Hey," he said casually as he sat down.

"What do you want, Eric?" I said icily.

He ignored me and reached his hand out to Jenna. "I didn't get a chance to properly introduce myself at the funeral. I'm Eric."

"Jenna."

Eric smiled. "Great to actually meet the person I've been texting."

Jenna smiled back at him. "It's nice to meet you, too."

Their cheeriness annoyed me. It was as if they were both completely unfazed by what had just happened. "Should I leave you two alone? You clearly have a lot to catch up on." My chair scraped noisily across the floor as I stood up.

"Wait!" Eric reached toward me but remained seated. "Don't go. Please. I want to apologize." He gestured to the chair I had just vacated. "Give me two minutes."

I grudgingly took my seat again. "Fine, two minutes." I crossed my arms over my chest and leaned back.

Eric exhaled loudly and ran a hand through his short brown hair. "Your deal with Victor shocked the hell out of me. But I get it. You did what you had to do."

"Why didn't you say that in front of them?"

"They'd already made up their minds. Nothing I said would change that."

"Still would have been nice. That's what friends are supposed to do."

"Yeah, but they're my friends, too. They'd never talk to me again if they knew I was okay with what you did." Eric idly drew circles with one finger on the tabletop. "I can't give them up like that. If I side with you, I'd lose control of my own group—of my own way to fight against Victor. So where would that have left me?"

I wanted to find fault with his choice, but he was just trying to keep the fight against Victor going. And that's all that really mattered. "So you don't think I'm Victor's spy?"

"Hell, no! You had something bigger to bargain with, and I know for a fact that Victor never got that information from you." He reached his hand across the table and held it out to me as a peace offering. "Thanks. I owe you for that."

My hostility fizzled away as I shook his hand. "You're welcome."

Jenna looked quizzically back and forth from Eric to me. "What are you talking about?"

"Nothing," I said. "The less anyone knows, the better."

Eric nodded in agreement.

Jenna tossed her hands up in the air and fixed me with a withering glare. "Do you know how frustrating it is being your girlfriend?"

"Sorry, Jenna. I just can't."

"Can you at least tell me what it means that you've joined Victor?"

"I didn't join him," I snapped. "I've been forced to work for him. Whenever there's a time glitch, I have to fix it."

Jenna's brow furrowed. "Weren't you already fixing a whole bunch of glitches? How does this change things?"

"Yeah, I fixed a bunch of glitches. But there were also months where my jump device was stashed away and I completely ignored it because I freakin' hate time jumping. Who knows how many other glitches I missed? But now I can't skip any. It doesn't matter if I'm sick or on vacation or still recovering from the wounds of my last jump—it's now my job and only my job. And if I slip up in even the slightest way, Victor could kill me, both of you, the entire group, and pretty much anyone else I've ever talked to."

Jenna paled while Eric's jaw dropped.

"Yup," I said. "That's how I bought my life—by selling my freedom."

"What about Sam?" Jenna asked. "Is she part of this too?"

Eric's brow furrowed in confusion. "Who's Sam?"

Inwardly, I cursed. Jenna was probably the smartest person in my school. Yet she had an annoying habit of bringing up things that didn't need to be brought up. "She's my time-jumping partner," I said.

Eric blinked a few times, then slapped his palms against the table—a loud, hard smack that made people turn to look. "You have a partner you've never told me about? A girl?"

"You didn't know about her either?" Jenna shook her head. "Don't feel bad. He told me only a few days ago that Sam was a girl." Jenna's eyes narrowed and her voice dripped venom.

I raised my hands defensively. "I should have told you both about her. And I'm sorry I didn't. But I promise I won't hide stuff from you anymore"—I looked straight into Jenna's eyes—"unless it is necessary to protect someone's life."

"All right," Eric sighed. "If I'm going to help you, we need to come clean. No more secrets or any more of this 'need-to-know' crap."

"What?" Jenna said. "Both of you just pulled that on me."

Eric ignored her and looked me squarely in the eyes. "Agreed?"

"Agreed," I said. "And exactly how do you want to help?"

"I don't know," Eric said. "Like I told you before, my plans were to go time jumping with you. I thought we'd be a team, fighting Victor's guys as they plundered the past." He shifted uneasily in his seat. "Guess you don't need me for that. But there has to be something I can do. I'll be damned if I'm going to just sit on my ass and watch Victor win."

"What about your dads? Aren't you worried Victor will do something to them if he finds out we're working together?"

Eric snorted. "If I don't do something now, they'll be dead in a few months anyway."

"I want in, too," Jenna said.

"Uh-uh. No." Eric shook his head. "Terrible idea."

"It's too risky," I said.

Jenna's back stiffened. "From what I understand, I'm at risk just being your girlfriend." She looked around the coffee shop to make sure no one was listening, then leaned in close and lowered her voice. "Not to mention you keep telling me how the whole world is doomed if Victor wins. So what's riskier: sitting here on my butt doing nothing or helping you stop him?"

She had me there. I looked up at Eric, but he merely shrugged. "She has a point."

"Fine," I sighed.

Jenna threw her arms around me. "Thank you!"

I winced as my sore ribs stung under her overly enthusiastic embrace. "Okay, so we're the Three Amigos. Now what?"

Jenna released me from her hug, then looked at me with a wolf-like smile on her face. The look she got when she knew what she wanted and wasn't going to let anything stand in her way. "We'll think of something. We're smart, and we have nothing to lose. And, best of all, Victor thinks you're under his thumb now, so you don't have to hide from him anymore."

She made it sound so easy, as if the three of us would spend a night or two brainstorming and just figure out some way to defeat a worldwide conspiracy rooted in centuries of history. Would she still be so optimistic when I told her the full scope of Victor's plans, or would we actually figure out the one weakness that we could exploit to bring his entire scheme crashing down?

Only time would tell . . . and unfortunately it was running out.

CHAPTER 28

Like a crumbling monument to apathy, Sam's house stood at the end of the street, second last on the right. Weeds sprouted from the unmown lawn, and a set of bald tires leaned against the front step, while the roof had a sag to it that I didn't remember. This place seemed to deteriorate a bit more every time I visited—just like my relationship with Sam.

I climbed the cracked concrete steps and stood on the landing. Butterflies fluttered in my stomach like they always did when I visited Sam, and with a trembling finger, I rang the doorbell. How would she react when she saw me? What if her awful stepdad answered? Was anyone even home? So many terrible possibilities.

A few seconds later, soft footsteps padded toward the door—too light to be the slob her mom had married. The door opened and Sam stood there, dressed in a loose blue T-shirt and a baggy pair of gray track pants, her red hair cascading in a wild tangle over her shoulders. My pulse still quickened at the sight of her, and my palms got so sweaty I had to wipe them on my pants.

"H-hi," I stammered.

"I was kind of wondering when you'd show up." She leaned casually against the door frame, looking neither angry nor excited to see me. She gave off a heavy *meh* vibe, which, considering everything that had gone on between us in Greece, was a good thing.

"Am I that predictable?" I asked, trying to keep the conversation flowing.

"Yeah. You are. You've visited me after every other time jump, so I figured you weren't going to break the pattern."

"I know I said this in Greece, but I need to say it again. I'm really, *really* sorry about what I said about your dad. It's not true. I'm positive he loved you."

Her cheeks flushed. "I'm actually kind of . . . embarrassed about how I handled that. We were on a time jump and you're my partner. I never should have abandoned you, no matter how much you hurt me. The second I landed at home I said the words to send me back to Greece, but the stupid jump device decided to land me much farther down the coast and two days after I left you. It took me hours to run back to the battle." She clenched her fists in front of her chest. "You could have died because of me. So I'm sorry too."

"The important thing is you made it back in time to save my ass—again." I gave her a hopeful two-thumbs-up. "So are we good?"

"We are." She fixed me with a hard look. "But promise me we'll never argue like that on a jump again."

I raised my hand. "I promise."

She peered closely at my face, no doubt noticing the fading bruises, then her gaze dropped to the splint on my left fingers. "What happened to you?" A tinge of concern was in her voice. "You didn't have those in Greece."

"Victor and I had a chat. He had questions and didn't like my answers."

She shook her head, and a tired smile played across her lips. "So . . . not trying to sound rude or anything, but why are you here? Hopefully not just to apologize. Did you come all this way just for your jump device? I could have FedExed it back to you."

"Don't worry." I held up my hands. "No drama this time. I'm actually here to talk to your mom."

Sam's brows arched. "Did you hear that they added this really cool feature to phones where you can actually call people and talk to them? It saves you hundreds on travel costs."

"Ha ha, very funny. I need to see your mom in person. I need to see her reactions. I need to be able to press her in case she gets evasive."

"So nothing about you traveling all the way here just to interrogate my mom strikes you as the least bit dramatic?"

"I meant that there wouldn't be any drama between you and me. I know this sounds strange, but . . . I have to ask her something about your dad."

Sam crossed her arms over her chest. "And why can't you ask me?"

"Because I honestly don't think you have the answers I need." I reached into my backpack and took out a book. "I almost forgot. I brought you something."

She turned the book over and smiled at the familiar image of a werewolf and a vampire on its cover.

"In order to save over two thousand years of culture and literature, I had to burn your copy when you left it behind in Greece. So I kind of owed you another one."

She thumbed through the book and her eyes narrowed. "Have you been reading it?" She looked like she was trying hard not to laugh. "Some of the pages are dog-eared."

"No!" I said . . . but probably a bit *too* emphatically.

"I knew it!"

"Just a few pages at the airport . . . and on the plane."

She put her hands on her hips and tapped her foot. "How far did you get?" Her eyes had a mischievous sparkle to them.

"I'm not telling."

She chuckled again. "You read the whole thing, didn't you?"

"Maybe . . ."

"Does your precious little girlfriend know her big hero reads books like this, or do you hide that from her, too?"

"Hey! I actually told her about you."

"*Everything?* Even what you said to me after Mongolia?"

"Yup."

"Really?" Sam asked incredulously. "How'd she handle that? Are some of those bruises on your face from her?"

"She was angry, but we worked it out."

"Wow . . ." Sam shook her head in disgust. "That's pathetic. You wouldn't catch me staying with a guy who said he loved someone else."

"It's not pathetic!"

"Uh-huh. You keep thinking that." She moved out of the doorway and waved me inside. "My mom's in the kitchen."

The usual pile of shoes lay scattered across the foyer floor, and the faint odor of must and cigarettes hung in the air. I kicked off my shoes and followed Sam toward the back of the house and the kitchen.

As we passed the living room, I noticed that her stepdad wasn't in his usual spot in front of the TV. "Did you finally kill him and bury his body in the woods?"

"Not yet," Sam said flatly. "He's on a hunting trip. I'm hoping he and his buddies all get drunk and shoot each other."

In the kitchen, Sam's mom was washing dishes. Marlene almost always wore overly tight jeans and shirts—and today was no exception. She turned her head at our approach and brushed a strand of black hair away from her cheek. "Oh . . . it's you," she sniffed when she saw me, like I was some annoying stray cat begging for food.

Not the best greeting, but better than the one she had given me the first time we met.

"Hi, Marlene." I flashed her a smile. "Can I talk to you?"

She leaned back against the counter and shook a cigarette from its pack. "You're talking to me right now, ain't ya?"

"If you don't mind, I want to talk to you about your first husband's friends."

She jabbed a finger at me. "First off, he was my *ex*-husband. And second, nothing good will come from dredging up the past. Although, judging by those bruises on your face, that don't scare you none."

"Please, I'm desperate."

"You're wasting your time," Sam said. "All she knows is booze and bingo."

"Watch your mouth, girl," Marlene snarled at Sam. With slow, practiced motions, Marlene lit her cigarette, inhaled, and blew out a cloud of smoke. "Whaddya want to know?" she asked me.

"Did Robert ever mention someone named Victor?"

Her eyes narrowed. "Yeah. There was a Victor that used to come 'round our house in the early days. Why?"

"Do you know his last name?"

"He never told me, but I'm pretty sure he's the same one who's running for president." She pinched the bridge of her nose and shook her head. "Geez . . . did I ever pick the wrong one. The loser I chose couldn't find two nickels to rub together, and there's his friend, about to run the country."

"Do you remember what kind of stuff they'd talk about?"

"Nope. They kept themselves real quiet when I was around. Which was fine by me. I didn't want to know. Robert was an unhappy man, so he couldn't have been up to no good."

"Did Robert ever tell you what he and Victor were doing?"

Marlene snorted. "He never told me nothing, and if he did, I didn't listen. The man was a born liar, and there's only so much lying a person can take before they give up believing." I winced, thinking how much I'd lied to Jenna.

Marlene leaned back, with the heels of both her hands pressing down on the counter's edge behind her. "Anything else you want to know?"

"Robert must have had notes or books or something, right? And Steven probably took them after Robert was killed. But what happened to them after Steven died?"

"I burned 'em," Marlene said, full of defiance. "Every last one."

"What? Why?" I sputtered.

"Because I didn't want Samantha getting any ideas. Fat lot of good it did—she managed to find that stupid time-travel thingamajig anyway. And look at her now." Marlene waved a hand toward Sam. "Does that girl look happy? Nope. She looks just like her father and brother—miserable."

Beside me, Sam stiffened. "Dad was always happy with *me*. Maybe he was just miserable whenever he was around you."

Marlene's head bowed, and she stared at the faded linoleum under her feet. "I know you hate me, girl. But everything I ever did was for you."

"Everything you did?" Sam fumed, her face turning red. "Since when does leaving your family count as being a good mother? The only reason you even took me back is 'cause Steven died. And look at this crap heap you dragged me to!" She waved her hand around the kitchen. "And let's not forget all the money you've taken from me, or the fact that the creep you married refuses to fix the bathroom door lock just so he can 'accidentally' walk in whenever I'm taking a shower. So thanks, Mom . . . Thanks for everything."

Marlene's lips curled as if she'd just chugged sour milk. "You think it's easy for me? Do you know what it's like raising a daughter who won't even give me the time of day? I'm sorry I'm not your father. I'm sorry I left you. But I'm not a bad person. I'm your mom. I love you, Samantha. If only you knew the things I've done for you."

"Like what?" Sam crossed her arms over her chest.

"I . . ." Marlene turned her back to us and stared out the window over the sink. "Another time," she said softly.

"I knew it!" Tears welled up in Sam's eyes and her cheeks turned red. "Even you can't think of anything nice you've ever done for me!" She stomped toward the back door.

"Sam! Wait!" I cried, but she tore off into the backyard, racing toward the forest that sprawled behind her house.

I stood there watching her through the screen door—running again, like she always did. Before Mongolia, I would have gone after her and tried my best to just listen and be there for her. But if I tried that now, would she still want that, or should I just give her space to cool down?

"I hate that tattoo of yours," Marlene said quietly. "And I really hate that Samantha's involved with all this mess. But I can tell you love her. And no man should let the woman he loves run away like that." She flicked her hand toward me in a shooing gesture. "Don't just stand there. Go get her!"

I dashed out the back door. Sam was nowhere to be seen, but I knew where she'd go. Through a gap in the trees, I found a well-worn path leading deeper into the woods. I ran along it, brushing aside the maple saplings and ferns blocking my way. After a few minutes, the trail ended at the bank of a slow-moving stream, where a large fallen tree lay next to the edge. Sam sat facing the water, with her back resting against the tree trunk and her knees pulled up to her chest.

This clearing brought a flood of bad memories to mind. It was here that Sam had ripped my heart out and tossed me aside after I told her I loved her. But that was my problem. Right now, she needed me.

Gingerly, I sat next to her, the rough bark of the tree trunk pressing into my back. She looked at me with teary eyes. "Why did my dad have to die? Why did I have to get stuck with *her*?" She uttered the last word like it pained her to even say it.

There was a sadness in Sam's voice that I'd rarely heard before. I'd never seen her look so vulnerable. I wanted to hold her tightly, to comfort her, and to assure her everything would be all right. But there was still a huge divide between us, and I didn't want to make it wider by doing the wrong thing. "Yeah, it sucks," I said instead. A nice safe answer.

She rested her head on her knees and turned her face my way. "When do you have to go back?"

"I got a one-way ticket—I'm not sure where I'm going next. Why?"

"Do you want to stay over tonight?" She wiped her eyes with the back of one hand.

Huh?

I ran her words over again in my head, making sure I'd heard them correctly. "What happened to keeping things strictly professional?"

"I know that's what I said, but right now I just need a friend. I'm so lonely here. I don't want to be stuck alone in the house with her."

"Will your mom be okay with that? I'm not exactly her favorite person."

"She'll be too drunk to notice, and I'm long past caring what she thinks."

A few months back, I would have jumped at this invitation, but now I wasn't sure how to answer. Was this some sort of weird test Sam was throwing at me? How would Jenna react when I told her that I stayed over?

Sam sensed my hesitation. "Please?"

No matter how distant Sam had been over the last three months, no matter how much she had pushed me away, I still couldn't say no to her. "All right."

For a moment, the only sounds were birds calling to each other in the trees and the gurgle of the stream as it trickled past. I closed my eyes and tried to bask in the calm, to just feel the sunlight on my face as it poked through the leafy canopy. This blip of peace was the closest thing I'd had to a vacation in months.

"Why were you asking my mom all those questions?" Sam asked, destroying the moment.

"Because Victor is going out of his way to protect you, and I want to know why. It might be a weakness we could exploit."

"And you think my mom would know the reason for that?" Sam snorted. "When it comes to time jumping, she'll never have anything helpful or nice to say."

"It's okay. I might be able to get the information from another source."

She lifted her head. "Who?"

"Do you remember that jerk Chris in Greece?"

"Ugh!" She visibly shuddered. "How could I forget?"

"Well, I took his jump device. I've already arranged the swap."

"Where's Chris?"

I stared at the ground and shook my head. "He's not coming back."

She gasped. "You didn't."

"Yeah. It turns out Jerry was his dad. He was a bit displeased, to put it mildly, that Victor let me live."

"Oh, geez . . . I'm sorry." She rested a hand on my arm. "Are you okay?"

"No. Not really. I ordered Chris's death. Just waved my hand, and all these spears slammed into him. I've killed lots of people, but always in self-defense or to save history. But how do I justify this? He was annoying? He had something I wanted?" I exhaled slowly and stared at my hands. "I didn't wield the spear, but his death is on me."

"Did you really think we could defeat Victor without shedding some blood?" She looked at me with a mixture of sadness and pity. "You've been watching too many superhero movies if you believe that. People are going to die, and it sucks that it will be at our hands. But if we actually want to defeat Victor's plan, do we have any other option?"

"I know we don't. But every time I come back from a time jump, another little part of the old me is gone and I've crossed some line that I never imagined I'd cross. Each time, I make excuses for my behavior so I don't end up hating myself. But at what point will I look in the mirror and see a complete stranger staring back at me?"

Sam grabbed both my hands. "These doubts prove you haven't lost what makes you Dan." She gave me a weak smile. "Besides, we're a team. I'll tell you if you've gone too far."

"We're still a team? Even after Greece?"

"Of course. Sure, we both did some stuff we regret, but we apologized to each other and no one died, so I'm not ready to break this team up. Are you?"

"Hell no!"

"Great!" She squeezed my hands tightly. "Now tell me what happened with Victor . . . the full story."

I told her everything I'd learned from Chris and Jerry about how Victor's guys were using time jumps to create a huge secret organization that stretched back hundreds of years, and how Chris died but Jerry managed to escape. I told her about Stewart and Tim rushing off to kill Victor, my kidnapping and subsequent beating, the deal I had to make with Victor to save my life, Stewart and Tim dying, and how Jerry used his lies to turn my little group against me.

"Wow! That's quite the week." Sam pushed her hair back from her face with both hands. "And you think the only reason you're still alive is because of me? And that my mom might know something? Even if my mom had some huge secret to reveal, like I'm her love child with Victor, so what? What would you actually do with that information? I mean, Victor's guys are manipulating history. How could *anything* my mom told you help us stop that?"

"I don't know. I'm grasping at straws here." I tossed my hands up in frustration. "The more we learn about Victor, the stronger he seems."

Sam looked me squarely in the eyes. "Our plan has always been to get information from Eric's dads and see if we could find something they missed. Can we just stick to the plan and see what they've got?"

"But what if they have nothing? It's June now; elections are in"—I counted off on my fingers—"five months. We're running out of time. We need to come up with some radical ideas."

Sam leaned her back against the tree trunk. "I hope you're not thinking about that mythical city you saw in the time stream."

"It's not mythical!"

"Has anyone other than you seen it, been there, or even heard of it?"

"Well . . . no. At least not that I know of."

"Gee, you're right, Dan," Sam said with mock seriousness. "That doesn't sound mythical at all. I should have said delusional."

"It's real, Sam! I've seen it twice."

Sam raised her hands. "Okay, I believe you. But can we leave traveling to the city that no one but you has ever seen as Plan B . . . or C . . . or Z, and stick with seeing what Eric's dads have to offer? Then we can make a plan for our next jump."

"Next jump?" I looked at her in surprise. "You realize that I have to go on all of them now, right? Are you still going to come with me—on all of them?"

"Of course. We're a team." She smiled at me, and a there was a sparkle in her eyes that I hadn't seen in a long time. "Besides, who else is going to save your from your own stupidity?"

I didn't take the slightest offense at Sam's comment. I sucked at time jumping. To me it was one nightmare after another. It was only luck and Sam's incredible skill that had kept me alive. And ever since my "meeting" with Victor, I'd had this nagging feeling of dread hovering over me that my luck was about to run out. But knowing that Sam would be going back with me replaced the dread with hope—maybe I wouldn't die after all. "Sam? You're awesome."

"I know," she said nonchalantly.

We sat with our backs against the fallen tree, staring off into the forest. The silence didn't feel awkward; it felt like how things used to be on our first two jumps, before things got complicated between us.

After a few minutes, Sam jerked her thumb toward her house. "Want to ditch the forest and head into town? You know, grab a pizza or something?"

"Food? Always."

CHAPTER 29

Sam had always described her town as two gas stations and a grocery store dumped in the middle of nowhere, with absolutely nothing to do around them. It turned out her picture wasn't far off the mark. But somehow we managed to kill a few hours getting food, playing mini-golf on a run-down course that was partially taken over by possums, and just talking. It felt kind of weird to be having this much fun after how distant Sam had been lately, but I tried not to overthink it.

After stopping by my motel to pick up my backpack and to check out, we got back to her house around nine. We found Marlene passed out on the faded green couch, the TV on and an empty wine bottle lying on the carpet beside her outstretched hand.

Sam lifted her chin, stared straight down the hallway, and stomped past the living room, not uttering a word until we reached her room. "Make yourself comfortable," she suggested as she rummaged through her drawers. "I'm going to get changed."

She headed off to the bathroom, leaving me alone. I changed into pajama pants, then looked around while I waited for her to return. It still seemed odd that the deadliest woman I knew surrounded herself with a room full of unicorn posters, stuffed animals, and figurines, but

I knew her father had given her all of them, so mocking her collection was out of the question.

Sam returned a minute later in a long, loose T-shirt and flannel pajama pants. She hopped onto her bed and tapped the spot right beside her. "Let's watch a movie. I have one I think you'll like."

Bed? Beside her?

I took a step back. "What's going on here, Sam? For the last three months, you've been about as friendly as an automated answering service. And I get it—but now you're acting like none of that happened." I held my hands out to my sides. "Don't get me wrong. I *want* things to go back to how they used to be between us. But I'm so freakin' confused."

Sam twirled a lock of red hair around a finger and began chewing on the ends, not responding for a few seconds. "When we had our fight in Greece, you said I had no friends . . . that I pushed everyone away." Her voice was quiet and she avoided looking at me. "I was angry at the time, but . . . you were right." She bowed her head. "You're my only friend. And I pushed you away too. I just . . . miss you." She looked up at me and her green eyes were heavy with sadness, but she raised her brow hopefully. "Friends again?"

I smiled. "Of course. I miss you too. I hope—"

She raised her hand to cut me off. "Just friends, though. Nothing more."

My smile didn't fade. "Got it. So what's the movie?"

She reached into the drawer of her nightstand and pulled out her laptop. Tilting herself so I couldn't see her screen, she logged in, hit a few keys, and then proudly turned the display my way. The opening frame of *300* showed on the screen, ready to play.

"No way! I love this movie."

"I know." Her eyes sparkled with mischief. "Since you had such kind things to say about my book choices, we might check out the Oscar-worthy masterpieces you like to watch."

"Oh . . ." I hopped onto the bed next to her and she set up her laptop between us. "There might be a *few* historical inaccuracies," I admitted.

"You mean this isn't going to be an incredibly accurate representation of the original battle?" she said with mock surprise. "I'm sure the acting will be great, at least." She chuckled, hit play, and lay down next to me, so our heads shared the same pillow and our shoulders were touching.

"Thanks for staying," she said softly.

"No problem."

For the rest of the movie, I lay next to Sam, laughing at the bad acting and ridiculous battle scenes and comparing the actors to the real-life men who had heroically given up their lives for Greece. But most of the time, I didn't even watch the screen, I just studied Sam's face out of the corner of my eye. The way her lips curled when she smiled, or how the corners of her eyes creased when she concentrated. And the more I watched her, the guiltier I felt. What was I doing here with her when Jenna was waiting for me back home?

When the movie ended, Sam snapped the laptop shut, then turned to me with a smirk. "So that's your favorite movie, huh?"

"It's not my *favorite*. I just . . . like it." I shrugged. "So what great movie masterpiece is *your* favorite?"

Sam laughed. "Wouldn't you like to know?" She got up from the bed and placed her laptop on the nightstand. "But you'll have to wait to find out. I don't think I can stay awake for another."

"Are you heading to bed?" It was past eleven, but tomorrow was Sunday, so who knew if Sam had any other surprises planned?

"Yeah. I think so." She rubbed the heels of her palms across her eyes. "I had kind of a busy week, and I haven't gotten caught up on my sleep yet."

I was sort of relieved—I wasn't really looking for more situations where I'd feel guilty over Jenna. "So uh . . . where do I sleep?"

She pulled out an extra comforter and pillow from the top shelf of her closet and passed them to me. "Any spot on the floor's fine. Except by the window—it leaks when it rains."

I laid the comforter beside her bed, then we took turns using the bathroom. As I lay down on the floor, she slid under her unicorn comforter. "Do you need one of my awesome unicorns to cuddle up with tonight?" She chucked a purple plush toy at me that caught me in the side of the head before rolling to a stop.

I pitched it back at her but missed. "I think I'm good."

"Good night, then!" She flicked off the lamp beside her bed, plunging the room into darkness.

"Good night, Sam." I lay there on the floor, staring up at the ceiling, and not feeling the slightest bit tired. The day had been a huge emotional roller coaster. As much as I wanted things to be back to normal between me and Sam, it still felt weird to just go from zero to a hundred like that. And what was to stop her from changing her mind and banishing me back to the barely-a-friend zone?

Why did Sam always have to be so confusing? Jenna didn't play all these games.

A pang of guilt wrapped around my chest. Why had I even stayed at Sam's? She said she needed a friend, but was that the only reason I was there? Did some delusional part of me think she'd somehow change her mind about me?

I couldn't keep doing this to Jenna. Either I accepted that Sam and I had no future and fully committed myself to Jenna, or I cut Jenna free so she could find her own happiness. I had to make a choice.

The next morning, I woke to the smell of fresh-brewed coffee and the glow of sun shining through the window. I opened my eyes, expecting to see Sam still sleeping, but the bed was empty.

A glance at my phone showed it was nine thirty. I wandered to the kitchen, figuring Sam might be making us breakfast.

She wasn't there, but Marlene was—at the table playing solitaire, a cigarette sitting in the ashtray in front of her, smoke curling up from the tip. Dark circles hung under her eyes and her hair fell haphazardly around her face, twisted out of shape from her night on the couch. "Samantha's gone," Marlene said without looking up.

"Since when?"

"About twenty minutes ago."

"Do you know when she'll be back?"

"Knowing her, probably not till nighttime." Marlene flipped a card onto a stack.

"Okay . . ." This was awkward.

"That's Samantha." Marlene gave out a sound halfway between a chuckle and a snort. "That girl's like a dang cat. Only gives affection when she wants to. And even then it don't last long." She motioned with a card toward the counter. "Coffee's over there."

I poured myself a cup and then stood next to the sink, trying to decide if I should wait around for Sam or go find her.

Marlene waved to the seat across from her. "Sit for a bit. I wanna talk to you."

I warily sat down. "About what?"

Marlene leaned forward and put both hands flat on the table. "You need to learn to let sleeping dogs lie." There was a sternness to her voice I hadn't heard before. "Coming in here and talking about Robert ain't never gonna lead to nothing good, especially with Samantha around."

"Sorry. I just wanted to know about Victor. I didn't want to stir up anything."

"I know you didn't mean no harm." Marlene's tone softened. "But understand that Samantha ain't never gonna hear nothing bad about her father. She can't accept that Robert was a born loser. Couldn't hold a job. Couldn't keep no promises. And definitely couldn't hold a family together. Anything he was involved in wouldn't have amounted to no good."

I took a sip of my coffee. "Did you really throw *everything* away? Or did you just say that so Sam wouldn't ask for it?"

Marlene dragged a hand through her hair the same way Sam always did. "Nope. Got rid of all his damn stuff. Like I said, the man was never up to no good. And poor Steven just worshipped him, and followed along the same shady path. Those two were thick as thieves. I did my best, after Steven died, to keep Samantha clear of all their doings." Her lips curled in distaste. "But she found that damn time-travel stick before I did."

"You said Steven was on a shady path. Do you have any idea who might have killed him?"

"Nope," Marlene replied flatly. "Probably just some drunk." She hugged her coffee mug with both hands, holding it close to her chest. "You probably should be going now. Who knows when Sam will be back, and I'm heading to town. I can't have you here alone in the house."

"No problem. Thanks for the coffee."

I took my mug and headed for Sam's room. When I opened my backpack to grab a change of clothes, I found a note on top of them. It wasn't pink or purple, or anything fancy like Jenna would use—just a simple sheet of lined paper that looked like it had been torn out of a school notebook.

Dan,

Yesterday was fun. We should do it again someday. Unfortunately, I have to work all day today, so I guess I'll see you on the next time jump.

Sam

And, just like that, our reunion was over. No touching goodbye, no chance of another great day—just a short, impersonal note hinting for me to leave. I sighed and changed into my jeans and a fresh T-shirt. It was always like that with Sam—a brief moment when she let her walls down and let me into her life, before raising them up and casting me out again.

I left before Marlene could drop any more not-so-subtle hints. As I stood on the street outside, I mulled over my next move. For a second, I thought about visiting Sam at work, but she'd already said her goodbye in her note. Showing up at her work would only make me look desperate and needy, as usual. Better to just head back home.

I gave one last look at Sam's house, pulled out my phone, and arranged for a ride to the airport. Then I just stood there at the side of the road, thinking about my visit. I'd hoped Marlene would tell me more about Sam's dad and why Victor went out of his way to protect Sam, but that ended up being a huge waste of time. The only good thing that came out of the visit was that Sam and I seemed to have restored our relationship to pre-Mongolia levels. Hopefully, she wouldn't change her mind and start ghosting me again.

I texted Jenna to tell her I was heading for the airport. A few seconds later, my phone showed a video call coming in from her.

"You're coming home already?" she asked as soon as her face came on screen. "Is everything okay?" I could hear the unspoken question in her voice. She wanted to know if something had happened between me and Sam. And who could blame her? She knew I loved Sam, but she still hadn't argued one bit when I told her I was going to visit.

"Yeah, everything's fine. I'm just done here."

"That was quick." There was an unmistakable note of optimism in her tone. "Did you get all the answers you were looking for?"

"Not really. Overall, a disappointment."

"That's too bad. When do you think you'll be home?"

"Hopefully tonight." A gray hatchback turned onto Sam's street. "It looks like my ride's coming. I'll text you when I have a flight."

"Have a safe trip." She paused and I could see the hopeful look on her face. "I love you."

For a second I froze. There was no way I could escape answering this time. "Um . . . thanks," I said, then silently cursed at my weak response. Even after how much I'd hurt Jenna when I'd told her about Sam, she still said she loved me. And her voice had a little lilt at the end; she clearly hoped I would say the words back. She deserved a better response than a grunted thanks, but what? I definitely felt something for her. It wasn't the same thing I felt for Sam, but was that Jenna's fault? Despite being nearly inseparable over the last few months, I had never allowed her to be number one in my heart—I had always been holding that spot for Sam.

Come on, Dan. There's no future with Sam.

I swallowed hard. "I . . . I love you too," I blurted before I could over analyze things and chicken out.

Jenna eyes widened and her entire face glowed with happiness. "I . . . I . . ." This was the first time I'd ever seen her at a loss for words. "I can't wait to see you again."

"Me too." I smiled. "But I gotta go. The car's here." I quickly ended the call, tossed my stuff in the trunk, and then slid into the back seat.

As the car began the long drive to the airport, I gazed out the rear window. Even though I had made my choice, it still pained me to watch Sam's house recede into the distance, as if this was the final goodbye, the end of an era. I would still see Sam on time jumps, but I was pretty sure this was the last time I'd ever see her home. Despite some of the painful memories I had here, I also some had some that I would cherish forever, and I would miss visiting. But if I wanted to give my relationship with Jenna a serious chance, I couldn't keep coming here. Then there was the other issue that hovered over me like a dark storm cloud. In only a few short months Victor would unleash his worldwide destruction, and would this street, as I knew it, even exist after that?

I turned away from Sam's house. I couldn't look back any more. I had to look forward—to stopping Victor. And my only hope now was the time-jumping archive that Dave and Brian still owed me. Those files had cost me my freedom to Victor and had earned me a permanent enemy in Jerry. Time to find out if the information they held was worth the price.

CHAPTER 30

At the far end of the dirt road, just visible through a field of waist-high grass, stood a decrepit barn. Its clapboards had faded to a dull gray, and the roof had long ago rusted to a dark orange-brown. It looked like the place had been deserted for ages. It also looked like a perfect trap.

I stopped in the middle of the road and turned in a slow circle, one hand above my eyes to shield the sun's glare. The grass rustled gently and insects buzzed among the tall stalks, but otherwise, nothing stirred. If someone was hiding in the fields nearby, I couldn't see them.

I also couldn't see Dave's minivan or any other sign that he or Brian were there, which was weird, considering they were the ones who had forced me out to this little piece of forgotten countryside.

It would have been so much easier for us to just meet up at some coffee shop in town. We'd sit down, grab a coffee, they'd pass me the laptop, and then all would be done. But no, they insisted that we meet up here, saying it was the only place we could be sure that Victor's men wouldn't be watching us.

I wasn't even allowed to drive all the way here. I had to ditch my car at some sketchy gas station, then hike for about an hour through mosquito-infested woods.

With anybody else, I would have just refused the meeting. But I was so desperate for the information they owed me, I couldn't say no. Besides, the three of us had a history of meeting at weird places and times. These guys were paranoid with a capital *P*—but considering they were ex-time jumpers who had managed so far to survive Victor, I couldn't fault them for being overly cautious.

After adjusting the straps of my backpack, I set off again. A metallic rustle came from the backpack as the various weapons inside shifted. I allowed myself a brief smile. The three of us also had a history of trying to kill each other. If Dave and Brian were planning something, I'd be ready.

I crept to the side of the barn and peered around the corner. A small door stood slightly ajar, with Dave just visible through the gap, standing in front of a workbench that ran along one wall. His long gray hair was pulled back in a ponytail, and he wore faded jeans and a plaid flannel shirt with the sleeves rolled up. He had a kind of old-farmer look to him, like he'd dressed to match the meeting place. In his hands he was holding a dust-covered sword, which he was attempting to clean with an oily rag.

The sword had probably been a decent weapon once. Now, though, its blade looked dull, and the steel had lost its shine. I watched him for a few more seconds, trying to spot anything that would warn me of a trap, but Dave looked cool and calm, almost nostalgic, as if polishing that sword brought back fond memories.

My knuckles rapped sharply on the door, and Dave's head snapped up. "Hey! I wasn't sure you'd find the place." He seemed genuinely pleased to see me, but he could also just be a good actor. It was still too early for me to let my guard down.

I took a step inside the barn, just enough to see its interior but still keep a view of the outside. A cluster of fluorescent lights bathed this side of the barn in a cool, sterile light. Opposite the workbench, a row of wood pegs ran about waist-high above the floor, with spears, swords, axes, and staves standing between them. A layer of dust coated the weapons, and thin strands of cobwebs seemed to bind them together. In the center of the floor, a large rectangular area had been covered with blue gym mats. Cracks ran through the vinyl covers, and loose foam lay strewn across the floor from where mice had been chewing at the mats.

"I almost didn't. Not exactly easy to get to."

"That's why I chose it. It's safer out here. I bought it ages ago at a foreclosure auction for dirt cheap. But I haven't set foot in here in years." His eyes flitted over my bruised face and the splint on my left fingers. "You look like crap."

"I've had better days." I made a show of looking around the barn. "Where's Brian?"

"Getting supplies." Dave pulled a wad of steel wool from a drawer and attacked some rust spots on the sword's tang. A fine cloud of reddish dust sparkled in the beam of sunlight penetrating the dirty window. "You can come in. I'm not going to hurt you."

My eyes narrowed, but I didn't move. "What's with all the weapons?"

Dave's gaze slowly scanned the far wall and a brief smile lit up his face. "This is where we used to train."

"Used to? Why'd you stop?"

"Victor," Dave sighed, as if merely saying that name took up most of his energy. "He only wanted people loyal to the 'grand plan' to be time jumpers." Dave's jaw clenched, and he attacked the rust with rapid swipes. "I wasn't going to swear allegiance to his little band of homicidal maniacs, and I wasn't giving up time jumping either." He stopped scrubbing and glanced up to the dark recesses of the barn. "Brian and I tried to fight him. We tried to rally the other jumpers to help us. But you know how that turned out."

I did know. Victor had knocked them off one by one, either by murder or threats.

Dave tossed the sword onto the bench, where it landed with a hollow thud in a puff of dust. "The bastard ended up sending us a picture of Eric at his grade school, with a big red X drawn over him." Dave winced and shook his head. "That was the day we gave up our time-travel devices." He took a sad look at the weapons on the wall and the damaged mats. "Why bother training if you're never going to need it?"

He reached under the workbench and pulled out a black laptop. "Anyway, here's your payment."

Dave slid the laptop along the workbench toward me. "I heard through the grapevine that Chris Lucadamo didn't make it back from a jump." He pointed to my bruised face. "That from Jerry?"

"Yeah . . . he wasn't happy." I flipped open the laptop. A little yellow sticky note had been stuck to the top corner with a username and password.

Dave looked at me intently for a second, his expression unreadable. "What do you want this for anyway?"

"I'm looking for something specific." The laptop's screen lit up and I entered the login information. However, instead of seeing a normal computer screen, I was taken directly into the time-jumper archive app. With shaking hands, I typed in my dad's name and hit search. A moment later, his smiling face looked back at me from the photo on the page. I swallowed hard and felt a tightness around my chest as I read about all his achievements. How he had jumped at least twenty times to exciting spots in history.

I paused and turned my head away when I reached the end of his career.

Cause of death: Stabbing (Victor Stahl).

"Yup," Dave said. "Some of that's gonna be pretty tough to read. If there's anything particular you're looking for, maybe I can help you find it?"

I waved my hands helplessly at the monitor. After everything Jerry had told me about how Victor's guys were tweaking the past, I didn't know if anything in this mountain of information would actually help. "I *was* kinda hoping to find something that might help me stop Victor."

Dave snorted. "You're going to be disappointed. If I had that, I'd have used it myself."

"What about the jump device I gave you? You must have some plan for that."

"Nope." He bowed his head as if he couldn't look me in the eye. "That's my own personal escape pod. For now, I'll stick around in this time period and hope Victor chokes on a sandwich or one of his bodyguards decides to kill him. But as soon as that murderous prick wins the election, I'm going to catch the next time glitch, jump back into history, and just forget all about this world."

I could feel my jaw drop. "You're just going to abandon Brian and Eric?"

"Trust me, I'm not proud of my decision, and Brian isn't too happy with it either. But I'm done fighting. I don't care where the jump rod takes me. Anything will be better than staying here and watching Victor's plan unfold."

His words hit me like a slap in the face, and any respect I had developed for him crumbled to dust. "Do you have any idea what I went through to get that stupid thing? Why don't you fight Victor with it?"

Dave's head snapped up. "Listen, you arrogant little snot. I've been fighting Victor since before you were born." He jabbed a finger at me. "I've lost my friends, my time-travel device, and the last twenty years of my life, but the cold, hard reality is that he's won. If I couldn't kill him before, how am I going to kill him now that he has around-the-clock security?" He leaned back against the workbench and crossed his arms over his chest. "What am I supposed to do?"

"I don't know. But you don't give up. You keep fighting. You do . . . something."

"Like what? Die a needless death like your friends Stewart and Tim?" He flicked his hand dismissively. "Typical teenager. Complain about how adults do things but have no clue how to fix it themselves."

"Hey! Just because *they* were stupid, it doesn't mean I am. I *do* have ideas."

"Great, let's hear 'em." He waved his fingers toward me, urging me on. "I've heard *every* dumb idea imaginable, so let me tell you now why yours won't work, instead of you finding out by losing two more friends."

I shifted uneasily. Should I tell Dave what I really thought might work? Sam thought it was crazy. Would Dave just laugh at me too?

I stared at the top of the workbench. "Well . . . do you remember when we first met and I told you about a city floating in the time stream?"

Dave nodded.

"I want to go there."

I braced myself for some sort of mocking response, but Dave just stood there with his brow furrowed and one finger slowly tapping, with the rhythm of a leaky faucet, off the top of the workbench. "You've seen this city how many times? Once?"

"Twice."

The tempo of his tapping increased. "And you're sure you could find it again?"

"Yeah, all I have to do is—"

"No!" Dave raised both his hands. "Don't tell me. I don't want to know. The less I know about it, the better it is for you."

"So you believe me?"

"Yeah." His voice sounded distant, as if his mind was elsewhere. "And if there really is a city, then the last thing you want is for anyone else to know how to get there."

"Why?" A tiny flame of hope ignited in my chest. "What do you think it is?"

Dave scratched at his stubbled jaw. "There are three great mysteries of time jumping: Who created the devices? How do the things actually work? And why do glitches happen in the first place? People have been trying to answer these questions for ages. If you did see a city in the time stream, and you could get to it, you might get those answers."

"Right, that's what I'm thinking. Do you think I should go for it, or not?"

"I can't tell you what to do. All I can give you is advice based on my own experience. And I know for sure that trying to kill Victor in the present is next to impossible—we've tried repeatedly and failed. So what have you got to lose?" He gave me an encouraging smile. "It's one dumb idea that hasn't been tried, far as I know."

"But don't you want to know about this place? What if I fail? Don't you at least want to know how to get there?"

"Nope. If you fail, I will for sure." He spread his arms out wide. "Look at me, I'm over fifty, I'm overweight, and I haven't trained in years. My days of fighting and adventure are long past."

"But I don't even know if I'll survive trying to get there. There's this huge free fall and—"

Dave scoffed. "All the more reason I'll never go." He looked thoughtfully at the rusting weapons ranged along the wall. "But I'll help you. You name it, I'll get it for you. This city could be the break we need. If you want to stop Victor, you owe it to the world to try."

Horrible memories of that city flooded into my thoughts. The wind in the time stream viciously attacking me like it was a living thing. The terrifying freefall toward the city's central square. The huge garbage pile littering that same square, as if everything lost in the time stream ended up there. And the corpses lying amid all the garbage. I couldn't believe that horrific place was my best hope of stopping Victor.

"All right," I sighed. "Now if I can just figure out how to get there without dying in the process . . ."

"How big a drop is it?"

"Think skydiving into a parking lot."

"Ouch . . ." Dave ran a hand across his chin. "Parachute?"

"Wind's too intense, I think."

"Think? You need to know for sure."

"All right." I nodded. "Next time there's a time glitch, I'll check it out."

Dave picked the sword off the table and went at the rust again with his steel wool. "So what now? You got your archive. You have an idea. Anything else I can help you with?"

"I don't know. I might have questions about the stuff in the archive if you don't mind me hanging out a bit."

Dave shrugged. "Stay as long as you like. Happy for the company."

I grabbed the laptop and plunked myself down on the floor near the door. Searching the database, I found Sam's brother Steven fairly quickly. Under Cause of Death: Hit and run (unknown). I was kind of surprised at that one; I honestly expected one of Victor's men to have been the cause. Maybe Jerry had been telling the truth when he said that none of them were involved with Steven's death?

Next, I searched for Sam's dad, and within seconds Robert Cahill was staring out at me from the screen. I skipped all his time-travel achievements and went straight to the Cause of Death section: Multiple arrows.

Huh. No name or person associated with it? My dad's had Victor's name. Steven's had "unknown"; other people had "killed by locals." Why was Robert's blank?

"Hey, I think you're missing something here," I called to Dave.

"Whose page?" Dave asked in a distracted sort of way, clearly more interested in the sword.

"Robert Cahill."

The briefest blip of silence interrupted the rhythmic rasp of Dave's polishing. "What's missing?"

"It says he died from multiple arrows. But it's missing who shot the arrows."

Dave's body shifted ever so slightly. To an untrained observer, he'd still look relaxed, but I'd experienced too many fights not to notice the subtle change. He stood more lightly on his feet, and his hands curled almost imperceptibly around the sword's hilt. "Hmm . . . That is strange."

I set the laptop on the floor and slowly stood up, as if stretching my legs, before settling into my own casual stance. I didn't know why Dave's attitude had changed, but if he attacked, I'd be ready. "Do you happen to know who killed him?"

"Nah. Don't think we ever knew."

Something in his tone told me he was lying.

"Are you sure? I heard he was killed on a time jump, so it had to be someone in the community."

"Maybe Brian remembers." He casually lifted the sword off the workbench, pretending to inspect the blade for more rust.

C'mon, Dave. Don't do it.

"Great . . . thanks." I bent and reached into my backpack as if making room in it to put the laptop away. My hand closed on cold, sharp metal. "I'd appreciate it."

"It's important to you?" Dave's jaw clenched.

"Yeah, it really is."

Dave spun toward me, sword in hand. At the same moment, I sprang to my feet, three throwing stars in my hands. About ten steps separated us. Advantage me.

Dave's eyes focused on the star in my right hand, which hovered by my ear, ready to throw at the slightest movement. "One shuriken isn't going to stop me."

"It will if I bury it in your forehead," I warned.

Dave's eyes went from the shuriken to his own sword. I could tell he was calculating the distance between us and trying to figure out if he could reach me in time.

"Don't make me do this, Dave. Put the sword down."

His face twisted with hatred. "I can't believe you joined Victor after what he did to your father." He thrust his chin out defiantly. "So are *you* going to kill me, or is your little coward of a boss actually going to show up?"

"Wait . . . you think I sided with *Victor*?" My voice dripped with revulsion. "I'm trying to *kill* him. I'd never join his band of murderers."

"Then why are you here?" Dave challenged.

"To pick up the stupid laptop! You're the one who pulled a sword."

"And you're the one who brought a bag of weapons to a simple laptop pickup."

"You invited me out to some murder barn in the middle of nowhere! This place looks like the set of a horror movie! And based on our history, can you blame me for being cautious?"

A slight smile crossed Dave's lips. "No, I guess not." He lowered his sword a fraction. "If you're not with Victor, then why are you asking about Robert Cahill?"

With slow, exaggerated movements, I dropped my right hand to my side, though I still gripped the throwing star in case Dave made any sudden movements. "Why is his death such a secret? Victor won't tell me. His ex-wife won't tell me. Even Sam doesn't know what's going on."

"Sam?" Dave's brows lifted in confusion. "Who the hell is Sam?"

"His daughter."

Dave sucked in his breath as if I'd just revealed to him the location of a buried treasure. "You know where Samantha Cahill is?"

"Yeah. She's my time-jumping partner."

Dave raised the sword again and pointed it at me. "Now I know you're full of it!"

With my bandaged left hand, I clumsily reached for my phone and thumbed through my pictures. I picked one from our recent mini-golfing, placed my phone on the workbench, and slid it across to Dave.

"I'll be damned," he muttered as he studied the picture. "Those eyes and that hair are pure Robert. Does Victor know about this?"

"Yeah. It's probably the only reason I'm still alive. He wants me to watch out for her whenever we jump. Although, to be honest, she usually saves me."

Dave zoomed in on the picture and examined it closely for a few seconds. Then he began to chuckle to himself, almost like a madman. "Samantha Cahill is alive, a time jumper . . . and your partner." His shoulders sagged, and he dropped his sword onto the workbench, its metallic peal echoing through the quiet confines of the barn. "I never could understand why Victor kept you alive. *This* finally explains it."

I exhaled slowly, releasing the tension from my body as I put the throwing stars in my back pocket. "So we're good?"

"Yeah, truce."

"Can you please tell me what's going on, then? Why is Victor protecting Sam? And what happened to Robert?"

Dave scratched his jaw and looked me up and down. "You asking for yourself or for her?"

"Both, actually."

"You'd be better off not knowing," he warned.

"Nope. If I can jump through time and save history, I can handle the answer of who killed Sam's dad."

"Fair enough." Dave nodded. "But how do I know you won't run right back to Victor with the information?"

I slammed my fist against the barn's wooden door and a dull thud echoed inside the building. "Because he's a nutjob planning to kill billions of people! What more do you need?"

Dave took another glance at Sam's picture and then slid the phone across to me. "Okay. Eric said you took a massive beating at Jerry's hands in order to protect me and Brian, so I guess I can trust you. But it doesn't leave this barn, kid. Promise?"

"I promise."

Dave drew a hand down his face. He looked tired, as if he'd been carrying a huge burden for a long time. "You really want to know who killed Robert Cahill?" He jabbed a thumb at his chest. "I did."

My mind felt fuzzy, as if someone had just punched me in the head. I fully understood his words. I understood the thumb proudly aimed at his chest. I just couldn't understand what it all meant. "Y-you?"

Dave threw back his head and blew out a big breath. "Yeah, me. And that's my death sentence if Victor ever finds out."

"Why would Victor care?"

Dave laughed. "Now I *know* you're not working for Victor." He bent down and slid a blue plastic cooler out from under the workbench. "Come on, let's talk." He flipped a light switch, and a series of lights came on at the rear end of the barn, revealing a small sitting area with two wooden chairs, a plain coffee table, and an old, worn couch that was probably home to thousands of bugs.

Dave planted himself in one of the chairs and opened the cooler, pulling out a bottle of beer. "Want one?"

"No thanks. I'm good."

"Suit yourself." With a quick flick of his wrist, he opened the bottle and set it down on the table in front of him. "Sit." He leaned back in his chair and propped his feet up on the table.

Warily, I sat down. *What's going on here?*

Dave tilted back his bottle, polishing off about half of it in one guzzle. "I knew this day would come. A secret like that couldn't stay buried forever."

I leaned forward in my chair. "You're serious. You killed Sam's dad? Why?"

"I remember the moment so clearly . . . I don't think I'll ever forget it. That was the one point in my life when I could have done something big, and I failed." Dave swirled the bottle and watched the remaining beer circle around inside it for a few seconds. "It was early evening in a forest outside medieval Krakow. I don't know how I managed to sneak up so close without him noticing, but he was right there, hunched over his fire, with his back to me—a perfect target. And Robert was nowhere around."

"Wait. Weren't you aiming at Robert?"

"No." Dave gave me a wry grin. "I had bigger game in sight—Victor. He and Robert were time-jumping partners."

My head snapped back as if I'd been punched. "Partners? But Robert was on our side."

Dave shook his head and his lips drew tight. "No. No, no, no. Sorry, kid. Robert was rotten to the core."

I gaped incredulously at Dave as my mind tried to make sense of this news. Could Sam's dad have been working *with* Victor? No. Dave had to be wrong.

"Anyway, I had that bastard lined up, and he had no clue I was there." Dave drew his arm back like he was pulling an invisible bowstring. "I was so excited about taking him down that my hands were shaking. I needed to take a few breaths to steady myself." He dropped his arm and shook his head. "That one little pause changed everything. Robert came back right then, and I don't know what tipped him off, but he pushed Victor out of the way just as I released my bowstring. The arrow missed Victor and hit Robert in the side. My one chance . . . and I blew it." Dave drained the rest of his beer and slammed the bottle on the table. "Victor took off into the forest like the cowardly little turd that he is, and I don't think he ever time-jumped again. He stays locked up in his DC office all the time now."

Dave exhaled loudly and tilted his head back to stare at the rafters. "As for Robert, the first arrow didn't kill him. So I shot him a few more times to finish the job. I have to hand it to him, he was one tough bugger. He still managed to jump home with all those arrows stuck in him." He reached into the cooler and opened another beer. "I read about his death a few days later. Steven must have called some of Victor's people to clean things up, because the news said his body was found in an alley and police called it a mugging gone wrong." He took another long pull on his beer. "And there you have it, the true story of how Robert Cahill died."

I wished I had accepted the beer so I could wash down the bile rising in my throat. I'd finally found out something I'd been dying to know, and it didn't make me one bit happier. I felt worse, like my entire universe had been upended. I wanted to shout at Dave and call him a liar, but I knew what he'd said was true. Only one thing didn't make sense. "Why would Robert save Victor? From what his ex-wife says about him, he doesn't seem like he was the type to sacrifice his own life for someone else."

"He wasn't." Dave snorted. "He was an annoying little weasel with the world's biggest chip on his shoulder. But his whole plan depended on Victor, so Robert had to save him."

"What plan?"

"*The* plan. This whole insane scheme to take over the world was Robert's idea. None of this would have happened without him."

"Uh-uh." I waved both my hands back and forth in front of my chest. "I don't believe you. Robert Cahill couldn't have come up with this plan. He didn't have enough power or money—"

Dave's chuckle cut me off. "Rich and powerful men don't dream up genocidal plans to conquer the world by wiping out half of it. Only a very small and very angry mind could think up something this hateful and bring it all together." Dave hoisted his beer in a mock toast. "And, let me tell you, Robert was as small and angry as they come. He couldn't hold a steady job, he couldn't hold his family together, and he wasn't even a good time jumper."

"Exactly!" I said triumphantly. "He was a loser. How could he do this?"

"Yeah, he was a loser. But he did know how to do two things incredibly well. One"—Dave raised an index finger—"think up outrageous ways to strike it rich quickly. And two"—he raised a second finger—"he had this almost magical ability to suck people into his schemes. Victor was one of those people who just jumped on his ideas. At first, it was just about stealing from history to get rich, but over time it morphed into something bigger, more dangerous."

"Wait a second." I held up my hand to interrupt. "If Robert started this whole thing in order to get rich, why was Sam's family always so poor?"

Dave shook his head in disgust. "Every time Robert made a few bucks from a time jump, he'd head straight to Vegas or Atlantic City. He had dreams of hitting it big, but the casinos just took his money and left him broke. Some of us tried to talk sense into him, for the sake of Marlene and the kids, but he wasn't the type to take advice from anyone. And the closer he and Victor got, the more Robert avoided the rest of the community." He snorted. "Unless he needed money, of course."

Dave spread his hands wide like a teacher at the end of a presentation. "And the rest is history. Everything Victor has gained in life—his money, his power, his fame—it's all because of Robert. He's the one who enlisted similar idiots to rob the past to finance Victor's political career. I'm pretty sure it was his idea to use the glitches to start building up alliances in the past. And I know for sure that Robert's the one who first resorted to violence, when he found out that too many time jumpers were against him. He's the one who caused this stupid war." Dave grimaced. "If I had only gotten to him a few years earlier, all this madness could have been stopped before it even started."

I tried to let everything Dave had told me sink in. Victor's genocidal plot to rule the world, the war in the time-jumper community, my dad's death—all these events were caused by the same evil mastermind: Sam's dad. I didn't want to believe it, but deep down I knew it was true.

Sam could never know; it would tear her apart. But how could I keep this from her? She was the only person I'd ever been completely honest with, and the mere thought of hiding something like this from her made me sick to my stomach.

The air inside the barn was suddenly stifling. I needed some fresh air and some time to think. Sam knew I was coming to pick up the laptop, and she'd be texting me soon to ask what I'd found out about her father. What would I tell her? And how could I use the information about Robert to my advantage against Victor?

"I . . . I gotta go." I stood from my chair and grabbed my backpack.

"You okay?" Dave asked.

"Yeah . . . I just got a lot to think about."

Dave lurched to his feet. "Let me give you a ride back to your car. It'll save you a long walk and get me out of this dusty barn for a bit."

"No. I'm good." I held my hand to stop him. "I . . . I gotta clear my head."

"I get it. No problem." Dave sank back into his chair. "If you ever want to talk, or bounce ideas off me, give me a call. I know this place is out of the way, but it's safe. Maybe we can even meet once and not try to kill each other?"

I gave him a half-hearted smile in return. "Sounds good." I slung my backpack over my shoulders and rushed out into the bright sunshine. After the gloom of the barn, the light was almost overwhelming.

I began picking my way through the forest, trying to figure out what to tell Sam. Why did it have to be her dad? The truth would crush her. But she had a right to know that everything we were fighting against stemmed from him, didn't she?

This was the hardest decision I'd ever had to make, and there was no one I could turn to for help. I had to figure this out for myself. Either tell the truth and completely destroy Sam's world, or hide it from her and let her continue living a lie.

Would I want to know the truth?

I thought of my own dad, and how so much of my life as a time jumper revolved around memories of him and I together. Us sparring together. Our trips to museums. His daily lectures on history. He had shaped so many of my decisions. How would that change if I found out he was allied with Victor, and my entire childhood was a lie?

My gut clenched at the thought. I'd be crushed. I'd probably smash or throw away everything that reminded me of him. Every happy memory I had would be questioned. I'd wonder if he had truly loved me and had been looking out for me, or if he had been manipulating me and molding me to become like him. I'd probably be so devastated that I'd end up quitting my fight against Victor and just running away into the past like Dave planned.

No matter how much it pained me to hide the truth from Sam, I'd have to bury this secret. I couldn't rip away the only happy memories she'd had of her childhood. And selfishly, I couldn't risk her quitting time jumping. I had no hope of surviving future jumps without her.

I took a deep breath and exhaled slowly. This was another line I never imagined I'd cross—not being truthful with Sam—but deep down I knew I'd made the right decision. Eventually, she might find out about her dad, but I couldn't be the one to take away her happiness.

For the first time since I'd left Dave's barn, my mind was calm enough for me to notice the forest around me. The trees were mostly oak and on a small slope. With the sun shining through the leafy branches, and the weight of the backpack over my shoulders, it almost felt like I was back in Greece again, picking my way through the forest near Thermopylae.

For a few steps, I closed my eyes and walked between the trees, remembering all the heroes I'd met in Greece. Areus. Charilaus. Maron. Dienekes. Leonidas. All the Greeks who had stayed behind on the last day of Thermopylae. Although I knew it was just my backpack pressing against me, I could almost imagine Areus's shield in my back, giving me strength and urging me on when the battle seemed bleakest. He had been my friend, and he had willingly sacrificed himself for the good of Greece and for me.

What was I willing to sacrifice to defeat Victor?

I'd already sacrificed my freedom to the sick bastard, so he wouldn't kill me or my friends. I'd definitely sacrificed my ethics. In killing Chris, I had stepped over a line I had never wanted to cross.

But was I willing to sacrifice my life?

That was a question I didn't know how to answer. And hopefully, I wouldn't have to find out. Despite Sam's skepticism, I believed our only path to defeating Victor was the city in the time stream. Once she saw that it was real, I was positive we could figure out a way to survive the bone-crushing freefall without becoming smears on the pavement. And, if Dave was right, and the city did contain all the secrets to time jumping, we might be able to figure out a way to stop Victor.

Now I just had to wait for another time glitch.

HISTORICAL NOTES

The Battle of Thermopylae occurred in late August or early September of 480 BCE and was part of the greater Greco-Persian Wars that lasted from 492 to 449 BCE. The wars themselves were caused by the expansion of the Persian Empire under Cyrus the Great, who had conquered the Greek-inhabited region of Ionia, on the west coast of modern-day Turkey, in 547 BCE. For almost fifty years, this region remained under Persian control, but the region rebelled in 499 BCE. After many years of fighting, the rebellion was crushed, and the Persians decided that the best way to stop further rebellions was to conquer all of Greece. A period of war followed, with both the Persians and the Greeks winning different battles, and no side gaining the advantage. In 480 BCE, Xerxes, ruler of the Persians, decided to personally lead one of the largest invasion forces ever assembled, and this army met the Greeks at the Battle of Thermopylae.

The main source of information for this battle is Herodotus, a Greek historian who lived from 484 to 425 BCE. He wrote the *Histories*, an extensive history of the Greco-Persian wars. He traveled far and wide to confirm the information in his book and, because of his dedication to accurately recording the past, earned the moniker "the Father of

History." Unfortunately, even though the events he records are regarded as mostly true, his counts of men in battle are usually exaggerated, so they need to be taken with a degree of skepticism. For instance, Herodotus says there were two million Persian soldiers at Thermopylae, while modern historians put the number at closer to 200,000. On the Greek side, however, Herodotus was fairly detailed in his numbers, so we know that there were roughly six to seven thousand Greeks at Thermopylae, standing against that huge force of Persians.

The Greek forces at Thermopylae came mainly from the south of Greece, since the north of the country had already been overrun by the Persians. Although the Spartans sent only a small force of men, they were given overall command of the army because they were known as the best warriors in all of Greece.

To be a Spartan meant spending your life training for battle. At the age of seven, male children were sent to the *agoge*, Sparta's education and training program, which used harsh, extreme, and sometimes cruel methods to prepare boys to be Spartan citizens and soldiers. They spent their entire childhood in the *agoge*, learning hunting, stealth, warfare, and athletics, and only at around the age of twenty were they considered old enough to go into battle. By this time, they had already led a life of hardship and struggle. The ancient historian Plutarch said of the Spartans: "They were the only men in the world for whom war brought a respite in the training for war."

Many Greek cities sent forces to protect the pass at Thermopylae, and the Spartan contingent was actually one of the smallest groups present. The Spartans could not send more men because of the Spartan Festival of Carneia occurring at the time. This festival was held in honor of Apollo Carneus, and during the festival, the Spartans were forbidden to engage in warfare. King Leonidas realized that the Persians had to be stopped, however, so he decided to go into battle by himself, and he took his personal bodyguard of three hundred men with him. The members of his guard were all older men who had fought in many

The Spartan Sacrifice

battles and had already fathered children. Leonidas and his men went into battle knowing there was little chance they would return home.

As for the battle itself, history records that when the two armies met at Thermopylae, the Persians waited four days before attacking. No one is sure why they waited so long. Herodotus writes that King Xerxes of Persia was so put off by seeing the Spartans fearlessly combing their hair and wrestling before battle that he held off in order to build up his own courage. The more likely reason for this delay is that Xerxes was waiting for the rest of his army to catch up with the vanguard. Since he commanded such a large force, it would have taken time for the slowest troops to catch up with the fastest.

When the battle finally was joined, the Persians were savagely beaten back on the first two days. On the third day, a large group of Persians managed, with the help of a Greek traitor, to navigate a path through the mountains and come out in the rear of the Greek forces. Upon hearing this, many Greeks chose to flee, but the Spartans and some of their allies remained to hold the pass for as long as possible. The historical sources do not fully answer why Leonidas chose to stay when he had ample warning of the Persians attacking from behind. Herodotus says that an oracle foretold that either Leonidas would die or Sparta would fall, so Leonidas chose to sacrifice himself for the sake of Sparta. Although this sounds heroic, it is not likely—so the question remains.

The Spartans and their few allies fought valiantly against the Persian forces. But since they were caught between two armies, they were all surrounded and killed, except for the Thebans, who surrendered.

Herodotus records that when Greeks came later to the battle site to bury their dead, they found over two thousand Greek bodies. This number would include, of course, the nine hundred or so helots that the Spartans had brought with them. As for the Persian dead, it is believed that around 20,000 Persians lost their lives at Thermopylae.

This book leaned heavily on the *Histories* by Herodotus for most of its details. As someone who was born only four years after the battle, and who traveled extensively through the lands of ancient Greece, Herodotus would have had access to oral histories and survivors of the battle. For extra details, I also used the accounts of Diodorus Siculus, a Greek writer from the first century BCE. Although he was writing almost four hundred years after Thermopylae, he was known to have drawn extensively from other historians whose works are no longer extant. The two sources do not always agree, so in cases where they diverge, I used the events I considered most likely to have happened.

The impact of the Battle of Thermopylae is both negligible and far-reaching. From a military sense, it did nothing for the Greeks but buy them a few extra days. The Persians were not stopped but continued their invasion into Greece, where they sacked Athens and conquered other Greek cities. The Persian advance was only halted a few weeks later at the Battle of Salamis, where an Athenian-led navy scored a huge victory against the Persian fleet. With his navy destroyed, Xerxes decided to leave Greece, and he instructed his general Mardonis to finish off the conquest of the country. The Greeks and Persians fought again on land at the Battle of Plataea, a year later, where a force of Greeks, led this time by the full Spartan army, soundly defeated the Persian army, bringing an end to the Persian invasion of Greece.

The defeat at Thermopylae is significant for its moral victory. It showed that a small force, with the right terrain and the right mindset, can hold off a much larger opponent. In addition, the battle gave the Greeks a rallying cry to fight around. It showed them that the Persians were not invincible, and that a brave and motivated defender could exact a bloody price.

A few final notes. Many of the names in the book are from the actual history. For the Spartans, Leonidas, Pantites, Dienekes, and Maron were all recorded to be at Thermopylae, while Megistias the Seer of Acarnania and Demophilus, the leader of the Thespians, were also recorded to be there. Many jokes were attributed to Dienekes, and I tried to include

The Spartan Sacrifice

them here, as well as adding a few quips of my own that I felt suited his style.

The poem the Spartans recite during battle is by the Spartan poet Tyrtaeus, who lived during the seventh century BCE. Although there is no written record of the Spartans actually reciting this poem at Thermopylae, the Greek author Athenaeus said that the Spartans "in their wars recite the poems of Tyrtaeus," so I thought it plausible that they would have recited this particular poem before the heavy fighting at Thermopylae.

ACKNOWLEDGMENTS

Writing a book, and especially the fourth one in a series, is definitely not a solo project. There are so many people who helped me bring this book from the original rough ideas to the final creation. My wife, Pam, deserves the biggest shout out for all the support she has given me over the years. She reads my books almost as much as I do, constantly giving me feedback and helping me bring out the depth in scenes. She also is a huge promoter of my books on social media, and regularly creates content for me when I just want to run away from the entire social media world.

My children, Leah, Arawn, and Calvin, have been the inspiration of the series from the beginning, and have all contributed in their own way to the books. Although they are no longer teens, they gave me great insight into the teen world of today, helping me understand how teens talk, dress, use technology, and react to situations. They have also been huge fans of the series and have made their own suggestions for where Dan and Sam should end up in the past. This particular novel was inspired by Arawn. He actually wanted them to end up in ancient Egypt, but I couldn't think of a good story line for that period, so we settled on ancient Greece instead.

For over twenty years, I have been fortunate to be a member of an incredibly supportive writing group. A long time ago, someone gave our group the name WIHW, which stands for Writing Is Hard Work. The name doesn't exactly flow off the tongue, but it is fitting. This group of dedicated writers is the first to see the poorly written drafts of my chapters, and they have given me countless improvements over the years. I am grateful for the detailed critiquing and helpful feedback that Tom Taylor, Cryssa Bazos, Connie Di Pietro, Jay Stewart, and Gwen Tuinman provided on this book.

I am also fortunate to have two incredible editors, Peter Lavery and Maya Myers. Sometimes it is kind of disheartening to see how many improvements on grammar, punctuation, and story they find, especially after I've already done countless revisions on my own at the recommendations of my family and writing group. But Peter and Maya always manage to elevate my writing a few notches, and for that I am incredibly thankful.

I am also thankful for my publisher, Imbrifex Books, who have been huge supporters of the series from the beginning. They have been great to work with and have always asked for my feedback on things like back cover text and front cover design, In addition, they have done so much work to publicize my books, and the awards won by the first books in the series could not have been done without Imbrifex's support. I am truly grateful to them.

Finally, I would like to thank all the readers who have been following along with the adventures of Dan and Sam. Writing a book is a huge task, and writing a series even more so. But knowing that there are so many people who enjoy the books is not only humbling; it is also encouragement to continue plugging away at my keyboard.

Happy reading!

ABOUT THE AUTHOR

Ever since his mother revealed that he's descended from Vikings, ANDREW VARGA has been captivated by history. He has studied extensively, read hundreds of history books, watched numerous historical films, and earned a BA from the University of Toronto with a specialist in history and a major in English. Andrew has traveled across Europe, explored famous castles, museums, and historical sites, and over time, has built a collection of swords, shields, and other medieval weapons. He currently resides in the greater Toronto area with his wife Pam, their three children, and their lively mix of two dogs, two cats, a turtle, and some fish. It was his children's passion for reading—especially historical and fantasy stories—that inspired Andrew to begin writing this series. Outside of his writing and editing work, Andrew enjoys reading more history, playing guitar, and participating in any sport that gets him away from his computer.

Connect with the author online:

🌐 andrewvargaauthor.com

📘 @AndrewVargaAuthor

📷 @ andrewvargaauthor

This is the fourth book in the JUMP IN TIME book series. **The Last Saxon King** was published in March 2023. The second book, **The Celtic Deception** was published in August 2023. The third book, **The Mongol Ascension** was published in September 2024. The fifth book, **The Orleans Ordeal** will be published in August 2026.